EMPE AE

THE LAST VIKING, VOLUME 3

JC DUNCAN

Boldwood

First published in Great Britain in 2024 by Boldwood Books Ltd.

Copyright © JC Duncan, 2024

Cover Design by Colin Thomas

Cover Photography: Colin Thomas and Alamy

Map Designed by Flintlock Covers

The moral right of JC Duncan to be identified as the author of this work has been asserted in accordance with the Copyright, Designs and Patents Act 1988.

All rights reserved. No part of this book may be reproduced in any form or by any electronic or mechanical means, including information storage and retrieval systems, without written permission from the author, except for the use of brief quotations in a book review. This book is a work of fiction and, except in the case of historical fact, any resemblance to actual persons, living or dead, is purely coincidental.

Every effort has been made to obtain the necessary permissions with reference to copyright material, both illustrative and quoted. We apologise for any omissions in this respect and will be pleased to make the appropriate acknowledgements in any future edition.

A CIP catalogue record for this book is available from the British Library.

Paperback ISBN 978-1-80549-829-2

Large Print ISBN 978-1-80549-831-5

Hardback ISBN 978-1-80549-827-8

Ebook ISBN 978-1-80549-828-5

Kindle ISBN 978-1-80549-830-8

Audio CD ISBN 978-1-80549-822-3

MP3 CD ISBN 978-1-80549-823-0

Digital audio download ISBN 978-1-80549-825-4

This book is printed on certified sustainable paper. Boldwood Books is dedicated to putting sustainability at the heart of our business. For more information please visit https://www.boldwoodbooks.com/about-us/sustainability/

Boldwood Books Ltd, 23 Bowerdean Street, London, SW6 3TN

www.boldwoodbooks.com

CAST OF CHARACTERS

The Kingdoms of Norway, Sweden and Denmark

Afra the Constant: Elder of the bandit brothers who follow Harald.
Eric 'Sveitungr' Alvarsson: The narrator, Harald's closest companion and follower.
Harald 'Hardrada' Sigurdsson: King of Norway 1046–1066, half-brother of King Olaf, and claimant to Danish and English thrones.
Halldor Snorrasson: One of Harald's Varangians, cousin of Ulfr.
Ingvarr Hakonsson: Son of Hakon.
Jarl Hakon: Petty jarl, attending the Thing in Tinghaugen with his son.
Jarl Halfdan: Lord of Tinghaugen.
Rurik: One of Harald's followers.
Thorir the Cuckoo: Younger of the bandit brothers.
Ulfr Ospaksson: Varangian with Harald Hardrada, one of his senior warriors.

The Kyivan Rus

Olga: Kyivan palace attendant and Eric's wife.
Yaroslav the Wise: Grand Prince of the Kyivan Rus.

The Byzantine Empire

Aki Freysson: The second in command of the Varangians.
Arduin: Leader of the Lombard allied forces in Sicily.
Bardas: Greek mercenary commander.
Georgios Maniakes: Byzantine nobleman and general.
John the Parakoimomenos: Palace eunuch. Brother and close advisor to Emperor Michael IV.
Maria Arantios: Byzantine noblewoman.
Michael Dokeianos: Byzantine officer.
Michael IV the Paphlagonian: Emperor of The Romans.
Petar Delyan: Bulgarian rebel and self-proclaimed emperor.
Styrbjorn the goat: Komes of the fourteenth bandon of the Varangians, the Warborn.
Sveinn: Komes of the second bandon, the Wolfhounds.
Theodora Porphyrogenita: Sister of Empress Zoe.
William de Hautville: Norman mercenary leader in the service of the empire.
Zoe Porphyrogenita: Wife of Michael IV, Empress of the Romans.

The Emirate of Sicily

Abdallah Ibn Ziri: Emir of Sicily.
Abu'l-Qasim Ibn Ali al-Kabali: The Emir of Syracuse, vassal of Abdallah Ibn Ziri.

PREFACE

Harald Hardrada's rise in the Varangian guard in the mid-1030s was meteoric, by all accounts. The sources disagree precisely when he came to command the guard, and how, and what specific rank he held, but one thing is sure: By the summer of 1038 he had served the empire in a great number of battles, sieges and skirmishes, and covered himself with glory to become an extremely powerful figure in the imperial court.

At the end of *Raven Lord*, Harald Sigurdsson had just returned from his trip to Jerusalem where he had been tasked with protecting Empress Zoe's sister, Theodora, in her pilgrimage to the Holy Land. They had gone as far as the river Jordan but were betrayed and set upon by local bandits and rogue soldiers who were acting under the orders of Zoe to ensure Theodora did not return home alive. Zoe feared Theodora would be used to replace her as Emperor Michael IV's wife by John, the ravenously ambitious brother of Emperor Michael.

Harald and his Varangians managed to protect the imperial princess, but only with enormous sacrifice and the final help of a mysterious band of mercenaries that had been shadowing them throughout their travels.

These mercenaries were revealed to be commanded by none other than Bardas, Harald's sworn enemy and rival from his time in the Kyivan Rus. Bardas and his employer, Maria, had once been set on usurping the throne of the empire for themselves but in the ever-shifting alliances of court politics had allied themselves with Michael and had been sent to the Holy Land to protect Theodora from Zoe's assassins.

This turn of events ended up with Harald and Bardas reluctantly fighting on the same side for the same purpose and saw Harald's favourable relationship with Zoe shattered by the knowledge she had been willing to let him be killed if it meant removing her sister as a threat.

The palace court is a web of factions fighting for control. John, through his brother Emperor Michael, seeks to found a new family dynasty. Empress Zoe seeks to retain the power of her own Macedonian lineage. The noblewoman Maria will use any potential avenue to power, having already tried manipulating the empress's sister Theodora into usurping her sibling, hoping to then replace the ageing princess and become empress herself.

Harald, sick of the plotting and scheming by the emperor and empress, forced them to come to an accord. He would keep the peace between them using his power and position in the guard, and would no longer be a pawn in their internal struggle for power.

Now, as the year 1038 comes to a close, it is only a matter of time before one of the factions makes their next attempt for absolute power, and tests the peace enforced by Harald Sigurdsson – the protospatharios of the Varangians and the wielder of the Emperor's Axe. Harald's new-found power is certain to be brutally put to the test, and even as conflict once again brews inside the palace, unrest and rebellion threaten the far-flung provinces, and even the capital itself. Harald's duty to defend the seat of power of the Roman Empire is about to get far more bloody and complicated.

PART I

ASSASSIN

1

TINGHAUGEN, NORWAY; SPRING 1098 AD

Ingvarr rested the axe head for a moment on the gnarled, hacked old stump. Blowing hard and eyeing the pile of chopped firewood. Was that enough? He thought so. The nights were cold and they liked to keep a good fire in the late evening, but it did not need to burn for long.

'He's around here somewhere, is he?' Ingvarr looked up in surprise as he heard the familiar voice on the other side of his tent. The old, sonorous tones of Eric Sveitungr, the now ancient warrior who had once accompanied Harald Hardrada on his great life's adventures.

He was surprised because the old man had spent the late afternoon and evening on each of the previous two nights in the great hall, entertaining the gathered men with tales of Hardrada's life. But it was barely noon, and he didn't understand why the old man would be in their camp outside the town.

There were shuffling footsteps and Eric appeared around the side of the simple wool-panelled tent that he and his father were sharing for the week, one of half a hundred in the camp that had sprung up around them.

'Ingvarr, there you are,' said the old man brightly.

'Eric, what, what do you need?' Ingvarr looked at him uncertainly.

Eric continued as if he had not spoken. 'I am going to start my story early today. It is such a fine day, isn't it? Yes. A fine afternoon and I feel the energy burning in me such that I haven't felt in years.' Eric smiled excitedly and rubbed his hands together. 'So fine I felt like walking all the way out here. It invigorates the blood of an old man, a good walk.'

'You came out here just to tell me yourself that everyone is gathering?' Ingvarr replied, flushed with pride at the special treatment.

Eric looked at him for a moment and then laughed deeply until he coughed. He waved a hand at the young man as he recovered his breath and then shook his head. 'No, no. No one is gathering yet. That is why I asked for you as I passed the camp; I need someone to run round and tell everyone that I will be starting earlier today. Outside, in fact. I will sit under the great tree where the Thing will be held in three days, just outside the town, and wait for enough to have gathered.'

Eric smiled happily and nodded to himself. 'Yes, today I will tell my story in the sun.' He looked at Ingvarr expectantly. 'Well, go and gather everyone.'

Ingvarr looked left and right and stammered. 'Everyone?'

'Yes, everyone.'

'But... I don't know where everyone is.'

Eric nodded serenely. 'That is why I need you to run around the town and find out. I'm sure you will do fine.' Then he turned around and walked away again with his slow, deliberate gait, leaving Ingvarr utterly perplexed.

He put the axe down and went to find his father and told him what Eric had said.

'Why would he make me do this?' he asked in a borderline petulant whine. 'What did I do to deserve this task? How can I gather the entire town? Who will listen to me?'

His father, Jarl Hakon, gave him a dour frown. 'Why are you complaining? He does you a great honour. It is a test, and you are already failing. You shame me, boy.'

Ingvarr's jaw gaped a little as he tried to process that way of looking at it. 'It is an honour? How?'

'He came all this way to give you the chance to call a meeting on the field of the Thing, to be seen and heard, personally, by all the great men and warriors of the realm gathered here... and you come and complain about it?'

Ingvarr looked morose and foolish and stared at the ground. 'I didn't think of that.' Then he looked up with a new twinkle in his eye. 'It is really an honour?'

Hakon nodded solemnly. 'Such an honour that if you do not do it soon, I will take the task myself, and gladly.'

The fear of losing this precious new thing that he had not known he possessed until that moment brought fear into Ingvarr's eyes and he straightened bolt upright. 'No! I will do it.' But then he faltered. 'I am only afraid no one will listen to me.'

Hakon put a meaty hand on Ingvarr's shoulder. 'Only showing your fear will make men hesitate to heed you. Speak firmly, with respect and confidence to your elders, and trust me, boy, they will accept your invite.'

Ingvarr nodded enthusiastically, his face flush with the great weight of his duty.

'Well, off you go then – don't keep Eric waiting.'

Ingvarr turned and ran off between the tents, and Hakon heard his voice calling out the message as it receded into the background.

Hakon stood there with an amused grin as a shorter figure

came out from behind a tent and joined him. Hakon turned and nodded to the old man. 'Thank you, Eric, he will love you for this.'

Eric smiled slyly. 'My pleasure, Jarl Hakon. He had to suffer the mockery of the entire hall last night, and I felt he deserved some recompense.'

Hakon laughed. 'He deserved it, but thank you anyway.'

'Walk with me back to town, will you? It would be terribly embarrassing if I were to stumble on the path and be late for my own meeting.'

'It would be my pleasure, Eric. It would be my pleasure.'

The two men walked slowly through the unsown fields back towards Tinghaugen in companionable silence for a while, but then Eric glanced over at Hakon several times and saw the jarl was deep in thought.

'What is it, Hakon?'

'Hmm? Oh, well, honestly I am still uncertain about letting my son go on this campaign.'

'What campaign?' Eric asked innocently. 'The Thing has not taken place; perhaps there will be no campaign.'

'Everyone knows the king intends to call a campaign to the Southern Isles, a big one.'

'How does everyone know that, without the king announcing it?' Eric asked, and Hakon knew the old man was toying with him.

'I assume because the king has made sure rumours of it are spread, to make sure it is not a shock when he proposes it.'

'That is likely true, in part. But what if he merely intends to gauge the reaction of his people to the idea before having to actually suggest it? It has been thirty years since the men of Norway went across the sea as one army, it is a very great thing to ask of them. By spreading the idea by rumour first, he can avoid proposing it and it being rejected in the meeting if he feels the reaction will be poor.'

Hakon nodded slowly. 'And thus avoid potential embarrassment.'

'Exactly.'

Hakon turned to Eric. 'And you are here to advise the king, so you have told us.'

'Yes.'

Hakon raised an eyebrow. 'But you will not tell us what your advice will be.'

Eric smiled and shook his head. 'My advice for my king falls on his ears first – and only his, if he so chooses.'

Hakon grunted. 'That is very correct and honourable, Eric.' They walked a few more paces. 'But I wonder, why did you come so early? Nearly a week before the king arrives. I believe your home is not so far away and you could have come later.'

Eric shrugged nonchalantly. 'I had nothing else to do, and it was a chance to meet with lords of the realm such as yourself.'

'And to sway us in advance of the king's visit?'

Eric feigned hurt with his bushy, furrowed brows. 'Have I attempted to sway you?'

'Not directly.'

'Well, there you go, then. I am merely telling a story to pass the time.'

They were nearly at the meeting field now, the rows of benches sitting in the shelter of the great oak tree at the top of the field where the speakers would stand. They could see a few men were already arriving ahead of them.

'Just telling a story, Eric, on the field of the Thing itself?'

'Yes.'

'A story about the king who lost his life and his army in a foolish invasion of England. An interesting choice, don't you think, before a meeting where you expect your king to call for a large invasion of the Southern Isles near England, perhaps England itself?' Hakon gave Eric a searching look, and the old man stopped by the outer row of benches, out of earshot of the few who were already there.

'You sound like you might disapprove of King Magnus's intended invasion? But you are here anyway, why?' Eric asked, deftly avoiding the question.

'I will support my king in whatever action he chooses. It is my duty.'

Eric nodded. 'Good man, that is honourable and proper.' Then he gazed at the tree, the very tree in whose shade, over thirty years before, Harald had stood and announced to the meeting of the lords of Norway his intention to invade England. Eric's eyes were sharp, but his hand clenched his walking stick with white wizened knuckles. 'Let me tell you, Jarl Hakon, that in my experience while any sworn man must do as his lord commands – and, in fact, to put all his strength, effort and blood into that task – it is not only acceptable but right to try and help his lord know the truth and make the best possible decision.' He looked at Hakon and his eyes betrayed a hint of sadness. 'I dedicated my entire life to that truth, and as you see, I am yet still alive.'

'So you are here to influence the people's opinion before the king arrives, to counter the rumours of a great campaign he has spread?'

Eric smiled, and the sadness in his eyes disappeared. 'My friend Hakon, I am just an old man here to drink ale and tell stories, and the king is just a lord doing his duty for his people and country.' He waved at the increasing number of people arriving at the field. 'Come, sit near me. I think I will be starting before long.'

Hakon was far from convinced, but he could see Eric would not be drawn any further. He helped the old man set up a high-backed chair under the tree, facing the rows of benches, and then sat down at the front as the field started to fill.

Eric chatted to men as they arrived and greeted him, and Hakon made small talk with a southern jarl, who was whingeing half-heartedly about the privations of Danish traders monopolising the fur trade to Sweden, something he hoped to speak to the king about.

Finally, a hundred or more men were gathered, with more coming in, when Ingvarr arrived at a jog, his face flushed and red.

'Ah, my boy, you have done well,' said Eric, waving the boy to a seat next to his father.

Ingvarr grinned broadly at the praise and Eric cleared his voice to speak to the whole crowd.

'I think it is time, my friends, that I should start, for you all have better things to do than to stare at an old man in silence, no?'

There was a patter of polite laughter and Eric nodded, then drew himself up in his seat to begin recounting his story.

2

CONSTANTINOPLE; SPRING 1038 AD

Well, at the start of the year of our Lord 1038, we had every reason to celebrate. Harald had become one of the most powerful men in the empire. For saving Princess Theodora and defending the Church of the Holy Sepulchre in Jerusalem he was loved by the people and the Church – and both of those things mattered deeply in the empire, let me tell you. He was admired and respected by the army, for what soldier does not admire a great military hero, and he was feared by the emperor and empress for his power.

Yes, at the time, we did not consider deeply how dangerous it was to be loved by the army, Church and people, and feared by the rulers. We enjoyed their fear, it made us powerful and arrogant and, above all, rich.

But in the palace, things had never been worse. The emperor, mostly under John's influence, and empress were like caged animals, desiring only to tear each other apart to become the sole ruler. Harald was the only thing preventing this, and though he could keep them physically safe from each other he could do nothing about those caught in the vortex of the power struggle.

Both factions were seeking to align powerful members of the court on their side, using whatever means necessary, for the moment they were able to break free of Harald's restrictions.

Thus the emperor and empress were united only in their fear of Harald's power, and their hatred for each other. So they competed to earn our allegiance, hoping that when we finally broke our oaths and turned to take the throne, it would be them, and not their spouse, who we chose to support in their internal civil war they were so certain we would join.

Am I saying we were going to break our oaths and seize power? No, never. But Michael and Zoe did not truly believe that, could not in their bones believe that, because to the Roman ruling class, there is no such thing as an oath that cannot be broken if it is advantageous to do so. They knew that either of them would seize power in Harald's position, so they assumed we would do the same.

Well, we were aloof to much of that, for much as the co-emperor and empress could not think like us, we could not think like them. Not then, not yet.

So what did we do? Well, we performed our duties guarding the palace impeccably, and we enjoyed the generous, overflowing bounty of gifts that the royals bestowed upon us. Truly they were intended as bribes but we did not care; we were mercenaries and gold was our purpose in life and we were swimming in a river of it.

And swimming in the deepest channel was Harald, who took one quarter of everything given to the guard. Men grumbled about it in dark corners, but Harald saw it as his due for he was the reason we were being so well rewarded, and there was so much silver and gold flowing that no guardsman wanted for anything, so the grumbling was muted.

But all that imperial wealth created a new and increasingly serious problem: What to do with it?

Along with the loot Harald had amassed during our campaigns against the wealthy Arabs in the east and the Holy Land, we now had a treasury that would make even a provincial governor green with envy. And it was all just in boxes and sacks in the basement of the barracks, behind a single locked door only two fingers thick of old wood. It was relatively safe while we were there, but if we were ever sent abroad, it would be too tempting a target for another powerful player in the city to overlook.

It was during a night of raucous celebration on one of the many feast days enjoyed by the city, where those not on duty gathered in the barracks for a rarely allowed night of drinking and feasting inside the palace walls, that Harald was sitting with me and leaned in to ask me something with the sort of face I had come to recognise meant bad news.

Now, you may ask, why was drinking and feasting rarely allowed inside the palace walls? Well, because Harald was determined not to let our riches destroy the guard. His enforcement of discipline was ruthless, and it was the right thing to do. Men hated him for it sometimes, but we all knew that if we let ourselves become fat and lazy through debauchery that we would suffer for it on campaign. We still had the pride to understand that, despite the temptations that were available to men with our fat purses.

'Eric, I have a question for you.' He wasn't drunk. Harald was seldom drunk; it was too undisciplined to become drunk for Harald to allow himself. He was really very boring as a drinking companion, perhaps something I have never made clear.

'What?' I said with a pleasant smile, because I, unlike my

lord, was very much drunk. A state I enjoyed on a perhaps overly regular basis.

I saw his brief look of annoyance at my dulled wits but he carried on anyway.

'It is the question of what to do with our treasury,' said Harald in a serious tone.

I waved my hand at the rows of men on benches and trestles, eating and drinking like heroes. 'I like what we are doing with it so far,' I quipped.

Harald did not find that funny and he scowled at me. 'I should talk to you about this when you are fit to converse.'

That cut me. I shook my head clear and wiped the smile off my face. 'No, I am ready now. I apologise.'

He stared into my eyes for a moment and then nodded. 'We must secure it for the future, find a safe place for it away from the politics and machinations of the palace.'

I furrowed my brows and shrugged. 'We have no safe place outside of the city. No one we could trust.'

He nodded. 'Not in the empire,' he said with great meaning.

I understood him immediately. There was one man in the great circle of the earth that Harald respected and admired above all others, perhaps even the only man Harald considered might be superior to him.

'You are talking of Yaroslav?'

'Of course.'

'You would trust him with our wealth?'

'Yes, as long as he gives his word, and there is something suitable in it for him.'

'A portion of it.'

'Yes, but I suspect that will not be enough.'

'What else will you offer?' I asked.

Harald made the sour expression he always made when he

was thinking and didn't like the direction of his thoughts. 'He will want an alliance. Once he sees my wealth – and he will already have heard of our success – he will judge that I am on the path to regaining a throne. Perhaps he will believe it is the imperial throne, perhaps he understands it will be my brother's throne of Norway. Regardless, he will want to secure a future alliance.'

'And? Is that a problem, would an alliance not also benefit you?'

'Yes, it would. My interests do not lie in the Rus so I do not expect us to ever be enemies.'

'So, we will go there and ask him to keep our treasury safe in return for an alliance?'

Harald shook his head. 'I cannot go.'

My jaw dropped like a stone. 'You want me to go alone? To Yaroslav?'

'Yes.'

I sputtered in protest. 'He will take that as a grave insult! That you would send me to ask a favour, not even going yourself? He would barely speak to me the last time we were there. He is the Grand Prince of the Rus and I am just a Varangian officer!' I protested so loudly that other men seated nearby looked up to see what was wrong. I did my best to get control of myself, forcing a neutral expression and leaning in closer to Harald.

Harald shook his head carefully. 'No. I am the commander of the Varangians and I cannot abandon the capital on a private mission to meet with a foreign ruler. It would be seen as treachery. Impossible. Yaroslav will understand that.'

'Your brother told me to stay by your side. Send someone else on this errand.' The thought of going to the Rus alone, to meet with the great ruler, sickened me.

'Who? Who else would I trust?'

'Afra,' I said, jerking my head at the Norwegian, who had been with us since before the battle of Stiklestad in Norway eight years before, and was Harald's closest confidant after me.

He and his brother Thorir had also been lifelong bandits, and continued to put those skills to regular use for Harald, so asking him to trust our entire wealth to them was a rather desperate decision.

'Send a bandit to treat with a king?' Harald smiled. 'It is an amusing idea, but that really would insult Yaroslav. No. He knows you were my second, he will accept you. I have already sent a letter.'

I deflated. 'You have already written to him saying I am coming.'

Harald nodded sagely.

'Why, before even telling me?'

'Because I knew you would refuse if you could.'

That hurt me. I never refused Harald anything if it was in my power to give. That was my place, my oath, my role in life – to support and protect Harald in all things. I have said it many times: I am called Eric the Follower, and damn those who use it as an insult, because it is honourable and I earned that name the hard way.

'I would not have refused your order,' I complained.

'You just tried,' replied Harald without malice. And it was almost true.

'I was only arguing, it is my place to dissuade you from stupid decisions.'

Harald smiled warmly, for one of his strengths was being able to see when he was wrong. 'It is, but on this I am correct. You will take our treasury to Yaroslav, and make a pact with him if needed. Offer him one fifth of the wealth to keep it safe. He will accept. He is not a man to barter. It is a fair offer, and he has no reason to refuse.'

'And what if he makes other demands for your allegiance?'

Harald smiled. 'Use your judgement. If he wants Norway as an ally when I take the throne, agree to it. If he wants us as allies now and to betray the emperor, refuse it. Nor will I be his vassal or his proxy, but a partner. Do as our honour and our oaths demand. I am sure you will do well.'

I bowed my head, appalled, but I could not protest further.

'Take fifty good men and one of our ships from the harbour. I will write all the permissions. But you will have to travel in disguise, with no imperial regalia or symbols. You will appear to be Norse mercenaries to any who see you, or you will attract all the wrong attention.'

'And what if the emperor and empress find out Varangians are travelling to the Rus? Even if it is just me, not you, will they not assume it is a plot?'

Harald nodded. 'Yes, which is why I will tell them what is happening and why.'

I was shocked. 'But you said we should travel in secrecy, yet you will tell them?'

'They will find out either way. They should hear it from me, but I will do so after you sail, to avoid arguments about allowing it.'

'They will still think it is a plot.'

Harald shrugged. 'They think everything is a plot. Come, Eric, enough of this. I have planned it all, you will be fine.' He put his hand on my shoulder. 'Let us enjoy the evening and celebrate with the men; tomorrow we will talk further.'

He smiled and joked with a couple of men who passed by, and then Halldor Snorrasson stood up, pointing at Harald with a decorated silver ale mug that must have cost as much as a good horse.

'To Harald and the glory of the Varangian guard!' roared the Icelander and his cousin Ulfr Ospaksson stood up and joined him.

'To Harald!' Ulfr said, and men all around joined in enthusiastically as Harald smiled and waved at them to sit down and stop embarrassing him.

Styrbjorn, the komes of the fourteenth bandon, came over, smiling broadly, and planted himself down in the seat opposite across the broad table. 'To you, Harald.' He slurped his ale noisily.

I liked Styrbjorn. He was a veteran guardsman, a firm supporter of Harald, and we had fought together for years. He was as good a Varangian as you could find, and as disruptive and ill-disciplined as Harald would ever allow.

Have any of you ever had a dog that was so poorly trained and behaved that you considered casting it out, but it was so charming, lovable and ferocious in defending your home and your family against threats that you kept it anyway? Yes? I see from your smiles that some of you have. Well, that was Styrbjorn. He was known as the Goat as he was as greedy, as stubborn, and as hardheaded as any goat you could ever meet. But there was no better man to have at your side on campaign. He did not have the discipline of Sveinn or Aki, but his wild behaviour and battle skill made him very popular in the ranks and there was no questioning how effective the fourteenth were in combat.

'Styrbjorn, I see you are in fine spirits,' said Harald with a slightly worried glare.

'I am, Commander. And I thank you for all you have provided for us.'

'Are you satisfied, Styrbjorn, with the festivities?' I said sarcastically, because Styrbjorn was famously never satisfied with any amount of luxury or debauchery.

'No, but only because no women are here. Other than you, of course.'

We clanked our mugs together and laughed at the insult, because that is what you had to do with Styrbjorn. There was no point getting into a war of words with him because nothing pierced his thick goat-hide skin at all.

'Have you anything to confess to me, Styrbjorn, while you are here?' asked Harald with a raised eyebrow, as I worried that the man would do something to offend or provoke Harald just to see what would happen.

Styrbjorn feigned shock and leaned back. 'I have done nothing! I am a changed man since our last meeting,' he said with a toothy grin.

'Well, I have not had a report about you from Aki for at least a month, so maybe it is true and I will have to consider some sort of reward.'

Styrbjorn nodded smugly. 'Nothing too big, just a simple gesture of thanks will suffice.'

I rolled my eyes and looked up as one of the kitchen boys arrived with a steaming platter and bowed his head at Harald. 'The cooks sent this for you. It is a spiced and honeyed bird, stuffed with figs and lemon. It is very popular with the court circle, and the cooks wanted to do something special for you.'

Harald smiled at the boy, who was clearly a bit nervous to be talking to the commander in person. 'Thank you, boy. Tell them I appreciate it. It will make a change from our normal, simple meals.' Harald nodded his thanks at the servant who smiled broadly and left in a hurry.

I laughed because Harald avoided the trappings of the rich citizens of the city. He liked his food simple and hearty.

Styrbjorn's eyes, however, lit up, and he leaned over the platter, sniffing at it almost like a goat would. In fact, *exactly* like a goat would.

'Off you go, Styrbjorn!' Harald said with a pointed finger.

Styrbjorn laughed and gave Harald a rude gesture with his hand to his nose that I would find hard to explain, but essentially questions the receiver's manhood both in size and functionality. Then he snatched up his mug and, with a final amused glare, skulked off back to his table. I was glad he was gone for he had seemed likely to cause an upset.

Harald poked at the elaborate platter of stuffed bird disparagingly. Then something caught his eye and he looked across the feast to see Afra was coming towards us and he abandoned the platter. 'Ah, I need to speak to him.'

'About my trip?' I asked.

Harald looked at me reproachfully and nodded before getting up.

Of course, he had planned the trip with Afra. Afra was Harald's problem solver for anything that required less honourable actions than we were willing to do ourselves or knew how to complete.

But it was hard to be angry, because Afra was brilliant in his own way, and also perhaps my closest friend in the guard.

I sat there alone, my addled head full of annoyance at being sent all the way back to the Rus and away from this place, when Styrbjorn hustled over, looking to where Harald was and seeing Harald's inattention. Before I could react he grabbed the steaming, stuffed bird and just grinned at my open-mouthed outrage.

'The commander said I deserved a reward!' he said, before taking a bite of the thing, his eyes and posture daring me to try and stop him.

I think I was about to but his brows furrowed and he pulled

the bird away from his mouth and eyed it in distaste, before spitting out the chunk he had already chewed off. 'Fruit doesn't belong in meat,' he said, with an air of complete disappointment.

'I thought you would eat anything?' I said.

'Not this rich man's fruity meat. I have standards, Eric.'

Then he shrugged, his smile returned, and he gestured to the table he had been eating at. 'Someone will want it though, can't give it back looking like this.' And he sauntered off.

'What was that?' Harald came back and saw my anger.

'Styrbjorn took that stuffed bird that the cooks made for you!' I said in drunken outrage.

Harald looked at the man and shrugged. 'I didn't want it.'

'That's not the point.' I hissed. 'It's a question of respect.'

'Oh, he is just trying to get a reaction. Leave him be until he really causes a problem again. It won't be long, I'm sure.'

I muttered but settled back into my seat, giving Styrbjorn's back one more foul look. To my fury, he turned at that moment and saw me, giving a delighted smile and a wave in return.

'I don't know if you should allow him to get away with so much; it will encourage men like him to ill-discipline,' I said to Harald.

'Eric. Focus your efforts on controlling them when it matters, and giving them a little space when it doesn't. He doesn't push at me because he disrespects me; he is just having fun and getting to feel a little independence.'

'It still feels like he is disrespecting me,' I grumbled. 'He waited until you were gone but flaunted it for me.'

Harald laughed deeply and drank from his ale. 'I didn't say anything about him not disrespecting you, Eric.' Then he slapped me on the back with a friendly grin. 'I doubt he gives a shit what you think.'

3

I woke the next day to a pounding in my head, a pounding that would not go away. It was often the case, ever since the great blow to the head I took in the Rus falling off a siege ladder, that I would get thunderous headaches, especially after drinking. I opened my eyes and rubbed them, then my temples, and then I realised the pounding was at the door not on the inside of my drink-addled skull.

'Eric!' shouted a muffled voice.

'What?' I growled, trying to lever myself up, cursing whoever had disturbed my rest. I glanced at the window and saw that it was barely light outside. It was far too early on a day off-duty for anyone to be disturbing me.

'Eric, Aki has sent for you!'

I groaned again. Of course, it was Aki. Aki was the second in command of the Varangian guard and a long-serving thorn in my guts. He had been the most senior komes of the guard, leading the second bandon, when Harald and I arrived from the Rus. He had taken an instant and vicious dislike to Harald for his arrogance, his insubordination, and his status as a prince that gained him so much favour with so many people.

Aki had no great family name; he had become the most senior bandon commander by his skill, discipline and dedication. When Báulfr the Broad, commander of the guard when we arrived, had died in battle against the Arabs, everyone, even Harald, had expected Aki would take over.

But the emperor had other priorities, and he had appointed Harald as he saw in him a potential threat and ally in power. That had backfired spectacularly, but regardless, Aki had been the one cast aside to make way for Harald's ascent.

Harald had recognised Aki's value, however, because despite the discord between them no one could deny Aki was a fearsome leader and disciplinarian, and Harald valued both. And he respected Aki's willingness to stand up and disagree where he thought it important. So Harald had made him second spatharios, the second in command of the whole guard, and given him the responsibilities of discipline, administration, and taking over command if Harald was absent or fell in battle.

Well, all that is to say that Harald might have respected and valued Aki, but Harald didn't have to answer to him like I did. I fucking hated Aki. I was certain he was particularly hard on me to punish me for being so close to Harald. It was not worth the pain it would cause me to refuse to come when Aki summoned me, despite the searing effects a night of drinking was having on my skull.

'I'm coming!' I blurted out.

'It's urgent! He is in the barracks of the tenth!' the voice called, and then I heard footsteps running away.

I dragged some clothes on, deciding I would receive less admonishment for not being in full uniform and maille than I would for being late, and headed down towards the south wing where the tenth bandon had their quarters.

When I approached, I could see something was wrong. Men were milling around outside; there was anger, confusion and grief in the crowd.

'Make way!' I called, and men stood aside. I might not have been a komes, but I was the standard bearer of the Varangians, and although I had no men under my permanent command, in reality, I was subordinate only to Aki and Harald himself.

I went through the door, nervous now, and peered down the length of the barracks. The room was mostly empty, but I could see a few men were still in bed, motionless and comatose from the night before, and a couple were moaning and rolling in their beds. The smell of vomit was in the air.

I was furious. The men should know better than to allow themselves to get into this state. Aki was going to flay them for this when they shook off their hangovers. I saw the man himself stooping over a bed, inspecting the motionless resident of it with a look of pure fury.

I stopped in front of him and made the salute. 'I am here as requested. I apologise for these men, it is a disgrace.'

Aki looked up at me in furious disbelief. 'What?'

I was confused. 'The men who are still asleep and hungover. It is not acceptable. I...' I looked at him as his face grew taut and he looked around the room again.

'Eric, these men are not asleep,' he finally said.

'What? But...' Then a cold hand gripped me and I looked more closely at the man they were standing over. He was on his back, a splash of drying vomit soaked the sheets near his head and was spattered on the floor. His face was the colour of the whitewashed walls, and his eyes were open and bloodshot.

'They are dead.'

I stepped back, appalled, and then looked around the room in a daze. There were three more motionless figures, and now that I was not busy admonishing myself they were so obviously dead, not sleeping. Even as I looked, two of the Greek doctors were tending to one of the moaning men, trying to get him to drink water. They did not look hopeful.

'What happened?' I said breathlessly. Then I looked back at Aki. 'Where is Harald?'

'He is in the palace, he left just before dawn. I have sent for him. As for what happened, we don't know. The doctors say it must be poison. But who would poison these men? There is no pattern, they are not enemies, they are not all friends.'

A horrible, churning ball of understanding erupted in my stomach, and I looked around again. 'Where is Styrbjorn?'

'Who?'

'Styrbjorn the Goat.'

'Fourteenth bandon? Probably in their barracks across the courtyard. Don't worry, though, we have already checked. It was just men of the tenth. Among the rest nothing more than sore heads and hangovers, a few throwing up their guts,' Aki said. 'Now, I need you to—'

'Was Styrbjorn one of the ones throwing up?' I asked, cutting over Aki, who glared at me in annoyance.

'Why do you care about Styrbjorn? Eric, we have four dead men here and two more dying and I need you to focus so we can find out what happened.'

'I think I know what happened,' I muttered, rushing for the exit and pushing my way through the crowd again, running across the courtyard until I reached the fourteenth bandon's quarters.

'Styrbjorn!' I shouted, and I pressed past a sea of confused guardsmen until an unsteady voice answered me.

'Here.'

I went towards the voice, finding Styrbjorn sitting on the edge of his bed, head down, looking as sick as the dog he was. He looked up at me and his face was pale. He tried to stand up but his legs wobbled and he cursed weakly.

Aki had followed me, and he pushed in alongside and glared at me and then Styrbjorn, eyes demanding an explanation. Styrbjorn looked horrified.

'I'm sorry, Second Spatharios. I must have had more than I thought. I will shake it off, I promise.' He tried to lever himself to his feet again but simply couldn't, and he slumped down with a look of confusion and shame.

'Explain what you know, Eric,' said Aki, but he was not angry any more. He was smart and he could see something was wrong with Styrbjorn beyond having too much to drink.

'Styrbjorn, who were you drinking with last night? The ones at the table that shared the food with you?'

Styrbjorn looked up with a defiant shake of his head. 'I'll not name names to share my trouble, I'll take whatever is coming myself. It wasn't them who got me so drunk.'

I knelt down to get eye-to-eye with Styrbjorn, and the smell of sickness was all over him. 'You don't understand, Styrbjorn, you aren't in trouble. But I need to know who you shared that food you took from Harald with,' I asked in a kindly voice, and it disarmed him.

'Some lads from the tenth,' he whispered. Then he looked up at Aki. 'Why?'

I stood, my hands shaking. I looked at Aki nervously. 'We should speak outside.'

Aki took one look at Styrbjorn and then at the several dozen men gathered around us. He measured the options then he grunted. 'It's too late to keep this a secret. Those men have been poisoned. We are under attack. Turn out the guard, I want everyone who can hold a weapon in armour on the square, now.'

Then he nodded at a couple of the nearest guardsmen. 'Get Styrbjorn to the tenth barracks, take him to the doctors there.'

Styrbjorn looked up at me helplessly as two men pulled him to his feet. 'It's poison, isn't it?' he whispered, gaunt and afraid.

I nodded. 'Meant for Harald.'

'Am I dying?'

I looked at him for a long moment. It's one thing to face death in battle, it's quite another to have an invisible horror working its way through your guts that you cannot face or fight. He was terrified, and I couldn't lie to him. I shook my head. 'I don't know, Styrbjorn. I've got to go and get the commander.'

And then Aki and I turned and rushed back to the square and started shouting orders. Men were running to and fro already, going to get their equipment, and those who were the fastest were already assembling on the hard-packed earth where last night we had been celebrating, now arming for a war we had not started, against an enemy we did not know.

'First fifty, go with Sveinn to the palace and find Harald, bring him back here. Go!' Aki shouted at the small crowd of fully armed men and nodded to Sveinn who saluted and set off, roaring orders at the mixed group of guardsmen behind him.

I doubt Sveinn even knew what was happening, but it didn't matter.

Aki turned to me. 'Eric, go and arm. There is nothing we can do now until we have news from Harald.'

'Could this be the start of an attack on the palace?' I said. 'They plan to kill Harald and then use the confusion to take the emperor?'

Aki nodded. 'It is possible. I will send the first full bandon to go and reinforce the first at the palace. But I need you ready to lead if there is a fight, so go, hurry.'

I nodded and ran for the stairs leading to my quarters. I suddenly realised my hangover was gone, my head was clear. The battle rush will do that like nothing else.

I powered up the stairs and went to my room. We always had our equipment out and ready to use at a moment's notice, it was our entire purpose, and we practised and polished and prepared. But it takes help to get a full maille hauberk on quickly, and I swore and struggled in my room alone as I wrestled mine on over my tunic, finally shaking it over my shoulders and buckling my belt around my waist. Something inside was twisted and uncomfortable, but I didn't have the time to fix it.

I jammed my helmet on and strapped on my sword and seax, before eyeing the bare pole that would normally hold the guard's standard before admonishing myself. We were not going into battle; there was no place for the great purple banner of the guard.

I rushed down the stairs again and found three of the four banda that were stationed in the barracks on the training square in full battle gear. Even as I rushed out, Aki despatched the second to go and patrol the perimeter of the barracks area of the palace grounds.

He had not returned to his quarters to get armed; two men had brought his equipment out and were dressing him even as he shouted orders.

I jogged over to him, and as I got there the gates opened and Harald and Sveinn came through at the head of a couple of dozen men. He saw us and immediately strode over, his face stormy.

'What has happened? We are under attack, who from? Sveinn wasn't able to explain.'

'He doesn't know, and really, neither do we,' said Aki. 'Four are dead, a few more are dying. It's poison.' He looked at me with a hint of uncertainty and then back at Harald. 'It looks like it was meant for you.'

Harald's eyes twitched and his mouth curled as he thought, then his gaze flicked up to meet mine. 'The stuffed bird?'

Damn him, he had worked it out so quickly. It had taken me ten times as long to make the connection.

I nodded. 'Yes.'

'Styrbjorn is dead?'

'No, he didn't eat enough, but a group of the men shared it out.'

Harald's temple pulsed and his expression darkened like thunder. 'Where is the boy?'

'The boy?' asked Aki uncertainly.

'Yes, the boy who brought it to our table.'

Aki looked at me and shrugged. I slumped. 'I hadn't thought to get him... It's all been so quick and—'

Harald cut me off with a gesture of annoyance. 'No time for excuses. Let's go to the cookhouse, now.' He looked at Aki. 'Some of the men are still alive?'

Aki nodded.

'Send to the palace for Afra, he might know something about this poison. Maybe he knows someone or something who can help them.'

* * *

We arrived at the cookhouse, a squat, low building near the servants' quarters behind the barrack complex, with twenty fully armed men. There was an open door and we went through it into the kitchens, finding the head of the cooks talking to a half dozen other men in low, urgent tones.

They all looked up in shock as Harald, Aki and I barged in with half a dozen guardsmen.

'Commander, what... You have already been told?'

Harald's eyes narrowed and he motioned at the men to block the only other exit from the large room.

'Told what?' he said icily. 'What do you know?'

The cook looked around nervously. 'Two of the lads had a fight. One of them is dead, the other ran.' He bowed his head. 'I'm sorry, I didn't think it was so important to tell you straight away, I wanted to understand what happened first. They might have been arguing over a girl, you see – one of them was sweet on this young thing from the washhouse and—'

'Enough.' Harald cut him off with a sour expression and a shake of his head. 'I don't care about any of that. Show me to the body.'

The nervous man instantly stopped his babbling and nodded, pointing at the now-blocked door. 'It's in the storeroom at the end,' he said in a hushed tone.

We filed quickly down the indicated corridor and came to the furthest open door. Inside, half leaning against a barrel was the body of the boy who had served Harald the stuffed bird. He had obviously been dead for most of the night.

Harald scowled. 'That's him, isn't it.'

I nodded.

'So they silenced him before he could say anything.' He went back out of the door and pointed at the cook. 'Where did you get this boy?'

The cook shrugged. 'I don't choose them – the palace provides us with whoever we need.'

'And the other one, the killer, who was he?'

'I don't know, Commander, he hadn't been with us long. Valens. Nice boy, easy-going, did what he was told.'

'Where was he from?' Harald asked irritably.

The cook quailed under the stare and shook his head. 'I don't know, I never thought to ask. He really just fetched things from the stores.'

'He didn't cook?'

'No, Commander.'

Harald scowled and advanced on the cook, towering over him. 'So who cooked the stuffed bird with the figs that the dead one served to us?'

The cook's eyebrows knitted together in confusion despite his fear. 'Stuffed bird? What... I don't understand.'

Harald searched his eyes, looking for a lie or deception. 'Last night, that dead boy served me a stuffed bird, said it was from you, a special treat the nobles like. It was poisoned, intended for me. Who cooked it?' He grabbed a handful of the cook's clothes as he spoke.

The cook dissolved into frantic babbling as he finally understood the magnitude of what had happened. I was unable to discern all the terrified jabbering that spewed from his mouth, but he was furiously denying anyone had cooked a stuffed bird in his kitchen the night before.

Eventually, Harald believed him enough to drop him with a disgusted sigh and he looked at Aki then back at the cook. 'In future, we will supply our own workers. Get rid of these ones.'

Aki nodded and the cook wailed in fear as a handful of guardsmen were directed to take the wretched man and his assistants away.

It was a ridiculous thing to say, in my opinion. We had no easy way to find trustworthy staff in the city on short notice, and the Vigla was in charge of who was and was not allowed into the palace grounds. But we weren't going to argue with him on the spot. I just hoped Aki didn't have them all executed before we realised we needed them back. Harald had left that part of the order quite vague.

'Come, let's go back to the barracks,' Harald said, striding back down the corridor as the cook's wails receded into the background.

* * *

Afra was waiting for us in the courtyard when we arrived and his face was dark.

'Commander,' he said with a nod.

'Do you know what it is?' asked Harald.

Afra shook his head. 'No, it's not my expertise.' He hesitated. 'But I know someone in the city, someone who supplies such things. He might be able to tell me.'

Harald nodded, trying and failing to mask his distaste.

'What of the boy who brought you the food? A cook's boy?' Afra asked.

'Dead.'

Afra nodded without any surprise. 'To be expected. And the one who killed him?'

'Another boy, called Valens. Killed him last night and fled. I want him found.'

'He will be dead or gone, Commander,' Afra said with a shake of his head, but then he saw the intensity of Harald's stare and nodded meekly. 'But I will have Thorir look anyway.'

'Was there anything else that could help our search?'

Harald nodded. 'Yes. The poison was on a stuffed bird. Stuffed with figs, honeyed and spiced.'

'What kind of bird?'

'I don't know, some sort of goose, maybe. I didn't taste it,' he said with a dour expression. 'Anyway, the cook says it didn't come from his kitchen, so it was brought in by one of the boys. How could they do that? How could they carry that through the palace grounds unnoticed?'

Afra jerked his head towards the servants' area of the palace, out of sight beyond the southeast side of the barracks. 'Easily. In the servants' quarters, every manner of things is being carried around, in and out of the palace. They have their own gate and it would be easy to smuggle a platter of food in.'

'The bird was steaming hot, freshly cooked,' I said brightly.

Harald nodded. 'Yes, it must have been cooked here.'

Afra looked interested. 'There are not many kitchens in the palace grounds. Yes, I should be able to find someone who saw something. Good, thank you.'

Harald nodded, satisfied, then he looked at me. 'I was meeting with the empress when I was disturbed, I will go back. Come with me. Bring twenty men.'

'What if there are further attacks?' asked Aki.

Harald shook his head. 'Someone went to great lengths to hide who did this; they wouldn't bother if it was a wider attack. No, this was just targeted at me, and I am certain who is behind it.'

I blanched. 'The emperor?'

Harald flicked me an angry look for saying that out loud in front of Aki and Afra, but shook his head. 'I don't think so. He needs me too much.'

'It's a fucking outrageous accusation, Eric. Some would call it treason,' growled Aki, who was not so involved in all the palace intrigue as we had been the previous years, and was still deeply loyal and perhaps a little naive.

'It is,' agreed Harald placatingly. 'Eric is tired, worried and hungover, and his judgement is compromised. He won't make such accusations again, will he?' Harald glared at me.

'No,' I mumbled. 'Of course not. I apologise. As you say, it is the situation that has got to me.'

Harald nodded. 'Good. Come, then, I need to get back to my meeting.'

4

As we walked back through the palace Harald was quiet and restrained. When we passed the entrance to Michael's half of the palace he stopped and stared at it for a moment.

'Ah, hell, I will know the truth of it.'

'What? Harald, no. The empress will be waiting.'

'She can wait a little longer.'

'This is not a wise thing to do, Harald.'

He ignored my entreaty and marched to the doors, getting a snapped salute from the four guardsmen at the entrance.

'Harald, don't do this,' I hissed, following him closely. 'You cannot make accusations without proof, and we have nothing!'

'I don't need to make accusations, I just need to see his eyes when he sees me and I will know the truth.'

I could suddenly see how angry he was. He had been holding it in as we reacted to the situation, but now it was bubbling to the surface, and Harald's anger was a hard thing indeed to contain.

The guards opened the door without a question being asked, and why wouldn't they? They were Varangians and there was nowhere in the palace Harald was not allowed to go unhindered except the very innermost chambers of the emperor's quarters.

I struggled to keep up with his lengthy gait as he strode through the vast complex, through the courtyard that led to the hall of nineteen couches and past, into the corridor that contained the hall of war and the great offices of the emperor's closest advisors and generals.

'Where is John?' Harald snapped at a guardsman as we passed.

The wide-eyed guardsman pointed further down the hall, and Harald ploughed onwards, ignoring my quiet protests.

John the eunuch, the emperor's brother and closest advisor. Since Harald had humiliated him in front of Zoe and Michael the previous year he had avoided another confrontation and kept out of Harald's way. But despite the cuts in his power and influence, John was still the emperor's closest advisor and his chamberlain. And nothing was more certain than that he hated and feared Harald in equal measure.

Harald reached the next set of doors but they were unguarded, and then we turned the corner and spotted two Varangians of the first bandon guarding a door. 'That will be it,' Harald said under his breath.

He marched over to them and they shared a surprised look and snapped their salute. 'Protospatharios,' one of them said. 'What is wrong?'

'I need to see John immediately. Open the door.'

'Yes, Protospatharios, I will ask.'

'No, you will open it for me.'

The men gave each other a worried look, and then one of them pulled a key from his belt and unlocked the door.

Harald didn't wait, practically barging through into the outer office, where a surprised servant was standing frozen mid-stride carrying a tray with a jug and some fruits.

Harald ignored him and ripped past the thick curtain that separated the two rooms, with me following on his heels.

I was in the room in time to see three alarmed faces look up from a table. John and two nobles I did not recognise.

John's eyes went wide and for a second he flicked his gaze towards the door on the other side of him, gauging the possibility of escaping. But we were already too close, and nothing makes a man look guilty more than running.

John collected himself and stood from the papers he had been discussing with the two other men, who were looking confused and nervous.

'Not expecting to see me this morning, eunuch?' said Harald in a voice that dripped menace.

'Certainly not in this manner,' replied John. Then he turned and whispered to the two nobles, who looked perplexed but nodded and then turned to leave.

Harald allowed them to exit the room, never taking his eyes off John.

John straightened up, all signs of being intimidated gone. 'So, what is it? I hear there was an incident this morning. You had the guard out in the palace grounds?' he asked mildly.

Harald strode forwards, stalking up to the eunuch like a leopard. 'It was you. I know it was you,' he said in a guttural whisper.

John made an admirable effort not to react to Harald's advance, but he did start to sidestep away, hands clenched behind him.

'What was me?'

'Only you could have placed those boys in my service.'

John furrowed his brows. 'You need to explain what you

mean, Protospatharios. I am a busy man and I don't have time for whatever you are refusing to say.'

'Yes, you think you are so clever. You think by arranging the servant's death you are safe. But you made a mistake, eunuch.' Harald leaned right in and smiled his wolfish smile. 'The cook's boy talked before he died. You need better assassins.'

There was a flicker of fear in John's eyes, and they fluttered as his body tensed. It was only there for a moment but it was enough, and then it was gone and his body and his gaze relaxed.

'You will have to explain. Pretend I am dumber than you. That might be difficult, but you will manage.' John tried to speak with bravado, but I could see he was shaken.

Harald sneered triumphantly, waggling a finger. 'I knew it was you.'

John's gaze hardened. 'And how will you prove your accusation? I know nothing about any cook's boy. What did he do, poison your food?' It was gloating, daring Harald to overreach.

'And how would you know that is what happened?'

'Because I am not a fool and you are.'

The two of them stared at each other, neither giving ground verbally or physically.

'You don't have any evidence of anything, do you? So what if a dying boy said something. Who will hear his testimony?'

'No one. But it doesn't matter. This won't be decided in a court.' Harald wagged his finger at me. 'Come, Eric. We have all we need from this one.'

'You have nothing, and you know it!' said John, and his voice was higher than normal.

Harald marched from the room, and my gaze lingered on John just long enough to see him swallow hard before I followed Harald through the curtain.

* * *

'That was stupid,' I said bluntly as we walked back towards the empress's quarters.

'No. Before I was suspicious; now I am certain.'

'We have no proof.'

'Maybe not, not yet. We shall see what Afra finds out.'

We could not discuss it further because we had reached our destination, and a very angry-looking attendant impatiently waved us through the familiar doors and into the presence of the empress of the Greeks.

'My apologies, Basilissa, there was an incident but it is resolved,' said Harald, bowing deeply to Empress Zoe in the shaded garden of her extravagant quarters.

Zoe looked neither perturbed nor relaxed, maintaining a studious neutrality at the explanation. Walking out in the middle of an audience with the emperor or empress was not something that was done. But she was managing to hide her displeasure well.

'You may sit, Araltes,' she said, using the Greek version of Harald's name as always. It would be beneath the dignity of the empress to use foreign words.

Harald nodded and took the available stool as Zoe relaxed back into her heavily cushioned lounger.

She still exuded magnificence. It was four years since we had arrived and I had first laid eyes on the famously beautiful empress. It was not, in fact, fair to say that she was just purely beautiful; her entire presence was impressive. From the perfection of her clothes to her complete confidence, and the impeccable attention given to her hair and the special colourings and lotions she was rumoured to apply to her skin that kept her looking like a woman half her true age.

Not that I was sure what her true age was. It was something of a polite secret, but Harald believed it was at least fifty.

'What was the nature of the incident, Araltes?' she asked casually.

'Nothing I need to concern you with, Basilissa.'

'I would ask you not to lie to me, Protospatharios. Anything important enough to rush from a meeting for is something that I should be concerned about.'

Harald nodded in acceptance. 'An attempt was made to poison me. It was discovered this morning.'

Zoe's eyes flicked up, showing her first emotion. Was it fear? Concern? I am not sure, but it was something. It was quickly repressed.

'Do you know who the culprit was?'

'I do.'

'Not Michael, I hope,' she said calmly.

Harald shook his head after a short pause. 'No, Basilissa. I believe it was John.'

Zoe's chin rose a fraction. 'I see. What evidence do you have?' She looked excited now, unashamedly, for John was her enemy too. She had ordered Harald to kill him at one point, a command Harald had refused in order to keep the peace between her and her husband.

'None.'

'Oh, how disappointing.' Zoe relaxed back into her chair with what passed for a frown on a face that always showed so little of her emotions. 'So you will do nothing about it,' she said. And it was an order, not a question.

Harald squirmed in his seat. 'Yes, for now. But my men are searching for the culprit, and if he leads me to John...'

'Then things will be different, but until then... Nothing.' Zoe tapped a finger on her leg. 'Now, how did your people fail you so badly that poisoned food reached you? Incompetence or treachery? Who checks your meals?' she flicked an accusatory glance at me and I winced.

Harald stretched slightly, clearly feeling foolish. 'No one checks my meals.'

Zoe raised an eyebrow. 'Then they are prepared separately?'

Harald looked even more squeamish and Zoe sighed like she was talking to a child. 'So what do you eat, and how was it supposed to be kept safe?'

'I just eat what the men eat, from the same kitchen. So, no one can poison me easily or deliberately.'

Zoe rolled her eyes. 'How have you survived this long?' Then she signalled to her attendant Hypatia, who came over to help her to her feet elegantly.

'Come with me, young Araltes. I am going to educate you on survival in this city for one who has dangerous enemies.'

Harald got to his feet sharply and followed Zoe, glancing at me in curiosity. We followed the empress through the garden and into the side area of the empress's part of the palace, near the servants' quarters. She led us to a door and Hypatia knocked while Zoe stood patiently waiting.

The door was opened by a servant who was very much surprised to see the empress, and who bowed dramatically and deeply, then shuffled aside so that we could all enter.

Inside the empress turned around and gestured around her. I scanned the room. It was quite large. A long table stood in the centre, covered in all manner of exquisite utensils, serving platters and plates. There were no low windows, only high ones along the rooflines, and they were small. Far too small even for a child to climb through.

On a wooden counter at the back, next to a clay hearth and oven that was gently smoking, were an assortment of plates of food of various kinds. Along the other wall was a shelf with fine glass jugs and ceramic jars, and a large metal box beaded with water that betrayed it contained ice.

There were four people in the room, besides the ones who had just entered. Two servants and two armed guards.

'This is where my food comes from,' Zoe said to Harald. 'Anything I eat, anything I drink, it comes from this room alone.'

Harald looked around, thinking. 'But it cannot be cooked in here, there is only this simple hearth.'

'Precisely. The food is prepared and cooked in the kitchens, by staff who are highly trusted. But even then, anything that leaves the kitchen to enter this room is tasted first, and then the food is left for half a day to check that nothing happens to the tasters, for some poisons are quite devious and slow. Only once the tasters have been checked and are in good health can food enter this room through that door.' She pointed at the far side of the room. 'Nothing goes into this room through any other way. Once food is in here, it is safe.'

'And the two guards and the servants check nothing happens while it is in here.'

'Precisely. Each pair checks the other is not breaking the rules, and all are heavily checked before they are trusted with this task.'

'But then everything in here is stale,' added Harald, eyeing a platter of bread.

'Indeed. Everything I eat is old, cold or boring. If I want it heated, they heat it on the hearth, but it barely helps revive much of it. That is one of the many sacrifices I make for my position. I am the richest woman in the world, but I can only eat something if I ask for it half a day in advance, and even then, it is often ruined by the time it reaches me.'

I regarded the entire room with distaste. Harald looked

around in fascination. 'And who do you think would dare to poison you?'

Zoe laughed. 'Araltes, they are so many I do not even bother to consider their number. This is the reality of rule in the Roman Empire.'

'And does Michael do the same?'

'No. He is too decadent and too newly empowered to accept this, but John keeps him as safe as he can,' Zoe said with obvious contempt.

Harald nodded slowly. 'I see. I had never considered something this... complex.'

'Well, now you must. The first time they failed, the second time they will learn. Will you?'

Harald bowed his head slightly at Zoe. 'I will, and I give you my thanks.'

Zoe just tutted softly and made her way to the door again, headed back into the garden with everyone in the room scurrying to either get out of the way or follow her.

As we strolled back through the lavish gardens, Harald was thinking deeply. Finally, Zoe reached her seat and turned while Hypatia rearranged her clothes to be ready to sit.

'Basilissa, why are you helping me with this? Would it be so awful for you if the next attempt on my life succeeded?'

Zoe gave Harald a thoughtful look. 'I am not happy with you, Araltes. You overstepped your bounds when you constrained me. But, I understand why you did it, however misguided, and furthermore I am confident whoever replaced you would be worse for me. So no, I do not wish your death. Not at the moment.' She added that last bit casually as if it were really a minor matter to her. Which, terrifyingly, it probably was.

When they had met the first few times there had always been warmth, and perhaps even a hint of flirting, from the empress to

Harald. And he had been intoxicated by it, I had seen that as clear as spring water runs.

But now Zoe was disdainful and cold, and it was clear that nothing was forgiven or forgotten. Yet, they needed each other still. It was a very odd and uncomfortable situation. I hated it, as I hated all politics.

'Is there anything else you wish from me?' said Harald with precise politeness, lowering his eyes from the empress.

She examined a fingernail and then slowly gestured for him to leave. 'No. I will save the original subject of our meeting for another day. I am tired and you have taken too much of my time. Try to avoid any of these disturbances in the future.'

Harald bowed. 'I will indeed try.' And then we bowed and left.

* * *

We returned to the barracks to find Afra and Aki waiting for us.

'How are the men?' Harald asked, and Aki shook his head. 'All the ones poisoned except Styrbjorn are dead. The doctors came, Afra's man came. Nothing could help them. Styrbjorn lived because he spat his mouthful out, but even that brief moment was enough to sicken him.'

Harald looked angry and glum. 'What was the poison?'

Afra looked worried. 'We don't know. Whatever it was, it was extremely potent.'

'Your man couldn't recognise the results?'

'No. If we had some remains of the food, perhaps he could have smelled it, but everything is gone.'

Harald nodded in resignation. 'So, we need to find the kitchen.'

'We don't,' said Afra with a shake of the head.

Harald looked up. 'Why?'

'A cook from the senate house kitchen was found floating in the Golden Horn this morning, with his head caved in.'

'Shit.'

'Yes.'

'So, what do we have, anything?'

Afra shrugged. 'No cook, no poison, no poisoner. We will keep looking and asking questions, but whoever organised this was well prepared. I doubt there is anything left for us to find. The boy Valens is gone, and it was undoubtedly a false name anyway. We are very unlikely to find him.'

'Damn. Well, we will need to change the way I am fed,' said Harald with a sigh. 'I have received some advice on that, we will discuss it later.'

'You have?' said Afra in surprise. 'From who?'

Harald gave him a blank look.

'Oh, I see. Well. I will get back to Thorir and see if he has any ideas.' Afra nodded and left.

'Aki. I want guards on the cookhouse at all hours now. No one comes or goes who isn't recognised.'

Aki nodded.

Harald winced. 'And Aki?'

'Yes?'

'You didn't kill the kitchen staff, did you?'

Aki shook his head with a wry smile. 'Of course not. I have them locked in a storeroom. I thought you might want to keep at least some of them.'

Harald smiled. 'This is why you are my second, Aki. Well, if any of them were guilty they would have been killed before we reached them. Go and release them, they have the evening meal to prepare for the men.'

'And what will you eat?'

Harald thought about it for a moment. 'I will go and eat at a tavern.'

We both gave him a questioning look and he shrugged. 'What? They can't have poisoned all of them in advance.'

'You still want me to go?' I stared at Harald in disbelief as we sat in a tavern halfway down the second hill that flanked the processional way.

'Yes. Why not?'

'Because you are being attacked, and they will surely attack again.'

'And how will you being here help? Are you going to be my food taster?'

That was a good point, I hadn't thought that through. I just didn't want to be anywhere else while he was in danger.

'No, but I can organise guards, check staff... Anything that helps.'

Harald sipped his watered wine irritably, and I saw him give it a brief suspicious look first.

'No, Afra can do all of that better than you. This situation just makes getting my treasury out of the city more important than ever. If I have to leave in a hurry, I may not have time to save it if it is here.'

Damn, that was a good point. I hated his logic, because I was so hot-headed and made my decisions largely with feel and instinct, and he was so often cold and careful and made me feel stupid. Unless he was angry or threatened – then he had a habit of losing his calm and I became the voice of reason. Bah, it was why we were such a good pair. At least one of us was almost always thinking clearly.

'I thought you would be happy to go to Kyiv anyway? Finally, you can be reunited with your wife.' He gave me a disapproving look because he knew that my rash and rushed marriage to Olga in Kyiv had been quickly and rather dishonourably pushed from my mind when I left for Constantinople. I had never considered, when I asked her to marry me, that I might soon be exiled from the Rus for half a decade. I had not been able to bring her to the city, it was too dangerous. So I had sent her letters and money when I could but had not received a reply for a while, not since before our expedition to the Holy Land.

I squirmed. 'Truthfully, I fear it. She will be furious with me, and she is right to be.'

'Then divorce her.'

'And lay the shame of that upon her? No, I couldn't.'

'Surely it is better than the shame of being married, but never seeing her husband.'

I shook my head in denial. 'I send her enough money to make sure she lives well.'

'You put her in storage the way we put our ships in storage. It is unbecoming,' said Harald with distaste, and I did not reply because it was true. 'Anyway, it is your business, not mine. I just thought you would be happy to resolve the matter one way or another.'

I think I just slumped in my chair and sulked, taking a deep draught of my wine and not caring if it was full of poison because that seemed a better option than sailing back to the damn Rus.

It's a long way. Did I ever explain to you properly just how far it is from Constantinople to Kyiv? Well, I don't know exactly, it's so far, but it has to be a thousand miles by ship. That is nearly a month's travel to get there and back in the most perfect conditions, and conditions were never perfect.

'I don't want to discuss it further, Eric. I need this done and I need you to do it.'

I nodded into my cup of wine. What else was there to do?

5

We launched one of our two longboats from the shipyard. We had used them infrequently over the four years we were there, but we periodically sent fifty men at a time of our core warband, the blood-marked and those close to us, to launch them, take them out and practise with them.

Why? Because Harald liked them and didn't want to sell them and buy Greek-style ships. It was part of our blood, sailing longships, and he had the wealth to pay the extortionate harbour fees.

I had fifty men with me, and we sailed with all our war gear but kept it wrapped until we left the harbour. It was silly, frankly. Anyone who saw us leave knew who we were. But none of them knew we carried a bilge laden with a fortune in gold and jewels. We had taken extraordinary care to conceal that by stitching all of it into bags inside of our rolled and packed maille hauberks and inside our belongings.

No one would think twice seeing us lugging our heavy armour shirts down to the ship and laying them under our seats.

No one would hear metal clinking over the sound of all our metal clinking.

I thought it was the idea of a master of problem-solving. But then I would, because it was my idea.

Ha! I was not just a ferocious wielder of spear and sword; I was a great thinker sometimes too, back when I was young and my mind had not lost its sharpness like a spear left outside in the rain for a season.

Sorry, my old mind is wandering. I won't waste your time sitting in this sunshine relating to you the journey to Kyiv. It was dull. I disliked sailing voyages even then. Bah, don't look at me like that! Not all of our people are born to love the sea. It is large, cold, wet, and full of things that would eat you if they had the chance.

It took over two weeks to reach Kyiv and it was my first time going up the Dnipr, against the stream. Ten days of much rowing and little sailing, hard work. We all arrived there exhausted, sore, and desperate to get into the city and away from our oars.

The first thing that happened when we arrived at the docks was the grand prince's trade inspectors came to assess our cargo for taxes.

Now, we weren't about to let those thieving bastards see the colour of our gold, so we flatly refused.

'The grand prince is expecting us. Everything in this ship is a gift for him, and him alone,' I said, glaring at the Rus official.

He was used to being glared at; he was a tax collector, after all. But he was less used to being glared at by fifty armed men, and he didn't care to press his argument more than was necessary to be able to claim he tried. So he sent word to the palace and told us not to leave our ships. That suited us; we didn't want to go anywhere while our precious cargo just lay there.

Eventually, a court official came down the hill and he spoke to the tax collector and sent him away after a short conversation.

'Eric Alvarsson?' he said, looking at us.

'That's me,' I said, standing. 'I am here to seek an audience with Grand Prince Yaroslav.'

'So I understand.' The official looked me up and down with a polite smile.

I sighed. 'I was in the prince's guard for several years. I know the process. We will find lodgings and await an audience. Is it likely to be in the next week or so?'

The official looked amused. 'The grand prince requests your presence at once. I am to escort you to the palace.'

'He what?' I mumbled.

He repeated it more slowly as if I were simple. 'He requests your presence... at once.'

That stunned me. The grand prince had never received anyone at once after they arrived when I had been in his guard. Not ever.

'What of my crew and cargo?'

'A detachment of the guard is coming down to escort you all to the barracks. Your ship will be safe here. You are able to carry all of the, uh, gifts?'

The man obviously knew what we were about. Harald had explained it in his letter to the prince.

'We are.'

'Good. Have your men wait here, and come with me.'

'Do I have time to change? I've been sailing for two weeks.'

The man looked displeased. 'I'm afraid my instructions are clear – you are invited to come immediately.'

I raised my eyebrows and looked down at my tunic. True, I had washed myself in the river a few times, but I was hardly fit for a grand prince.

Well, it wasn't my choice. Bemused, and after leaving Halldor with orders, I followed the man up through the city and into the whitewashed citadel with its cathedral and palace.

How small it was to my eyes then! The first time I saw the white city of Kyiv with its shining, domed cathedral I thought it was the most magnificent building in the world. But it would fit entirely inside the great cathedral of Hagia Sophia and leave space to spare.

* * *

I was shown through the familiar corridors of the palace and into the prince's quarters. It was comforting, in a way. Nothing had changed. The hangings, the carpets, the furnishings and the guards. It was like I had only left the day before, and four years had not passed.

I was shown to the very seat that Harald had sat in for his private audiences and I sat on the edge, barely brushing the fabric with my arse before the door opened and Yaroslav walked in. That shocked me a little. The room hadn't changed, but Yaroslav had. His hair was noticeably greyer, his limp more pronounced, his modest belly stretching more defiantly at his buttons.

His eyes were the same, however. Intelligent and searching, full of fire and force.

I stood and snapped out the customary salute of the Rus palace guard.

'Good man, you haven't forgotten your time in my service,' said the prince with a smile, limping over to his grand chair and sighing as he lowered himself into it.

I waited until he sat and nervously took my own seat again.

That was the first time for me. The first time I had ever had a meeting with one of the world's great rulers, on my own. Prince Yaroslav, Emperor Michael, Empress Zoe, King Anund Jacob; I had met them all, been spoken to by all, however briefly. But never as the one they were dealing with, just as Harald's man.

'I apologise, Your Highness, for my state. I have just completed a long voyage and did not think to prepare for my arrival properly.'

Yaroslav waved my apology away. 'I had to see you immediately, as I am leaving tomorrow for three weeks' hunting. Now, I have little time, so to business.' He eyed me sternly. 'Your troublesome prince is doing well for himself, I hear. Commander of the Varangian guard?'

I nodded nervously. The prince did not seem happy.

'And he sends you for a favour from me? The last master he so dearly insulted.'

I quailed. My lip wobbled, I think my hands might even have shaken. Is there shame in it? No. None of you knew Yaroslav. He was more terrifying than any battle. I would rather face ten rows of sharpened spears than the disapproval of the only living man Harald truly looked up to. He had the living force of raging rapids and all its terror.

'The balls on him!' Yaroslav's broad face cracked into a smile as he slapped his thigh. 'Ha! I knew he was destined for great things, but to hear the reports my people send? The conqueror of the Arabs, the saviour of the Church of the Holy Sepulchre, the protector of the emperor and empress of Rome!' He laughed heartily. 'By God, I am glad I sent him away from my city – he would have been a caged lion here, and turned on his tamer all too soon. Is the world itself even big enough for your master?'

I smiled in relief. 'I am not sure, Your Highness.'

'Well, he now sends me an offer, and I consider it short of fair.'

'Oh. I apologise.' I was unsure how to respond.

'Yes. He wants me to keep his money safe, and in return, all I get is a tax of one fifth of its value? A little on the low side for such a favour.' He tapped his fingers on his leg in contemplation, although I was savvy enough to know that whatever he was going to say, he had planned it long in advance. The appearance of thinking was just for show.

'I suspect he thinks an offer of alliance will make up for the rest of the value.'

I nodded.

'But why? An impressive young man he is, but a throne he does not have. What value is there for me in an alliance with the head of my enemy's palace guard?' Yaroslav sat back and spread his arms questioningly. 'I see none unless he intends to betray his rulers and help me in any future conflict?'

'He does not, Your Highness.'

Yaroslav threw me an irritated glare. 'I know that, young man. He is not an oath breaker and I am not foolish enough to think it.'

'I apologise, Your Highness,' I said, lowering my chin.

'Hmm. So, he expects any value in an alliance to come in the future. He still intends to take the throne of Norway?'

I was nervous about this question, and I had expected it. The king of Norway at the time was the boy Magnus, and he was very much the puppet of his mother and some powerful jarls, who were very much the clients of Yaroslav. There was an implicit conflict between Yaroslav's aims for Norway and Harald's.

'That is still his rightful quest,' I said, with more pride than perhaps was necessary.

'That could cause me a great deal of problems, a war for Norway. Not in my interests at all.' Yaroslav shook his head firmly.

I said nothing while he stared at me, pretending to mull the problem over.

Then he looked to one side and tutted. 'But perhaps the boy Magnus can be peacefully moved aside, with my encouragement.'

I sat up a little straighter. Here it was: Yaroslav was gently easing what he wanted from this deal into the conversation. I had watched this game enough times to recognise that the terms were about to be presented.

'That would be interesting to Harald, I am sure, and much appreciated.'

'How much appreciated?' Yaroslav shot back, quick as a fox after a bird.

I tried not to look nervous. 'If Harald regains the throne of Norway, he swears he will be an ally and friend to the Rus. Moreover, any further wealth he earns in the empire he will send to you, and give the same tribute as already offered.'

Yaroslav watched me, waiting for more.

I was flailing, because I had no more to offer.

'That is it?'

'Ah, yes, Your Highness. That is what I have been instructed to offer.'

Yaroslav stared at me, and his fingers lightly drummed on the arm of the chair.

'It is not enough,' he said finally. 'I am disappointed your master did not foresee that. Did I overestimate him?'

I tried to hide my concern. 'I apologise, Your Highness. What else would you suggest?'

Yaroslav didn't bother making a show of thinking it over. 'An alliance is not enough. I would not help a mere rebellious prince take over the throne of Norway. I already have an ally there. But for a son-in-law, I would consider it a much more worthwhile act.'

I paled. 'A son-in-law?'

Yaroslav nodded gravely. 'I am old, Eric, and I am only getting older. I have set up sons as powerful princes, ready to take over after I die. My daughters are coming of age, and they will help secure my influence and my sons' future power outside of my borders. My eldest, Anastasia, is marrying Duke Andrew, an exiled claimant to Hungary's crown.' Yaroslav smiled. 'Andrew is very much like your Harald; young, angry, brilliant. With my support and his own wits, he will take the throne of Hungary. My dear Agatha is promised to Edward, the grandson of King Aethelred of England, also an exiled prince who has sought my protection, but will soon be ready to reclaim his throne.'

Yaroslav waved a hand in the air, counting off countries as he went. 'My wife's brother rules Sweden, I have married my sister to King Casimir of Poland. So both are safely my allies.'

My mouth started to fall open a little in awe of the scale of his ambitions and plans, being laid out in front of me like a map.

Yaroslav nodded contentedly. 'I have two daughters left. Elisiv, and young Anne. Two more countries to bring into my family; two more alliances to seal my legacy. Perhaps I will secure a prince of the Franks for Anne?'

He made a nonchalant expression and stared at me intensely. 'Finally, I offer Elisiv to Harald, to join our houses in the bonds of blood and friendship.'

'My God,' I uttered, without meaning to. I looked at my hands, still filthy from the day's rowing. They were shaking at the magnitude of it. Harald thought in terms of countries; this man's ambition spanned continents.

'Your family will rule half of Europe,' I finally stammered out.

Yaroslav nodded and his eyes twinkled. 'We will. And I was the fifth son of a minor prince of the Rus.'

I shook my head to clear it. I had abandoned the niceties of language and title, I was so engrossed in the scale of it all. 'Harald will not agree to be your vassal.'

'He does not have to. I do not seek his vassalage, Eric. I do not intend to rule all of these countries, only to secure a web of alliances that will dominate Europe, helping all of us to thrive against the threats that surround us.'

I nodded slowly. 'And at the centre of that web, the Holy Roman Empire. You do not seek any alliance with them.'

'I do not.'

'You will break their power, isolate them.'

'Without my armies even marching against them. With four wedding gowns, I will defeat them.' His satisfaction at his plan broke through into his smile, almost lecherous in its self-delight.

I nodded. 'But then, what will your armies do? Surely you expect to expand your...'

The final piece of the puzzle hit me and I blanched. 'The Empire of the Greeks. That is your true target.'

Yaroslav shrugged nonchalantly. 'I could not discuss such a thing with a member of the Varangians.'

'That would make you an enemy of Harald!'

'Only if he were still there,' Yaroslav emphasised.

I slumped. 'And not if he were here or in Norway, married to your daughter. Is it really all so... simple?'

'I am impressed, Eric. I did not expect you to understand. Harald would, of course. Perhaps he suspects some of this already. But yes, I have made my plans, and I wish Harald to be a part of them.'

'And if he refuses?'

'He would not,' said the grand prince confidently. 'But I

require your decision now. He wrote to me that you were authorised to make a commitment in his place.'

'But my prince, he will be forced by honour to tell the emperor of this danger, if I relay to him what you have said to me.'

'And you will indeed be honour bound to relay it.'

I nodded, worried now. I possessed secrets that kingdoms would kill to know, or protect.

Yaroslav tried to put me at ease. 'Harald is honourable, but he is also clever. His oaths are to protect the emperor while he is the commander of the Varangians, are they not?'

I shuffled uneasily in my chair. The precise oaths we took were deeply held secrets, ones I will not even reveal here to you, but that was close enough to their meaning. 'In a manner, yes.'

'Then it is simple. I swear on my honour not to take any hostile action against the empire while Harald is there, if he commits to marry my daughter and my other terms. Then, he does not need to report a threat that does not exist while he is under oath. The threat only arrives once he has left. In return for his agreement, I will keep his fortune safe as requested, and, when the time is right, help him secure the throne of Norway he so keenly desires.'

Yaroslav sat back with a satisfied slump. 'Do you have any other concerns?'

I gaped for air like a fish. I had come expecting to promise an alliance of friendship between the Rus and Norway in the future, and a little storage of silver and gold. Yaroslav was asking me to seal Harald into a world-spanning web of alliances that could dominate Europe for the rest of our lives, perhaps even beyond.

And, I would be committing him to a marriage he had not anticipated.

'Your Highness, can I not take these terms to present to him?

It is beyond anything he and I discussed.' I was practically pleading. So much for Harald's advice to try and be calm and unflustered.

Yaroslav shook his head. 'No. That would take months, and anyway, I know his answer and so do you. He simply cannot refuse these terms. I know that because I wouldn't. Do you really wish to sail all the way back with that answer? Or does he truly trust you to make this decision in his place?' Yaroslav leaned in, looking at me sympathetically. 'Does he truly trust you, Eric?'

I lifted my chin proudly. 'More than any other living man.'

Yaroslav nodded once. 'Then we are agreed, are we not?'

Ah, what was I to say? The great prince was right; I had no choice and nor did Harald. We could be Yaroslav's enemies, and be forever excluded from our homeland, or we could be his family, and be part of his plot to rule half the world.

What would Harald do? Well, you all know. I shook hands with the greatest man in Europe and left his palace.

I had one more duty to attend to before I left the city. One I feared even more than meeting Yaroslav because it was a thing of such shame and dishonour.

I went to the Norwegian merchant who lived in the city and ran a fur and amber trading business near the docks. He was the man to whom I had sent letters and money to pass on to Olga.

'Eric! By God, I thought you were dead.' He smiled and we clasped arms even as I looked at him in concern.

'Why did you think I was dead?'

'Well, the letters and money stopped coming.'

I blanched. 'When?'

'Oh, the start of last year?'

Over eighteen months ago, then. I had been on campaign in the east twice, and I knew that had left stretches of many months between chances to send anything, but for him to have received nothing for over a year meant at least two had not reached him.

'I have sent to you twice in that time.' I looked at him suspiciously, and he raised his hands defensively.

'Don't accuse me, Eric. I'm far too wealthy to risk stealing from you.'

I nodded bitterly. 'Then someone stole them on the way.'

'That isn't surprising. It's not exactly safe sending silver this far in the trading boats. Lots more captains less scrupulous than me, lots of pirates about. Anything could have happened.' He gave me a sympathetic shrug.

'Well, where is Olga?'

'Oh, gone. Last time she came to check with me was nearly a year ago.'

'Gone? Gone where?'

'Off to live with family.'

'Where?'

'She didn't tell me.'

'Didn't you ask? How am I supposed to reach her?'

'You aren't. She told me if anything else came from you, to keep it for myself.' He looked away from my shame. 'I'm sorry. She said if you weren't dead it was better if she didn't know.'

'So, that's it?'

'That's it. Did you really expect it to continue like this?'

I shook my head miserably. 'No. I think I came here to end it.'

'Well. It's ended by the sound of it.'

I was wracked with guilt, top to toe. I could barely look at the merchant. 'Did she... Was she well?'

'She seemed fine, Eric. But we were hardly friends. I just passed her your silver and letters.'

It was shocking to find that my wife had abandoned me.

More shocking to know that truly I had abandoned her first, and that for all those years she must have felt as I was feeling in that moment.

I managed to thank the merchant before I slunk away with the weight of the dishonour, and went back to my men.

6

I arrived back in Constantinople in May of 1038, exhausted from the voyage to and from Kyiv, and filled with worry about telling Harald what I had agreed.

We pulled the ship from the water and set it under cover. It was an older ship, but it had managed the long journey well.

We marched up through the city to the palace and reached our home. Nodding to the guard on the gate of our barracks I asked him, 'Where is the commander?'

'He is here, somewhere. He returned not long ago.'

'From where?'

The guardsman just shrugged.

I thanked him and walked through the stone-arched gate with my men behind me. There were a number of men training in the yard and they stopped as we filed through. Excited greetings were called out and I smiled and nodded at my men to release them from the formation to go and talk to their comrades.

They would take care of themselves. I had more serious

matters on my mind. I headed for the back corner of the barracks and the stairs that led to Harald's quarters.

I found him in his office with Aki, poring over a list of new recruits. With the wealth pouring into the guard, prospective recruits were flocking to try and join the ranks. Most of them were the Rus and Norse warriors we wanted, but inevitably many had only the most tenuous claims to either Norse blood or experience in battle.

The numbers were so great that Harald had set up a separate camp outside the city walls just to check suitability before they even made it to the barracks to be questioned and tested.

Far more than half of the prospective recruits were not even worthy to get to that stage; Harald and Aki were being extremely particular.

So the guard's ranks were refilling fast. Six previously dormant banda had been refounded, and all the rest strengthened until their ranks were full. The guard now had twenty-three flags with men to follow them, and although many were still in training and not fit for combat, almost four and a half thousand men followed Harald's orders.

He kept his core units – the first, second, seventh, tenth and fourteenth – in the barracks in the palace. These were the banda he trusted the most, commanded by men he knew well and many of them containing veteran men of the blood-marked, the warband who had come with us from Stiklestad, through the trials of the Rus, and stayed with us in the empire. There were also all the men who joined during that journey.

Another six units were garrisoned nearby in the palace or the wider city. Four were training in temporary camps outside the walls and the others were scattered on missions or garrisons throughout the empire.

'Eric?' Harald looked at me with concern as I entered. 'I did not expect you back yet. You reached Kyiv?'

I shot him a resentful look and nodded. He really doubted me? I still craved his approval, you see. I'm not sure when I stopped, but it certainly wasn't by then.

'Yes. Everything as you ordered.'

'Remarkable. The winds must have favoured you every day of the journey.' Harald did not look pleased; in fact, he looked oddly nervous, perhaps even guilty.

'No, but I was granted an audience with Yaroslav the very day we arrived.'

That got a raised eyebrow. 'Really? Then I imagine your news is very good, or very bad. So, tell me.'

I glanced meaningfully at Aki.

'What, you don't trust me, Eric?'

'I trust you, Aki, this just doesn't concern you. Some of it is very... personal.' I looked at Harald. 'I can return later.'

Harald shook his head and stood up from the list. 'No, Aki has this in hand.' He gave Aki a moderately apologetic look and the second sword picked up the list and left without a word of complaint, just an annoyed glance at me on his way past.

'So?' Harald asked impatiently.

'Yaroslav agreed to keep your treasury safe, and to a future alliance,' I said, my tone making clear that wasn't all.

Harald's eyes narrowed. 'What else.'

'It's quite complex. Please hear me out before you react angrily.'

Harald stiffened. 'What did you agree to?'

I swallowed. 'You are promised to be married.' There was silence for a moment and then Harald nodded.

'I expected that might be the case. To whom, Anastasia?'

I was wrong-footed by his casual revelation that he had predicted a marriage. It was infuriating. If he had predicted it, he could at least have told me. Maybe he was worried if I expected it I would give in too easily? Bah, it was all schemes inside schemes with Harald, and I never fully understood his mind. I shook it off and replied, 'No, she is promised already to a Hungarian duke. Yaroslav has promised you the hand of Elisiv.'

Harald frowned. 'Elisiv is a child.'

'That is how I remembered her too, from last we met. But Yaroslav presented her to me and I was surprised. She is almost a woman now. She is fourteen, and quite charming to look at, if a little cold.' I tailed off. 'I do not think she shared her father's enthusiasm.'

Harald thought about it and shrugged. 'Her enthusiasm is not required.'

'So, you are not angry?'

'No. This is normal between great families. It is interesting that he has promised another daughter to a duke though, and not a king.'

'An exiled duke.'

He looked up. 'What?'

'Yes, and another daughter to an English exile.'

Harald stood, his eyes creased together as he thought about it, then they widened. 'By God, he is building a stable of rebels.'

'Exactly.'

Harald paced to and fro behind the desk. 'He has, what, two other daughters? So, he can back two more rebels. Even if only most of them are successful, half the countries in northern and eastern Europe will be ruled by men in his debt, married into his family.'

I smiled. It was wondrous how fast he put these things together.

'When does he need me to come and marry her?'

'He put no limit on it.'

Harald nodded. 'I don't have enough wealth yet, nor will I go and be married to a girl who is barely a woman. So, a few more years. He won't object to that?'

'No.'

'Did he tell you what he intends to do with this grand alliance he is building?'

I nodded, and I became nervous again. 'He did, but I am unsure if I should tell you.'

Harald's eyes widened. 'He moves against the empire?'

'I didn't tell you that.'

'It's the only potential enemy you wouldn't tell me about, because of our oaths to protect it.' He furrowed his brows at me. 'But Yaroslav knew that so how does he expect to avoid conflict with me?'

'He promises not to do anything until we leave imperial service.'

'Ah, of course. So I could argue to myself it was not in my oath to warn them of the danger.' He grunted. 'It is a poor argument.'

'What is our other option? If we warn them, the deal is broken and Yaroslav keeps our silver and we have nothing.'

'Indeed.' Harald scowled. 'For now, we will do nothing. The threat is not immediate.'

I smiled in relief. 'So, you are content with the arrangements?'

Harald looked up at me with a hard expression. 'I told you to have my money stored safely. You promised me in marriage to a child, tied me into the junior partnership of an alliance with a man who intends for his family to rule the entire known world and has the power to make it happen, and forced me to consider breaking my sacred oath to protect the empire in order to save my personal fortunes and ambitions.'

He held my gaze as I shrank under the reprimand, but then he smiled. 'I expected worse.'

'You bastard.'

Harald laughed and shook his head. 'The ambition of Yaroslav, though!'

'I know, it's on the border of madness.'

'It's magnificent,' said Harald with a sigh of contentedness, as if he had not heard me.

Ha! That was Harald. As I told you, there are good reasons he led and I followed. I looked at him while he mulled over the scope of Yaroslav's plot.

'I need to go to my quarters, and wash.'

Harald snapped back into the present like he had forgotten I was still there. 'Hmm? Yes, yes of course. Come and find me later, I also have things I need to tell you. But it can wait.'

That pricked my interest, but not in a pleasant way.

* * *

'Afra!' I said, spotting him near the palace's eastern bathhouse talking to a man in a fine but understated dark green tunic that I did not recognise.

Afra looked up at me partially in alarm, then smiled as he saw who it was and gave the stranger a single nod of dismissal. 'Eric! I heard you were back, and so soon!'

We embraced. You would not have believed it if I had told you at the time, when I first related to you meeting the grizzled old bandit, that we would become firm friends. Afra the

Constant had been everything I thought I did not respect: An outlaw, a thief, a murderer and a masterless man.

But he turned out to be honourable, in his own way. He liked to say it, that being known as 'the Constant' was merely an outlaw's way of saying he kept his word, both to his friends and his enemies. He was rough, uncultured, rude and impudent. But he was also resourceful, brave in his own way, loyal and intensely intelligent. Intelligent in that fierce, cunning way that a lion is intelligent. Always watching, silent, careful. Deadly. I loved him for all of it. He was the most useful man I ever knew.

His brother, Thorir the Cuckoo, was not my friend. I don't say this to disparage him; I just don't think he had friends. While Afra was big, gregarious, and quick-witted, Thorir was a living statue. He was slim, balding except for when he was wearing a wig, and had a face that was both ill-defined and unremarkable. He made an art form of indifference and blandness.

It was all part of his great skill. Thorir was a thief and a spy of the highest order. He could disguise himself with ease, pass unnoticed in a crowd, learn languages in weeks and seemed never to find a door he could not unlock or bypass. He was, frankly, quite terrifying.

'Who was that?' I asked, nodding towards the man in the green tunic.

'Ah, one of my associates,' Afra replied with a wink.

'Oh, yes. What sort of associate?'

'One who is most effective if no one knows who he is.'

I rolled my eyes. Afra maintained a circle of spies, informants and other useful people in the city. It was intensely useful to us, but infuriating how he would never tell me anything about it.

'Untold secrets cannot be spilt,' he would say. And it was true, but it irked me nonetheless.

'Fine. Well, tell me how it has been while I was away. Has Harald been attacked again, or got himself into more trouble?'

A troubled look crossed Afra's face and I caught it before it was gone. He shrugged. 'No, no more attacks, but only because we caught two in the budding.'

'Two! What?'

'Another poisoning, a poor attempt I think only made as a show of threat. And a servant with a blade who tried to get into his presence at night two days later. That one was much more serious. I think, in fact, the poisoning was cover for the real attempt.'

'My God, and how was he stopped?'

'With a seax in his chest.' Afra shrugged. 'He tried to get past a guard who was too alert.'

I frowned. 'This is madness.'

'It is normal, in this city.'

'Then I can't wait to leave.'

'Don't pray too hard on that, Eric. Leaving the city means war and war is tedious and full of misery and death.'

'You are getting fat and lazy, old man. War is what we do!'

Afra shook his head and smiled. 'I am, as you say, too old for war. But luckily for me, the first bandon doesn't go to war unless the emperor does, and I don't think he is going anywhere.'

I frowned. 'Why?'

Afra looked around, judging what to say. 'I should really let Harald talk about all of this, but the emperor is in declining health. A life of debauchery is catching up with him.'

My eyes widened. 'How bad is he?'

Afra nodded his head from side to side. 'Not so bad yet, but enough that the first vultures are starting to circle.'

'That sounds dangerous,' I replied dumbly, unsure what to make of the vague answer.

He patted me on the shoulder. 'Enough of it. I will let Harald say to you what he wants. My duty is to guard the royal family, not to gossip about them. Tell me, how was your journey? I hear you got Harald married.'

I gaped at him. 'How can you already know that? I only told Harald just before I left to come to the bathhouse!'

Afra smiled. 'A lesson for you. You told one of the crew with you, and they told others, and then one of them told me. This is why you don't tell secrets.'

I frowned. 'I only told a couple, in confidence. I trusted them!'

Afra nodded. 'Untold secrets cannot...'

'Be spilt. Yes, yes. Keep your smugness to yourself.' I shook my head ruefully. 'I'm glad it wasn't an important secret.'

'Soldiers and secrets are like whores and your last gold coin; just because they want them, doesn't mean it's a good idea to give it to them.'

I laughed and shoved him roughly. 'Do you have any other words of wisdom for me before I go and wash?'

'Only that you should, indeed, wash. Or it would take more than gold for a woman to get this close to you.'

And then he walked away with a delighted chuckle.

I didn't speak to Harald until the next day. He was out of the barracks, I was exhausted, and I went to sleep before he returned.

The next morning I went up to his office to find him alone, poring over a list of expenditures on equipment for the new recruits. Harald had hoped to be able to give all of the paperwork and administration to Aki, but despite his second in command doing most of it, there was too much for Harald to escape it entirely.

'Money is missing,' he complained in a tired voice as I entered. There was a goblet of watered wine on the table and a jug, which struck me as odd. Harald usually only drank on certain evenings when he felt no danger of being needed for action. Which was almost never, so he rarely drank. To see the work getting on top of him to the extent that he was drinking during the day was quite shocking.

'Money? Missing where?'

'We are paying more for new equipment than the equipment we are actually receiving.'

'Ah.' I nodded in understanding. It seemed like fairly standard pilfering of the sort the empire thrived on. Someone in the chain between the guard's treasury and the armoury was skimming funds. It was a long chain of people. I didn't envy him working out who it was, especially since it was probably more than one.

'Is it enough to matter?'

'I think it is measured to be little enough that no one would care.' He looked up at me with a dark expression. 'But I care.'

'So I see,' I said, nodding at the wine. I reached out to pick up the cup and he angrily swatted my hand away.

'No,' he said tersely, surprising me with the force of it.

'I'm sorry. Since when are you so protective over your wine?'

Harald glared at me, his brow twitching. 'You do not drink wine from my cup, in my office. Do you understand, Eric?'

I was taken aback completely.

'Say you understand.'

'I... I understand.'

Harald gave me one good glare and then went back to his

paper. 'Standards of discipline and respect have to be enforced, even with you. You are too familiar in front of others.'

I fumed. It was true, of course. I was too familiar. But of course, I was! I had been with him since the first time he swung a sword, and he was only alive because of me. Bah, I was such a prideful youth.

As I stood there fuming, about to storm out, a guardsman came to the door and looked in. 'You have a visitor, Commander.'

Harald looked up. 'Who?'

'John the Parakoimomenos.'

I gaped and looked at Harald.

Harald glared at me to be silent and then nodded at the guard. 'Show him up.'

'What the fuck is he doing here?' I said as soon as we were alone again.

'I suspect he has come to gloat at me for the latest attempt on my life, or to complain. He complains a great deal,' Harald muttered.

'Then why let him in?'

'Because not to would be petty.'

Well, that seemed a logical reason to Harald.

'Shall I go?'

'No, stay. He is less insufferable if there are witnesses.'

John finally arrived up the stairs and came into the office. I could see he was brimming with outrage.

'Protospatharios,' he hissed, making Harald's title sound like an insult.

'What are you doing here, John?'

'You have turned away every man I have sent to talk to you,' John said. 'So I am forced to come here myself. If I didn't know better, I would assume you wanted to see me.'

'I cannot express in words how wrong that is,' Harald said,

finally deigning to look up. 'I turn away your people because I don't care what they have to say. I am not your servant, your lackey or your guard, and nothing you do or wish to do has any interest to me.' He looked down again at his paper. 'The only reason I didn't have you turned away at the gate is because it gives me mild pleasure to do it myself. Begone.'

'You sulk like a child, Harald. Both our lives would be easier if you just—'

'Died?' Harald flicked his predatory eyes up as he interrupted the thin eunuch.

John didn't miss a beat. He smiled thinly. 'Yes. But until that blessed day, you will stop interfering with the free flow of goods and servants into the palace grounds. It is causing the royal household enormous inconvenience.'

Harald looked at him with a furrowed brow. 'What do you mean, exactly?'

'Do not pretend to be stupid. You are having every servant and cargo into the palace grounds stopped and searched, and many are being turned away without explanation. It is causing chaos to my people. The palace cannot accept this any longer.'

Harald shrugged. 'There have been three attempted assassinations, all conducted by such servants and using poisons or weapons smuggled into the palace. So, now they are all checked.'

'It is the Vigla's duty to keep the palace boundary secure and make such checks, not the Varangians.'

'The Vigla were shit at it, otherwise there wouldn't have been problems. But regardless, I really don't care what you think. If you want me to stop searching servants, stop using them to try and kill me.'

It was conversational. Harald didn't look perturbed at all. More bored. It was infuriating John.

'I didn't do any such thing,' he said. But it was a rote, almost lazy denial. 'Regardless, the emperor has instructed me to stop this disruption. You are the cause, thus you will stop. Or will you disobey the emperor?'

'You aren't the emperor, John. You might wish to be, but you really don't have the balls for it.'

John took a deep breath and glared at Harald, shaking his head in disdain. 'Childish insults. Really?'

Then he looked down at the table, glancing at the mug of wine. 'Mighty Harald, sitting here with his papers and drinking his sadness away. Reduced to competing with me for power by harassing my people. It's pathetic.' He leaned forwards and looked at the wine. 'Are you not even going to offer me any refreshment?'

Harald didn't even look up from the paper, he just reached out calmly to take the cup and move it towards himself, out of John's reach. 'You won't be here long enough to need it. Regardless, before I shared my wine with you I would share it with stray dogs.'

John leaned back, his face reddening slightly. 'The emperor commands you stop this blockade of the palace.'

'Did he write that down? Or am I taking your word for it?' said Harald, putting his hand up and suppressing a yawn.

John's face went a deeper shade of red and he stood up straight. 'I thought you were better than this.'

'And I thought you would be gone by now.'

John glared at Harald, then at me, and then turned to storm from the room. As much as such a slight man can storm anywhere. Perhaps it is better to say he wafted out.

I looked at Harald in amusement as he took a draught of the wine. 'He really does hate you enough to kill you.'

Harald looked back at me and frowned. 'Don't make light of it. He is the most dangerous man we know.'

'So why provoke him?' I chided, for I thought he was indeed being petty, as John had said.

'Because the other option is capitulation.'

It was a fair point.

'He pushes at every seam of power. Despite Michael's promises to me and Zoe that John's power would be curtailed, it only expands, and Michael is supine, powerless to do anything.'

'So what will you do?'

Harald shook his head. 'Keep pushing back.'

'How can I help you with John?'

Harald looked at me uncertainly and then shook his head. 'You cannot. This isn't work for you. Afra is dealing with it.'

I mulled that over for a moment.

'Harald, did you even want me to return from Kyiv? I thought I was doing my duty well by returning so quickly, but you could not have been less pleased to see me back and now you don't need me?'

Harald huffed and glared. 'I am too busy to deal with this, Eric. I am under constant attack, drowning in administration and petty concerns caused by the recruitment efforts, and one or both of the people I serve are either happy to see me killed or are actively involved in the attempts. And here you are, complaining and wasting my time with your unasked opinions. You know what I need from you, Eric?'

I was too angry to answer.

'I need all the ships out and cleaned, made ready to sail. I need the seventh and tenth banda training in battle formations with their new men, and I need the whole guard prepared for going on campaign, but Aki is too busy with the new recruits. The influx of new men makes us powerful, but slow and unprepared. Go and make us ready for war. Leave John to me.'

'Prepare the ships? I am sworn to protect you. You are under constant attack, and you want me to go and recaulk hulls?'

Harald spread his palms. 'You want to know how you can help me, Eric? That is how. I haven't forgotten your oath to protect me but it was not an oath to constantly second-guess and chide me! There are tasks that need doing, and that is the one I have assigned to you. Will you defy me or will you do it?'

I snapped out a salute. 'Yes, Protospatharios. If those are your orders I will carry them out.'

'Good! That is the response I need from you more often.'

I stormed from the room. And I did it with a great deal more style than John had managed.

7

Well, I wasn't going to be left accused of performing my duties poorly. So I gathered a hundred reluctant men from the barracks and went down the next day to haul one of the guard's ships out of the water and clean it. In an ideal setting, all the ships would be out of the water for winter, but there were too many ships, and too few sheds.

Luckily the guard did not own many ships ourselves, just enough to transport a bandon or two around to a new garrison or city. When we went on campaign it was the navy of one of the local themes that would be tasked to carry us.

But I spent a very dull and hard week cleaning and preparing the half dozen ships we owned, including our two longships. Then I spent several more weeks training with the seventh. I was no longer a member of the seventh, but I still felt very attached to them and the komes, Ulfr, was happy to have me with them as long as I did not overrule him or interfere with his command.

I barely saw Harald. He spent most of his time in his office and I was not about to go up there again. A formal written order came from the palace to order the Varangians to stop searching servants and deliveries at the gates. Harald changed Afra's orders to search servants and goods randomly as they walked about the palace instead, arresting anyone who was deemed suspicious or was caught with anything they should not have. Technically, this was not against his new orders.

He was right to send me away; I would have been scathing in my opinion of that. It was both ineffective and petty. I could sense his helplessness in dealing with John, who was gobbling up the power in the palace once more at remarkable speed. There was a rumour that one of his brothers was being put in charge of the treasury accounts, a position of extreme power in the court.

I was walking past the gate of the barracks one afternoon when the great door opened and a small party of men walked in, escorted closely by four guardsmen. John was at the head of the visitors, along with a couple of his personal guards, and some other officials. He was berating the guardsman for some perceived slight.

'He is here to see the commander. I've sent word up that he is waiting, but he refuses to, uh, wait,' said the harassed guardsman, looking at me pleadingly.

I smiled. 'I will take him up.'

I looked at John. 'Leave your guards here. No one goes in armed except us.'

John sneered at me but motioned with his hand for the armed men to stay, and gestured at me to lead the way. He and his two assistants followed.

We went up the stairs and I saw Afra coming out of the office. He gave me an oddly stilted nod and walked off, going into one of the other rooms down the hallway.

I entered the office with the unwelcome visitors in tow.

Harald looked up and he was clearly surprised to see me, and then looked at John and scowled. 'What is it this time?'

'No niceties, then?' said John.

'Your lackeys can wait outside,' Harald replied, pointing at the staff. 'As can you, Eric.'

'I would prefer they stay; better for both of us to have witnesses. This won't take long, but much longer if we argue about who is allowed to listen.'

Harald tapped a forefinger on the desk a couple of times and then relented with a sigh. 'If you promise to be quick, then.'

'I do. You arrested a man yesterday in the palace grounds as part of your banned searches of palace staff. I need him back.'

'Which one?'

'Well, I don't want you to know, so simply release all of them.'

'No. I wouldn't even if I could. Is that all?'

John paused to try and control himself and advanced towards the table. Harald eyed his goblet of wine and moved it away slightly. John saw the movement and scowled. 'I'm not here for your wine. I'm here for my man.'

'Well, you can have neither.'

'You will release them.' He clicked at one of his assistants, who produced a scroll. 'I have a signed order this time, from the emperor.'

Harald took the scroll and unrolled it suspiciously. 'You got the emperor to sign an order for the release of some servants who were caught with contraband in the palace? Seems extraordinarily minor to bother the emperor with.'

'The emperor is my brother, you dull Norseman, I simply asked him. Now he commands you.'

Harald shrugged. 'I can't release them all.'

'You must!'

'Well, I had two of them hanged. So, no, I can't.'

John looked appalled. 'You had two hanged? Why?'

'They had weapons on them. Any chance the man you wanted was armed?'

John simply grew more furious.

'Ah, that is a yes,' said Harald sagely. 'Well, your man is probably dead. In future, don't send servants with weapons into the palace.'

John put both hands on the table. 'My man was armed because he was carrying important papers, and men would kill for those papers. Where are they?'

Harald looked up, pursing his lips. 'I don't remember any papers. What was in them?'

'You know perfectly well! I am sure you read them, found they had nothing to do with you, and kept them. I want them returned!'

Harald narrowed his eyes and leaned forwards. 'Do you have written orders for me regarding the papers?'

I think something in John broke. His eye twitched, his knuckles went white. Then he exhaled deeply and Harald shook his head.

'You will have to come back with written orders regarding the property of the executed men.'

'Ah, very clever. You think this will work? You think you can frustrate me enough that I simply give up? I will get those orders, and I will get those papers.'

'Not at the moment, you won't,' said Harald, flicking his eyes to the table behind him, where I noticed a heavily folded clutch of papers. John saw it too and grunted in anger.

'Those are mine. Give them to me.'

'Those are mine, and I will not give them to you until ordered to do so. You see, John,' said Harald, leaning forwards. 'You can't have what's mine. And I can make anything mine if I choose to.'

John leaned forwards as if to shout in Harald's face but then caught himself, staring Harald down with his hands trembling in fury. Then he darted his hand out and snatched the cup of wine from the side of the table. Harald tried to slap it out of his grip but was too slow, rising to his feet with a surge of anger.

'Don't you dare,' he growled like an enraged leopard.

John smiled manically and raised the cup to his lips, and took a quick and deep gulp before Harald could do anything. He smacked his lips contentedly and put the fine silver goblet back down again.

'You see, Harald, I can also have whatever I want.' Then he coughed and a look of fear crossed his face as Harald advanced on him around the table.

John looked at Harald oddly and then forced a smile onto his face. 'I see this is a waste of my time. I will return with that order.'

Then he snapped his fingers at his two assistants and hurried from the room.

I stood in the corner, wide-eyed at the whole extraordinary affair. Harald's bad temper disappeared in an instant, and he took a deep breath and looked at me in concern. Before I could ask why, Afra came back into the room, looked at me for a moment and then walked over to the table. He picked up the cup and inspected it.

'Did he drink it?'

'Yes.'

Afra peered inside and nodded. 'It should be enough.'

My stomach lurched like I had been hit with a storm-wave, and I almost lost my balance as my head swam.

Afra produced an identical cup from his tunic as I watched in shock. He placed it on the table and put a little wine into it from a jug. Then he gave me another look, almost apologetic, and hurried from the room.

'Harald,' I gasped. 'What have you done?'

Harald looked at me sadly. 'I wish you hadn't been here for that, Eric.'

'What have you done!' I asked more forcefully.

Harald raised his chin. 'For how long was I supposed to be attacked and ignore it? I struck back.'

'Poison. You poisoned the emperor's brother,' I said in a deathly whisper, too scared to even say it out loud. It was still too loud for Harald, who hissed at me and then moved to the door, looking around and closing it with us inside the room.

'He tried to kill me, Eric. He chose the weapons, I won the fight.'

I stared at him forlornly. 'Zoe told you not to, she told you not to take any action. Oh, God, you have made yourself a traitor.' I felt sick.

'I have done nothing of the sort.'

'This is why you wanted the ships ready, this is why. We will have to flee.'

'You are too naive, Eric. This is the way of the court and the game of power. I will not have to flee. With John gone, Zoe and Michael will need me more than ever.'

'But Michael will know you killed his brother! How can he forgive you?'

'How will he know?'

'You gave him the poison!'

'What poison?' asked Harald. Gesturing at the cup, sitting there innocent and clean. 'And I gave him nothing. He stole some wine from my cup. Wine that I was drinking, wine that dozens of men have seen me drinking over several months.'

I stepped back, seeing the scale of it. 'You have been planning this for months?'

'This is why I wanted you out of my way, because I knew you would not be able to deal with this. But it had to be done.'

'You provoked him to draw him here, taunted him with the wine, goaded him into drinking it. Why? Why such complexity? Why do it here?'

'Afra tried to get poison into his food or drink, but his security is far too careful, and a violent death would cause too much trouble. The only way to get him to take poison was to get him here, into the barracks. And he would never have taken anything I offered him. He was too careful.'

'So you angered him, and his anger and his pride overcame his care.' I was almost impressed, but I was too appalled. 'Poison is a woman's weapon, Harald. How could you consider this?'

'It was the only way. And it was Afra's plan.'

I shook my head. 'And what now?' I looked at him with new panic. 'When will he die? How long will it take?'

'Long enough for him to be back in the palace, long enough for there to be doubt over where the poison was taken.'

'Oh, God, we must prepare the banda. There will be chaos when the news gets out that John has died.'

'No!' Harald snapped. 'You will do nothing, do you understand? We will not prepare, we will be unprepared. To be prepared would be an admission of guilt. If chaos occurs, we will react to it as needed.' He hissed in frustration. 'I really did not want you involved in this, but John forced my hand by bringing you up. It would have risked the whole plan to force you to leave, it would have seemed very odd to him.'

'It was my decision to come up,' I said defiantly.

Harald shrugged. 'It doesn't matter. You are inside now, which means you are one of only four men who knows what just happened, and you will remain silent about it to your grave.' He glared at me. 'Swear it, Eric.'

I baulked. 'Swear it? You would force me to take an oath on a low crime? You require me again to commit my loyalty to you? Haven't I done enough?' I shook my head angrily. 'No, I will swear nothing.'

He scowled at me for a moment and then gritted his teeth and grunted in anger. 'Then you will remain in the barracks until the news arrives. You will go to your quarters, and eat with the men and appear completely normal as if it were any other day.'

'And not the day the man I follow turned to poison to break his oaths.'

'I broke no oath,' Harald said, almost shaking with anger. 'I have no oath to that wisp of shit who tries to have me killed. He is not the emperor, he is just his mutilated brother, not even a man.'

'Killing him is an attack on the emperor himself!' I said, just as angry.

'Killing him will save the emperor from his plots! You think John serves the emperor's interests? You think he will care for Michael once he has killed me and then Zoe? My oath is to keep them both safe and alive, and John is the biggest threat to that, a threat I have ended. If you cannot accept that, go to your quarters and remain there until you are called and tomorrow you can leave the guard and my service and go elsewhere.'

'That's how it is, is it Harald? I must accept everything you do, or leave.'

'That is exactly how it is.'

I was shaken. I had no inkling for a life outside of Harald's company. 'And what of your promise to your brother?' I said.

Harald stepped back and shook his head, pointing at me. 'Do not bring him into this. This is unworthy.'

'No. You told him you would listen to me, that I would help guide you. What happened, Harald?'

'I did not tell him I would be a slave to your advice, Eric. I knew you would advise me against this action so I refused to even hear it. I have taken your advice before, and if you can get past this I will take it again someday. But now, you will take my orders and you will act as if nothing is wrong. You will go down into the barracks and be seen to be calm and acting as normal, and then you will go about your duties. Do you understand?'

'Yes... Protospatharios.' I choked out the words.

Could I abandon him, even over that?

No, I could not. Nothing is so hard as being loyal when your whole being screams at you to abandon your master. Harald and I were tied by blood and loss and it was not a bond I could break so easily.

They call me Eric the Follower and damn you, I earned that name.

8

We went downstairs and Harald chatted and joked with men in the training square and spoke to the guards. I went and joined in the training, sparring with some new men who might have been older than me but were as fresh as new-cut hay. But I was distracted, and one of the cocky bastards put me on my arse, which seldom happened. I was a fabulous swordsman, as I am sure I have told you a half dozen times.

I wish I could still prove it, but my traitorous hands can barely grip a hilt these days, let alone dance the dance of steel and blood that made me famous. Bah, the more I claim it the less you believe it, I know. When I was young and strong I also heard withered old men telling stories of their glory over their cups, and I also didn't believe them.

I went to my room as soon as I felt I could slip away. Luckily, with my position on Harald's staff, I had my own chamber. I just sat in it and worried, free from prying eyes.

* * *

Finally, I dragged myself out to get my evening meal and found the Icelandic cousins joking and laughing with a group of the men as they ate. I got some food of my own and went over to join them.

'What's wrong, Eric? Are you so miserable to be back here with us better men?' said Halldor, komes of the tenth bandon. The Icelander was a fickle one, sometimes sullen and quiet, other times irrepressibly and annoyingly jolly. Apparently, it is something about Icelanders. Maybe it is their home. Fire and ice, a world of two extremes. Perhaps it is in their blood because I have noted it with many of them.

I made a gesture at him which I doubt you are familiar with because it was a Greek peasant's insult, but you put your finger here behind these two while they are joined. It's a little hard to explain but in general terms, it advises the recipient to go and fuck a goat... or maybe that he does already fuck goats. You know, it has been a long time and I am not sure. Regardless, it was one of my favourite gestures.

The men around Halldor laughed and he mimed being greatly offended. It was good not to actually be offended, or someone would start rumours that you did, in fact, mate with goats.

'I am just looking forward to another week cleaning ships and training children like you, Halldor.'

Which was a weak insult because he was older than me and a very experienced warrior. But it was passable because he just laughed and moved his attention elsewhere.

Harald appeared and walked around the tables, stopping to talk to a couple of the officers. He came to sit near me, but I ignored him.

As we sat there and ate, the gates opened and a guardsman in full armour came over at a run, straight to Harald. It was one of the first bandon, one of Afra's inner palace guards. A palace official was in tow, looking stressed and nervous.

I tensed, but Harald just smiled and waved the man over.

'Commander, I have an urgent order from the palace. They require your presence at once.'

Harald's brows narrowed. 'So urgent I cannot finish my meal?'

Men were still going about their food and talking. There was nothing unusual about a guard coming to talk to Harald.

'Yes, Protospatharios. Immediately,' replied the official.

Harald nodded and stood, stepping back from the table and taking the guard a few steps back. 'What has happened? Is there a threat?'

The guard looked uncomfortable and leaned in to whisper. I could barely hear it over the sounds of the men.

'One of the emperor's advisors has died... Poisoning is suspected.'

Harald stiffened and leaned back to stare searchingly at the guard's face. Then he bit his lip and turned to Halldor and me, the nearest officers. 'Halldor, turn out your bandon, quietly. Armed and armoured. Stay in the barracks unless I send for you.'

'Turn out? What is happening?'

'I don't know yet, something at the palace. You might be needed.'

Then he turned to me. 'Eric, bring whoever is on duty in the guardhouse and come with me, now. No rush, just quickly.'

I nodded and stood, walking quickly over towards the large room by the gate where twenty men were always waiting, fully kitted up, ready for any eventuality. It was a very boring duty, almost nothing ever happened. When I went through the door and told them all to stand up and follow me there were actually small exclamations of joy.

We filed out of the guardhouse and caught up with Harald, the guardsman of the first bandon and the palace official. We did not jog, but we walked fast enough that the little official was huffing and half running to keep up with us, tall men used to fast marching for days at a time.

When we arrived at the inner palace we saw men with torches everywhere and a dozen or more guardsmen at the gate.

We rushed over and Harald nodded to the man in charge, the flag bearer of the bandon. 'What is happening?'

'I don't know, Commander. The whole of the first is out on guard. Afra is in the emperor's quarters.'

'The emperor is safe?'

'He is.'

'Good. Here, take these men and add them to your own. More are preparing in the barracks, if you need them.'

'Thank you, Commander. I will send for them.'

Harald nodded and then motioned at the official to lead the way. He turned to look at me and bit his lip in indecision. I think he was about to order me to stay with the men but I nodded and jerked my head at the gate. I was going with him, and I wasn't giving him a choice.

We strode through the inner palace and to the emperor's quarters at the back, passing guardsmen in every corridor and in every entryway.

'Can you tell me anything more of what happened?' Harald asked the official.

He shook his head. 'I was just sent to get you.'

Harald grunted and we carried on until we reached the door to the emperor's office, where four guardsmen stood on watch. One unlocked it to allow us through.

Harald went in with me close behind, and the first surprise was we saw Zoe was there with Hypatia, and she had a face of thunder.

Then the emperor stood up from his chair behind the grand desk where he read and affixed his seal to laws and dictates, and he glared at Harald in silence.

'Basileus, Basilissa. What has happened? Are you both safe? Who has died and is there any chance of an attack?'

'I doubt it,' said a thin, raspy voice. And John stepped out from behind a curtain.

Harald stared at him in shock that he was not able to disguise. My jaw clenched and my eyes widened.

'You seem extremely surprised to see me, Harald.'

Harald tried to recover. 'I am not, I am surprised by everything here. What has happened?'

'Your face says you know exactly what has happened,' snapped the emperor, nodding at John. 'I did not want to believe it.'

'Basileus—'

'Stop it, I don't want to hear it,' said Michael.

'Well, I do. What is the problem?' said Harald defiantly. Not giving any ground.

'The problem is that you poisoned me,' croaked John, and I could see he was not well at all, and his voice was hoarse.

'You seem very well for a man who has been poisoned. Are you sure you do not just have a fever?'

John laughed, and that made him cough again. John smiled. 'Ah, well, I am familiar with poisons – a man in my position has to be. I smelled it as soon as I drank your wine and knew immediately what it was. So I left and went to purge myself, and took remedials, and so I survived what would have killed a horse.'

'I gave you no wine at all.' Harald looked at Michael. 'This transparent pack of lies is wasting your time. John wants rid of me, and this is merely a plot to do so.'

'Yes, yes. It was very clever, Harald. I admit, I was furious with myself when I realised what I had done. To drink poisoned wine from your own cup! Ah, you are smarter than I thought, which is no great admission because I thought you as dumb as a rock.'

'I will not stand here and be spoken to like this,' snarled Harald. 'This man came to my office, was rude to me, stole my wine, and now claims an attack. It's pathetic.'

'Yet, you were shocked to see him, Harald?' said Zoe from behind us, and Harald stiffened and gave her a hurt look.

'He was hiding behind a curtain. It confused me, that is all.'

'Not very convincing.' drawled John.

Harald looked furious. 'And why are you so familiar with poisons, John? As a man who has been through two attempted poisonings recently, and only has one enemy in this room, I am curious.'

John smiled more broadly. 'I am only knowledgeable so that I can detect them in case of an attempt on the life of my brother or myself.' He bowed his head slightly. 'A wise precaution, it turns out.'

Harald snorted. 'There is no proof. You offer nothing more than the very theories that were refused when I presented them when you tried to poison me.'

'No, Harald. You made the mistake of being there when the poison was given.'

'Again, you speak without proof.'

'Perhaps.' John snapped his fingers at one of the guards behind us who I had just heard arrive. The man came forward and he was gingerly clutching the silver goblet from Harald's office as if it would bite him. He must have gone to fetch it just after we left.

John took the goblet and peered inside, finding there was still wine in it. He sniffed at it cautiously.

'Well?' the emperor asked.

John frowned. 'I am not sure. My nose is full of the fumes of my stomach.'

Michael sighed. 'There is an easier test.'

He walked over and took the goblet, marching to Harald and handing it to him. 'Drink it,' the emperor ordered flatly.

Harald shrugged and took the cup, was about to drink it all and then he paused.

'If you are telling the truth, it will be safe to drink,' said Michael. Now that he was close, I could see how weak the emperor looked. His eyes were sunken and lined, and one cheek quivered slightly.

Harald looked sharply at John, then he lowered the cup. 'No.'

'What? Well, then you pronounce yourself guilty,' Michael said with finality. 'It is your cup, your wine.'

'How do I know John did not have poison added to it on the way? For none was in it before. It would be a very clever way to be rid of me, making me drink this and seeming to kill myself with my own poison. The perfect murder, in fact. I should have seen it sooner. This entire affair is a ploy, ideal for such a devious mind. He snatches my wine, pretends to be poisoned, the only evidence for which is his own word, then poisons the cup and makes me drink it to prove my innocence. I die, and appear to be proven guilty by my death.' Harald looked at John with a smile. 'So clever I can only commend you for it.'

Michael frowned and paused, looking at John. Then he shook his head furiously and knocked the silver goblet to the ground, where the wine sprayed and ran across the marble, and puddled in the cracks.

'Saints damn the pair of you!'

'I have done nothing!' protested John.

Michael turned on his brother. 'I believe you that this attack was real, and maybe it was indeed Harald, for we all saw his face. But I also know you are probably behind the attacks on him, him and so many others.' Michael was spitting mad now, and breathing so hard he had to go and lean on his desk. Two attendants rushed out to support him.

John looked shocked. This had very suddenly taken a turn he had not been expecting.

'Brother, he tried to kill me!'

'Oh, then prove it!'

John stared at Harald in anger. 'I will. I can question his men. I can draw the truth from them.' He pointed an accusatory finger at me. 'Starting with his bedwarmer.'

I don't know what shocked me more – to be threatened with torture by John, or to be accused of being Harald's lover.

Well, it was everything I could do not to draw my sword and cut him down on the spot.

'Enough!' said Zoe stepping forwards. Then, more quietly, 'Enough. I was hoping for an honourable confession, but clearly, that will not happen.'

'This can still be put to the court,' hissed John, seeing his victory slipping away.

'No, it cannot. I will not put the head of the imperial guard on trial because you have a cough and a personal vendetta,' said Zoe icily.

'Perhaps you won't have a choice,' said John, and Zoe looked at him the way a cat looks at a mouse while he is deciding whether to finally kill it or play with it some more.

She softly shifted her gaze to Michael. 'Husband, I know he is your brother, but if he talks to me again like that I will have him killed, and not with poison, either.'

Michael paled a little; he was terrible with threats of violence. Really a weak man. He nodded and waved at John irritably. 'I apologise. He is distressed from his sickness.'

'Good.' Zoe did not look at John again as the man simmered in the corner, seeing the last chance of his victory slipping through his fingers.

'Husband, I will speak with you in the morning and we will resolve this. I promise.'

Michael nodded enthusiastically.

Harald looked calm again, but Zoe cast her glare on him with full force. 'Come with me, Protospatharios. Now.'

Then she swept from the room with her attendants and Harald following, and with me bringing up the rear.

We walked through the palace in silence until we reached the empress's chambers, and Zoe sent everyone away except for her attendant Hypatia, Harald and me.

The regal mask fell away and a furious face appeared from beneath the carefully made-up visage. 'I told you not to do anything!' she said, jabbing her finger at Harald, who looked at her defiantly.

'I did noth—'

'Oh, a pox on your denials, Harald. Don't do that here. Do you have any respect for me?'

Harald swallowed and looked at her for a moment and then his shoulders sagged a little. 'He left me with no choice, Basilissa.'

'Fool!' she screeched. 'You have no idea what you have done.'

'He intends to kill you, Basilissa. But he knows he has to get rid of me first! What was I supposed to do, ignore his constant attacks?'

'Yes!' shouted Zoe. 'You angry little man, you were supposed to do as I commanded – stay alive, and do your duties. I was working on another solution and you have ruined it. Ruined it!'

She was towering over him, backing him up with her unleashed rage. It was like a street cat seeing off a pampered family dog. Harald was physically retreating from her fury.

'I... I apologise, Basilissa. But this situation can be recovered.'

She took a deep breath and patted at the hair that had come loose in her anger. A single delicate curl. 'Perhaps. But not with you.'

Harald looked staggered. 'What does that mean?'

Zoe shook her head sadly. 'I don't know yet. I will have to speak to Michael tomorrow when he is calm. I will try and offer some form of mission away from the city. Perhaps I can keep you from being removed from your position and exiled.'

'I saw how Michael deferred to you, you can have whatever outcome you wish!'

Zoe shook her head irritably. 'When I am in the room, yes. Michael is clay in my hands. But the moment I leave he is John's creature.'

'But he admonished John. Maybe he has lost the emperor's trust.'

'That did surprise me, and it is the only reason I can hope to keep you from being exiled or put in chains.'

Harald was taken aback and he stared at the floor, looking totally lost.

There was no sympathy in the look Zoe gave him. 'You brought this upon yourself, Harald. You overreached in a game you do not fully understand. Go, get out of my sight. I will do my best to contain the damage you have caused.'

Harald practically shuddered. 'Yes, Basilissa.'

* * *

They summoned Harald to the war room the next day. It was a sombre walk. We avoided the direct route in case John had decided to make a spectacle of it. Instead, we went south through the inner palace, past the domes of the imperial church and the magnificent Chrysotrinklinos.

The great, three-storey octagonal building was the rarely used formal throne room of the palace that towered over the royal family's quarters and loomed over the skyline of the seaside walls from the outside. We rarely had cause to go there, and, I noted sombrely, may not have to ever again.

We entered the inner palace from the seaward side, past the older wings and into the central buildings where the great war room lay. I walked silently with Harald, dressed in our best tunics and cloaks, and we were met at the door and escorted through into the centre of the ancient building to the room where, just six months before, Harald had lured the two rulers and enforced peace terms on them, with Harald as the power broker.

It was deliberate, of course, to reverse the roles for Harald's humiliation in the same location. But, short of an armed uprising, there was little we could do.

The doors were standing open waiting for us, and I followed Harald as he strode unhesitatingly through and found the emperor and empress seated together at the long table, with John leaning against the great painted map on the wall that showed the empire and all its territories, cities, roads and fortresses.

There was no seat for Harald, and I stood at the back of the room while he walked forwards and stood smartly in front of the emperor and empress.

'Harald, we have discussed the matter of your duties in the palace and recent incidents, and we have decided it is best if you leave the city,' said Michael, shifting nervously in his seat as Harald towered over them.

'As you command, Basileus. Do you require assistance selecting my successor?'

Michael was taken aback by Harald's calmness and he shook his head. 'We are not dismissing you, Protospatharios. It is our opinion—' Michael nodded uncertainly to Zoe as he said it '— that your past service to the empire outweighs any possible misjudgements you might have made.'

I looked over towards John and saw that he was ashen-faced and surly. Clearly, he had not recovered from his poisoning, nor was he happy with the situation.

Michael continued. 'It is better, I think, for a man more suited to war to be sent to join one.'

Harald's eyes flicked to Michael, and his posture straightened slightly.

'John, would you explain?'

Harald turned round reluctantly to look at John, who stared at Harald for a moment before pointing to the map. 'Sicily,' he said, tapping the map at head height, pointing at the great island south of Italy. 'Currently ruled by the Moslems, but separated from the Caliphate of Egypt. Seeing an opportunity, we recently sent a strong fleet and also a small army under Strategos George Maniakes to try and secure a base on the island, with the aim of capturing it for the empire.

'Strategos Maniakes is currently in Italy raising forces from our Italian allies, and hiring mercenaries, to conduct this campaign. He needs more men, Harald. And who better to send than the Varangians?' And he finally smiled.

Harald looked back at Michael. 'If you send the Varangians to Sicily, who protects you here?'

'We will only be sending half of the Varangians. The rest will remain in their garrisons and protect the city. I know you have recruited a lot of new men, so we can bring in more from the surrounding cities to replace them.'

'How can I command the guard if it is split in half? Who will keep the city secure?' protested Harald.

'Your second, Aki Freysson, will remain here and command in your place, under the emperor's supervision,' said John, unable to contain his glee. 'Don't worry, I have already spoken to him and he is fully prepared for this duty.'

Harald gulped and went silent. The message was clear. They were just sending an expendable portion of the recently expanded guard, and the portion most loyal to Harald. The city would be stripped of the men who answered to him and he would be replaced in all but title. Aki would finally take command of the Imperial Guard, and undoubtedly be a far more pliable and controllable commander.

I felt Harald's pain. This was exile. Exile to the furthest reach of the empire, so far in fact that it was not even in the empire, to a campaign so unimportant the imperial army was not being committed, just a small force and whatever locals and mercenaries could be scraped together.

'You will take ten banda of the guard and sail for Italy. Once there you will join George Maniakes' command and help him secure Sicily for the empire, and you will only return when you have done so. Do you understand your duty, Protospatharios?' asked the emperor with a little more trepidation in his tone than he perhaps would have wanted.

But Harald was already defeated, and he knew it. 'I do, Basileus.'

'And will you carry it out faithfully?'

'I will. The guard obeys, Basileus.'

'Good.'

Michael stood and Harald bowed as the emperor left the room. Zoe stood too and went towards the door without saying a word to Harald, or barely even looking at him.

Harald was left standing there, shoulders slightly slumped. I went over to join him. John came over, although at a slightly cautious distance.

'You came close, Harald. If I am honest, much closer than I ever expected.' He smiled, the happy, confident smile of victory.

Harald looked at him in distaste. 'You are a fool if you think this is over.'

John smiled more broadly. 'You are being sent on a campaign that cannot be won, to an island no one cares about, with a general who has no troops. It is over, Harald.'

'He has me, and a fleet. You know nothing of war, eunuch.'

'Ah, yes, the fleet. Interesting you mention that. Do you know who the admiral is?'

Harald's eyes narrowed. 'Some lackey of yours?'

'Close! Well, in fact, my brother-in-law.'

'You would risk your brother-in-law's reputation to sabotage this campaign?'

John nodded happily. 'Oh, definitely. He is quite useless and I care nothing for him, but he is so desperate to please me. I'd say he will do anything I ask, to earn my favour.' The emphasis was dripping with malice.

John stepped away from the table. 'Best of luck, Protospatharios. I am not sure we will be seeing each other again.' And then he headed for the exit at the far end of the room, following the emperor.

Harald stared at the eunuch's back for a while and then turned to me, and his eyes were dulled. 'Come on, Eric, let us go and prepare.'

I had nothing encouraging to say to him, so I followed him to the corridor that led back into the courtyard and out of the inner palace.

When we went outside Zoe was waiting for us. She gently waved at the guards and attendants nearby and dismissed them with that gesture so that we were left alone with her.

'Sicily, Basilissa?' Harald asked in a tired voice.

'Yes.'

'Was that truly the best that could be agreed?'

Zoe's expression clouded. 'You have no idea how hard it was even to negotiate that. Two thousand men of the guard? You claim to be a great war leader, Harald. I've bought you an opportunity, at great cost, to redeem your name. If you make a success of this campaign you can return a hero again.' She looked up and down the corridor. 'But do it quickly.'

Harald gave her a long, hard examination. 'You believe this can actually succeed? John is so confident it cannot. Two thousand men cannot conquer an island that size.'

'John expects you to fail, and hopefully to die. You will not be able to trust the fleet; I expect the admiral will have orders to prevent you from either succeeding or returning home. But, I know something John does not,' said Zoe.

Harald's eyes bored into hers. 'What?'

'I have arranged instructions, and funding, to hire the best mercenaries in the Mediterranean for this campaign.'

The corner of Harald's mouth turned up in a smile. 'Who?'

Zoe smiled – a small, cheeky smile. 'You will like them, Araltes. They are Normans.'

Harald smiled, fully this time. 'You know that Normans are kin to the Norse, and almost as skilled in battle?'

She nodded.

'There are not so many of them, a few hundred, but they have their own local troops and I will ensure more aid is sent to you. Above all, Araltes, I know you are capable of wondrous things. Prove me right, and John wrong.'

Harald blushed like a boy in his first love. 'Basilissa, I could kiss you.'

Zoe put a hand on his face and smiled at him affectionately. 'And if you return victorious, Araltes, I think that you shall.'

Then she took her hand off Harald's face and elegantly strode away.

Harald looked at me, and the great wolf of ambition was in him and it grinned at me with Harald's teeth. 'Come, Eric. Let's gather the men and get to sea. We have an impossible war to win.'

PART II

CONQUEROR

9

STRAIT OF MESSINA, OFF THE EAST COAST OF
SICILY; JUNE 1038 AD

I remember standing on the prow of one of our dromons – the big imperial galleys – my hands resting on the head of my war axe with its haft planted on the planks at my feet, watching the oncoming Sicilian shore and thinking it was the most beautiful land I had ever seen.

On the shore lay the harbour town of Messina, our destination, draped across the sloped coastline in elegant white and red. Behind the town was a wall of forested mountain ridge that ran from the end of the island on our right all the way south almost out of sight. The ridgeline appeared to rise directly from the beach, but our scouts assured us that it did not and that there was a narrow coastal belt of relatively flat land a thousand or so paces broad at its narrowest.

I suppose I should explain what, and I shall briefly.

Well, we sailed for Italy just a few days after our meeting with the emperor and empress, our constant preparations for war paying off and ensuring we were ready. We sailed west towards the empire's lands in southern Italy for two weeks, found the army of Maniakes sailing south towards Sicily and joined him. He was glad to have us, although wary of Harald. He surely remembered from the Antioch campaign of two years before that Harald was both a capable commander and likely to be a thorn in his side if they ever disagreed.

Harald, for his part, accepted the command of the strategos without complaint. Maniakes was a hero of the empire, and titles I didn't bother to memorise dripped off him like gold from a queen. He was the lord of Italy, the supreme general of the East, the master of something important in the court that I forget the significance of, and other things.

Why was such a respected and successful Roman general sent with us on a campaign John intended to fail? Well, for much the same reasons as we were – because he had grown too powerful, and the rulers of Rome do not tolerate too much power in the hands of lesser men.

We remembered him from the Antioch campaign as well-educated in the Roman way of war, careful to the point of passiveness, calm and decisive in battle. Honestly, Harald respected him, despite their later relationship. Harald respected anyone with genuine skill in leading an army in war, and only a fool would claim, as many later tried, that Maniakes was a poor general. Cautious, yes, and arrogant certainly. But strategically and tactically thoughtful and competent.

We needed the city of Messina as the gateway to the island. It dominated the narrow strait through which our ships would pass and was the perfect location for a foothold. A good port, and close to the empire's land in Italy.

The two main cities of Syracuse on the southeastern tip of the island and the capital Balarm in the west were too strongly defended to capture from the sea.

But Messina was not walled. So, eschewing an unopposed landing somewhere else along the shores of the island, Maniakes had decided on a brutal and immediate assault on the beaches outside the city of Messina itself. The advantage was that the forces of the Emir of Sicily, Abdallah Ibn Ziri, had little warning and little time to react, allowing us to seize a vital port and base for the campaign.

Harald was delighted. It is exactly the sort of plan he would have made. A single, bold thrust with surprise, speed and violence. So I stood behind him under the imperial banner of purple and gold, with half a bandon of the seventh at our backs and the other men of the guard spread across twenty ships to either side. There were another eighty ships of the fleet behind us, all packed with soldiers ready to disembark. Almost the entire army – ten thousand men. Only the baggage train and a small guard force remained in Italy, waiting for our victory to cross.

We stood in the cool sea breeze and sweated gently in our armour. It was a cloudy day and I was grateful for that because it was high summer and the days were often furnace-hot.

'Wait for my signal, guardsmen!' shouted Harald at the eager ranks behind us, all waiting for the crunch of keel on rock and sand to know that we had arrived and it was time to get off the ship. But jump too early, before the ship had stopped, and you would risk drowning or being run over by the beaching vessel.

There was a bump as the underside of the bow glanced off a rock, and then a pause as a wave lifted us, and a great thud as it deposited the bow onto the beach.

The great weight of the ship and the last heave of the oars ground us another ten feet up the smoothly sloping sand and then the ship shuddered to a halt. Four men at the front dropped broad, rope-tied ladders over the bow.

'Move!' shouted Harald joyously, his face alive with delight at the prospect of being in battle again, and he didn't wait for the men to react, he just jumped to the bow, swung himself around on one hand, and scurried down the ladder like a rat.

I was too slow to claim the second spot behind him, and I jostled with a wave of my excited brothers to clamber out of the high bow. Others were jumping down into the shallows from the lower parts of the side of the ship. A few arrows fell around us and I saw men go down, but still it was not so many, for there were twenty ships like ours disgorging men onto the beach, eighty more coming on behind, and not enough archers in all of Sicily to stop us.

'Form up!' shouted Harald, and dozens of us ran up the beach to join him. Those with shields and spears made the wall where he stood, and those with long axes stood behind, ready to cut over their comrades' heads or to be released through the wall to break the enemy.

'Form columns of attack by bandon!' shouted Harald.

Up and down the beach a dozen or more formations like ours were forming and rushing to join us as we marched towards the town, just a hundred paces away and the komes relayed his order to their banda, gathering together their men and pushing out into the scrubby grass behind the beach, angling towards the edge of the town.

The enemy were waiting on the edge of their settlement, the streets and alleys barricaded with timber and furniture. Their archers were clambering onto rooftops and perching on balconies.

It was a brave show of defiance from the outmatched garrison, for they had no hope of victory. Looking back on it, I wonder why they put up such a fight. Perhaps they thought this was only a raid and we could be dissuaded. Perhaps it was simply because they were defending their homes and felt they had no choice.

'Advance!' ordered Harald once there were several hundred

of us around him. Other ships of the army were unloading behind us, but Harald wasn't waiting. The guard was leading the way.

We marched up towards the buildings and the arrows came for us. We shivered behind our shields and forced our way forwards. My armour saved me from an arrow that came from an angle past my shield and hit me in the chest, but other men were not so lucky. There were cries and curses as steel heads punched through maille and flesh, and we left our toll of men on the path as we advanced into the teeth of the defences.

Finally, the front ranks reached the hasty barricade in the street between two buildings and we roared and surged forward, hammering at the defenders with axes, spears and swords. Archers leaned over the roofs above us and shot men point-blank with terrible effectiveness.

Styrbjorn led a charge of men from the fourteenth, throwing themselves at the barricades, smashing the obstacle and its defenders aside with wild rage.

Styrbjorn had never fully recovered his wild, carefree spirit from the poisoning that had killed so many of his friends. In camp, he was quiet and perhaps even gloomy. But in that battle, he was proving still to be fearless and courageous to the point of recklessness.

I understood. I think he was trying to drown his regret in the blood of his enemies, a form of revenge to take the place of the revenge he could not get on the true culprits of his misfortune.

A guardsman was shot in the shoulder in front of me, and, roaring with outrage he dropped his shield, turned, and threw his spear at the archer, who was skewered and pitched forwards into the mob below with a soundless scream.

Styrbjorn, miraculously untouched in the maelstrom, burst through the last of the defenders in the street and a great howl of anger and victory went up from our ranks as we rushed into the streets of the town with nothing left to oppose us.

The brief battle was over, but the fight was not. We ransacked that fine town and took our tax in blood and treasure for their daring to defy us. The shattered remains of their garrison fought us in alleys and courtyards, or individually in homes and bedrooms, but it was futile. The only homes that were spared were those whose owners could shout for mercy in Greek, or show us signs of the cross, for many Christian Greek families still lived there, left behind when the empire retreated fifty years before.

* * *

The army made a makeshift camp directly above the beach that night, right where our ships had landed. We recovered our wounded and buried our dead, giving the final mercy to any enemy found alive and then dumping their corpses in a hastily dug trench above the beach.

We felt secure there beneath the wooded slopes. The mountains were not impassable to a few men on foot but could not easily be crossed by an army. That made us relatively safe in our new base other than from the north and south, where an enemy would have to advance down the narrow coastal strip and be at a great disadvantage.

Men came to see Harald to praise him, and he received them as if he were the general, although he had the good sense also to go to Maniakes and congratulate him on his victory, and to hand to him a significant tithe of our loot that we had taken from the town.

'The guard earns its reputation, once again,' said Maniakes, standing and walking out of his simple open-sided tent to receive us. There was a small crowd of staff officers and hangers-on around the strategos, as befitted a man of his power and position, and they watched nervously as the two men faced up to each other.

Harald smiled and saluted smartly, then bowed his head slightly. 'It was a bold and simple plan, Strategos. I merely carried out my part as ordered.'

That earned a pleased smile from Maniakes and a patter of appreciation and relief from his entourage.

'Your orders were to wait for my forces to land before you began the assault, but you did well regardless. Give my thanks to your men.'

'They will appreciate that, Strategos,' Harald said, ignoring the careful criticism in the general's words. But Harald always regarded the plans of other men as advisory only.

Harald inclined his head slightly and walked away, with me following him with a childish grin. 'That went well.'

'It did.'

'Harald Sigurdsson!' a voice called, and we looked aside to see a pair of men in fine maille walking towards us with their own retinue behind. They got closer and I recognised them as the Normans, William and Drogo de Hautville, minor nobles who had come south with a mercenary band for similar reasons to us. Seeking fame, riches and power.

I liked William immediately. Mostly because he was so similar to Harald. Harald, for the same reasons, was immediately wary of him, like two stray cats meeting in the street. His brother, Drogo, was clearly the junior sibling, quiet and restrained, but a fabulous warrior.

'William.' Harald nodded politely in greeting.

William's men had been assigned to land behind us and assault the town. When Harald had done that alone, he had denied them a large portion of the loot they might have expected to take. It was a recipe for a blood debt between two mercenaries, but William's smile seemed genuine and his demeanour didn't display a trace of hostility.

'I suppose I should thank you, saved me some nasty fighting there.'

'I thought you loved a good fight, you Normans.'

'It's true, we do! But it seemed more polite than to accuse you of stealing our opportunity for glory and gain.' He clasped arms with Harald. 'Next time, we will have our chance, I am sure.' That comment was a little more pointed, and his stare a little more forceful.

It was a very diplomatic way of conveying his displeasure, and I thought it well measured. I liked him even more for that.

'I am certain you will, William. There are surely many more great battles to come and even greater towns to seize.'

'Precisely, and we shall make the most of it. Please, come to my tent and speak to me of the battle. I have some excellent French wine fresh out of a ship from Bordeaux. You will find it much better than the Greek stuff you are forced to endure.'

Harald smiled thinly and nodded. 'I have duties to attend to but...' He looked at me. 'Eric can deal with it temporarily.'

I gave Harald a smirk that only he would understand because he hated small talk over wine and was only being diplomatic.

The two brothers took Harald away as I walked back to our camp near the shore. The great men could drink wine and talk of their heroism, but the soldiers like me had bodies to bury or burn, and hundreds of men to organise into watches and patrols.

10

'Why aren't they moving to face us?' said Maniakes with a troubled expression. 'Do they have more men coming, or are they merely waiting for us to move out to the north to set upon us in more open ground?'

'Perhaps they know they cannot win by attacking us?' Harald said, looking around the tent where the leaders of the army were meeting.

It was eight days since the capture of Messina, and the port town was now flush with imperial soldiers, ships, supplies and everything else that comes with an army to a captured town. There was even a new harbour master to marshal the great fleet and the supply ships.

The Emir of Sicily had mustered his army from all over the island, which outnumbered us perhaps two to one, and marched it to a small town just the other side of the mountains on Messina's western side. We had expected him to round the northern edge of the mountain ridge and then attack us, where we could defend the narrow strip of land and negate his numbers.

But the enemy had simply sat in that town for three days and done nothing while our scouts watched from the forest.

'Perhaps he is simply incompetent,' suggested Arduin, and Maniakes looked at him in disapproval.

Arduin was a Lombard nobleman, and leader of the large force of southern Italians that were notionally allied to the empire, but were in reality a small client state and being used as auxiliaries in a campaign where the empire didn't want to use proper thematic forces.

The Lombards were an odd bunch. Few of them spoke Greek and none spoke Norse, so I have almost nothing to say about them, except that they were odd-looking, odd-sounding, and odd-behaving. Not really like Greeks, but also nothing like Normans, Norse or even other Italians.

'Do not underestimate our enemy, Arduin,' chided Maniakes.

'I do not, I merely accept the possibility that these men are simply unsure what to do, and unprepared to face us.'

'I have faced the Moslems before, Arduin, and I assure you, they were both brave and competent.'

Arduin shook his head, almost rudely. 'These are not the same men as the Arabs of the east, Strategos. They are a weaker branch of the same tree. They have not fought a proper war in a lifetime.'

'If they were so weak, they would not have been able to take this island from the empire.'

'Bah, that was politics, Strategos. Taking advantage of a moment of turmoil in the empire. Believe me, my people are familiar with them.'

'Then why haven't you conquered them yourselves?'

Arduin smiled and gestured around the group. 'We are too few, and were waiting for allies.'

Maniakes grunted, but I could see he found the argument at

least somewhat convincing, and he rose to his full height and looked around the group.

He was a tall and broad man, Maniakes. Not so tall as Harald, but definitely broader, bulkier. Not muscle – I do not pretend he was some great warrior, and in fact, I am not sure I ever saw him fight. But he was imposing nonetheless.

'Then perhaps we should consider moving around the mountains to face them, instead of waiting for them here,' Maniakes finally said, and William and several others voiced their agreement.

'There is another way,' said Harald, stepping out of the tent to look up at the forested ridge. He pointed with a finger. 'The enemy is just three miles on the other side of that ridge.'

'That ridge cannot be crossed by an army. We can get neither horses nor waggons up there, nor march in any formation whatsoever. Even if we crossed it on foot we would be trapped on the other side with no water or food,' said Maniakes with a sneer.

'True, we would not be able to sustain ourselves over there, nor hold territory. But do we need to?' Harald looked around the group.

'What do you mean?'

'Well, is our objective not just to force the enemy army to fight? Once they are defeated, that is it. This is a big island, but not so big that they could raise another army if we destroyed this one.'

'Correct.'

'Well, let us march over that ridge at sunrise, defeat their army, and march back the next morning. If every man carries nothing but a single meal and water for a day, we won't need horses or waggons. We just win and return. And, to improve our situation, the enemy will also assume we cannot attack from that direction, and we will have surprise and be uphill. The forest is thick and it will cover our approach until the last moments.'

Harald looked around, waiting for someone to object. No one did. William smiled happily.

Maniakes looked troubled. 'It might work, Harald, but it is deeply risky. If we are defeated there will be no safe line of retreat. We will be massacred as we try and file back over the mountain on a few narrow paths.'

'Then we should be sure not to be defeated,' said Harald with a smile.

'This is not the correct way, Harald. I know you have read the imperial doctrine. This kind of risk is how you lose campaigns.'

'Then what does the doctrine say?'

Maniakes breathed in deeply and furrowed his brows. 'To secure our position, defend it, maintain a line of supply and retreat, and wait for an opportunity for advantage or greater numbers to attack.'

'Will we get more troops?'

'No.'

'Will we gain some other advantage?'

Maniakes huffed. 'That is uncertain. If the enemy moves away again, we could follow them.'

'And if they don't move?'

'If they don't move we must remain here, or risk losing our port and our line of supply and retreat.'

'I don't see how we can win the island by simply defending this port indefinitely.'

Maniakes pointed a chunky finger at Harald. 'The primary goal of any imperial army or navy is to avoid losing battles, and thus we must avoid taking great risks.'

Harald nodded. 'Then, perhaps, that is what needs to change in order to recover Sicily. We can wait here for something to change, or we can force that change.' And he uncrossed his arms and pointed at the mountain again. 'That is where you can find the means of change, Strategos.'

Maniakes grumbled and looked at the ridge again, and I could see he was being swayed. Finally, he leaned back and nodded. 'We will do as Harald suggests. Go and prepare your men, we will leave at dawn the day after tomorrow. Written orders will follow with your dispositions for the march and the battle.'

He pointed at his second in command. 'Bring me the scouts who have been over the ridge, I want to know the land.'

* * *

'I'm surprised he is doing it,' I said as we walked back to our camp. 'He is so cautious.'

'I really gave him no choice, he would have looked a fool in front of our allies to just sit in town refusing to even attempt victory. I have forced him into a decision.'

I looked at Harald with a squint of concern. 'Have you ever considered using persuasion, not force or coercion, to get your way?'

Harald looked at me blankly as if he had not. Perhaps it was true.

I shrugged. 'It might sometimes be more appropriate, is all I mean.' And then I walked away back to my tent with a smile.

Climbing the ridge was awful. It was a hot morning, and although the trees sheltered us from the sun they did nothing for the heat or the dampness in the air that assailed us and dragged us down. It wasn't the tallest of mountains. In fact, it was really just a sharp hill, but the terrain was rugged and nasty, and the paths we followed suited for goats and herders, not men in full armour.

We finally reached the crest and it was already well into the day. Some of our scouts met us at the top, men who had been up there for two or three days watching the enemy in the valley below.

'Have they moved?' Harald asked, panting from the climb.

One of the men shook his head. 'They are still camped around the town down there.'

'Good. Go back and watch them, I need to know when they see the Normans.'

'As you command,' the scout said and then went off at a jog.

William de Hautville and his Normans had been sent with his three hundred mounted knights around the mountain to appear on the plain below the enemy at around midday. It would not look like an attack – three hundred knights were too few to attack an army – but it would at least draw the enemy's attention.

So the orders Harald had received were to lead the army across the mountain, hide in the forest and wait for the Normans to appear at the bottom of the valley beneath the town, then move out to advance down the hill. The imperial troops would move out on the left, the Lombards on the right, and we would all attack the enemy camp together. The Normans were to cut off the line of retreat to the coastal plain and ensure the victory was decisive.

A simple plan, and simple plans are often best.

But the enemy spotted us.

How? Our scouts had cleared theirs out of the forest, or so we thought. Perhaps they saw glinting in the trees or maybe it was just dust in the wind. I don't know, and it didn't matter. Suddenly horns were blaring and flags were flying and the enemy army was moving like a colony of ants around the town below us, pouring out of their camp and shifting positions from the north to the south to face us.

With our entire army in the forest, unable to see where the other contingents were, or see signal flags and with trees muffling the horn sounds and mixing them with the enemy, we could not decipher any orders that might have been signalled to us.

'We should attack immediately before they form up fully,' said Harald, punching his palm with a fist, staring down the hill.

'The rest of our army will not be ready yet.'

'They might be rushing into position, they might even attack without us. Imagine the shame of that?'

'Harald.' I grabbed him by the shoulder. 'Do not charge us down that hill, early, alone, into ten times our number.'

He glared at me for daring to speak to him like that, and I saw in his eyes that he might do it just to defy me. In fact, I was sure he would do it.

He growled and wrenched himself free of my hand, staring down the valley and grumbling as the enemy organised themselves into a strong defensive line. We could see it was too late, the surprise of our arrival was lost.

'We will live to regret this. We should have acted before it was too late,' he finally said, kicking the ground in disgust and stalking off into the trees where the men were hiding.

I stood there watching for a while and finally, in the distance, I saw a haze of dust and the glitter of weapons and armour. The Normans had reached the bottom of the valley.

I shall never know what went through the emir's mind for sure, but I can guess. He had received reports of an enemy force in the forest above him on the mountain, where no army should have been able to pass, but he would not have known how many.

Fearing a surprise attack he had redeployed to face it, but no attack had come.

Then he had seen, in full view, a force of cavalry appear to his rear down the valley, their numbers obscured by distance, dust and heat haze. By imperial doctrine, that should have been the vanguard of our army, and he surely expected to find the rest of us advancing behind them. I assume he determined the force in the forest to be a ruse, a distraction.

I thought it remarkably stupid at the time, but after a short while, most of the army that had formed up to face us above the town turned and rushed down the valley to face the new threat.

'Harald!' I shouted, looking back into the trees.

'I see it,' he said, jogging across to join me. His eyes were alight with excitement. 'Do I have your permission to attack now, Eric?' he asked.

He turned to shout to our signaller before I could give a response, and at his command, the Varangian guard swept out of the trees and started advancing down the valley.

As we got out into the open, I saw on our left and right the rest of the army appear from the tree-line, and, below us, the enemy dissolve into disorder and confusion.

A good general would never have allowed what happened in the town of Rometta, but control of their army dissolved in front of my eyes before the first man put steel into a foe. Cramped into a narrow valley, with conflicting reports of enemy to the south and north, the enemy army dissolved into individual contingents, each reacting to what they could see.

Maniakes, on the other hand, had taken his staff to the top of the low rise on the side of the valley and could see the entire battlefield. Flags flew and horns blared their messages, and on our right the Lombards changed their course, angling away and disappearing over the hill into the next valley as we and the imperial troops continued towards the town.

'He sends the Italians to make a flanking march, to crush the town in a noose,' Harald said with obvious approval.

Behind the town, I could see a scattering of waggons and horsemen fleeing out onto the road to the south, trying to get out of the trap. Later, I would find out Emir Abdallah himself was in that party. The coward abandoned his army to escape before the battle was even decided.

Despite the chaos in the town below us, there were still thousands of men in formations turning or moving to face us, and I could see horsemen riding back and forth, trying to get order into the chaos and form a coherent line.

They wouldn't have time. Harald judged the distance as we reached the valley floor a few hundred paces away from the first enemy group. 'Hold together! Don't break the formation, we go together until the town!' he shouted, and men took his orders right and left along the line.

We didn't charge, we didn't roar down the hill with axes high and legs pumping. Have you ever seen a muddy slope collapse after heavy rain? It seems slow and unlikely to go far, but it is unstoppable and consumes everything it touches.

That was us. We marched into those half-panicked enemy formations one by one, and we consumed them. Most battles are hard, honestly, even the great victories. But at Rometta we barely broke our step. Each time we encountered formed enemy we stamped into them with our shields and weapons up. Our spears licked out and axes rained down on their heads, our enemy died, and our feet stamped forwards again.

I can't remember a single man I killed that day, although it must have been a dozen. None was remarkable enough to make an impression on my mind. I am certain no one laid a blade on my armour, which is also remarkable in such a battle.

We rolled slowly down that valley, steadily obliterating anything that faced us. Slowly enough, in fact, that the imperial troops on our left, facing less resistance and moving faster, curled around the left side of the town and into the enemy camp, driving retreating formations back into our path, where we hit them from the sides and rear and shattered them.

Then, as we reached the small town on its hill, the Lombards appeared from the crest to the right and swept down in a mad, breakneck charge, routing the last semblance of the enemy resistance and driving them up into the streets where the ferocious Italians turned the streets red with the blood of the defeated enemy.

'Halt!' shouted Harald, holding his spear high and stopping our line outside the town. Men looked at him in what approached outrage, for their blood was singing with the joy of an easy victory and they wanted to continue, to finish the slaughter and pour into the enemy camp. But Harald shook his head. 'Let our friends clear the field; we have already won.'

* * *

The valley and the town that afternoon was a charnel house. It was a massacre the likes of which I had never seen in such a small area. Maniakes' staff counted fifteen thousand enemy dead and the small stream through the valley ran red and black with blood and offal.

The entire army of Moslem Sicily was destroyed. We made piles of their weapons as high as a man, stacked their flags and banners and burned them, and the smoke carried the power of the emir away into ashes and dust.

We in the guard had lost barely two dozen men to death or serious wounds, and the only complaint we had was there was not a drop of wine to celebrate with, because the enemy did not drink it, and anyway the imperial troops had looted their camp and would have drunk it all even if there were.

Harald gathered the guard together and moved us up the valley to make camp in the shelter of the forest, away from the stench of death that smothered the valley like a blanket as the imperials and the Lombards looted the camp and the town and celebrated into the evening.

We stripped our armour and lay on the soft forest floor on blankets and made fires, ate the food we had brought with us hanging from our belts, and drank the last of our water. We would regret it in the morning, but it was not far to march home and by noon the next day we would be back in Messina.

As we lay there, laughing and talking and hearing men boast of their prowess in the battle, as soldiers always do after a victory, a dozen horsemen made their way up the valley towards us in the fading light and I saw that it was William. Half the horses were loaded down with barrels.

Harald stood up and went to greet him. 'You were a little late, William,' Harald said with a glare.

'And you let the enemy spot you too soon,' countered the Norman, and then both men smiled and clasped arms.

William let go and gestured back to the horses. 'We brought water with us around the coast, and I thought your wild Northerners could use some. All that killing looked like thirsty work.'

Harald's eyes widened as the Normans unstrapped the small barrels and carefully lowered them to the ground. 'Ah, William. You have made a thousand friends with this. Killing so many is indeed thirsty work and my men were going to awaken parched and grumpy.'

William beamed. 'It is my pleasure.'

'Did you arrive in time to wet your sword?'

William laughed. 'Barely. It was just scattered survivors and fleeing men, but we had our sport.' His eyes sparkled with joy. 'And we caught half their baggage train trying to leave. You would be amazed what their nobles saw fit to bring to war.'

Harald nodded. 'So, your men will sleep happily tonight.'

William nodded. 'I gave a portion of the loot to the strategos, of course. Should I set aside some for you? I know you did the hardest fighting, and I do not wish to leave sour feelings.'

Harald shook his head. 'We keep what we gained by steel, and so should you. None here will resent you for it. Only the empire's nobles insist on taking what they did not earn.'

William grinned. 'I am glad to hear you say it.'

'Keep your wealth, but thank you for the water, William.'

The Norman untied a leather-wrapped flask from his horse and passed it over to Harald with a wink. 'For your men, water. For you, wine.' And then he saluted and led his horse away down the slope, leaving us with the barrels and the flask.

Harald sighed. 'They are almost like us, these Normans, but yet they are not.'

'In what way?'

'I would never make our men drink water while they watch us drink wine. These Norman knights have become too full of themselves. They are nobles first and warriors second, whereas we are the opposite.' He sounded disappointed.

Harald threw the flask at me. 'Find a man in the seventh who earned that today and let him have it.'

I turned the heavy flask in my hand and nodded. 'More than one, I think. Or we will be carrying him over the ridge tomorrow morning.'

11

'Admiral Stephen, thank you for joining us,' Maniakes said with a subtle but very clear sneer.

Maniakes had called a meeting at his new headquarters in the grandest building on the harbourfront in Messina, where I stood quietly at the back of the shaded balcony and waited while Harald and the army's other leaders gathered.

It was five days since the great victory at Rometta. With his army shattered and having narrowly escaped the battle with merely his life and a few of his officers and aides, the emir had ridden to his capital in Balarm and abandoned the rest of the island to fend for itself.

Stephen had been last to arrive. I knew that Stephen was raised to the rank he held simply by merit of being the eunuch, John's brother-in-law. What I did not know, and what was causing such a look of distaste on Maniakes' face, was how obviously and completely he was out of his place in such surroundings.

His tunic was richly made and decorated, but he was somehow wearing it wrong. His cloak sat poorly on his hunched shoulders, and he constantly looked nervous, unsure what to do or say. He nodded cautiously to Maniakes, mumbled some sort of greeting, and then walked over to the corner before pausing, visibly contemplating if he should stand somewhere more prominent, and then awkwardly sidling up to stand near Maniakes, where he looked less like a confident leader and more like a man waiting to be executed for a crime.

'I hear he was a shipyard worker a year ago,' whispered the Greek officer next to me. He shook his head slightly. 'A hull-scrubber in an admiral's uniform. It's a disgrace.'

I nodded subtly. 'I am told this campaign is the first time he ever went to sea other than to cross the straits outside Constantinople. Now he commands a fleet?' I did not bother to contain my distaste.

Maniakes looked at the admiral in annoyance, but then he cleared his throat and leaned forwards over the simple map laid on the table. He waved at all the officers to bring them closer.

'We now control the northeast of the island. The enemy has no army left to put in the field to face us, and probably will not for a year or more, but that is not to say victory is complete.'

He tapped his finger on the bottom edge of the map. 'The Ifriqiyan shore lies this way, and there, possible allies for our opponents. Fortunately, Emir Abdallah of Sicily has been quarrelling with the Zirid emir who rules Ifriqiya and is theoretically his overlord. So it is possible they will not send aid at all, but we cannot be sure of it. Despite their animosity, I am certain they would rather their own people ruled here than us, even if they are rebellious, and we must assume they will send an army, even if they eventually do not.'

'When can we expect that army, if it comes?' asked Harald.

Maniakes shrugged. 'Not soon. Their lands are vast and their forces very spread out. I expect not until after the winter storms have passed at the start of next year.'

'So we have six months to capture the island?' said Harald with a pleased nod.

'That won't be possible,' Maniakes replied firmly.

'Why not?'

'Their army may be destroyed, but Sicily is hard land full of few roads and good fortresses, and they will take a considerable time to reduce, one by one. We cannot get to Balarm or Syracuse without capturing at least half of them first. From the records of the empire when we ruled here last there are sixteen forts, towns and cities with defensible walls, and a number of smaller places besides. Most of them here, in the east. We cannot hope to take so many in six months.'

Harald looked unamused but held his tongue.

'No, we will be methodical and work our way south, taking each fort and town as we come to it, while the emir cowers in Balarm to the west.'

William spoke up. 'What if we move west, besiege Balarm and kill the emir. Will the island not surrender?'

'No. There are several local leaders who hold little love for Emir Abdallah and have no reason to care that he is dead.' Maniakes tapped the southeast corner of the island. 'The most powerful of them is here, at Syracuse. The largest city on the east coast. The lord of Syracuse controls the entire southeastern part of the island, and we must defeat him as well.'

'Can we take the city from the sea, as we did at Messina?'

'No, Syracuse is well fortified. As it should be; we built the walls. They are comprehensive, and cover the sea as well as the landward side.'

William stood back and nodded. 'I see. And the landward approaches?'

'Each pass into the area of Syracuse is well defended and several smaller fortified towns must be taken in order to reach it. It will be a full campaign, but we have the men and the time to achieve it. I wish to capture that city before next summer, but first, we will secure the interior and cut it off from supply, and also from the sea.'

Maniakes turned to Stephen. 'Admiral, that is your task. I want a complete blockade of Syracuse. Nothing in, nothing out.'

Stephen looked alarmed to have been asked something but nodded.

'Have you ever conducted a blockade, Admiral?' Maniakes asked.

Stephen stiffened and had the self-regard to look insulted. 'No,' he finally admitted.

'Many in your fleet will have, so please send to me your three most senior officers so I may plan with them.'

It was outrageous. He had just cast Stephen, the admiral appointed by the emperor himself, aside in favour of some of his subordinates. It was correct, of course. Stephen was wholly incapable of performing his duties, but to humiliate him like that in front of the entire leadership was... another surprisingly bold decision by the strategos.

Stephen just stood there and quivered in fear and impotent anger. Maniakes ignored him and carried on. 'A small garrison will remain here to guard the port, and I will write to the emperor asking for the resources to fortify the town here.' He looked up. 'We will be marching south in two days. We have adequate supplies, animals and men. Do any of you have questions?'

* * *

Harald was in a dark mood as we returned to the camp. 'I know you are disappointed with the cautiousness of his campaign plan,' I said. 'But maybe it will progress faster than expected?'

'What?' Harald looked at me irritably. He clearly hadn't heard me at all.

'I can see you are disappointed with the meeting.'

'No, it's not that. I expect caution, it is how Maniakes is.' He shook his head. 'The problem is his treatment of Stephen.'

'But Stephen is useless; a muttering, terrified labourer dressed in an admiral's finery.'

'Yes, I know that, everyone knows that, but he didn't have to make it so clear in the council.'

I was taken aback. 'Do you feel sorry for him?'

'Of course not. I would drop him into the sea and forget he had ever existed if we didn't need him.' He stopped and grabbed me. 'But we do need him. Without him and his fleet, this campaign is unwinnable. If Maniakes quarrels with him he will be further inclined to sabotage this campaign beyond whatever poison John has already trickled in his ear. Maniakes needs to be more careful in his treatment of him.'

'Ah, I see. Perhaps tell the strategos that Stephen is intended to undermine us?'

'Don't be foolish, Eric. Maniakes won't tolerate even a hint of such betrayal. He would confront Stephen and create the crisis, making himself look the instigator at the same time.'

'You think so?'

'I know so. Maniakes has the mental flexibility of a rock.'

'Can't he just replace Stephen?'

'No. John was too careful. Maniakes has absolute power of Italy and all its forces, but those ships are from the themes of Samos and Hellas, and he has no authority to appoint their admiral or directly command them. If Stephen decides to leave or is forced to, the fleet will go with him. And there is nothing we can do about it.'

The Greek's way of doing things was a complete mystery to me. Imagine giving a general ships to rely on, but that he could not directly control? Madness. But much the Greeks do is mad to us, and the careful division of power was deliberate, done to ensure no challenger to the throne could ever gather a strong enough force to his banner. No one man alone besides the emperor could gather both an army and the fleet to move it.

'And you are sure we cannot win without the fleet?'

Harald shook his head and increased his pace as if to flee from the stupidity of my questions. 'It's a whoring island, Eric.'

The first serious town we encountered marching south along the coast was Taormina. It was half the size of Messina, and its wall was not high enough. We took it with ladders. It was an unremarkable assault but it cost us over a week in siege. We then started passing along the northern flank of the great smoking mountain Aetna that dominates the northeast of the island.

We spent a week passing its looming shadow, clearing villages and preparing to besiege the next major settlement that stood to the north of the mountain, a large town called Tiracia, and that is when Aetna started belching smoke from its hazy tip. We were alarmed because none of us had ever seen such a thing before, although we knew about it from our local guides, who were not in the least perturbed.

That night, as we settled into camp preparing to besiege the fortified town, the tip of the mountain started spewing fire, like sparks from a brazier. Great fountains of fire were belched into the air, curving and fading gracefully away and then exploding into incandescence once more as they landed on the slopes. I sat up for most of the night and watched it, as did many of the men, for it was so utterly terrifying and magnificent.

I can understand, standing under that great black tower of rock and soil, watching it spew fire into the night sky, how the long-dead Romans believed in pagan demons of fire and water and other such things. A mountain that spews fire and smoke from its peak like a blacksmith's forge, but a thousand thousand times the size? How can you imagine such a thing if you have never seen it, and once seeing it, how can you understand its power without knowing that it is surely our Lord God's creation?

Maybe some of you have been to Iceland – I hear there are such mountains there also – but it was the first and only time I have seen such a thing in all my long life, and I was in pure awe of it. How puny we are, we mortals and our armies, compared to the power of the Lord and his creations.

The mountain simmered and smoked and gouted flame and fire, and we surrounded the town and set stakes and dug ditches and cut trees to clear ground and all the things a besieging army must do.

This town of Tiracia was a serious fortress, and we were not sure how to tackle it. The imperial engineers tried first by making engines to throw stones, but the trees nearby were too small and twisted, and the walls too thick and well made, and that approach was quickly abandoned.

We tried throwing up earthworks and trenches so we could get close to the walls for a storming by ladders, but the base of the wall had a spiked ditch and the first ladder assault by the imperial troops was futile and bloody.

So we settled in to starve them out. With no relief coming for them, it would be long and dull, but the end was inevitable.

***

Harald was displeased, to say the least, as a month ticked away and the enemy showed no sign of surrendering. Nor would Maniakes agree to split his forces and send half to besiege somewhere else. He felt it would leave both halves too weak, and risk disaster if an enemy force did manage to gather and come to confront us.

I suspect more that he was concerned about losing control over the half he was not with and did not trust any of his senior officers to have that much power.

Harald signalled his displeasure by being as unhelpful as he could get away with. He did not refuse orders, exactly, but the guard was slow to react, inefficient, and never volunteered for anything.

'If he insists we sit here and do nothing, nothing is what we will do,' Harald complained. A month passed, and then another, and it was nearly winter of 1038 and the town still defied us, and far from taking the whole island we had not yet even conquered the entire northeast of Sicily.

Finally, Maniakes announced we were going to break the siege in a week's time and move on to somewhere easier to capture. He needed to keep the image of progress and success going in his reports to the emperor.

Harald came back from that meeting seething with fury. 'We aren't leaving,' he muttered.

'That would be mutiny!' I said, trying to calm him before anyone heard him discuss it.

'Who will condemn me for refusing to flee in the face of the enemy!'

'John!' I hissed.

Harald grunted at me and walked off, down to the edge of the camp overlooking the siege-works that we were about to abandon. He sat there all afternoon and evening, refusing to see anyone, trying to break into the town with sheer force of willpower. He didn't even return for the evening meal.

'He's not in a good way, then,' said Halldor with a smile as we sat and ate.

'It doesn't bother me not to storm that bitch of a town,' replied his cousin Ulfr. 'No doubt it would be us called to do it, and I'd be more pleased to be told to mount that hideous girl you keep in the city than to scale those walls.'

Halldor gave Ulfr a hurt expression but everyone else there just laughed. The big Icelander had a famously odd taste in women. Ulfr always said Halldor's first love as a young lad had been a sow, and that he had never got over it being slaughtered for the family table. Every woman he swived since then had been an attempt to find that same love again.

'There is nothing wrong with her.'

'Aye, nothing at all. Leave him alone,' said Rurik, earning a thankful nod from Halldor. 'Most of us worry our women will have left us for another man when we get back. Poor Halldor here has to worry she'll have been taken by a farmer with poor eyesight, butchered, salted and hung up in the market.'

'Their eyesight wouldn't even have to be that poor,' added Ulfr with a gleeful grin.

Halldor jumped on him then, and the two men rolled and tussled in the dry grass, and only one of them was being particularly good-natured about it.

'Get off him!' I said, grabbing a handful of someone's tunic. 'You're both komes for saint's sake, set an example.' I was trying to sound stern, but it didn't help that I was still giggling.

Eventually, Ulfr kicked free and backed up, one eye swollen but still grinning. Daring Halldor to have another go.

But then Harald appeared out of the gathering gloom and the two men stopped, pretending nothing was going on, like children caught in the kitchen with stuffed pockets.

'Found a way in yet, Commander?' Rurik asked jovially.

Harald shook his head. 'Other than flying over the walls, nothing.'

Rurik nodded and then looked up, pointing at a small flight of sparrows headed towards the town. 'Like those little bastards. Rats with wings, they are. Come out here to pick at our crumbs and then fly back safe for the night.'

Harald looked up in confusion and watched as the birds went towards the town.

'What?'

'Oh, nothing. Just a joke.'

'No, explain.' Harald gave Rurik an odd look.

Rurik's eyes scanned his commander, not knowing what needed explaining. 'Those birds, they come out here every evening at mealtime, pick at our bread and our crumbs, then fly back to the town when it gets dark.'

'Why?'

'Well, to roost I expect.'

'Where in the town do the birds roost?' asked Harald.

'I'd be more likely to know where the emperor shits,' said Rurik with a shrug.

Harald stared at the town again, and we all looked at each other with odd expressions, like Harald had lost his mind a bit.

Then his eyes moved from the town to the mountain above us that was once again smoking and belching fire after a month's rest.

'They probably nest in the eaves under the roofs – in the rafters,' he said, with far more excitement than such a statement should generate.

'Uh, I guess so.'

Harald looked back to us and in the firelight, his face was grinning the wolf's grin. 'We need to catch some, tomorrow.'

'What?'

'Dozens, dozens of them.'

I stared at him like he had lost his mind. Then Harald kicked at the fire, scattering sparks and embers and causing a shout of protest.

He ignored it and took his seax out, raking a glowing coal from the base of the firepit. He laid it aside, by some grass, and it cooled and dulled, and then sat there smoking gently. Harald took a stick and laid it on the coal and stared at it. For a short time, nothing happened, and then the stick started to blacken and curl, and finally, puffed into flames.

Harald stood up, and the men were still staring at him like he had misplaced his wits, but I understood.

'We give the sparrows some gifts to return to the town,' I said.

Harald pointed at me. 'Precisely.'

'What are you talking about?' said Rurik, who was a much better fighter than he was a thinker.

'Tomorrow, we are going to trap as many of these birds as we can. We will get some wire and tie hot embers to them, and then release them.' Harald pointed at the town. 'They will fly back to the town. Now, we gave up on the idea of burning the town with fire arrows because of the tiled roofs. But if these birds nest underneath the tiles in the rafters, as I suspect, they will drop some of these embers on wood.' He nodded and grinned. 'And it's been a dry summer.'

Rurik's eyes widened. 'Will that work?'

'I think it might just burn them out. Get a good night's sleep. In the morning I want nets made, we will need a lot of birds.'

***

Maniakes was extremely dubious about the plan, dismissing it as ridiculous. But it cost him nothing and Harald had persuaded him to allow the Varangians to attempt to burn the defenders out of the town. So the next day we set up our traps.

'Now!' I hissed, and two men yanked at the ropes holding up the corners of the net, causing it to come slapping down to hit the earth, smothering the small flock of birds that was pecking at the crumbled bread we had left under the trap.

There was an explosion of avian panic and flapping wings as the birds tried to escape, but very few of them did, and the net writhed and shimmered as a few dozen birds tried fruitlessly to get out past the knotted string, abandoning the feast they had been enjoying.

'Yes!' I called, giddy as a child, and we moved quickly to secure the corners of the net so that nothing could escape.

'Go and get Harald,' I said, and Halldor nodded and went off to where Harald and Ulfr had set up a different kind of trap between some small trees.

Harald came back and smiled when he saw our captive birds, who were just beginning to settle a little.

'Excellent. Ours did not work so well.'

'Do we have enough?'

Harald shrugged. 'We will find out.' He looked at the horizon, where the sun had set but the sky was still bright.

'How long should we wait?' I asked.

'I'm not sure. It's not so dark now as it was when they were all flying home last evening. Make sure the fires are well-stoked. I'm going to check everything is ready in case this works.'

***

The sky darkened and Harald returned, fidgeting with his sword hilt as he watched the sky. 'Rurik!' he called out quietly.

'Yes, Commander,' said Rurik, coming from where the line of fires was crackling merrily.

'Do you think it is time?'

Rurik looked surprised to be asked. He looked at the horizon and then at the town. 'I'm not sure.'

'You noted these birds, you must have seen them fly back a few times. Is the darkness enough yet?'

Rurik stared hopelessly at the town again and finally shrugged. 'I think so.'

Harald did not look impressed. 'I need these damn birds to fly home, not to somewhere else.'

'Let's try a pair, and see where they go.'

Harald nodded. 'Fine.'

Two men carefully extracted two birds from the net and pinned their wings, holding them upside down while they wriggled and protested.

Another man came over with a decent-sized ember on an iron spike. It was giving off ferocious heat despite it being almost completely dull. Another man wrapped a thin wire around it, swearing as his fingers felt the heat, and then tied the wire to one of the first bird's feet.

The bird's protests only increased, and it wriggled at the indignity and heat of it all.

'Let it go!' said Harald, and the man turned it over and threw it into the air. The bird lurched mid-flight under the odd weight tugging on one of its feet and circled as it tried to shake it off. Then its instincts to flee took over and it flew off – almost exactly in the opposite direction to the town.

Harald swore furiously. 'Bring another,' he said.

'Wait,' I said, my eyes tracking the bird, which had arced around and was heading for the town. 'Look.'

There was a faint trail of smoke behind the bird, and Harald looked up and followed it and saw that it was heading straight for the besieged fortress. He whooped in excitement.

'Get more! Everyone, grab a bird or an ember. Quickly!'

Well, a few dozen men suffered burned fingers, some coals broke apart or fell from their wires, and one poor bird got tangled up in the wire as it took off and its feathers burst into flames mid-air, falling from the sky like one of the molten rocks from Aetna, hitting the ground in a shower of sparks and charred feathers.

But most of the birds took off with their smoking cargo trailing below them. And most of them flew towards the town. We could see a web of smoke trails, and the little glow of embers like fireflies in the night, receding into the night towards the walls.

Finally, all the birds were gone, and we all stood there, panting and nursing blistered skin, watching.

Nothing happened.

Nothing happened for such a time that we all started to look glum. Night fell, the torches on the walls of the enemy town were lit, and we all stood in dejected silence.

Then the enemy lit more torches, and finally, we realised some of them weren't torches at all because the blobs of light were too big and were spreading.

'It's working!' exclaimed Rurik in glee.

'Weapons!' shouted Harald. We all rushed to retrieve our steel and shields and the seventh bandon gathered and rushed down towards the town, picking our way along the road towards the nearest gate.

From the town, the glow of fire was spreading and we were close enough now to hear shouting and wailing.

The flames above the town grew and spread, towering over the walls and sweeping across the tightly packed buildings so quickly that we could see the progress moment by moment.

The roar of the fire overcame the shouts and screams of the desperate inhabitants. Some desperate souls jumped from the walls to escape the inferno until, finally, the gate nearest us juddered and then cracked open as a rush of people fought their way out past the desperate guards who were trying to keep the doors sealed.

The guards were overwhelmed and then hundreds of terrified people poured out of the gates. I saw some of the soldiers, lit up in the firelight, discard their own weapons and join the fleeing crowd.

We watched in rapt fascination as the fire inside the town approached the wall, driving the last people who were able to flee in front of it. They fled right into our lines, where our waiting men gathered most of them together in frightened groups to await Maniakes' decision on what to do with them.

The fire was so intense we couldn't get into the town before dawn.

We picked our way through the smoking ruins in the morning and found that over half the town had burned, the night wind driving the flames uphill but sparing the lower town and the southern gate, which had stood closed all night in the face of the tenth and fourteenth banda.

The fire at the upper gate had been so fierce it had burned the gates out from the inside.

The remaining enemy garrison surrendered without a fight, their position completely hopeless, in exchange for a promise not to slaughter the remaining inhabitants who were now mostly in our control.

But we didn't agree anything about their possessions, and a thousand gleeful men of the guard went over that town like a family of mice over a pantry, finding everything of value that we cared to take, tearing down hangings, levering up floorboards and cutting open mattresses and pillows in search of hidden valuables.

Only a rich town can afford such good walls, and that one did not disappoint us. We marched back into the camp, soot-smeared and smiling, and dumped five grain sacks full of loot at Maniakes' feet as his share, while William and Arduin and the imperial officers looked on jealously.

But we did not care. If they had wanted the spoils, they should have taken the town.

We had captured a major fortress without losing a single man to the enemy. Maniakes was pleased, Harald was delighted to enhance his reputation yet further, and Rurik was given a bag of gold coins the size of his fist as a reward for giving Harald the spark of inspiration. It was, in many ways, Harald's most glorious victory, not least because all of us lived to celebrate it.

12

Ah, I am in danger of getting lost in my story in Sicily. I should move on. We kept moving south and besieged and captured another half dozen fortresses and towns over the next six months. It was slow, boring, and none of those victories was so bloodless as the town we burned with birds.

Men died on ladders, men died in camp of disease and in accidents, ambushes and skirmishes. Added to that, we had to leave garrisons in some of these places, and the army was slowly whittled like a stick, until, in the high summer of 1039, Maniakes gave up the advance on Syracuse because we simply did not have the forces left to besiege it even if we reached it.

We had secured the northeastern third of the island, and only the great town of Catania blocked us marching on Syracuse from the north, and the route from the west was covered by a range of mountains whose passes were guarded with fortified towns.

To our delight, no reinforcements had come from the emir's overlords in Ifriqiya.

I think we were all too exhausted by a year's campaign to

complain. The bulk of the army retreated to Messina to rest, and Maniakes set off to Bari to raise funds and troops from the imperial themes of Italy.

What did we do while we waited for him to return? Bah, nothing interesting. We gambled, we rested, we trained. The town of Messina was filling with Greeks now. Traders, builders, soldiers' families, whores. All the people that follow a victorious army around.

We also found a constant influx of Sicilian Greeks coming from the lands we had conquered, and refugees fleeing the Moslem-held lands we had not yet reached. A large number of Greeks had been left behind by the empire half a century before when they abandoned Sicily, and their children were cautiously pleased to see us return. I will not say the Moslem lords abused them terribly, for honestly they did not. But they were an underclass, made to pay more taxes and denied important positions and ownership of much land, and they saw in us a hope for a better future.

So we welcomed them in, let them settle in the captured towns, and recruited from their men to plump the withered ranks of the imperial army.

Harald sent word to Constantinople for more guardsmen to come and refill our own banda, but an apologetic letter and two hundred new recruits were all we received in return.

Harald was furious for a week, but short of sailing back to the capital, which he was forbidden from doing, what else could he do? The emperor demanded that all the trained men of the guard remain to protect him, and would not spare any for us, or so Aki wrote. But we saw the hand of John behind it.

In the winter of 1039 Maniakes finally returned to a restless army with over four thousand new troops at his back, although some had been reluctantly pressed into service from among the already drained Lombards, and they were not enthusiastic, to say the least, reeking of mutiny at worst.

We received letters from Afra whenever he could find a ship going our way. He spoke of a worsening situation in the palace. The emperor was still unwell, less and less active, confined to his quarters except for short appearances at public events.

Zoe and John were at war over control of the palace court again, and although Afra believed Zoe was gaining the upper hand, he feared that would drive John and the emperor into some desperate act.

To add to the problems, there were rumours of dissent and perhaps future rebellion in Bulgaria, which the emperor, in his weakness, was unable to confront. Afra urged us to complete the campaign as soon as possible and return before the situation spiralled out of control.

By the start of 1040, after the new forces we had brought in, along with the recruits we had raised from the Sicilians, the army was whole again and larger than before. So, after time to train the new men, have equipment delivered, and prepare, we set out again in the early spring of 1040, and marched southwest towards the ring of fortresses that protected Syracuse, ready for the final campaign to capture the city. Maniakes decided to take the inland route in order to surround the coastal plain dominated by the city of Catania and cut it off before we besieged it. It was a sound plan, if typically cautious.

No one was more enthusiastic about the renewed campaign than Harald, and he practically harangued the rest of the army's leaders in every meeting and on every march to be decisive and make haste, to the point where he became quite isolated and disliked, and even William the Norman was perturbed by Harald's frequent outbursts and lack of patience.

I think his intolerance of wasted time is displayed best by what happened at the siege of one of the fortresses on the northeastern approach to Syracuse, a fairly formidable fortified town, built perhaps two centuries before by imperial engineers. It blocked our chosen path to Syracuse and we had to take either it or Catania before we marched on the city.

We set up siege around the town and sent envoys to negotiate their surrender. Among them, we sent leaders from nearly a dozen settlements we had previously captured or had given in to us. They were there to convince the defenders both that their situation was hopeless, and that if they surrendered, they would be treated well.

To Maniakes' surprise, all his entreaties were ignored, and for weeks nothing happened as we dug in around the town and they simply sat there giving no sign of weakness.

After the strategos finally gave up hope of them surrendering without a fight Maniakes took all the leaders of his forces out to a small rise five hundred paces from the walls to survey the defences to debate how to make a direct attack. The town stood against the northeast side of the valley, near a small river that ran along the front of the walls on the south and east. The only good approach to the town was from the northwest and west.

'It has good walls, and a proper defensive ditch and outworks,' he said, pointing at the freshly dug system of trenches, ditches and spikes surrounding the high stone walls on the open side.

'They have had a year to prepare for this siege,' said Arduin.

'It could take a long time to reduce this place by starvation; they will have good food stocks and well-water from the river,' added William.

Maniakes sighed. 'Perhaps we should move to the coast instead. Catania has less significant fortifications, or so the scouts say.'

'That will cost us weeks,' said Harald, shaking his head firmly. 'Your reason for taking this fortress first was correct. If we do not, the enemy can march on our flank at any time.'

'The enemy has no army to march on our flank.'

'That we know of. But they have had a year to gather. Do you trust Stephen to intercept any relief fleet?'

Maniakes scowled. 'No.'

'Well, then moving to Catania will do nothing but slow us down and increase the risk of being countered. If an enemy relief force arrives, we will have to quit the siege and a season will have been wasted. We are here, and we should take this fortress, rather than dither like old women and change our minds.'

Maniakes scowled and shook his head. 'I will not have this debate again, Harald. Victory is more important than the speed taken. This empire has been built over a thousand years and will continue long after your impatient life is over, and petty insults will not change that.'

'And if the coastal fortress is not to your liking? What then? Will we give up and march away for another year?'

'And what do you think we should do here? Starve them out? It will take months, maybe a year. They have all the water they like, and who knows how much grain in storage?'

'No, we will find another way.'

Maniakes fell silent and then nodded. 'Good. Those are your orders.'

'What?'

The general looked at Harald and smiled. 'The army is going to march to the coast and besiege Catania. You, however, I am tired of. I have been tired of you for a year but I am finally unwilling to listen to you for another moment. You are to remain here and capture this fortress, alone.'

Harald's brows furrowed. 'With less than two thousand men?'

'Should that be a problem for the guard?'

Harald bristled at the implication and then reluctantly nodded. 'I accept. I will take this fortress and then march on the city. Leave me a thousand of the new Sicilian levies, to garrison it once it is captured.'

Maniakes laughed. 'You really believe you will take it?'

'Yes. Are you really giving me orders expecting that I will fail?'

'Yes, in fact, I am. But I will have several months of peace in the camp while you do, which I count as a great victory. And if by some miracle you succeed, that will be a victory for me too for this fortress will be in our hands. So, yes, you may have a thousand of the new levies. They are not much use, anyway.'

Maniakes nodded to himself with deep satisfaction and stretched his prodigious bulk to its full height. 'My decision is made. The army will march tomorrow.'

'Strategos, may I stay with the Varangians?'

Everyone looked around in surprise at William.

'There are not many of us, and horses don't do well in sieges. You will not be hampered by our absence.'

Maniakes looked at the Norman suspiciously for a while but then shrugged as if it were nothing. 'You may, William. But if the protospatharios leads you into some disaster I will not be sympathetic and I will not compensate you.'

'I understand, Strategos.'

Maniakes looked at Arduin and his Greek officers. 'Good. Let us go and prepare for the march tomorrow. I look forward to a quiet and orderly march without our northern friends.'

They walked off, trailing the big general, and William walked over to Harald with a smile. 'So, what is your plan? How will you take it?'

'I don't have a plan yet.'

William's smile faded. 'You don't have a plan? I stayed assuming you had some clever plan and I could help you and share in its glory.'

Harald shrugged apologetically. 'I have no plan, only necessity. We have to complete this campaign soon. I need to conquer this island and return home. I cannot do that at the pace the strategos sets. We will all be old men by the time he finally marches on Balarm.'

'I understand that, Harald, but desire alone will not get us into that town. Do we have enough men left to assault those walls? I do not think so.'

'No, we do not,' admitted Harald, rubbing his chin and staring at the town. 'But we must make sure they don't know that. I want the garrison convinced that we will attack frontally. We will have the levies start the assault works, make trenches, cut trees to prepare ladders and everything else.'

'What will be the point of that?'

'Well, then I will use the time to think of something else.'

'What are you hoping for, perhaps to do the trick with the birds again?'

'I have seen no such birds in this valley. In any case, we need to capture this fortress intact. We can't burn it down.'

Harald looked at me. 'Come, bring half a dozen men. We are going to walk around this place and find its weakness. Because it isn't on this side.'

* * *

We spent the rest of the day circling the walls, well beyond arrowshot. We gazed at each angle, we climbed the slope above the town to the east with some difficulty, and realised it was completely impractical for an assault by armoured men.

The river was not very wide, but it was annoyingly deep and relatively fast-flowing, and the bank on the fortress side was high and near vertical. Assaulting from that direction would be nearly impossible.

That just left the side facing the open plain, which the enemy had heavily reinforced. It was a difficult prospect, made impossible with our small numbers.

We did not have any more luck on detailed inspections the day after the army left. We considered a ruse to draw the garrison out, by pretending to march away the next day as the rearguard. But the fortress commanded such good views of the valley that it could never work. Even if the garrison foolishly sortied to pick over our camp, they would see us return to fight them with easily enough warning to retreat behind the walls again.

Half our small army fruitlessly started building up the siegeworks facing the open side of the walls, while Harald sat down with some of us to discuss a new plan he had.

'They rely on the river bank to protect that entire flank. The wall there is smaller, less well-manned, and has no ditch. That is the only side we could attack.'

'How?' William looked at him dubiously. 'We cannot cross that river and attack with ladders, not underneath their gaze.'

'No, not a full assault, but I want to see if we can use that bank as cover, maybe for something smaller. I will go and scout the place tomorrow before dawn. If there is a way into that fortress, it will be on the river side. I need you to arrange a distraction, mass some men for an attack, something like that. I want their eyes off the river for a while.'

'As you say, Strategos,' replied the Norman.

Harald gave William an odd look. It wasn't clear if he had said it in mockery or deference.

'Quiet,' whispered Harald, as someone behind us slipped and fell. I heard muffled grunting and then silence.

'Sorry,' murmured the figure behind me. It was Halldor.

We edged down the riverbank. None of us was wearing armour, just carrying shields to defend ourselves should a rain of arrows come our way. But nothing had happened yet and we were close enough to shoot. The walls loomed over us, fifty or so paces beyond the high riverbank on the other side.

There were six of us, all officers. We carried a single small ladder, just long enough to get us to the top of the bank. Harald stared at the wall and I followed his gaze and in the dim moonlight, I could see enemy on the ramparts. This garrison was alert, and not foolish enough to leave the walls undefended, even there by the river.

We waited there for a while in the shelter of some small trees and bushes on our side of the river, until finally, we heard some shouts of alarm from inside the town towards the northwest.

'They have seen William's men,' said Rurik next to me.

The figures patrolling the ramparts above us all did the same thing, the same thing anyone does after many nights of total boredom as a sentry: They all looked towards the sound of the action.

'Now,' hissed Harald, and we crouch walked down the gentle

slope of the riverbank and into the water, ladder carried between us.

We did not run. Running through the water would have given us away. We slowly waded through the surprisingly cold flow, trying to avoid splashing or losing our footing on the uneven riverbed and falling.

We managed to reach the other bank without trouble and without a rain of arrows greeting us, so we all gathered there on the narrow strip of gravel and sand under the high riverbank, now out of sight of the walls.

'Get the ladder up,' said Harald, and we carefully swivelled the rough wooden thing around and leaned it on the earthen bank, which was about twice the height of a man.

Harald put his foot on the rung first, but Rurik stepped up and shook his head. 'I'll test it, Commander.'

Harald grunted but acquiesced, stepping aside and letting the stout Swedish komes carefully go up the ladder while we braced it. He reached the top without a problem and slowly raised his head peering left and right.

He looked back down and nodded to signal that it was good to move, and then crept over the top. He disappeared and then Harald followed, and the rest of us waited at the bottom for what seemed like an age while they scouted the walls above. There was limited cover up there, as the enemy had cut back all the trees on their side and what was left was bushes and rocks in the gap between the river and the wall.

Eventually, as the sound of shouted orders on the north-western wall faded away, signalling the feinted attack was over, a dark figure appeared at the top of the ladder and started climbing down, and then another.

Harald dropped to the ground next to me, expressionless in the darkness.

'Well?' I said, eager to know.

His dark visage shook. 'It's not good. The ground up there is bad, uneven, rocky. And they have cut ditches and sowed spikes and traps that we could not see from far away. A surprise escalade in the darkness would be impossible, it would be slow moving and discovered before the ladders hit the wall.'

'And a full assault, in the daylight?'

'A massacre.'

I slumped against the bank, disheartened. We did not have any other plans to test.

As I leaned on the bank, a chunk of it broke off and fell with a thud, and everyone froze, waiting to see if it had been heard.

After a time, there was no shouting from above. The earth was solid but soft. It had made little noise falling away.

'I'm sorry,' I said, gingerly backing away from the earth.

Harald came towards me but instead of berating me, he examined the wall of earth. Then he poked at it, and dug a hand in, pulling away another lump.

'I assumed this bank was stone, that this end of the walls was built onto the rock of the hillside.'

Harald got his seax out and stabbed it into the hard-packed earth, levering it and breaking a bigger chunk away. His teeth flashed in the dim light. 'We can dig in this. And if we can dig in this, we can probably dig under the wall from here. It's only fifty paces away.'

I looked at the bank again, and then where we were. 'But how? Here?'

'We need to go, it's getting lighter,' said Rurik, padding over.

Harald's shadowed head nodded. 'Yes. We will talk later. Leave the ladder down here hidden under the bank and let's go.'

* * *

Harald gathered his most trusted komes on the highpoint of the land just outside camp on the way back. Styrbjorn, Halldor, Sveinn, Ulfr, Rurik and I. Harald pointed at the riverbank where we had climbed. 'Look how close to the walls it is. We could dig from there.'

'But they would see us, they could easily stop us once they did.'

Harald shook his head. 'Now that I've been down there, I think we can approach the entire way up to that spot on the far side of the river, at night, instead of crossing it in view of the walls. We wouldn't be able to do it with our entire force unseen, but with two dozen men, at night, unarmoured and carrying picks and shovels? I think it could be done.'

We all stared at the river again.

'But they will hear us,' said Ulfr.

'No. That earth is soft and we could dig quietly. And once we are inside the bank the noise will be muffled.'

'And what about the dirt we dig out?' asked Rurik.

'We just put it in the river and let the waters take it away,' said Halldor with a grin.

Harald nodded. 'If we work carefully, and move men in and out only at night, I think we could dig under their walls without being detected.'

There was silence as we all contemplated it, then Ulfr nodded and grinned manically. 'It's just crazy enough to work.'

'It's not crazy, Ulfr – it's careful. We must be precise and methodical and take only the calmest, most disciplined men,' chided Harald.

'So I'm not in charge of the digging, then,' said Ulfr with an even bigger grin.

'No,' said Harald, and he set his mischievous gaze on me. 'Eric will be in charge of the tunnel.'

13

Well, I hate digging. I hate digging in the day, in the sun, on my own land and with good hot food in my belly. A soldier does a lot of digging in his life. Much more of soldiering is about digging than it is about fighting. You dig latrine ditches, you dig defensive ditches, you dig trenches for sieges, you dig wells, you dig to fill in ditches that the enemy has dug, and you fill in ditches that you have dug but now your commander has decided that we need to be twenty paces away instead.

But none of those things are nearly so bad as digging a tunnel. And no tunnel digging could be worse than doing it at night, in silence, right under the nose of the enemy.

I led the first group of a dozen men along the riverbank three days later carrying nothing but tools, waterskins, a little food and some wood for making braces. We rubbed charred wood on every bit of skin and crept up the river like shadows, often having to wade.

It took a long time, but Harald had been right. We were almost always out of view of the fortress and would be almost impossible to detect.

We reached the spot under the bank near the walls and carefully set all our tools down. We had cloth-wrapped everything, and I picked up a shovel.

I looked at the dark wall of earth in front of us with unease.

We had discussed how best to make the tunnel, and fortunately, some men in the guard had experience with such things because the empire often used undermining during sieges, although not normally like this, starting so close to the enemy. The man I was given to advise me was a lithe veteran of the second bandon called Bjorn. Men called him the Breaker, but I didn't know why. He had been in the Varangians for more than a decade and had taken part in an undermining against a rebel fortress in the Aegean, which made him an expert compared to me.

He explained to me the methods the Greek engineers had used, and we came up with a plan to copy them. We began by cutting a small hollow into the bank, slowly and carefully, and building an entranceway of two pillars and a lintel, packing them in hard with earth to make a strong opening into the bank that was unlikely to subside.

Then, we took turns in pairs digging at the earth inside the portal. We progressed slowly, only digging a couple of paces deep in that first night and putting in a pair of supports to keep the new opening secure. While two men dug, others carefully put the earth we dug out into the river, letting it be washed away.

Before dawn, we hid all the tools in the entrance we had created and carefully made our way back downriver before heading to camp.

* * *

Look, I shall not tire you with a story of digging, for it is not interesting. I shall move to the conclusion of that month of scrabbling in the dark and the dirt to make you understand what we were achieving.

From what we could see from the hillside, we were aiming for a small cluster of store buildings and stables twenty paces inside the walls. We believed that would be our best chance of getting into the town unseen.

We dug until the length of the tunnel was as close to right as I could judge it. Then for another night, under Bjorn's direction, we made several chambers near the end, so men could wait close to the exit, ready to pour out into the town.

Finally, we painstakingly dug upwards at an angle, making a ramp towards the surface, really not knowing how far above us that was and having to go slowly, probing with a slim metal rod. On the third night, the rod reached stone across the entire surface of the roof of the tunnel. We had reached the surface.

'I never want to see a shovel again in my life,' I said to Bjorn, having to suppress a manic giggle and remembering there could be enemy just a few paces above our heads. 'Let's finish for the night and return to camp, let Harald decide.'

Harald listened carefully while I described the situation. When I finished, Harald nodded and turned to William. 'I think we are ready, then. I will take a single bandon, the fourteenth, up the river and into the tunnel, it's all we can hope to sneak in without being seen. Two more banda will wait across the river to come across quickly and follow us. You, the rest of the guard and the Sicilians will be ready to storm the gate if we get it open from inside.'

'And if you don't get the gate open from inside?' William asked.

Harald shrugged. 'I don't care. March to join Maniakes. It won't matter to me. I'll be dead.'

'You should be leading the main force, Harald. Don't risk yourself on this.'

'If I didn't have you here, William, I wouldn't. But I know you can handle the army, and I know my men will believe in this plan far better if I prove I believe in it too. So no, I will go through the tunnel. You take the rest through the gate.'

William nodded slowly, giving Harald a deep look of appreciation. 'The words of a true war leader, not just a strategos.'

Harald cocked an eyebrow. 'So it was an insult then, when you called me that.'

William laughed. 'Not an insult, Varangian. Just probing you. I will go and prepare my men and the levies. Who will lead your men coming to the gate?'

Harald looked around the little group and nodded at Sveinn. 'Sveinn and his second bandon will lead the guard.'

Sveinn raised his chin and nodded in thanks for the position of responsibility. 'As you command, Protospatharios.'

'And I need two mad bastards and their banda to come across the river and through the tunnel after us,' Harald added.

Halldor grinned like a hyena and leaned over to punch Ulfr in the shoulder. 'He means us.'

Harald nodded. 'I do.' He paused before continuing. 'You all have your orders. Prepare carefully. I will be leaving the camp this evening with the fourteenth, and we will attack before the sky lightens in the east. William, Ulfr – be ready and in position with your forces long before that.'

'Should we not go with you, up the river?' asked Ulfr.

'No – it is too likely we will be spotted, six hundred men

going up the river. Wait on this bank, and be ready to cross when you see my signal. I will send a man to wave a torch from the entrance to the tunnel if we successfully break in.'

'As you command, Strategos,' said Ulfr, with a lot more confidence than I felt.

* * *

Getting two hundred men to the tunnel entrance, in full armour and carrying all their shields and weapons, was a fraught experience. I think it is only the will of God that we were not spotted, and luck that it was quite a dark night with a good wind blowing whose moans and rustles must have washed away the sound of our travels.

However it happened, we managed to get to the tunnel without raising the alarm, and Styrbjorn, Bjorn and I went to the end first with a half dozen men, into the chambers dug there. The rest of the bandon huddled on the riverbank out of view of the fortress.

It had taken us far longer to reach the tunnel than we expected, and it was not long before we intended to attack, judging by the progress of the half-moon across the sky.

'We are late, we must dig fast.'

'If we dig quickly, we risk being heard,' said Bjorn.

'Everything about this risks a great deal.'

'When shall I bring the men into the tunnel?' asked Styrbjorn.

'Not yet – there is nothing to breathe in here for more than a dozen men. They can come in just before we attack.'

Styrbjorn nodded. He went back down the tunnel to the river to rejoin Harald and the rest of the men.

Bjorn and I dug the slope upwards to find a way up, quickly

and as quietly as we could. We were soon exhausted from digging in the cramped space, and two men took over from us as we rested in the chamber below, waiting for them to break the surface so we could attack.

Well. I have waited for many attacks in my lifetime, and it is never restful or pleasant, let me tell you.

But waiting underground, with no light but a single torch, breathing in the foul air and the vapours of the burning oil, knowing how much earth and rock was poised above you, ready to crash down without warning and crush you, knowing that we might emerge into a trap and be slaughtered, or have burning oil poured down into the tunnel to roast us all alive…

It was the worst wait I ever had, and it went on forever as my heart pounded and I just longed for Harald to come and tell me we had to either begin or leave.

I turned my head to where the figure of Bjorn sat in the flickering darkness. 'Bjorn?' I whispered.

'Yes?' the old guardsman replied quietly.

'Why are you called the Breaker?'

'Ah, yes, many men wonder that.'

'Well?'

'If I told you, it wouldn't be so interesting.'

'Is it interesting?'

'It must be interesting, otherwise, you wouldn't be asking.'

'Well, I could always ask the other men.'

'You could, but few of them know, and those that know won't tell.'

'Why?' I asked, perplexed.

'Because then it wouldn't be so interesting,' said the older man with a distinctly youthful giggle.

'I don't understand,' I huffed, and his giggles only got louder. 'Is it because it is embarrassing?'

'No, it does not embarrass me.'

'Is it simply that you were a rock breaker before you joined the guard?'

'No, my father was a farmer and I was too.'

'Then how did you come to join the guard?'

'I was shit at farming and good at fighting.'

I smiled in understanding because so many men ended up as warriors that way. 'So what did you break? An oath, a jar, someone's head?'

'Those are all good guesses, but none true.'

'Then what?'

'Ah, I have a principle not to tell anyone without something in exchange, and that, I won't break.' And he giggled to himself.

I knew this must be a well-worn joke for Bjorn, getting people who asked him tied in knots for his amusement. And truthfully, I didn't care, I just wanted to take my mind off the waiting. But... the more he wouldn't tell me, the more I wanted to know.

'What would you trade it for, then?' I asked. 'What do you want in exchange for you telling me why you are called the Breaker?'

'Hmm. I see you truly need to know. Then I will trade it for that fine ivory brooch you wear,' he said, pointing at my chest.

I thought about it for a moment. I felt ridiculous, but the brooch was not so valuable. I had bought it in Constantinople from a stall selling them by the dozen. I grumbled for a moment and then nodded, unclasping it and handing it over.

Bjorn grinned, teeth white in the darkness, taking the brooch and giving me a wink. Then he flexed his hands and snapped the damn thing in two, giggling manically at my outrage before dropping the broken halves on the floor like they meant nothing to him.

'That's it?' I gasped in an outraged whisper, staring at the broken pieces. 'It's just a child's trick; you get people to ask what it means so you can do that? You whore's bastard!'

He just nodded his head and laughed harder, jamming his arm into his mouth to muffle the sound. And I, feeling very stupid, went back to silently contemplating the coming attack.

Finally, the two men came back down the slope, breathing hard. 'We are ready to break through.'

I nodded and tapped the man sitting near me. 'Go and get Harald and the fourteenth.'

14

Soon the silence in the tunnel was broken by the sound of rustling equipment and pattering feet, and Harald came down the tunnel in a puddle of torchlight, and behind him, the faint light of the tunnel was completely blocked with the shadows of men.

It was time.

I nodded at Bjorn, who gave me a wink in the semi-darkness, and we went up the ramp together. It was just wide enough for us both when we dug it, but now, in armour and with our swords in our hands, it was desperately cramped.

We carefully scraped away at the edges of the hole around the underside of the stone until the gap was big enough for a man, and in the process, we found a joint between two flagstones and they subsided slightly, causing us a moment of panic, but then held firm. A small crack appeared between them, and dust and fragments of rushes showered us. It was good news. We had found some sort of open space or room, and nothing was weighing down heavily on the stones.

'We will push them up,' I whispered to Bjorn, and he nodded.

There was no place to drag the stones down past ourselves. Everything had to go up.

Then I looked back down the ramp with great difficulty and signalled to the next man that we were ready.

'Go,' came a whispered command a few moments later, and I heard the men below starting to move up the ramp.

I looked at Bjorn, stuck in that space with me, close as lovers, and we braced ourselves and pushed firmly but slowly up on the stone flag, gritting our teeth as it ground against the stones around it and dust and debris poured into the ramp, little stones tinkling off our armour.

Then the flagstone was half up and I could see a completely dark room above. I could tell nothing about it or its size, but no one stabbed me in the face or poured burning oil on my head, which was a profound relief. So I steadied the stone and waited while my comrade moved the other one.

We carefully put the stones down on the floor to the side and I climbed up into the space, peering around in the near-total darkness. As my eyes adjusted to the gloom I could see that the room was a small store of some kind, and I could see the faint outline of a door. Men were coming into the space behind me, so I went to the door and opened it as quietly as I could.

I went into the next room, sword first, and I could make out racks with shelves on. On the shelf nearest me was a bundle of something, then to my abject horror the bundle made a noise and moved, and I froze.

A cascade of realisations hit me. The shelf was a bed. All the shelves were beds.

It was a barracks. We had dug up into the storeroom of a barracks.

The bundle sat up and spoke more loudly, and another voice answered from somewhere else in the darkness. The second voice sounded irritated. A third joined from close beside me and that voice sounded scared.

The man on the bed in front of me got to his feet and stumbled towards me in the darkness. He realised something was very wrong in the faint light leaking out from the torch in the tunnel in the room behind me.

I shouted and made a wild swing at him with my sword, and all hell broke loose.

When I have told this story in the past, and I have told it many times, I have always said that I let out a mighty roar to terrify and confuse my enemies.

I am certain the truth, which I am now humbled enough by age to admit, is that I bayed like a terrified goat. Regardless of the noise that poured from my mouth, the result was the same: A scream of pain and fear from the darkened man in front of me as my sword slashed across his arms and ribs, and complete chaos all around the room as men awoke and realised that death was in the room with them.

I have told you before that I was a great swordsman, but as I waded into that room in darkened, terrified fury, trying to cut some space for my fellows to follow, I killed more bedposts and blankets than living enemy. They had no idea what was happening, just awakening to screams and crashing in the night. I had no idea where they were because what little I could see was completely lost in all the movement.

I think I put another enemy on the ground. I was knocked over by someone running in panic and I got a good stab into them while we flailed on the stones.

As I scrabbled to my feet I could hear the voices and roars of my fellows behind me as they came into the room, and then light poured into the space as someone brought a torch up the ramp, which only made matters worse, for I finally saw how big the barracks room was.

There were probably sixty beds in that vast stone chamber, and men were rolling and jumping out of all of them, milling in confusion or grabbing weapons.

The single torch waved and darted behind moving, fighting forms, casting insane shadows that flittered around the room, dancing with bunks, hanging clothes and enemy in a chaos of light and darkness where I could barely tell human from furniture, let alone friend from foe. I could see enemy spilling out of the bunks and arming themselves in the chaos, far outnumbering us.

There were perhaps ten of us in the room at that moment, with more scrabbling up the ramp behind us. Good enough odds for Harald. He howled an order at us and we charged into them.

We should have died in that room. Even unarmed, fifty of them should have been able to take us down under their sheer weight and then secure the hole. But we were fully armoured, glinting in the firelight, howling like demons and spewing from a glowing, firelit portal with steel and death and surprise. I don't blame them for panicking, I don't blame them for trying to flee, and I don't like to remember the feeling of cutting my way through their defenceless backs as we rushed to make it to the main door before someone had the good sense to seal it from the outside and trap us.

We climbed over their writhing bodies and scrambled to the opening. I was there first and I cut down a man with an oil lamp, who was still just staring wild-eyed into the chaos, and the lamp fell onto a wounded man in bedclothes whose chest promptly burst into flames.

I kicked and cut my way through the door and found myself in another large room, some kind of eating hall with benches and tables. It was empty except for a few fleeing figures, all headed for another door at the side of the room.

I ran after them, trusting they would be fleeing to the outside, and went through the archway, finding myself in a moonlit courtyard and facing four fully armed men who were coming my way, mere paces from the door.

We all stopped dead, and they were more surprised than I was, so I went at them before they could make any decisions.

I assumed my comrades were with me, but I did not know. Perhaps I should have retreated inside instead of attacking, as I did not even have a shield, but then they might have closed the door and sealed us in. You have only an instant to make these decisions, and my choice was to attack, hoping my comrades were at my shoulder.

I thrust my sword into the one on the far left first because he was the greatest threat to my open side. My sword plunged into his throat as he shouted at me in outrage, reducing his shout to a gurgle. Then I whipped my sword out and across at the others to try and catch anyone too slow to react. My blade clattered off the spear of a man who was trying to poke me in the chest.

All three of the others had their weapons out now and were coming at me, and my sword was high and to my right and my side was exposed, the side one of my comrades should have been covering. But there was no shield appearing at my side, and I wasn't going to die with a spear in my back, so I swiped my armoured free arm up, knocking aside a thrust at my face, and jumped in towards the central man, bringing my sword back around and jabbing it into his chest.

His armour held against the weak thrust but he was knocked off his feet. I almost joined him as a weapon hammered into my side and I stumbled.

I half turned towards the threat to try and deal with it and then someone speared me in the back.

That one hurt. It was a good, strong thrust and it broke through between two plates over my kidneys and I felt that it was caught in my maille, but the blow was still agonising. I lashed out with my sword at the limit of my reach and the guard who had put his spear through my armour was too slow to pull back to stay out of my range and I cut him across his face as I fell to one knee.

I saw the last two men coming at me to finish me off, and I felt a strange feeling of surprise. I was about to die, and I had been so sure that no one would be able to beat me.

'Eric!' a voice shouted, and Styrbjorn ran at me from the doors, his men pouring out behind him. He crashed into the man who had been about to kill me and I dragged myself to my feet.

The man I had cut across the face was fumbling around, trying to bring his weapon up, and I could see that only one of his eyes was ruined. He stared at me in fear with the other as he wiped blood from his half-severed nose.

The fool. He should have run. I cut his hand from his arm with an upstroke as he raised his sword to hack at me in panic, and split his skull with the downstroke as he stumbled.

I stood there, breathing hard and looking around, quite stunned to still be alive, and the pain from the spear blow to my kidney rushed through my chest. There was a trickle of wetness down the back of my thigh that told me perhaps the maille didn't completely catch the spear, but I tried taking a step forward and my leg worked, so I decided I would probably live.

'What were you doing, fool!' shouted Styrbjorn as he reached me, grabbing me and pulling me into his men. I finally saw maybe twenty enemy coming at us across the small square, with more behind them. Shouts of alarm were coming from everywhere now, and the noise of a fortress coming to life was all around us.

I was barely in the shelter of Styrbjorn's shield when they hit us, and we were fighting for our lives again.

There were too many of them and we were not in a formed line, standing there in a group with our men just pouring out of the door in no order, so the fight descended into a brawl around the entrance in moments.

I found I could not raise my right arm to strike from high, it caused a cascade of pain on my right side where I had been wounded. So I put my armoured left arm up as a pathetic shield and stabbed with my sword underneath it.

A guardsman was stabbed from both sides with spears in front of me, and thrashed like a hooked fish as he fell to his knees and howled in outrage. Another enemy had all the time he needed to carefully put his spear-tip through the Varangian's eye socket as I watched, helpless to intervene.

Our outnumbered men were being hacked at from every angle, and the only reason any of us lived for more than a few moments was our heavy armour and our shields. But armour is not perfect, and never can be, and another of our veterans slumped to the cobbles, hands wrapped around a spear that had gone in under his lamellar chest armour. Yet for each of us that fell, more of us were pouring through the door.

I took a nasty sword blow on the maille of my exposed arm and felt something crack inside. I howled in outrage at the man and lashed out at his sword hand to disarm him, but he was quick and pulled out of the way, and another man stabbed his spear into my armour and winded me.

I stumbled back, my broken arm clutched to my side. More men shoved past me, and I hissed and groaned as they jostled my injured side and my broken arm, and a wave of screaming guardsmen stepped over the bodies of our men who had fallen to buy them time, and they hacked into the enemy pouring into that square and hewed them down like wheat.

* * *

I had no part in it. My fight was over. But I could not go back down the tunnel, so I limped after them and watched as Styrbjorn led his men across the small, blood-splashed square towards the gate, and then Harald was pushing past and shouting at the men that followed to join him.

I looked around and could not gather the strength to follow as he and fifty or so Varangians disappeared down a street towards the sound of fighting. Men continued to stream past me, heading towards the gate, but they were distant to me, and I felt cold and alone. There was a deep fear in me, something primal and raw. I looked up over the rooftop of the low buildings in front and I could see figures moving on the parapet, torchlight wavering and figures falling in the dancing shadows.

I tried to move towards them through the flickering shadows in the square, but the shadows lengthened and stretched, and then the sky spun and misted and I could not understand the blackness, or how the cool, hard stone had ended up on my cheek.

* * *

'Eric?'

My eyes parted and the coolness of the stone was gone. Which annoyed me, because it had been oddly comforting.

'He is awake. Someone get Harald.'

'No, leave me here,' I mumbled. 'Go to the gate. You have to let them in the gate.'

'The gate?'

'He thinks we are still in the fortress,' said another voice.

'Eric, open your eyes,' said the first, infuriating voice. I just wanted to be left alone; whatever they needed could wait.

But the voice wouldn't shut up, and eventually, I opened my eyes to look at it and found the dull light of a cloudy sky, but even that hurt, and I tried to lift my arm to block it but could not.

'Where is my hand?' I asked in confusion, lifting my head to look down, and finding that my armour was gone and that I was on some sort of bed in an open-sided tent.

'Your arm is broken and strapped. Don't try and move it.'

There was a dull but overpowering wave of pain from my back as I relaxed my muscles to lie down, and I nearly vomited.

'Where am I?' I muttered as the wave of pain subsided.

'You are not dead, Eric Alvarsson, if that is what concerns you. Even though you should be,' said a familiar voice with a laugh.

'That wasn't what I asked.'

'We are in our camp. It is three days since we stormed the fortress,' replied the voice, and my confused mind remembered that the voice belonged to Ulfr the Icelander.

'I have been asleep for three days?'

'Asleep? God, no. You were in the middle lands, muttering and sweating and bleeding. But they must have rejected you, for here you are again.'

I finally opened my eyes fully and looked up at Ulfr's smiling face. 'The middle lands? I thought you were a Christian, Ulfr. Don't spout that pagan nonsense at me.'

The face of Ulfr smiled even more broadly. 'Of course, I am a

Christian, Eric. It is required for members of the guard to be Christians, so I am.'

I muttered, but it was not the time to argue about Ulfr's heretical beliefs. In truth, a number of the guard were unrepentant pagans, and some even wore the hammer token of their fallen pagan god under their tunics. But it was required by law for all guardsmen to be baptised Christians, so many of them secretly served two divine masters, which I always thought must satisfy neither.

At that moment the face of Harald appeared above me, and it was looking more concerned than amused.

'Eric, do you recognise me?'

'Of course I do. Why wouldn't I?'

'You didn't the last time you woke, just ranting about walls. The fever was still strongly in you.'

'Why?' I tried to look over my body again but I was terribly weak and I started to shiver.

'Your wound, Eric.'

'My wound? You mean my arm?'

Harald looked at me oddly and I screwed up my eyes as another wave of dull pain radiated from my back. 'Do you mean that spear prick in my side? Is that it?'

'Spear prick?' Ulfr laughed again. 'Eric, someone put a spear into your back. It's a miracle you could even stand, let alone that you survived until now.'

'That's enough, Ulfr,' said Harald irritably, and waved him away.

Harald looked down at me. 'You don't remember?'

'It was really that bad? I thought my armour stopped it. It didn't feel like a bad wound.'

'Well, it was. The Greek doctor said you would die, that your kidney was probably burst. The bleeding was too great.'

'Is my kidney burst?' I asked, horrified.

'Must not be.'

'Oh, well, that's good.' I saw the distress on his face and realised he had spent the last three days assuming I would die. Perhaps he still thought I would die. It happens often. Men recover from the initial wound and fever, and then just fade away or stop breathing in the night. Something having been broken inside them that the body simply cannot do without.

'What happened, in the fortress?'

'We took it. Styrbjorn got to the gate and we opened it. There was a nasty fight there against a big part of the garrison but Sveinn and the second bandon reached us in time to secure the gate for the rest of the army, and then it was over.'

I smiled. 'Ah, Styrbjorn, the old goat. He saved me in the fight in the courtyard. He fought like a hero.'

'He did. And he suffered for it.'

'He is dead?' I asked, a wave of distress overcoming me.

'No, wounded in the fight at the gate – not as badly as you, but he is in his tent and won't be leaving it for a few days. And his time as a mountain goat might be over. He took a big slash across his thigh, and he lost a couple of toes.'

'Toes?'

'Yes, someone dropped an axe on him.'

I grimaced. 'Nasty. How?'

'Styrbjorn killed the man holding the axe. He stopped holding it.'

I laughed at that and immediately regretted it as fresh, sharp pain radiated out from my back. A just punishment, I think, for laughing at the suffering of Styrbjorn.

Once I stopped huffing and groaning from the pain I sighed and looked at Harald again. 'So, what now?'

'When the army is ready to move we march to join Maniakes.'

'When will that be?'

Harald stood and looked around. 'When the wounded are fit to travel.'

'Do you mean me? When I am fit to travel?'

'You are far from the only wounded man, Eric, and not the worst either. It was a nasty fight.'

Well. He wasn't lying. He hadn't the heart to tell me, but on a bed a few tents away, Bjorn the Breaker was shivering and moaning, half his ribs laid open and festering. He wouldn't live to see the sunset. He died before I even knew he was wounded.

Nor was Bjorn the only one to die. The fighting around the gate had been vicious, the garrison stubborn. Nearly four hundred guardsmen had been killed or wounded. It was a heavy price to pay for the town, but it was the nature of war. We had been victorious and, most importantly for Harald, everyone had seen us do it when Maniakes had said we could not. He had cemented our reputation to the whole army, and his personal ferocity as a leader. For Harald, four hundred dead and wounded guardsmen was a fair price to pay. That is the calculation of kings and great men, and you can accept it or you cannot. I could.

15

It had been a rich town, and while I had been carried unconscious and bleeding from the central square, most of my comrades and the Normans had stripped the town of its wealth.

So when we finally marched east towards Syracuse, as I suffered the journey in a cart that was the most profane and heinous torture device I ever did encounter, the army was in high spirits.

The Sicilian levies had been left to garrison the fortress, and other than the effects of some very enthusiastic looting, it was still intact and strong. That would secure the northwestern approach to the city while we besieged the main prize, the ancient city of Syracuse.

We marched to the coast north of the great city and found Maniakes was concluding his siege of the coastal town of Catania, which was not well fortified and had surrendered after the first assault. Harald went down to meet with him and the other commanders, leaving me with our men, and returned with a dark expression I had not expected.

'What happened?'

'He seemed angry that I had succeeded. I suspect it is because it makes him look foolish, to have ordered me to do something he said was impossible.'

'He is jealous of you.'

Harald breathed out and nodded. 'It's not just that. The whole atmosphere in the meeting was bad. Maniakes blamed me for it, claimed with me gone it would be better, but clearly discord between the contingents has got worse in our absence. Arduin took me aside, complained that his men are being very poorly treated by the Greeks. He is struggling to keep discipline in the ranks, and they are not being correctly paid. Maniakes is taking some of the silver that is meant for them, and not giving them a fair share of the spoils from our victories.'

My jaw fell open. That was the height of stupidity for a military commander, to steal from your own men. 'How can he be so openly corrupt? We should take him back to the capital in manacles.'

'Don't be a child, Eric. The entire empire is corrupt. Everyone promoted to a position of power uses it to steal and enrich themselves. The courts would never rule against Maniakes for stealing from some auxiliaries from Italy or mercenaries from the north.'

I slumped back, furious. 'So, what will you do?'

'Well, William and I have agreed to take the portion of the spoils meant for Maniakes and give it to Arduin and his men. That should keep them in line, at least for a while.'

'But what about Maniakes? When you don't give him his share what will he do?'

'I don't know. He would make a fool of himself demanding the spoils from a victory that he claimed could not happen. But some men can be consumed by their pride and jealousy, beyond all sense. I pray Maniakes is not one of them. Still, we must take some precautions. I'm going to send what we have back to Messina, and then on a ship to Constantinople, where Afra will arrange for it to be sent to Kyiv.'

My eyes widened and I nodded. We had accumulated quite a considerable haul over the two years of campaigning. Then I suddenly realised where Harald might be going with that line of thought.

'No,' I said, pointing my finger at him.

'No what?'

'I'm not going. Not this time.'

Harald shook his head irritably. 'No, not you. You are too weak to travel anyway. I will send Styrbjorn. His injury is not healing well and he needs the palace doctors, or he might lose his whole foot.'

I nodded sadly. Styrbjorn lived for the guard. If he lost his foot, he would have to be dismissed.

'Maniakes will be furious.'

'Maniakes can suck a sword for all I care. Once our loot is gone he can't do anything about it.'

'He will complain to the palace.'

Harald shook his head and stood. 'I doubt it. It will make him look weak and petty.'

'Well, there will be trouble one way or another.'

'I know it, Eric. I know it. But he made this fight, and I won't back down from a man who behaves like this.'

Could I expect any different? Of course not. If Harald was a man to accept that kind of humiliation, none of you would ever have even heard his name.

* * *

After a few days, the army finally marched south, leaving more of our dwindling local levies to garrison the city.

Our Varangians were put in the vanguard, probably because we were fresh and well-rested, but perhaps also to keep us away from Maniakes.

We marched south along the coast and several minor towns and outposts surrendered to us without a fight, so it was not many days before we arrived on the hillside overlooking the city of Syracuse, the jewel of Sicily.

I am told, and I have no reason not to believe it, that Syracuse is older than Rome itself, and that they have written records in their great libraries that the city existed one and a half thousand years ago.

I find that hard to understand or believe, and certainly such a timespan is impossible for a man to contemplate, even at my age. But I saw the ruins of the ancient temples in Sicily – faded, depreciated ghosts of the ones that still stood in other parts of the empire, and those stones looked as old as time itself. So perhaps it is possible.

In any case, the Greeks valued Syracuse most highly of all the cities on the island, and the empire had built up its defences accordingly. It was a formidable place to contemplate trying to take by force, as we did when we arrived there.

The main part of the city was built on a sharp, pinched peninsula, almost an island, raised in the centre above the land it jutted out from. The rest of the settlement clung to the coast beside that island stronghold. The landside walls were tall and strong, and looked out over a small plain covered in farms that gave an attacker no cover or respite. There was a low hill behind that plain covered in an ancient necropolis, a colossal, ruined theatre, and other remnants of the city's Roman past.

The base of the walls of the city themselves was built into the rock of the peninsular, and all of the coast of the city was covered by a smaller, but still formidable, sea wall, including fortified breakwaters surrounding the twin harbours that nestled into the land on both sides and pinched into the centre of the city, almost meeting in the middle.

Not only were those harbours well-protected, but they formed a choke point in the middle of the city so that even if an attacker breached the outer walls, they would have to fight through a second, internal defence that was perhaps even more resolute.

* * *

When we arrived, Harald led the guard up onto the low hill several hundred paces from the outer boundary of the city and we made camp. The available flat area on the hill facing the city was not large, and no one wanted to make their camp near the necropolis, so the rest of the army made their camp in the low ground beneath to complete the encirclement of the city. That low ground was slightly marshy and fetid in places, An unpleasant place, as I am sure it was intended to be by the defenders.

They could have camped on the land further to the north, but then the city would have been completely open to the east, and the siege incomplete.

Maniakes called a meeting of the commanders to his headquarters, which he had placed inside the ruined theatre nestled into the side of the hill below our camp. It was not dissimilar to several in Constantinople, except clearly far more ancient, and abandoned by the Moslem rulers to the weeds and the goats, whose dung was everywhere.

Next to the theatre was a quarry with vertical cut walls as if made by God himself, such was the scale of it. The stones from that quarry, rich and white, must have been used to build the theatre and the ancient city. It was quite beautiful, even in its dilapidated, overgrown state.

There was a roaring fire in the middle of the bowl of the theatre and we gathered around it. The area had been hastily cleared of scrub and bushes and much of that material was being used to feed the fire.

When we arrived, one of Maniakes' Greek officers was arguing with him, while Arduin was sitting aside looking uncomfortable, and William was nonchalantly drinking from a substantial flask of wine.

Maniakes shot Harald a furious look across the circle of firelight and Harald relaxed down beside the fire with a contented sigh.

'Why did you take the best site for your camp, Harald? Should you not have given that to my men, in deference to your strategos?'

'My men are still tired and wounded from the siege. If you had respect, you would allow them the best ground,' added Maniakes' enraged subordinate, and the subject of their angry discussion became clear.

Harald pointed lazily at me, with my broken arm still strapped to my side, and my wound still stiff and bandaged. 'I also have wounded men. But I arrived first, so I chose the first site.'

'That is not a fair method of decision.'

'Nor is simply assigning the best site to your own men, along with the best loot, the easiest sieges, and the most praise in your reports to the palace.'

Maniakes breathed hard and sat up slightly at the affront. There was a poisoned silence.

Harald looked around and nodded contentedly. 'I know what is fair – let us draw lots.' He reached out to the ground and picked up a freshly cut stick the thickness of his thumb and the length of his hand that was left over from clearing the bushes.

He laid the stick on the ground and cut it into two equal halves with his seax, and proffered one half to Maniakes. 'Make a mark on your lot, I will make one on mine, and we will give them to a neutral party.' He looked around. 'Arduin will do. He will mix them up, place one in each fist, hidden from view, and I will select one. If I draw my own lot, my men stay where they are. If I draw your lot, tomorrow I will give your men my camp. That is fair, do you not agree?'

Maniakes looked dubious for a moment, but he could not argue. It seemed fair. He nodded and took the stick. He cut a mark into it with his knife and passed it to Arduin. But Arduin was on the other side of Harald, and I saw Harald sneak a glance at the lot as it passed him. Then Harald cut his own mark into his lot and also passed it to Arduin.

The Lombard put both hands behind his back and moved the lots back and forth quickly, and then brought out both closed hands, offering them to Harald.

Harald tapped one hand and Arduin handed over the lot. Harald held it up to inspect the mark on it and grinned, exclaiming in triumph, 'My men stay where they are.'

And then he cast the lot into the roaring fire.

Maniakes stood and protested. 'Why did you throw it into the fire, instead of showing it to me?'

Harald's smile faded. 'What do you accuse me of, Strategos?'

'I wished to see the mark and know it was yours.'

There was a nasty silence. Harald stared at the general in anger. 'You do not accuse me of dishonesty?'

Maniakes hesitated.

'Then before you accuse me of anything, look at the other lot Arduin still has, and see that it has your mark upon it.'

Maniakes flicked his eyes to the Lombard as I tried to withhold my smile. Everyone knew what Harald had done. Everyone. But Maniakes could not prove it. He reluctantly walked into the trap and took the lot and inspected it.

'Is that your mark upon it?' Harald asked.

Maniakes stared at it intently, but then nodded slightly. 'It appears to be.'

'I know you will be good to your word and that the matter is resolved without anyone being insulted. I gave you fair chance to take my camp, and that chance did not prove fruitful. Shall we continue with the matter of the siege?'

Maniakes glared at the lot as if it had betrayed him, and there was an expectant silence around the meeting as everyone watched to see what he would do. Then he abruptly cast his lot into the fire and returned to his seat.

'The Norseman cheats you!' hissed an angry Greek officer, stupid enough to say out loud what everyone knew to be true. 'He copied your mark, and burned his lot to hide the deception!'

Harald sighed and got slowly to his feet, unravelling like a snake to tower over the Greek officer, who looked up at him in alarm.

'I have killed men for less than that,' said Harald calmly. 'Much less.' He looked at Maniakes. 'I deny the accusation, my honour on my words. With your permission, Strategos, I will have his life in a test of skill with weapons, or his tongue if he is too cowardly to face me.' He said it in such a way that left no one in any doubt that he meant it. William the Norman grinned over his wine at the encounter. I am sure he wanted nothing less than to see Harald carve up the whingeing Greek officer.

'I will not allow duels between my officers!' Maniakes said in alarm.

Harald nodded and pulled out his seax, stepping towards the Greek. 'His tongue, then.' He grabbed the smaller man by the shoulder pieces of his armour.

'No! Harald, what use to me is an officer without a tongue? Release him... Please.'

Harald paused with the officer squirming in his grip, the Greek's eyes wide with terror. And he slowly turned his head to Maniakes.

'You know what it is to accuse the commander of the Varangians of dishonesty? Something must be done, or men will whisper that the honour of the guard is broken, and for the safety of the emperor, I cannot allow that.'

Maniakes looked furiously at the foolish officer and his hands were balled into fists. 'This man is wrong, I attest to it. You won the lots fairly and no man will question it or he will face my discipline. But we are at war, and I insist you release the fool.'

Maniakes immediately regretted making it a command, and his stance softened. 'I request it, Harald.' He grated out, humiliated.

Harald pretended to consider this deeply for a moment and then dipped his chin in acceptance, swinging the officer around and dumping him in front of the strategos.

The officer turned to protest to the general in outrage, but Maniakes backhanded him across the face with surprising force and sent him sprawling in a mess of limbs and dust.

'My officers will show better judgement and respect,' he spat, glaring down at the smaller man as he looked up in a shocked daze, one hand clamped to his cheek. 'Get out of my sight. Send your second to replace you.'

The officer dragged himself unsteadily to his feet and then, with a last poisonous look at Harald, loped away into the darkness.

William shook his head in glee and proffered his wine to Harald, who thanked him and took a deep, satisfied slurp to cement his victory.

Maniakes tried to recover his poise and continued the meeting, but I paid little attention. We had won our victory.

* * *

Over the coming days, it became clear that Syracuse was probably the most formidable fortress we had yet faced. Its walls were strong, well-maintained and built into the rock, making undermining or tunnelling almost impossible.

The seaward walls were likewise built directly onto the jagged, rocky shoreline, which was shallow and treacherous and sowed with large timber and iron constructions meant to snag any approaching ship leaving the channels. This made an assault from the sea very unlikely to succeed, even though a number of Admiral Stephen's ships were with us in order to blockade the city.

Through a number of boring meetings that I shall not recount to you every option was considered, and even Harald had no solution. Imperial records apparently recorded previous sieges, including the one a hundred and fifty years before when the city had fallen to the Moslems, and those sieges all took starvation and many months before they succeeded.

So the army settled in for a long siege, and Harald was deeply frustrated.

Harald was not the only one who was angry. Maniakes had been humiliated, and, with nothing better to do than sit around in camp feeling the scorn of other men, he took out his petty spite on everyone around him. Worst of all, when one of two ships carrying silver for the army was lost at sea in a storm, he gave the Greek half of the army its due silver and refused to pay the Lombards, Normans or Sicilians at all.

Us Varangians would be paid separately when we returned to Constantinople, so it did not affect us, but Arduin's men were on the verge of mutiny, and William's Normans threatened to leave the army and go back to Italy. It was a bad time, and the question was not whether we would be able to break the defences of Syracuse, but whether the army could be held together long enough to even try.

* * *

I liked to walk along the hill above the city in the early summer sun. It was good for my recovery to start exercising again, and I was still weak. I also liked the calmness of the ruins there, a thousand years old and still strong, which made me care less about our own, very short-lived troubles.

Harald joined me on this walk one day, and we went along the ridge until we reached the ancient, ruined fort at the eastern tip, which the Greeks said had been raised to defend Syracuse in the time before the Roman Empire even existed. It was still impressive, although its gates stood empty and its walls were broken in many places. But I could see how it would have dominated the plains to the east and protected the city from approach.

We climbed the biggest remaining tower, I with some difficulty, and stood at the top amongst the creeping plants and weeds that made their home on and between the old stones.

'Men have been fighting over this place for longer than we can imagine,' said Harald, gazing out over the city. 'I know it is also true of our homeland, but there we cannot see the evidence of it, only the sunken tombs of the old kings. Here, the remains are everywhere, the bones of old wars standing in the middle of our new ones.'

I looked at him oddly, because such contemplation was not normally something he indulged in.

'Why does that matter to you?'

'Because I wonder if this war of ours even means anything? Take the city or not, in a thousand years another man will stand here on these stones and look upon this city and think that his taking it is terribly important. But maybe it is not.'

'If it is not important, why are we here? What is all of this for?'

Harald stared out over the bay for a while before replying. 'Because I want men of Norway, a thousand years from now, to remember my name with pride and respect. And perhaps, in that time, when men gaze upon these walls and consider those who came before, they will know that I was here, and be humbled by it.'

'Why does it matter so much to you, what men think a thousand years from now, or even a hundred?'

'Because if a man is known and respected, is he even truly dead? My brother Olaf's body is in the ground, but the men of our country now revere him as a saint, have built a church around his tomb, and so his glory will last forever. I just want the men of Norway, when they speak of him with the fondness and respect that he deserves, to remember me also. And for them to do that, I must earn it, as he did.'

He fixed me with his piercing blue stare. 'Do you not understand that, Eric?'

And truly, I was completely perplexed by it, for I gave no importance whatsoever to what men said long generations from now. I had always believed Harald wanted power in his own time, and of course, he did. But there I was learning how highly he valued power that lasted well beyond his own mortal span.

But that is why he is remembered with love and admiration now, even more so than when he was alive. It is why, hundreds and perhaps a thousand years from now, men will still speak of the greatness of Harald Hardrada, while after I am gone, none but my grandchildren will remember my name.

* * *

We walked slowly back to the camp, and I was deep in thought, suddenly worried about my legacy, which is an odd thing to consider for such a young man. And I was still a young man.

'You know, none of it will matter if we fail here,' Harald said bitterly as we walked.

'If you had given Maniakes the camp he wanted, all of this might have been avoided,' I pointed out, perhaps not the most helpful thing I ever said to him.

'I know, but if I had merely backed down for him he would have taken more and more. His problems and personal flaws are his own, and not mine to fix for him.'

'You could have marked the lot fairly, and taken your chances,' I said.

Harald looked at me with feigned outrage. 'I *did* mark the lot fairly.' But then he grinned.

'Well, what do we do now? How do we get into this city?'

Harald shrugged. 'It will just take time.'

'And how much time? Until we conquer this place we are trapped here, unable to go back to Constantinople.'

'Yes, and that is what John and Michael wanted. This campaign was always meant to fail, or at least keep us away from the palace. This whole island is a fortress. We haven't faced an enemy army in the field for nearly two years, and yet we have captured less than half of it, or so I am told. It is hard to be sure because we have not even seen the other half. I thought they would surrender to us one by one, but each town is its own little kingdom.'

He turned to me. 'The Greeks tell me it took the Moslems over two hundred years to conquer this island. Two hundred!' He shook his head bitterly. 'We have been sent here to rot. Even if we take Syracuse, how many more fortresses are there to take? A dozen? It may never end.'

'Then what do we do? Abandon the empire and return home?'

'We do not yet have the wealth to do so.'

'Perhaps we can win your throne by strength of arms, not wealth.'

'We don't have the men for that.'

'Then perhaps we can find the men!'

'After fleeing this failure with our tails between our legs and abandoning our duties? Who would follow me? I wouldn't.' He was sullen. I slumped my shoulders in resignation.

'So we are trapped by this island, prisoners here.'

Harald took a deep breath and shook his head. 'No, Eric. Our enemies might believe that, but it is never true. We will find our opportunity and seize it. Believe it, for if you do not believe it, it cannot happen.'

Well, I don't need to tell you, I believed it.

16

For a month we sat and besieged Syracuse, and nothing happened. The enemy sat behind their walls, we sat in our camps and stopped anyone from entering or leaving, and our navy patrolled the sea with enough diligence to prevent all but the bravest and fastest enemy ships from entering or leaving the harbour.

And they were not big transports, resupplying the city with food. They were small, fast sailing vessels, probably carrying no more than messages, maybe pleas for help, or, worse, word that help was on its way.

Maniakes became completely cut off from the rest of the army, marinating in impotent anger and humiliation. Rumours openly circled the camp that the Lombards were considering rebellion, and William spoke to Harald in secret meetings that even I was not party to.

Several times guardsmen patrolling near the enemy city found arrows with notes attached to them in the ground, notes that indicated spies within our army were feeding information to the enemy. There were traitors in our ranks, and despite our best efforts to entrap them, we did not catch any in the act.

Eventually, the city gate opened and a party of soldiers and nobles appeared under the branch signalling they came for peace, waiting for our response to their invitation for negotiations.

Harald was not invited, specifically, but one of our sentries ran to tell him and he quickly armed himself and then ran down to the front of the imperial camp, dragging me in tow.

Maniakes had put together a group of his officers and was walking out to meet the enemy party, and William and Arduin were with him.

Harald joined the group and Maniakes' face betrayed his displeasure but he said and did nothing about it.

We met the enemy a bowshot or more outside our camp and stopped, just a half dozen paces apart, Maniakes doing his best to look confident and dominating, and the enemy looking far too relaxed.

'Strategos Georgios Maniakes, I present to you Abu'l-Qasim Ibn Ali al-Kabali, the emir of Syracuse, lord of these lands, servant of the emir Abdallah Ibn Ziri and follower of Mohammed, peace be upon him,' said the foremost man in flawless Greek. He was lavishly dressed and his headdress was decorated with large blue feathers that shimmered like the sea in the bright sunlight.

Despite his rich attire, it paled into insignificance compared to the trio of men behind him, the central one being the emir he was indicating.

'Have you come to surrender your city?' Maniakes asked, once the formalities were completed.

'No, Strategos, we have not. We have come to offer friendship, in return for you leaving and sparing your men a terrible summer in front of the walls that will yield you no success. We are well-stocked for a long siege.'

'If you were so well-stocked and happy for a long siege, you would not care if we remained.'

'Although we have no fear of you capturing the city, your presence does cause our people a few hardships and somewhat interferes with trade. We would simply rather not suffer the inconvenience,' the herald said with a friendly smile.

'I have orders from my emperor to return this city to Christian rule, but you and your people can remain, unharmed, if you agree to our overlordship. Or, you can face the fate of every town and city before us. No one is coming to help you. Our fleet controls the sea, and it is only a matter of time before my army crosses your walls. Believe me, Emir, you will want my army to cross those walls in peace, not in combat.'

There was a brief and fast-paced conference between the three very richly dressed men and then the emir shrugged, which ended whatever they were debating.

The herald turned back to Maniakes with a bow. 'We are not allowed by our faith or our lord to turn the city away from the control of the emirate, so we must decline. We will come and revisit our offer to you in another month, once the summer and disease have had their way with your men. You might find your way to being more reasonable.'

Then they turned and walked away without waiting for a reply, leaving Maniakes fuming on the path.

Harald caught William's eye and beckoned the Norman to follow us as we walked back to the camp and Maniakes angrily ordered his party to do the same.

'Well, that did not go well,' said William.

Harald looked around to make sure we were out of earshot. 'No, not for Maniakes. The emir is right; summer in this marsh will certainly drain the imperial forces. But, the emir is not as strong as he appears. He also must survive the summer and his people cannot drink seawater. It will be very difficult to dig a well on that tiny island, if not impossible. He must be worried to have come to negotiate so soon. Also, I learned something important there, something that Maniakes doubtless missed.'

'What is that?' William asked with interest.

'His name. Al-Kabali.'

'You remember his name? It was meaningless to me. They all have such long, indecipherable names.'

'I don't remember the rest, but I took note of that.'

'Why?' asked William.

'Because the Kabali family ruled Sicily for over a hundred years. They were the emirs of the whole island, now reduced merely to the area around Syracuse, and owing allegiance to the emir of Sicily in Balarm.'

'So?'

'The current emir of Sicily is not a Kabali, he is from a different family, one that has fought with the Kabalis.' William nodded thoughtfully.

I pressed my fingers to the bridge of my nose. 'So, the emir of Syracuse is the vassal of the emir of Sicily, who is the vassal of the emir of Ifriqiya?'

'Yes.'

'Is every lord of a two-pisspot town in this land an emir?'

Harald started to look annoyed. 'It just means lord, or maybe prince. It doesn't matter. What matters is the emirs of Syracuse and Sicily are not related, and the family of this Al-Kabali used to rule the whole island before Emir Abdallah usurped them.'

I looked at Harald in amazement. 'How do you know all this?'

Harald looked at me in annoyance. 'It is my duty to know all of this. The political fight is always as important as the military one. Our time with Yaroslav and in the palace should have taught you that by now.'

'So, the emirs of Syracuse and Sicily are enemies?' asked William, his eyes alight.

'Maybe not now, but in the past perhaps yes, and perhaps they could be again. We might be able to use this to turn the emirs against each other, and thus win us the city.'

'How?'

Harald looked at me for a moment, sizing me up, then he spoke to William. 'Let's go and talk to our Lombard prisoner. I think it is time he started talking to the enemy again.'

'Your Lombard what?' I hissed.

Harald nodded. 'I'm sorry, Eric. You didn't need to know. We caught the spy who was firing messages into the city, one of Arduin's Lombards.'

I stopped dead. 'I've had men out looking for him for weeks, but you already had him?'

'Yes.'

'Why keep it a secret?'

'Because if Maniakes finds out, he will assume Arduin is a traitor and banish him and his men, and the army will fall apart. So, we kept it a secret.'

'But... surely Arduin is a traitor?'

Harald looked at William and the Norman shrugged. 'It is hard to say. Arduin may not be aware of the spy. There are factions within his camp, and the man who sent this spy is not Arduin himself but one of his officers. Without questioning the officer, we would not know if he was acting alone.'

I nodded. 'This is all very well, but how can we use this to capture the city?'

'Well, we offer the emir something he wants, maybe to become emir of Sicily again if he allies with us. He can have the west of the island, and us the east,' Harald said.

'But we need the west, too!'

'Yes, but we can betray him later. What? You think I must uphold an oath made to the enemy? No, but let him think that.'

'That might work,' said William with a crooked smile. 'But we cannot let Maniakes know.'

'No, he would blunder into this and ruin it. It is a secret between us. Come, let us go and talk to our prisoner.'

Harald took us past the theatre and into the abandoned quarry behind, underneath our camp. There were a number of caves in the cliff, and he led us to a small one that wormed into the rockface. We found two Varangians there, mounting a hidden watch over a bound man tied to a ring embedded in the wall.

One of the Varangians was Rurik. He looked at me sheepishly and I glared at him.

'Just two nights ago I sent you out to look for the spy, and you reported you saw nothing?'

He shrugged his shoulders apologetically. 'I was just following orders.'

'Yes, and that is why I chose him,' said Harald in a tone that allowed no argument. 'Because I knew he would keep them. Now be quiet, Eric.'

I fell into a sulking silence, hurt not to have been the first Harald trusted. I was easily hurt, you see, in matters of Harald's trust and respect. I was never good with plotting or politics. I liked my enemy to identify himself and stand in front of me where I could kill him with my superior skill, or die if he earned that honour. That sulking around in shadows with lies and deceit was Afra's world, and sometimes Harald's. If I had been a little less proud it would have been obvious why Harald had kept me out of his plans, because he knew me better than I knew myself.

Harald leaned down to the captive, who quailed. I could see he had been tortured. 'Will you resume your messaging to the enemy?'

The man's eyes went wide with fear. 'I promise, I will stop. I swear it.'

'No, you misunderstand me – are you willing to resume?'

He looked lost. 'Why?'

'I need to send some messages to the emir, but I want him to believe they came from you. They will surely match the messages to see if the same hand wrote them. If you help me, I will not kill you.'

He nodded with pitiful enthusiasm. 'I will, I will write whatever you wish.'

Harald nodded sternly. 'Good. I will have writing materials and the messages I require written sent to you.' Then he looked at me. 'This man will take them.'

I nodded, hiding my unease at being taken into the plot.

'If you betray us, this man will kill you. Do you understand?'

The prisoner started yammering. 'I do, I will do no such thing... I mean, I will be loyal, or disloyal if you wan—'

'Quiet, cease your babbling. Just do what you are told, and I will not kill you.'

The man's head nodded so vigorously I worried it would detach.

'Good.' Harald stood up again to his full height. 'Eric, when I give him messages to write have them taken down at night and fired into the city. Make sure your men are patrolling that area and let no one else from the army do so. Collect any return messages and deliver them to me. Don't read them. Understood?'

I nodded fervently, with a little more dignity than the prisoner, but not much.

'Good. William, walk with me.'

* * *

I did as I was commanded and took paper and ink to the spy, then took his messages out to the fields in the dead of night where Rurik fired them over the walls into the city, for I could not pull a bow with my injured arm. I was curious what the messages said but did not break Harald's confidence by reading them.

A few hand-picked men patrolled the area to find and collect any return messages, which they did without question, despite surely suspecting it was part of a plot. Loyalty from your men is hard-earned, and nothing fills you with more pride or thankfulness.

This exchange of messages happened half a dozen times over a few weeks, and finally, Harald had concluded his deceptive conversation. He came down to the cave with me one night.

'The emir wants to meet with the traitor in the camp.'

'Ah, how is that possible?'

'You will see, Eric,' he replied with a tone that allowed no further questioning.

We arrived at the cave and found Rurik and another guardsman with the prisoner, who looked at Harald nervously.

'I have done what you asked,' he said.

'I know,' replied Harald blankly.

'And?'

'You have done well. As promised, I will not kill you.'

The prisoner slumped in relief.

We waited there for a while and then William arrived with several men behind him. My eyes opened in surprise as I recognised Arduin.

Arduin surveyed the scene with confusion and then fear. He turned to leave but found William blocking his path.

'What have you done, William?' he said nervously, struggling to maintain his composure.

William spread his hands to placate the Lombard. 'This is no trap, we just need to talk to you about something and could not explain it beforehand.'

'What is this?' he said, pointing at the prisoner.

'This is the traitor,' Harald said evenly. 'The spy who has been communicating with the enemy.'

Arduin stiffened. 'Are you sure?' I was not sure if I was convinced by his uncertainty.

Harald nodded slowly.

'You are here to accuse me? And then what, murder me in this hole? William, I do not deserve this!'

'Just hear him out, Arduin. He promised no violence upon you,' the Norman replied in a calming voice.

'I can't kill you, Arduin. I need you and your men with the army,' said Harald softly.

'Then what?'

'I need your help?'

'How?'

'I need you to be the traitor.'

That stunned Arduin and he stared at Harald, thinking and breathing hard.

Harald walked around the prisoner towards Arduin. 'I don't know if this man was obeying your orders, but it doesn't matter because the enemy believes it. I have been communicating with them on your behalf, slowly allowing them to convince me to betray Maniakes, and finally, promising your support.'

'You have done what?' Arduin spat, aghast.

Harald held a hand up. 'Please, let me explain. I need this siege to be over, and I need us to be victorious. The enemy now believes you are ready to betray us, and they have good reason to think that is the truth. You have been mistreated, your men abused and misused, your homeland subjugated. I know it is possible you really would betray the army, and thus the enemy also knows it is possible. Now they want to meet you, to arrange for your betrayal, and I want you to go to that meeting.'

'And betray Maniakes?'

'No. To betray the emir. This is their weakness, the way into the city. You will continue the negotiations and earn their trust. They will believe you because they want to believe you, because their position is not as strong as they portray.'

Arduin nodded slowly, his temple pulsing. 'This makes sense. But how will we do it?'

'They will be sending a small boat across the bay tomorrow night. You and two followers are allowed to go with them, to meet the emir.'

Arduin's eyes flicked back and forth nervously as he considered it. 'And how do you know I will do as you say?'

'One of my men will go with you.'

Arduin sneered. 'Of course, I see. You do not trust me.'

'I wish to,' said Harald earnestly. 'But you have to trust me first. Have I not been good to you?'

Arduin relaxed a little and nodded curtly. 'Certainly you won the affection of my men.'

'Well, we must learn to trust each other if this is to work.'

'Fine, but there is a hole in your plan. Your men look nothing like mine, and the Moslems will recognise it. They are familiar with us, we have been trading and fighting with them for two hundred years.'

'True, but my men look very much like the Normans. You will tell the emir that you are trying to bring William with you in this betrayal, but that he is unsure and needs to know more so has sent one of his men. Again, the emir will believe that, because he wants to believe it. It will be his ambition to corrupt William's forces too.'

'Why do you not come yourself?'

'There is a danger I would be recognised. I am very recognisable.'

Arduin breathed heavily. 'This is a great danger you are putting me in.'

'The danger to you should be limited. It will be my men patrolling that part of the shore, and they will ensure you are not seen by Maniakes.'

'And what of the emir?'

'He has no reason to harm you, and every reason to be your friend.'

'So you say. Well, what do you want me to say to him?'

'I will leave that to you. It should be easy, merely act as if you truly wish to betray Maniakes, and offer what you would offer if it were true.'

Arduin laughed at that, a little too hard. 'As you say, that will not be difficult.'

'My aim is to get him to allow your forces into the city, where we will turn on him. Work towards that goal. I believe he might covet ruling the entire Emirate of Sicily. We can offer to help him achieve that, but make no specific promises on this occasion. This is for both sides to test the waters and gain a little confidence. The more I let you work that out yourself, the more believable it will be.'

'I understand. So, what do I get from this? Helping you with this insanity that surely Maniakes has not been informed of.'

'I will ensure that your men get their fair share of the spoils in this, and all future battles. I will also make sure you get your missing pay first.' Harald looked at William. 'You too.'

The Norman smiled and nodded in thanks.

'I will also argue for better treatment and more independence for you and your people in front of the emperor himself when I return to the city.' It was a generous offer, and one Harald had in his power to give.

Arduin thought about it and then nodded. 'That seems fair. So, what now?'

'Now you earn the first piece of my trust.' Harald took his seax from his belt, and offered it to Arduin, hilt first, looking at the prisoner.

Arduin looked at the blade, Harald's stony expression, and the prisoner, who suddenly realised what was happening.

'You said you wouldn't kill me!' he pleaded, looking from Harald to Arduin.

'I won't,' replied Harald without even looking at the condemned man. 'For your betrayal, your lord will.'

Harald pushed the wicked-looking blade, shining in the firelight, towards the Lombard leader. 'I must know you can do what is required. I must know any previous thoughts of betrayal are behind you. Whether this man was acting on your orders or not, kill him and be cleansed of the stain of his treason.'

Arduin hesitated. 'This man is my kin, my tribe. His father has been a supporter of mine for my entire life.'

Harald put the blade in Arduin's hand and wrapped the reluctant fingers around it, before staring intently into his eyes. 'Good. Then I will know the deepness of your commitment.'

Arduin's jaw clenched and he took the blade away from

Harald. Rurik's hand clamped around the prisoner's mouth and stifled his last, horrified plea, pulling his head back and exposing his neck to that terrible, firelit steel.

Arduin leaned down, his eyes fixed and his hand steady, and the plot was sealed in blood.

* * *

Harald chose me to accompany Arduin and one of his officers. I cannot say that I was pleased, but I am not sure who else I would have trusted. So before I knew it I was crouching on the shoreline two nights later, and a small boat was gliding towards us in the near darkness of the bay.

The boat bumped into the sand and a man in the bow gestured at us to get aboard, and we did, as quickly and quietly as we could.

We were whisked back across the short stretch to the city harbour by four silent Arabs who did not even look at us. We passed under the walls and around the mole of the harbour with its guards and spikes and watchfires, and pulled into one of the many empty berths, where we were helped up onto the stone.

I had not worn any of my equipment, just a simple tunic and trousers. I didn't have a weapon, not even a knife; although we had not been forbidden to bring them, there was no point doing so and Harald had wanted to ensure nothing marked me out as a Varangian.

'Arduin the Lombard?' a man asked, and I recognised the herald who had met us outside the city weeks before.

'Yes.'

'Come, the emir is waiting.'

We were ushered into a building on the dock front, which surprised me. But then I realised that the emir would want as few people as possible to know there had been visitors, for he might have spies inside his walls too.

We went through into a back room which had been half cleared, crates and bags all pushed to one side. At a small, ornate table laid with drinks and fruits, a man was sitting in simple clothes. It was the emir. He smiled at us and rose with a small, humble bow, motioning to three stools arrayed in front of him.

We sat, and he sat after us. 'Please, refresh yourselves,' he said in a pleasant tone, and a servant poured us all some water that was infused with some herbs and fruits and was quite delightful. I would have preferred good mead to calm my nerves, but the Moslems do not have such things.

'I welcome you into Syracuse as a friend, Arduin of the Lombards. I wish I could show you my fine city, but...' He shrugged coyly. 'You understand.'

'I thank you, Emir Abu'l-Qasim, for the warmness of your welcome, and of course, I hope to see your city another time.'

'Good. So I understand you have dissatisfactions with your current commander?'

Arduin waited a moment before answering. 'I believe that is a good way of describing it.'

The emir smiled knowingly. 'I hear many things about George Maniakes, and none of them make me believe he is a tolerable man, even if he is a fine general.'

'Your information is good.'

'Of course it is, I pay well. Now, despite this, why would you risk turning against the empire? They are a fearsome enemy.'

Arduin swallowed. 'It is not certain yet, Emir, that I shall do anything. This is merely a conversation.'

'Of course.'

'But, if I were, it would be because without my men, and the

Normans, Maniakes is a toothless lion, and his are the empire's only forces in this part of their domain.'

'The empire will send another army, no?'

'If he loses this one? No, they will not.'

The emir leaned in, and his face and his eyes sparked with a keen curiosity and intellect. 'Explain.'

'Well, the truth is, the emperor does not truly expect Maniakes to succeed. They do not value Sicily highly.'

The emir was motionless for a moment and then slapped his leg lightly in satisfaction and sat back. 'It is exactly as I suspected, and as other sources have already told me. Thank you, Arduin, for your honesty. Maniakes is a trouble-maker, no? And the Northern mercenary. They are sent here to make sure they are not there,' he said, gesturing to the ground beneath his feet and then behind, in the direction of the empire across the water.

'Correct.' Arduin let the emotion show as his hands shook a little. 'Not only that, but the empire is preoccupied with other conflicts. Rebellion is brewing in Bulgaria, and that is a much greater threat than anything that could happen in Italy or Sicily. Regardless, I am tired of my people dying for this farce, to be a part of this politics. The risk to me may well be worth it.'

I swallowed hard. I could see the feelings were both real and deep. It was in that moment I decided that Arduin had, truly, been giving orders to the spy in our camp. I could not prove it, of course, but I became sure of it. It was quite a time later when I realised Harald, too, had been absolutely sure of it. That, in fact, Harald had relied on it for this plan to work, that only true feelings of treason from Arduin would convince the emir.

Ha, Harald was always so many steps ahead of me in such things.

'As you should be, as you should be,' said the emir with a sympathetic nod.

'But I will not trade one master for another,' said Arduin, shaking a finger. 'That is not what I am here seeking, and why this is still merely a conversation between men who need not be enemies.'

The emir nodded and spread his hands in offering. 'So, tell me, what is it that you want?'

'I wish to be rid of the empire in my lands.'

'That is a great and noble goal, my friend, and we wish it also. But, more immediately, what do *you* want.'

Arduin nodded. 'I want to end Maniakes' campaign, then take my men home alive and free of obligation.'

The emir tapped his finger on his thigh and thought about this. 'I do not wish to insult you, Arduin. But such simplicity, while admirable, is perhaps a little naive.'

'Why?'

'Well, you cannot simply walk away. There will be bloodshed before this is over, for all of us.'

Arduin nodded curtly. 'I am not a fool. What do you suggest?'

The emir swirled his cup as he thought about this, then he avoided the question and suddenly looked at me. 'What about the Normans?'

Arduin made to answer but the emir held up his hand politely but firmly. 'I wish to hear it from the Norman. He speaks the Greek tongue, I see him listening. Tell me, Norman, what does your master want?'

I was so nervous at the sudden and intense focus on me that I nearly froze up. I coughed and took a drink to buy me time to gather my thoughts and appear calm. 'My Lord William has similar complaints about his treatment, but his situation is a little... different.'

'Different how?'

'He is not a vassal, he seeks a more... solid incentive for changing his alliances.'

I tried to speak how I imagined a great leader would, in circles, avoiding the point. I think I really just sounded like a pretentious arse, but then, maybe that was the correct note to hit.

The emir smiled with slight distaste. 'He wishes to be paid.'

'Essentially, yes.'

'Ah, what a simple man a mercenary is. And he wishes, I presume, to be paid more than his current masters for the inconvenience?'

'Yes.'

'And tell me, Norman, why would he risk his reputation for a rise in his pay?'

I looked offended. 'He would not, if it were not for the many insults and mistreatments he has been subjected to. Nor have we been paid what was promised. If we are paid and treated correctly, we are steadfast and all know it. It was Maniakes who broke faith first.'

I jutted my chin out to convey my wounded pride.

'I see. And tell me, why is your Lord William not here to tell me this himself?'

I stared back at him. 'Because he does not know you or trust you, yet.'

The emir held eye contact with me for a while, his eyes boring into mine as I desperately tried not to give away any hint of my deceit, certain, the entire time, that he saw right through me.

Finally, he smiled and nodded. 'I think I can satisfactorily improve your lord's position, and, uh... earn his trust?' And at a small signal with his fingers, a man brought over a large silk-decorated bag, itself a beautiful thing, and set it down on the table with a telling thud. The emir indicated to it with a smile, and I opened the top, peering inside. To my open delight and wonder, it was filled entirely with gold. It was a staggering amount of wealth.

It also, of course, proved that the emir's dismay at being required to bribe William was performative. He had, of course, anticipated it and prepared for it.

'I wish to meet with your Lord William before we go any further with this,' said the emir. 'If he meets with me, all of this is his. Here, take a token of it to show him my gold is good.' He gestured to the bag and I helped myself to a large gold coin with a nod of thanks. Then the attendant took the heavy bag of gold away again, with my eyes greedily following it in a way that I did not have to feign.

Clearly regarding his interaction with me to be over, he turned back to the Lombards. 'Arduin, I believe we can be friends indeed, but this meeting has given me much to consider, and I wish to have a plan to propose to you in full, along with your friend, Lord William.'

Arduin nodded. 'I also have much to consider.'

The emir stood with a broad smile. 'Good. Then I am most pleased you have trusted me with this meeting, and I thank you for coming to my beautiful city to speak to me. I shall make another invite soon, by the same method as before.'

Arduin shook his head sadly. 'We cannot use that any more. My man was spotted and although he escaped, the Varangians now patrol much more heavily.'

The emir's face tensed a little bit, but he shrugged. 'A shame. How then?'

'It is too dangerous to communicate now, and I believe we need nothing but a time and a place for the meeting.'

'I see. Well, I think I will trust you with a little secret, as a gesture and to make these meetings easier and less likely to be discovered. At the base of the tower of the eastern side by the sea there is a small door, hidden from the outside behind a rocky outcropping. You should easily be able to approach it unseen and my men will let you in, say, on the seventh night from tonight? Shall I see you then?'

Arduin nodded. 'Thank you, Emir. You shall.'

17

Harald listened intently as we related the entire meeting to him in the morning. 'Good, good. You did very well. Do you think he suspected anything?'

Arduin laughed gruffly. 'I think he suspected everything. He is a very careful and intelligent man, that is clear. But I think also he believed us because as you said, he wanted to believe us, and what I told him was what he already suspected.'

'Fine, then our plan can continue.' Harald turned to William. 'Are you happy to go and meet with him next time?'

William nodded with a broad smile. 'For the bag of gold Eric describes? I would meet the devil in hell, naked as the day I was born.'

Harald suppressed a laugh and patted William on the back. 'Good man.'

'So, what do we offer him?'

'I suspect he will make the offer for us, but if not, say that you will help rid him of Maniakes and then take the island from the emir. In return, he will help Arduin take his homeland back.'

I thought that was a cruel thing to say when he did not mean it, and Arduin just looked at the ground and nodded in silence to acknowledge he had heard it.

'That should work. Now, what is the real plan?'

'We must get your forces inside the city, where we can turn on him.'

'I don't think that will work,' said Arduin. 'He is far too careful, too clever, and it is an obvious ploy. He will insist the treachery happens outside the walls.'

Harald frowned. 'What do you suggest?'

'We need a reason to get his main gates open, even for a small number of men,' said William. 'We can achieve nothing by this small door he describes. It will be easily defended from within. If we can get a body of men through the main gate, we can seize it and hold it while the army runs to support us.'

'Why would he ever let enough of us through the gate to achieve that?' asked Arduin.

It was a good question, and we all sat in contemplation.

'We could say the final treachery will be for a party of us to go through the main gate, which will be a signal to start the mutiny from our forces?'

'But still, he only needs to allow a small number of us in,' said William. 'I doubt he will agree to it anyway.'

Harald leaned back and considered it. 'I have a way, but someone needs to die. Someone important to you.' He looked at William. 'Your brother Drogo, perhaps.'

William's face fell and Harald chuckled. 'Only in pretence, my friend. Only in pretence. But the entire army must know about it. Come, let me explain.'

* * *

Well, Harald laid out his entire plan, and we all agreed to it after a great deal of discussion I won't bore you with. We had to assume the emir had other spies, so the planning for this mutiny was done with the utmost care, and was, of course, completely hidden from Maniakes.

Drogo was announced to his men to have a fever, and, over the next four days his 'condition' deteriorated and he was isolated in his tent. Finally, two days before the meeting, William announced tearfully to his men that Drogo had died of the fever that was widespread through the imperial camp. The news spread through the army, as Harald hoped it would.

William and Arduin, with one of the Lombards and I in tow, headed for the meeting on the agreed night, sneaking along the beach to the tower and hidden door that had been described, and being allowed in.

We were taken to a fine house near the walls, where in a richly furnished room, the emir greeted us. Arduin was smiling and glad, and William was stiff and his eyes were sunken. He had been keeping himself awake for two days in order to appear haggard and withdrawn.

The emir looked at him with sympathy. 'I am so sorry, Lord William, to hear of your brother's death.'

William looked up at the emir with surprise. 'How did you know?' he asked gruffly.

The emir gave us a knowing look. 'Please, I have other sources. They also relayed to me the sad news and I regret most heavily that we did not conduct this business sooner, and save your brother. Please, sit.'

We sat and William stared at the ground. 'I have other men who are sick,' he muttered.

'So I am told,' said the emir sympathetically. 'I hear the sickness is growing in the army.'

'We are here to end this, Emir,' Arduin said. And I saw the emir's eyes flash with quelled joy. 'But only if the terms are correct.'

The emir inclined his head respectfully. 'I intend them to be acceptable for all.'

'Then perhaps we should keep this short, for William's sake, because he has a brother's funeral to plan,' said Arduin with a sad glance at the Norman lord.

'Perhaps this can wait until you have dealt with your family affairs?'

'No!' said William firmly, raising his chin. 'How many more of my men will die waiting?'

The emir nodded. 'I understand. Well, then this is what I propose. Emir Abdallah has raised a new army to lift the siege. But on his own, he is not strong enough to defeat Maniakes. He needs Maniakes to be weakened before offering battle, and is awaiting a message from me confirming that I have succeeded in that.'

I did my best not to react to the news that the Emir of Sicily was preparing to relieve the siege, for we did not have any prior knowledge of that.

'When the emir arrives, Maniakes will be confident of victory and fight. However, if you desert him in the moment of the battle, and my forces join yours to attack Maniakes from the rear, the emir will surely be victorious.'

'So if we turn on the empire in the coming battle, what do you offer in return?'

'I will support Arduin as much as I can in your struggle with the empire, and pay you both handsomely.'

Arduin considered it and shook his head. 'It is not enough.'

'In what way?'

'I mean you no offence, but as Emir of Syracuse your reach is limited.'

'Well, I might persuade Emir Abdallah to help. With the Emirate of Sicily behind you and Maniakes defeated, the empire will be unlikely to commit sufficient forces to defeat you. They are, as you say, preoccupied.'

'Or Emir Abdallah might not. You cannot guarantee it,' said Arduin. 'Perhaps it would be better if you were Emir of Sicily.'

The emir raised an eyebrow and looked at Arduin passively. 'I am loyal to my lord Abdallah Ibn Ziri.'

'Your lord is the enemy of your family, is he not?'

'He was, once. But no more,' the emir replied carefully, and I could see how interested he was.

'You would not seek to have the Al-Kabali family rule the island again, with you at their head?'

The emir couldn't help it; his eyes sparkled with greed and lust at the idea. But he tried to make a noncommittal face. 'Even if such a thing were possible, why would you help me do that?'

'Well, if you were the lord of all Sicily, you would be able to help us secure our own freedom in Italy with much greater certainty. We could be allies, not just friends. Two strong domains on each side of the water, capable, together, of resisting the empire completely.'

The emir looked up and considered it deeply, and I could see the lure of it working its hooks into him, as Harald had hoped.

Then he shrugged. 'How would we defeat both Maniakes and Abdallah? Unless...'

'We let them destroy each other,' said William with a growl. 'Send your message to Emir Abdallah promising we will switch sides if he attacks Maniakes, but then do not. His forces and Maniakes will fight, and then we can destroy whatever weakened victor remains. We will then be the only army on the island, and surely we will secure it easily.'

The emir breathed hard and tried to contain his excitement. 'That... could work.' He paused a moment in thought. 'And then you will help me fight whoever remains, and secure this whole island?' he asked, wanting the comfort of repetition.

'Yes.'

'Hmm, it is ambitious.'

'Are you not an ambitious man? I am, and I see it in you too.'

'Yes,' blurted the emir, his face a rictus of indecision and excitement. 'This Ibn Ziri... This... betrayer. He stole this land from my family, he...' The emir gained control of himself and closed his eyes, breathing hard to calm his passions.

Then he opened them again and looked at us. 'You will have the chance to turn on me again, somewhere, as you have on Maniakes. How will I trust you not to do so?'

'Simply don't treat us the way Maniakes did,' rumbled William darkly. And the emir nodded.

'I want my own homeland, Emir Abu'l-Qasim, not yours. You know that is true,' added Arduin.

I saw the emir make up his mind. His posture rose, his smile was released, and he nodded firmly. 'I do, Arduin of the Lombards. I do. And I swear it, I will help you take your home back if you first help me with mine.'

Both men stood, and the emir was surprised when Arduin embraced him, but he returned it after a pause.

'There is one more thing,' said William suddenly. 'My brother.'

'Your brother? I don't understand,' the emir said.

'You have churches still, in this city?' William looked at the emir hopefully.

'Yes, we still allow the Greeks to live and worship among us.'

'Good.' William nodded soberly. 'I wish to bring my brother's body and lay him to rest in your biggest church. It cannot wait weeks until the battle. The weather is hot and...' William gulped uncomfortably. The emir looked quite moved by William's sorrow, and he nodded. He knew exactly what would happen to William's brother's body after two weeks unburied in the Sicilian summer.

'Of course, but... I do not wish to insult you, William the Norman...' The Emir looked genuinely pained.

'But you are worried at the risk of allowing us through your gates,' finished William with a nod of understanding. 'Just me and several dozen of my men to bear the coffin and make a respectable procession. We will come unarmed, in daylight.' Then he looked at Arduin. 'Perhaps Arduin can attend also, for they were friends.'

Arduin looked completely torn by that, but fortunately, the emir seemed to interpret his discomfort as grief.

He bowed, relenting. 'Of course, of course. Whatever you need, my friend. For friends we are to be.'

'Indeed,' said William with a smile, and I could see the shadow of the strain on his face.

* * *

'We cannot tell Maniakes until the last moment,' said Harald, digesting the news we had brought him. 'Even if he agrees to it, the spies the enemy still have might get word to the city in time to warn them.'

'So, we must tell him what we told the emir, that this is simply us taking Drogo's body to be buried in the city.'

'Indeed. We will have our men quietly prepare for battle. Maybe the rest of the army will notice, maybe they will not. Our camps are separate. Either way, they will notice when our men move down to the edge of the fields and prepare to rush the gate. So we will inform the strategos at the last possible moment.'

'He will be furious,' I said.

'It cannot be helped,' said Harald. 'And if this plan wins him the city, he will forgive us.'

'Who will command our forces?' I asked.

'Well, Drogo will command mine,' said William with a laugh. He was enjoying every aspect of this plan greatly.

'I have a cousin who I trust to bring mine,' said Arduin.

'And Sveinn will lead ours,' said Harald. 'Eric, you will come with me, along with twenty men. William, you bring ten of yours, and Arduin, twenty of yours. I think that is the most we can get away with. Bring only your best and toughest. The fight will be nasty. Wear whatever armour you can conceal under your tunics, and nothing else. No shields, no visible weapons.'

'It's going to be a terrible fight if they are prepared for treachery.'

'Yes, we must expect they will be prepared.'

'Does everyone understand what is required of them?' asked Harald, looking around.

'I hope your plan at the gate works,' said William with a grin. 'But if it does not, what a tale our deaths will make!'

* * *

'Fuck, this thing is heavy!' muttered Ulfr, struggling as he was under the weight of Drogo's coffin. Eight men carried the simple Cyprus-wood box, but they were suffering under its load in the heat.

'Drogo did love his food,' said William from where he walked in front of the coffin bearers, to a muted ripple of laughter from the Normans.

We were walking down the path towards the city gate, already halfway there. Our preparations in our parts of the camp had not gone unnoticed, and Maniakes had sent a furious messenger to ask why our men were arming, and then the imperial part of the camp had started arming too when the Lombards did.

Harald had waited until the last possible moment before sending a man with a letter to explain the plan. We just had to hope it was enough to avoid bloodshed in the camp.

We got closer to the gates but they remained steadfastly closed, and I started to worry the emir had seen through us all along. We were well within the range of the archers watching from the walls now, but they made no hostile move, just stared at us in curiosity.

Just as we were about to reach the gates they cracked open and started to be pulled back, revealing a line of armed men blocking the way. 'Be steady, be calm,' Harald whispered to us around him.

We stopped outside the gate and William and Arduin stepped forward, lifting their cloaks to show they were not armed, and those of us not carrying the coffin did the same.

The line of enemy suddenly parted and stepped to the side, and the emir himself appeared, in all his finery, with his entourage, and waved us in with a hasty gesture.

We resumed our slow march, the men behind us groaning under the load of the coffin. We reached the gate and passed under it with William and Arduin in the lead. The emir gave a slight bow to both of the leaders and smiled.

'I welcome you to Syracuse, Arduin of the Lombards, and William of the Normans.' He paid no attention to Harald, who was just acting as if he were one of William's Normans with the rest of us.

The emir saw Arduin's discomfort and he nodded sympathetically. 'I know that this is a day of mourning, but I hope it is the start of much happier times to follow. Come, bring your men inside the walls, and I will escort you to the church.'

Arduin nodded and stepped aside, waving to the patient column to continue. The men started their slow walk past us, and the emir noted the eight men struggling under the heavy coffin as it approached the archway.

'You bear a heavy burden in this, in more ways than one,' he said to William, who just nodded. And then he turned to Arduin, who could not meet his eye. 'But together we will free our people from this Greek menace.'

Arduin said nothing and did not move, just stared at the coffin. I tensed, and my hand strayed to the seax hidden at my back.

'Do you not welcome this alliance, Arduin?' said the emir, and he put his hand on the Lombard's shoulder and gently pulled.

Arduin turned to face the emir and his face cracked and a tear fell from his eye.

The emir looked at him in confusion.

'I'm sorry,' blurted Arduin, and the emir's face slackened before he looked more closely at the men coming through the gate, and saw their furtive glances at the guards.

'What have you done?' the emir whispered in shock, and then his eyes darted to the coffin bearers as they stopped in the middle of the gateway.

The emir backed away from Arduin, suddenly aware of the danger. 'What have you done!' he howled in outrage.

Then the men bearing the coffin dropped it to the ground with a thunderous crash.

So many things happened in that moment that I struggle to know how to relate it. The coffin burst open, revealing that it contained not a body but an entire bushel of swords packed in muffling straw. The back half of our column rushed in, grabbing at the weapons, even as the emir screamed at his men in their own tongue, pointing at the gate.

William went for the emir but he was too slow, and several of the emir's entourage bravely put themselves between their lord and his assailant. William was suddenly in a nasty fight, seax against swords, with several of his men rushing to help him.

Those of our men already through the gate turned and fell upon the guards lining the street with the knives, seaxes and axes they had pulled from hiding places in their clothes. There was a terrible slaughter as the enemy was caught completely unprepared by the speed and violence of the attack. In moments men with swords from the coffin joined them, and the slaughter was complete.

More men at the rear of the column killed the guards at the gate itself and secured the big wooden doors.

But the emir had not been unprepared, and, no sooner had we massacred the men at the gate than dozens of guards spilled from hiding places in buildings on either side of the street, and we heard shouts from above us on the wall.

The four panels of the coffin, fitted on the inside with straps for this purpose, were brought up as shields and twenty men formed a makeshift wall in the gate, where they would stand and hold until they died, or our army, who would already be rushing from the main camp six hundred paces away, arrived.

But the number of the enemy coming at us was significant, and they were shielded and armoured.

'To me!' roared Harald, stepping forward and raising a sword in the air. 'On me!'

Those who were finishing off the initial guards came back and formed a mass around him, myself included, and swords were hurriedly passed out to those who did not have them. We all stripped our cloaks from our backs and wrapped them around our left arms, in place of the shields we did not have.

Our job was simple – we were to protect the open gate behind us until the rest of our forces arrived.

The enemy surged down the street towards us, and Ulfr and Halldor, standing together beside me, roared their savage battle cry and ran forwards to meet the enemy, their cloak-wrapped arms held up in front, and their swords pointed forwards like spears, and we all followed.

The two sides clashed in a maelstrom of ferocity. Both knew that to lose was to die. There was no retreat for anyone, and the fighting was especially ferocious because of it.

I put my sword into a man who was hacking at the guardsman to my right, and both men went down in a spray of bone and blood. Ulfr split a defender's head in half, and Halldor ducked under his arm and stabbed his blade through the chest of another and then kicked him off the weapon to attack his next victim.

A Lombard to my right went down with an arrow in his back and that was the first moment I realised the enemy on the wall behind us was finally shooting down at us, but there was nothing we could do but suffer it.

I went towards Harald as a spear lashed at him. He batted it aside and sheared the arm from his attacker, but then went down in a rush of enemy as someone punched him in the face with a shield boss. I screamed at our men in fear and horror to get to him before anyone could finish him off.

I cut my way through the enemy, soaking up frantic blows on my still tender arm and the light maille I wore under my tunic.

I found Harald struggling to his feet, with enemy closing in on him, and I saw that he was in dire danger.

Halldor saw it too, and he jumped into the oncoming enemy with reckless rage, cutting down one attacker and kicking aside another as a dazed Harald got up and tried to defend himself.

One of the enemy stepped forward and cut at Halldor, and I felt sick to my stomach as the blow connected with his unprotected face. The big Icelander stumbled in shock, his hands falling limply to his sides, and then he sat down heavily on the bodies behind him.

Ulfr howled in rage at the sight of his beloved cousin falling, and he poured himself into the enemy like a storm into a forest, and his blade was everywhere. Half a dozen of us followed him into the tempest of blood and steel, and more men behind, and despite our lack of shields and armour, the enemy recoiled from us and then started retreating from us, and then finally broke.

A dazed Harald roared at us to hold as we started to follow them, and we reluctantly fell back to where he stood amidst the carnage. I looked around and saw that almost everyone still standing was hurt, and far from all of us were still standing. Ulfr was helping a dazed Halldor to stagger away, and his cousin's face was a bloody ruin.

Behind Harald, over the heads of our men at the gate, I could see the banner of Sveinn's wolfhounds bobbing and fluttering as the second bandon ran towards the gate, just a few hundred paces away.

There was a noise behind us and I turned to see a fresh wave of the enemy pour into the street, and the emir and his bodyguards were with them.

The emir was a brave man. He knew that he had to close the gate or the city was lost. And he put himself in command of his men and he came for us without hesitation.

'Shield-wall!' shouted Harald. The men at the gate had not been idle, having run out and grabbed shields from fallen enemy to add to the makeshift coffin panel shields, and now made a modest but respectable shield-wall inside the archway.

We all fell back to the gateway. The enemy on the wall had found some stones to drop, and several of our men went down under the impacts.

The enemy rushing at us down the street were no city guards or militia; these were the personal bodyguards of the emir, in fine armour and wearing plumed helmets, carrying spears and long, curved swords.

There was no prevarication. They came at us in a great body and hammered into our wall as one unit, smashing us back a pace and knocking several men from their feet.

Then we were in a terrible fight, pressed in under the arch, and our usual advantages of good helmets and long axes were absent. So we traded lives with the brave Arabs, losing men to overhand spear thrusts and sabre cuts, even as wicked Norse swords and seaxes worked their butchery in between and under the shields, thrusting into stomachs and groins and thighs.

The slaughter was terrible, but the numbers were on their side, and they pushed us back, men fell, and they pushed us back again.

William roared something in French to his men, and they formed a little group behind our struggling line. He pointed his sword at the emir, roared a howling, sky-searing war cry and charged.

His little band of men smashed through both lines, even as

the Arabs were getting their hands on one of the doors and trying to close it against the press.

Men and shields went tumbling without distinction for whose side they stood on, and William and his killers were through and into the press of enemy, inside the range of their deadly spears.

Harald shouted at us and we surged after them, following William as he hacked his way, life by life, towards the emir, who stood his ground and shouted at his men to get the doors closed.

But William was faster than them, stronger than them, more determined than them, and he cut down the last enemy between himself and the emir and aimed a vicious overhand strike.

The emir stepped aside and parried the blow away, cutting back neatly at William and striking him on the shoulder. William was only saved by his maille and roared in pain and outrage.

He attacked again, but he was tired from fighting and the emir was shockingly quick and lithe, a real swordsman. He hit William twice more and drew blood from his chest with a nasty thrust with the slim, curved sword.

Harald reached his friend and joined in the fight around the emir, half decapitating a richly dressed enemy who tried to come to his lord's aid.

More and more men tried to save their leader, and they abandoned the gates as their numbers thinned and the fastest of our men from outside the city reached us and put their shields and spears into the fight. The emir looked at us in tight-lipped horror as his men's attack finally stalled and our numbers bloomed, but he held his ground as the last of his guards rallied around him, and William pressed again.

William thrust for the emir's body and the enemy leader

wore the blow on his armour, then cut down at William with a blow that could have split his head in two. William desperately threw his free arm up to block the strike, and it should have severed the limb, but there was a ringing of metal and the sword shattered and bounced off, half of it flying away to clatter off a wall.

The emir only had time to stare at his broken blade in horror as William stepped forward and transfixed him with a vicious thrust to the chest.

He sank to his knees, disbelieving, his accusing eyes fixed on William's all the way down. Then his head tilted back and his mouth muttered a soundless prayer until the Norman kicked him off his sword to shiver and convulse in the blood-churned mud of the street.

The enemy did not give in when their emir died. They had nowhere to run and they fought for their city with determination and desperation as Sveinn led the rest of the Varangians into the streets, through the gate we had held at such a cost.

Behind the Varangians came the Normans and the Lombards, and they headed for the twin harbours, where they forced their way through the hastily organised defences there and deep into the city.

I didn't see any of that fighting myself for I was too exhausted to continue, and those of us who had survived around Harald pulled our fallen comrades from the street so they would not be trampled into the dirt.

Almost every single man who had gone through the gate with the coffin was wounded or dead. Except me, I was untouched. Maybe it just wasn't my turn that day. Who knows how fate decides these things?

Maniakes was so confused and outraged by events that by the time he was sure we were not rebelling against him it was too late, and the regular imperial forces never even entered the city. As the dim light of dusk fell, Syracuse was ours.

18

Harald spent that night ruthlessly clamping down on the ongoing looting of the city, using surly guardsmen to enforce discipline on the rest of the army. With many of his senior komes injured it was a difficult task, but by morning the city was largely at peace and had been spared the kind of widespread destruction that was typical after a hard siege.

The empire wanted the city intact, and many of its people were still Christian Greeks whose support would not be gained by destroying their city and looting their homes. Of particular importance were the two harbours and their warehouses. Restarting of trade was a high priority for Maniakes to show the invasion was worthwhile.

The emir's quarters, however, were ruthlessly looted, and his significant wealth largely recovered by our guardsmen.

* * *

The next day, most of the guard was still in the city, keeping order, but Harald had returned to our camp for the evening to join in our muted celebrations, which mostly consisted of lying around a fire, drinking to dull the pain, and retelling our own recollections of the fight around the gate.

'How is Halldor?' Harald asked Ulfr, who was there with us despite several nasty wounds to his arms.

'He will live, or so say the healers, but he will certainly be a great deal uglier than before.' Ulfr grimaced in a pained attempt at a smile. 'Although some would say that was not possible.'

'It is lucky he already favours such hideous women,' replied Rurik, and Ulfr coughed a laugh in return. The amusement was all bravado; Halldor's wound was sickening. The sword had cut right across his face, narrowly missing an eye but slicing his nose, both lips and chipping or removing a handful of teeth before carving across the other cheek. He had been lucky the blow was not heavier but he faced a long and painful recovery, and the very real chance of wound rot and a hideous death.

It was the kind of wound men truly fear to take. I am sure I was not alone in thinking a quick death would probably have been better than to live with such an injury.

'Ah, Varangians!' said a familiar voice in heavily accented Norse, and William strode into the firelight, a small barrel tucked under his arm. 'I bring gifts to the conquerors of Syracuse!' He smiled and set the wine down on the ground where a pair of men gratefully took it away to open it and distribute the contents.

Well, we were not children. We knew he was surely not there just to give us gifts, but to seek his share of the spoils. He was a mercenary; what else could we expect? And we had made promises to him.

Ulfr stood and thumped his bandaged left arm against his chest, ignoring the pain that must have caused. 'William the

Norman. You are welcome here.' He nodded profoundly at the Norman. 'You have the bravery of a bull and the arm of a hero.'

William's face lit up with genuine delight at the compliment and he gave Ulfr a little bow. 'I don't know your name, Northman, but with a greeting like that I am sure we are about to be friends.'

'I am Ulfr Ospaksson. Come and share a drink of your famous wine with me and we shall be friends indeed.'

William beamed. 'I shall, but first I must speak to Harald.'

'Bah, he is a poor drinking companion.'

'True, so it will not take long.'

William strode over to Harald and me and they embraced. 'Ulfr is right. Your fight with the emir is worthy of a great poem,' said Harald.

'Ah, thank you, but I remember you helping me.'

Harald shook his head. 'I barely got close to him. It was your victory, and a worthy one. He was a good swordsman.'

'Stunningly good. I did not expect it. He almost had me.'

'You broke his sword with your arm, if my memory is correct?'

William grinned.

Ulfr, quite drunk and clearly having decided not to wait for William to be done with Harald, was listening and interrupted.

'Yes, I saw that! We all saw that. You broke his weapon with your arm and then killed him with a perfect thrust. It was beautiful, a perfect kill.' Ulfr shook his head with an expression of delight and longing that a man might make when he thinks of a particularly magnificent woman.

'How did you do that?' asked Harald with a raised eyebrow. 'You must have bones of iron.'

'Yes, it is true.' Ulfr said, his eyes wide and unfocused in the evening light. 'Do you have a name, Norman?'

'You know my name,' said William confusedly.

'No, no. A *real* name, a name earned in battle.'

William shook his head.

'Ah! Well, I shall call you Iron-arm.' Ulfr waved his cup around vaguely at the gathering. 'And they all will too,' he said with great pomposity and seriousness. 'I have declared it.'

Harald looked embarrassed at Ulfr's drunken behaviour, but William just smiled even more broadly. 'William Iron-arm? I like it. I thank you for this name, Ulfr Ospaksson. It is worthy.' Ulfr gave a single nod, and then finally saw that the rest of us were waiting for him to leave, and he grumbled to himself and headed off.

'I am sorry about that. My men have been enjoying themselves all day. The Moslems may not drink wine, but they certainly trade in it. Despite my best efforts, a large amount was liberated from the docks.'

William smiled and jerked his head at the barrel he had brought. 'Where do you think I got that?'

'I assumed that was your personal wine.'

'No, I finished the last of that weeks ago. That was some Italian swill I liberated. Anyway, I came here to talk to you. I think we have a problem.'

'If it is with pay, we will make up the difference, don't worry.'

'No, no. It's not that. I have that plump purse of gold from the emir, and more besides. No, it's Arduin.'

'His men were among the first into the city, I'm sure they did well for themselves before I ended the looting and I have told him I will give him his share of what we took. So what is wrong?'

William shrugged. 'It's not his men that are the problem, it's him. Something has changed in him, since the fight at the gate.'

'He fought well enough, after he almost gave us away.'

That was a generous assessment. I was of the opinion that

Arduin did, in fact, give our plot away, albeit mere moments before we sprung the trap. But such moments cost lives in war. Nor did I see him take much part in the fighting. But Harald was being diplomatic.

'He is in a foul mood, and he refused to talk to me.'

'Why?'

'We made him pretend to gain an ally to help free his people, and then we made him betray that ally.'

Harald scowled. 'There was no betrayal, it was a ruse.'

'Still, it has affected him.'

'He will recover. He and his people have an overlord, it is a common thing. The empire is not such a terrible master.'

'True, although Maniakes is not the best representative of that.'

Harald shook his head. 'I will make sure they are fairly paid, and soon this victory will be complete and they will go home wealthy men, to the benefit of their people. They have nothing to complain about.'

William looked at Harald awkwardly for a while and then accepted it with a shrug. 'As you say.' Harald was too disgusted by the whole thing to study William's reaction, but I could see the Norman's sympathy was divided.

'Come, let us drink some of this wine you brought.'

William looked around and saw Ulfr was passed out flat on his back on a straw pallet at the far edge of the firelight, snoring loudly. He laughed. 'We won't have to share it with as many as I thought.'

* * *

The army stayed at Syracuse for nearly three weeks recovering. Harald did not even argue. The army had to recover from the sickness that had been rife in the ranks, and many of our men needed time to heal from their injuries or be shipped back to the city for those like Halldor who were too badly injured to continue with the campaign.

It made me morose. We had sailed to Sicily with two thousand fine guardsmen, and for two years all we had returned to Constantinople was a hundred or so men destined never to fight again, or to die lingering deaths of wounds that would not heal.

Far more than that had been put in the ground. War consumes good men like horses eat hay. Constantly, in great quantities, and thoughtlessly.

The news that finally persuaded Maniakes it was time to march away was when Admiral Stephen arrived in the city to report that an Arab fleet had bypassed his blockade and sailed to Balarm, depositing a small army there. The emir now finally had the forces to face us in the field again, despite our capture of Syracuse.

'I gave you *one* task!' shouted an enraged Maniakes at the admiral, in front of all the officers of the army. 'One task! And that was to stop the enemy from reinforcing the island.'

'The sea is very large,' said Stephen, comedically gesturing to the bay that spread out below the theatre. 'And I could not watch them everywhere.'

'The sea is large?' thundered Maniakes in disbelief. 'You have come here to tell me the sea is large? Are you an admiral or a fly-ridden imbecile? Not only did you fail to stop the boats sent from the city during the siege that must have been asking for help, but you also failed to stop the army that was sent in response to that request! You serve no purpose here whatsoever!' He grabbed the nervous little man by his fine tunic and shook him like a child and then threw him to the ground.

'If you hadn't married John's sister you would be cleaning the bilges of a fishing boat in some five-house village in Lesbos,' Maniakes shouted, red-faced and spittle flying at the man as Stephen cowered on the ground.

However much we all sympathised with the general's anger, for there was not a man there that had anything but disregard for the dockworker John had put in charge of the fleet, it was a profoundly stupid way of dealing with it.

'Take your fleet south and make sure nothing else reaches the island. Now!'

Later that day Harald and I stood in the old, ruined tower and watched as the fleet sailed away. It was not headed south along the coast. They went east.

Harald said nothing, but his face was drawn and glum. We are now on an island without a fleet to supply or support us. Eventually, as the sails faded into the horizon, he tore his eyes away from the wretched sight and we walked back to our camp.

The army marched regardless. Maniakes proclaimed that we did not need a fleet, and would march until we reached Balarm and finish the conquest of the island. He could no longer afford to take things slowly. Without the fleet, our only chance was to quickly defeat this new enemy army and then force the surrender of Emir Abdallah before the Arabs of the mainland could respond.

So we marched northwest, past Catania and into the great plain beneath the smoking mountain of Aetna. Our destination was the great hilltop fortress of Enna, reputedly the most formidable on the island and the key to the entire interior. Once that was captured, the way to Balarm was open.

We were on the road to Enna when our scouts found the enemy army marching east and we met the enemy near a hilltop town called Troina.

We pinned them in a valley below the town and they had no choice but to fight. Their numbers were perhaps half as great again as ours, but they were largely levies and it did not give us and our battle-hardened forces any concern, especially positioned uphill as we were.

Maniakes laid out his plan, which was very simple and classical. The main body of infantry, the Lombards and the Greeks, would advance down the hill in a broad line with the support of archers and skirmishers. The only cavalry we had – the Normans and a few hundred Greeks – would drive the enemy cavalry in on one flank, and then curl around behind and hit the enemy from behind as our infantry engaged them. The Varangians would form the reserve.

William Iron-arm was gleeful. His knights had spent much of the campaign fighting on foot and conducting sieges. He came up to Harald. 'I have seen the brilliance and bravery of your men, Harald. Now, my friend, you will finally see how we Normans fight.'

'Leave something for us,' Harald grumbled, for he was fuming that we were being held in reserve.

'I do not mean to offend you, Harald, but I hope not to,' William said with a grin and a slap on Harald's back, and then he walked away to join his men.

Harald was piqued, and he could not help but go to Maniakes. 'Why are you holding your best troops in reserve?' he asked. 'The enemy poses no threat to us here. They are on the defensive and the best way to win is to break them with a single decisive attack. We are the best troops for that!'

'This is the standard use of the Varangian Guard, Harald,' said Maniakes without looking troubled. 'You will remain in the reserve and guard the commander and the camp, and be used in case of disaster.'

'We guard the emperor in battle, and you are not the emperor!'

'Hmm, no, not now,' said Maniakes, still watching the army deploy.

Harald was stunned and he took a moment to digest it. 'That's it, isn't it? You are hoping to take the throne.' He put his hand on his sword. 'Is it treason you plan, Strategos?'

Maniakes had the sense to look alarmed, but also gave Harald a contemptuous stare. 'No treason, Protospatharios. The current emperor is sickly, and there is no successor. Who will the people turn to when he dies, other than the greatest general in the empire?' His eyes were slightly glazed, even manic, and I wondered if he were drunk.

'You really think you will be the next emperor?' said Harald in something that almost touched on respect, for he was to ambition as a moth to a flame.

Maniakes smiled. 'I am ready to serve if the empire calls. Now, I have given my orders. Carry them out.'

Harald walked away, eyes wide and his mind clearly racing.

'I can't believe it,' he said when we were out of eyeshot. 'He really believes he can claim the throne?'

'Why not?' I said with a shrug. 'The current emperor was a palace attendant; surely a general fresh from a successful conquest is a far better claimant? He will be a hero to the people.'

Harald laughed. 'I can't believe I didn't see it. It's so obvious now. And this is why John was trying to ensure this expedition failed. It isn't just about me; he has put all his rivals in one place and tried to have them rot here.'

'And we are destroying that plan with our victory.'

Harald swore. 'Despite Stephen's best attempt to end it.'

'You think the admiral let the enemy fleet past deliberately?'

'I am sure of it. And then he abandoned us at the first excuse. Yes, John is trying to destroy both our reputations for we are two of the only men in the empire powerful enough to stop him propping another family member up on the throne if Michael dies.'

I watched the army forming up in the valley below us while all the pieces fell into place.

'He will be a terrible emperor,' I finally said. 'He has no talent for politics, not that I have seen, anyway.'

'No, you are right. He is truly foolish.'

'But we need him to succeed, so that we can return to the capital.'

'But if he succeeds, he might be the emperor soon and we will be sworn to him, and that will not end well for us.' Harald cursed bitterly and kicked at the ground. 'We lose either way. Damn the mothers that bore these vain, little men. I will not serve this fool if he becomes emperor.'

'I think we can worry about this after the battle,' I said, nodding to where the imperial lines were finally advancing.

'I doubt we will have anything to do during it,' Harald replied drily.

Well, as usual, he was right.

I won't waste too much more of this glorious sunlight describing in great detail a battle we did not take part in, except to tell you that the Normans proved their worth a dozen-fold, and we watched them in amazement and respect as they picked the enemy army apart and tore the broken parts into bloody flotsam.

They first drove the light Arab horse from the flank with ease as the enemy, with no room to manoeuvre in the confines of the valley, were forced to fight the big, armoured Northern knights spear to spear and sword to sword and were utterly outmatched.

Instead of pursuing their shattered enemy to the wind, the Normans wheeled around in a beautiful display of discipline and horsemanship, rallying around William in the centre under his bright banner, and charged into the back of the enemy line before it even met with our infantry.

They shattered the left-most portion of the enemy in a single stroke, scattering most of the terrified enemy and herding them towards their fellows closer to the centre the way a shepherd's boy moves sheep.

The fleeing men fouled the formation of the next unit along, and then the Normans hammered into the mess and routed the lot, driving deep into the panicked mass and cutting a bloody swathe before, again, pulling back before they could become bogged down and overwhelmed.

A third of the enemy army was now broken, bodies littering the ground by the thousand, and finally, the enemy tried to adjust their formation to meet the threat of the wheeling, stinging Norman knights. But they were too slow and too late, and the onrushing Lombards caught their army in mid-manoeuvre even as William led his knights behind the enemy right wing for one final charge.

He shattered their right wing, driving them in towards the centre, where the whole remains of the enemy army were struck by the wall-formed Lombard ranks and hammered backwards. The fight spilt down the valley as the enemy tried to retreat, but anyone who fled in numbers was cut down by the whooping, jeering Normans. Anyone who tried to stand and fight was overwhelmed by the Italian and Greek infantry.

The victory was absolute, and we never laid an axe on an enemy. The Lombards pillaged the enemy camp as the Greek troops returned to our own on the ridge and Arduin and William came to report to Maniakes, who was watching with an oddly unhappy expression, despite the great victory his army had just achieved. Perhaps it was the fact the Lombards and Normans had done most of the fighting and not his own troops, or perhaps it was that William had exceeded his orders. Perhaps he was still stinging from Harald's lambasting his ambitions. I don't know what caused it, but the strategos was in a foul, silent mood when the two commanders returned to the camp and came to Maniakes' tent.

Arduin was beaming, riding a fabulous white horse he must have taken from the enemy, and waving to men left and right as he and William soaked up the plaudits for his men's performance from Varangians, Normans and Greeks alike. Maniakes' expression only soured further.

Arduin dismounted nimbly in front of the open-sided tent and untied a jewelled sword from behind the saddle of his horse. He came over towards Maniakes and held the sword up. 'I present the sword of the enemy commander.' When Maniakes did not move, he gave it to one of the general's officers, who took it and put it by Maniakes' side. The strategos remained silent, but his eyes drifted to the horse.

'What horse is that?' he snapped.

Arduin looked taken aback at the tone, and the area around the tent fell silent. 'The enemy general's horse. I killed him myself and took his horse as my mount.' Arduin beamed, but few around made any noise of appreciation any more. Everyone could see that Maniakes was furious, and the atmosphere was tense.

'I will have the horse with the sword,' Maniakes said.

Arduin's smile faded. 'I am sorry?'

'I claim everything that belonged to the general of the enemy. I am the commander of the army, I am due his possessions. You may take some other, lesser animal.'

There was a shocked silence around the gathering as Arduin looked around in stupefaction at the insult. He turned to William, who shook his head and glared at Maniakes in disapproval.

'Strategos, please, let me have this horse as part of my share. I earned it in battle. It is honourable.'

'Your share? I have not even determined if your men will get a share. All I saw was ill-discipline and men seeking glory above obeying orders, rushing to overtake my men, who rightfully should have taken the enemy centre and their camp.'

'Glory seeking? I was seeking victory, Strategos. I saw a weakness in the enemy created by William and I took advantage of it.'

'You had no orders!' cried Maniakes, and he stood suddenly, his face reddening. 'You seek each time to take the glory rightly belonging to the soldiers of the empire, seek to tarnish my victories with your own pronouncing and performing. All of you, you Varangians, Normans, Lombards. Mercenaries with no discipline!' He spat on the ground and there was a rumble of anger and shock around the gathering.

'I will have the horse and any other things you stole, and I will decide if you should have some other reward after this disgraceful display.'

I was open-mouthed in horror. Maniakes had completely lost his mind with jealousy and spite. Harald's fists were balled into rocks next to me.

Arduin's face screwed up in resentment and anger, and he shook his head. 'No. The horse is mine.' William turned to urgently whisper something in his ear but the Lombard shook his head adamantly.

People were starting to move around now, some to Arduin, to plead for him to give in, others to Maniakes to try and calm him.

Maniakes turned to one of his officers. 'Bring me the horse.'

The officer nodded reluctantly and walked over towards the white stallion, which was standing nervously beside Arduin, ears back, watching the men crowding around it with wide eyes.

The officer reached out to take the reins and Arduin, still talking to William, felt the pressure and yanked back reflexively to try and control the horse, causing the officer to be pulled forwards and collide with the horse's shoulder and neck.

The horse finally lost its cool and reared, whinnying in fright. It lashed its hooves through the air in front of it as Arduin tried to get control, and it kicked the unbalanced Greek officer square in the face and snapped his neck back like a twig. Everyone in the crowd heard the crack and saw that he was dead before he even hit the ground.

There was a moment of horrified silence as the armoured body crashed to the dirt, and then Maniakes looked at Arduin in abject fury. 'Seize him!' he roared, and dozens of Greek soldiers swarmed towards the Lombard, who looked panicked as he and he handful of men were surrounded and his arms were roughly grabbed.

'Don't do this, Georgios!' shouted Harald, shoving his way through the febrile crowd towards the general with me hot on his heels.

'Don't do this!' he urged Maniakes again, grabbing him by the arm and hissing in his ear.

Maniakes' eyes whipped around to meet Harald's 'He just murdered my officer, set the horse on him! It's treason!'

His eyes were wide and unfocused, and now I was close enough to smell his breath and it reeked of wine.

He was drunk. The man was as drunk as a three-copper whore. That shocked me more than anything.

'It's not murder, it was an accident. Everyone saw it. Think, Georgios, you need him! Don't do this. You need him to win this war!'

'I don't need him!' spat Maniakes, more outraged than before. 'I don't need you or him. I just need men to obey, *obey*!' he shrieked, and he struggled to get Harald's hand off him. Several of his guards came forward and wrestled Harald back. There was no sympathy in their faces and they were not going to let their strategos be manhandled.

'He is going to destroy everything,' said Harald to himself in despair, watching as William urgently whispered something in Arduin's ear, even as he was led forward.

'Strip him!' shouted Maniakes, pointing a finger at the Lombard leader, who nodded reluctantly at whatever William had been saying to him and stopped struggling, giving himself in to the men who were dragging him towards the strategos.

'It was not murder!' called William, striding towards Maniakes. He spread his hands and gestured to the Italian who was now kneeling in the dirt, all his clothes being torn from him by the uncaring hands of Maniakes' guards.

'Show wisdom as well as strength, Strategos. I beg you,' William said, closing with the general and taking one of his hands. 'This man made a mistake, but it would be a greater one to shed his blood here, and stain your victory forever.'

Maniakes seemed torn by this and William's deferential tone.

He stared at the now naked Lombard leader, who was kneeling in the dirt with his head held high and defiant.

Maniakes looked at William again, and then his eyes darted fearfully around the crowd, and even he could see how aghast many of them were, even some of his own troops.

He raised his hand to order quiet, and something approaching calm settled as the crowd waited for his judgement.

'Whip this man from the camp. Send him back to his men with nothing as a lesson for defying the orders of the emperor!'

His men did not exactly move enthusiastically at this disgraceful order, but many who had now arrived had not seen the incident and just saw the body of the officer and the captive foreigner, and there was no shortage of willing hands or spear shafts.

The humiliation that Arduin endured as he was dragged like a dog from the camp while the soldiers of the Greek themes beat him, whipped him and jeered at him angers me even to this day. He was a good man, a fine leader of his men and his people, and I almost wept to see him so unfairly degraded. Some coward stabbed him in both arse-cheeks with a spear on the way out, the coward's wound, and no man less deserved that stigma.

Once he was finally clear of the camp, and barely able to walk – battered, bleeding and dazed – William helped him up onto his own horse and walked him back down the valley to his men, leaving Maniakes once more as lord of all he surveyed – in his own mind at least.

19

The Lombards marched out of the valley the next morning. I had feared they would fight us and Harald had kept the men ready for most of the night. But they merely deserted, marching north where they would have to beg, borrow or pay passage back to Italy with whatever ships were at Messina. They would be able to afford it. They had kept almost the entire spoils from the enemy camp, except the twice-stolen white horse.

William came to see us in our part of the camp at dawn even as the Lombards were breaking camp to leave, and his face was glum as he dismounted by us.

'Could you not persuade him to stay?' Harald asked the Norman noble.

'I did not try.'

'Not at all?'

'No. Would you stay if that had been done to you?'

Harald grunted. 'No. Either I or Maniakes would not have survived the attempt of it.'

William smiled and nodded. 'Nor me. I am very fond of you,

Prince Harald of Norway. But this is where our paths must part. For now, anyway.'

Harald stiffened. 'You are also leaving?'

William nodded firmly. 'I will not stay and serve a man who both dishonours me and fails to pay me. I have no oath with him; he is not my master. I was here for gold and glory, and neither will be had now.'

'We are so close to victory, William,' Harald muttered hopelessly.

'Perhaps. But I am not paid for victory, just to fight. In any case, I have better opportunities in Italy. There are more of my brothers there, and we have another master willing to pay us. So I will go there and seek a different fortune.'

'You have more brothers?'

'Yes. Eleven, in fact.'

'Eleven!'

William grinned roguishly. 'My father was good at two things, fighting and fornicating. And as you have seen, I learned at least one of those things very well. Not that I can claim to have fucked anything as thoroughly as Maniakes has done to this campaign.'

Harald was too morose to laugh.

'Maybe we will return here, one day. One thing Maniakes has shown me is this island is ripe for conquest. Maybe my people will take it.'

'This island? You would fight the empire for it?'

William laughed. 'We both know the empire won't rule this island for long. It is a rotten carcass, and the Arabs will take it back when we are gone.'

Harald deflated like a punctured bladder because it was true, and it meant the destruction of all we had bled to achieve.

'We were so close,' he whispered again.

'I know, Harald. I know. Well, I have to ride, but I hope we meet again, perhaps on the other side of a battlefield. Now that would be a proper fight, eh?' He put his foot in a stirrup.

'Don't joke, friend,' Harald said indignantly.

William beamed as he mounted his horse. 'I am not joking, Varangian. What a glory it would be to fight and defeat you and your men. My family would sing of it for generations!'

And then he turned his horse with a deft flick of the reins and put his heels into it, moving with it like man and beast were one as it set off down the hill at a run.

Harald stared at the back of the receding Norman for a while and then shook his head and walked back to his tent.

I suspect the only reason the army did not pursue the Lombards and the Normans and bring the deserters to battle was that Maniakes was hungover and very late to rise, and even his own officers neglected to wake him and give him the news, such was their shame at him.

We marched towards Enna three days later and reached it after two more, and were wide-eyed at the fortress we saw. It was built into the heavens itself, perched onto a rocky outcrop above the valley with only a single narrow track leading up to its only gate. It was by far the most indomitable-looking fortress I had seen until then or ever did see.

Ignoring the seeming impossibility of taking the place, the greatly reduced army, now little over six thousand men, made camp across the sloping ridge that connected the town to the outside world and settled in for a siege.

Harald spent five days examining the place from every angle, even trying to climb the near-vertical cliffs at several points, and then another two days just sitting in our camp staring at it.

Finally, Maniakes overcame his pride and came to see Harald, bringing only a few of his usual entourage of officers and attendants to the rocky outcrop where Harald sat and stared at the great fortress.

I think Maniakes had finally found it in himself to be embarrassed at his behaviour, and the results it had brought upon us.

'So, how will you take it?' the strategos said, trying to strike a jovial tone.

'We cannot,' said Harald, rising from his rocky seat, too tired to be angry.

'You will think of something.'

'No. No, I will not. I have considered everything. Every trick I know, every technique from the manuals. They and I are clear about the answer. You can take this fortress by bribery or starvation, and no other way.' Harald looked at Maniakes with contempt.

'If you had twelve thousand men you could leave four thousand here to besiege it and starve them out in six months, while the rest of us marched on Balarm and hoped to force Emir Ibn Ziri to surrender. But you threw away half your army, so we can't do that. We would have to stay together with the small army we have left, and in the six months it would take us to starve this fortress into submission the emir would raise new forces and come and drive us away, and we are too few to do anything to stop him. If we ignore this place and march to Balarm they will close the mountain passes behind us and we will have no supplies while we besiege the emir. Nor can we bring them by sea because we have no fleet. We have no options. We have failed. You have failed.'

Maniakes recoiled at the cold, scathing assessment.

'Nonsense. We can still take this fortress, Harald. If we take it quickly we can still win Sicily!'

Harald looked up at the walls again and shook his head. 'Probably not. Even if we take this we might not take Balarm with whatever we have left. No. It's over.'

Even I was shocked by Harald's resignation. He never in his life thought victory was impossible. I found myself taking Maniakes' side, assuming Harald would find a way to victory. He always did.

Harald pointed a finger at Maniakes. 'You won't be here for long enough anyway, so it doesn't matter.'

'What do you mean? Are you threatening me?'

'No. But when news of the mutiny of your auxiliaries and the abandonment of your fleet and mercenaries reaches the capital they will replace you immediately, to try and limit the embarrassment. You will receive news of your relief long before the defenders here starve.'

Maniakes quailed. 'Are you sure?'

'Of course. John will have been waiting for any excuse to humble you, and you have provided it.'

'John was against me from the start!' Maniakes blurted, a wave of resentment gushing forth.

'Of course he was,' snapped Harald, sneering at the general like he was a naive child. 'And yet, we so nearly succeeded, until your foolish treatment of Arduin.'

Maniakes waggled a finger vigorously. 'Arduin was a part of it, sent here to undermine me! Those bloody Norman brothers too, and that useless whore Stephen. All sent to ensure I failed! Arduin provoked me, constantly. All he and the Normans did was try and steal my glory, undermine me, make me look bad in front of the men. They were sabotaging me from the start!'

'For the love of the saints, Georgios, no. You did all those things. *You* made yourself look bad, *you* undermined the army. You sabotaged yourself. Arduin and William were not your enemies until you made them thus.' Then he paused and made a conciliatory gesture. 'Stephen, yes, he was certainly ordered to thwart you.'

Maniakes looked lost. 'Arduin was not in John's control?'

'No.'

'William surely was?'

'No, he was hired by Zoe's people. And he didn't care about politics at all. He just wanted to be treated well and get paid, and you couldn't even do that.' Harald shook his head bitterly.

'You need to stop talking to me this way, Protospatharios! I am still the strategos of this army and you will respect that, even if you respect nothing else!'

Harald took a moment to think about it and then shook his head again. 'No, I won't. I'm leaving with my men. You are welcome to wait here for notice of your removal from command, but if you want my advice, that wait will be far more comfortable at Syracuse.'

'Leaving, leaving where?'

Harald pointed east. 'I'm going to Messina.'

'For what?'

'To wait for new orders somewhere that has a solid roof and a bathhouse.'

'You are marching away from my army for a bath!' shouted Maniakes in disbelief.

'Since I am forced to await the news of my humiliation, I might as well do it clean,' Harald said with a resigned shrug.

'This is mutiny!' whined Maniakes. 'I can have my men stop you!'

'Maybe it is mutiny, but no one will care. And I doubt your

men can stop me. I think half of them would join me if you ordered it. They are as sick of you as I am.'

Harald gestured to me to join him as he turned his heel on the flabbergasted general and walked away.

'You are too much of a fucking coward to try it anyway,' muttered Harald, but I doubt Maniakes even heard him.

Well, Harald was true to his word. We simply marched away and within a week were nestled safely and comfortably in Messina, where our grateful men found good accommodation in the half-abandoned town, and set about spending the money they had accumulated during the campaign with commendable efficiency, as soldiers always do.

In my life's experience, one thing is always true: A soldier cares far, far more about being paid than about keeping his pay. He will fight you like a rabid dog for his share, but part with it without thinking twice for a soft bed and a nice young thing to share it, or a month's worth of wine.

And thank God that is the case, because when the month is up and the silver is gone, that is the only reason you can ever get them back on campaign again. Rich mercenaries don't go to war very willingly.

We had not been resting in Messina for long when events outside of Sicily started to loom over us, and the shadow of war once more darkened the skies. I was down in the dockside warehouses going over a list of supplies with several komes when Rurik came in and gestured to me.

'Harald needs to see you.'

I looked up from the list. 'Now?'

'Now.'

I gave Sveinn and the other officers a knowing look and walked away with Rurik. 'Where is he?'

'Down by the harbour entrance.'

'What is it?'

'A ship arrived from Constantinople, some of our men were in it and they have news.'

I nodded. 'Good. We need more men.'

'We will always need more men.'

Rurik's tone was odd, almost despondent, and I took him by the arm to stop him and he looked at me with a dull expression.

'What is wrong? What do you mean by that?'

'It is nothing.'

'Horseshit. Tell me what is on your mind.' I was quite disturbed because Rurik was one of our most steadfast men. 'Come, Rurik, we have been together for over ten years, since Stiklestad. Tell me what is causing you this concern.'

Rurik stared at me and his face contorted slightly. 'That is exactly it, Eric. Ten years. We left our home ten years ago, with the promise we would return. But here we fought a failed war, unrelated to Harald's desire for the throne, or our duty to the defence of the emperor.'

'It is not unrelated, Rurik. To regain the throne we need men, to get men we need wealth and reputation. We are gaining both in service to the empire.'

'And when will it be enough?'

'I don't know. Rurik, you took an oath to see this through – we all did – and there was no promise it would be easy.'

'I know my obligations, Eric. But does Harald remember his? His promise to lead us home?'

I stood back, eyes narrowed. 'Of course he does. He will take us back when we are ready.'

'What do you mean by *us*, Eric?' he said, shaking his head.

'Do you know how many of the blood-marked are still with us here?'

I felt a cold seep of guilt. No. I had lost the habit of counting. In our campaigns in the Rus, losses had been high, and by the time we had left, we had only a little over forty of Harald's original one hundred and fifty men remaining to sail south to the empire. I knew more men had died in the many campaigns since, but I did not know how many were left.

Rurik nodded at my silence. 'I thought not. The answer is twenty-five. Twenty-five of us who stood shoulder to shoulder at Stiklestad and followed him into exile remain alive and under Harald's command. How many will survive to see our home again? Or will we all be spent, to the last man, in these pointless wars whose result does not matter to us? I hold my oaths to Harald, Eric. And I always will. But do something for me. Promise me you will try and get some of us home. We have given our lives to Harald's cause, but in return, at least some of us deserve to see our homes and the fjords again.'

His face was blank, almost resigned, and it cut me to the core to see a man like Rurik, who I had always thought was one of the strongest of us, reduced to this state.

'Rurik I...' I struggled to decide what to say. That I also wanted to go home, that we truly intended to, that Harald still cared about his men. But I realised none of that was what Rurik needed to hear.

'I swear it,' I said.

Rurik just nodded glumly and carried on walking.

* * *

When we arrived at the dock where the newly arrived ship was sitting, gently bobbing on the slight swell in the bay, I saw a number of figures in Guard cloaks standing around Harald, their backs to me. I got closer and one of them turned.

I grinned like a child seeing his father for the first time in months and loped over, taking Afra in a vicious hug.

'Easy, Eric,' Afra said with an embarrassed laugh.

'What in seven hells are you doing here?' I asked. 'Is the first bandon here with you?'

I looked around and saw my joviality was not shared. Harald was looking glum.

'What has happened?' I asked as I started to worry.

'There is a rebellion in Bulgaria. The leader has proclaimed himself the emperor of Bulgaria and separated his lands from the empire.'

I nodded. 'Why does everyone look so glum?'

'The emperor himself went to visit the army sent to fight the rebellion, and was present when it was defeated.'

'The emperor is dead?' I said in shock.

Afra shook his head. 'No, he is safe and back in the city. The imperial tagmata there got him safely off the field, but it was a close thing.'

'I see.'

Harald looked furious. 'The emperor went to war and we weren't even there to protect him,' he said bitterly. 'Our foremost duty.'

'So we are recalled now?'

Afra shook his head. 'You are not. In fact, I was removed from command of the first bandon by Aki and sent here, along with a number of other men who were plainly exiled for their loyalty to Harald,' Afra said with a dim expression.

'The guard in the capital is being utterly purged of men loyal to me,' said Harald with a furious tone.

'By Aki? How could he betray you like this! How is it in his authority to replace men you appointed?' I said, aghast.

'It is not. But Afra says he suspects the orders came from above.'

I growled. 'John?'

'Yes,' replied the bandit. 'He has used the shock of the defeat to seize power. He made himself the first minister after the emperor, and head of the treasury, courts, garrison forces, harbours and taxes. He has seized almost every lever of power in the city for himself.'

'The balls on that man!'

'Well, in a manner of speaking,' replied Afra drily. I realised what I had said and did not even find it funny, the situation was so serious. In the past, John had always controlled power more subtly, coercing and controlling from behind the scenes. But now he had effectively made himself emperor, with the sickly and now humiliated Michael just an arse to warm the throne and speak the words that John placed in his ears.

'I can't believe Aki would allow this.'

'I am... disappointed in him,' said Harald, withholding the fury I could see in his face.

'I thought Zoe was winning the war for the palace? You said as much.'

'That was last year, Eric. Things have turned badly for her and she has lost heavily since then. This rebellion has worked to John's advantage. The emergency lets him get away with things he would never previously have managed. Her supporters have been removed or bribed, her support in court has collapsed in fear of the purges, and all the undecided have moved to John's corner, desperate for unity in the face of the war.' Afra shrugged. 'She fought valiantly, but it is almost over. She is practically a prisoner now.'

'And we have lost our eyes and ears in the palace,' said Harald.

Afra's mouth twisted into a sly smile. 'Well, the funny thing is, when we left the city Thorir didn't arrive in time to get on the ship. He must have got confused about his orders. Typical of my brother, always just disappearing when you think you know where he is.'

A few of the men laughed, and Harald cast a firm stare around their faces. 'But you all saw him arrive here on this ship, didn't you?'

'Yes, Protospatharios,' they chorused.

'Good.'

Ah, loyalty is so precious. John may have cleansed the city of those faithful to us, but he might have made an oversight in sending them to join us in exile. He would have been better served to scatter them to the four corners of the empire. Perhaps he was complacent with the scale of his victory, or perhaps he just didn't think about it. Even the smartest men make mistakes. God knows, Harald was one of the most intelligent men I ever knew, and he made plenty of them.

'Well, I am glad to have you all here. I need all the friends I can get.' He smiled and embraced Afra, and then clasped hands with all of the several dozen who had come with him.

'Come, you will not be here for long, but we have good beds spare, and a little wine too.'

That got an enthusiastic rumble of appreciation. Soldiers are simple people, they really are.

PART III

VANQUISHED

20

MESSINA; JANUARY 1041 AD

We stayed in Messina all through the autumn and winter of 1040. We could not return to the capital – we had no orders to do so and Harald's request for instructions was answered a month later with a simple missive to support the governor of Italy, which was Maniakes when we sent the letter, and no longer Maniakes by the time an answer returned.

There was some good news from the east – the Bulgarian rebellion ground to a halt as its power-thirsty leaders, feeling victorious, immediately turned on each other. Of the three, the self-proclaimed Bulgarian emperor Petar Delyan killed his co-leader Tihomir, then replaced him with his cousin, a man called Alusian, who himself was completely defeated in a second battle with the imperial army. Alusian then tried to take over the rebellion by inviting Petar to a feast, drugging him and blinding him. Despite this, Petar retained control, Alusian was exiled and turned on his cousin, joining the imperial forces in exchange for amnesty from the emperor.

It is remarkable to me how greed and the thirst for power drive men to such madness. Regardless, it was fortunate for the empire, and for a while, the war stopped as both sides licked their wounds. You may wonder why I am explaining to you these things which did not involve us, but it was important, and you will understand later.

As Harald had predicted, shortly after returning to Syracuse after abandoning the siege of Enna, Maniakes was stripped of all his titles and ranks and recalled to Constantinople in disgrace, where he was arrested and imprisoned, before being quietly exiled. We never crossed paths with him again. His fall from power did not sit well with him and I hear he led some foolish rebellion some years later and was executed for it. A fitting end for such a vain man.

The new Capetan of Italy was one of his officers, a man called Michael Dokeianos, a minor noble from the northwest of Anatolia. We had had some contact with him in his duties as one of Maniakes' deputies during the two years on campaign, and he was a dour and competent officer in the way that many of the Greeks were.

We didn't receive any instructions from him for months, nor was Harald interested in seeking orders. We heard that he was busily shoring up the garrisons of the parts of the island that we had conquered and generally doing nothing that interested us. Eventually, he simply appeared in Messina by ship and came to meet Harald. He cut a very different figure to Maniakes, being slight, quiet and unimposing. It was a huge improvement.

'What is it that you need, Strategos?' asked Harald politely as we sat on a shaded veranda overlooking the harbour. It was very early in 1041, and we had been in Messina for nearly six months. Although it was a very pleasant place to spend winter, without the duties and rigours of the palace the men were getting bored and lazy, and discipline was starting to suffer. So Harald was not exactly unhappy at the prospect of being given something to do.

'There is trouble brewing in Italy. A revolt of the Lombards.'

Harald nodded. 'Another rebellion? I have heard rumours.' He looked up. 'Is it Arduin?'

Michael looked embarrassed. 'I had thought not at first. It was led by some local nobles in the north of the region. I made Arduin the ruler of Melfi, to try and compensate him and ensure his loyalty after what Maniakes did. I thought he would be a buffer between our lands and the rebellion.'

'That didn't work?' asked Harald with an amused grin.

Michael looked despondent. 'No. The moment he had the town and surrounding area under his control he simply joined the rebels.'

Harald let out a snort of laughter, which caused Michael's face to go rigid with annoyance, but he managed to control himself and continue.

'This rebellion now threatens to overtake all of our land east of the Principality of Salerno, and from there, it will threaten Bari. I must move to confront it immediately.'

'But you have so few men.'

'Indeed. The war against the Bulgarian rebels consumes the empire's attention. There is nothing left for us. I suspect that is why the Lombards chose this moment to act.'

'So you need me.'

'I do,' he admitted reluctantly. 'You have one of the last uncommitted forces in the entire western empire. Protospatharios, I am aware that you can probably refuse if I order you, and that after the way Maniakes behaved, I might even understand it. But, if I simply ask you, man to man, to come and help me secure the province, will you do so?'

Harald contemplated Michael for a moment as if he was considering refusing. Hah! Michael did not know Harald well enough at all. He was desperate for a fight, some way of making up for his association with the failed invasion of Sicily. He wanted to regain his reputation, and success in war was the only route he knew.

He nodded graciously. 'I will, Capetan.'

Michael breathed out and cheered up immediately. 'I am grateful, Harald. I am.'

'But, I must ask – if we are going to Italy, who will defend Sicily?'

'I will leave small garrisons in Syracuse and Messina, but the true answer is we are quietly abandoning the rest of the island. The palace is not interested in sending any more men to defend it. The empire simply has bigger problems and Sicily is not a priority. Perhaps it never truly was.'

Harald smiled sadly. 'So it was all for nothing.'

'Yes, I'm afraid so.'

'How disappointing.'

Michael just looked away.

'Well, when are we leaving?' Harald was not too troubled. We had all abandoned Sicily in our minds months ago, and gotten over the pain of that failure by then.

'As soon as possible, Protospatharios. Every day matters.'

We sailed a few days later, shuttling our small army across to the harbour town of Tarantem piece by piece, from where we gathered and marched to Bari. Along with the local forces and some levies, Governor Michael was able to raise a respectable army over the weeks that followed, but news kept coming in of the expansion of the rebellion, which now encompassed almost all of the Principality of Salerno and all the lands north of that, which I never visited and am not familiar enough with to describe to you.

While we defended the capital of Bari, Michael marched out with a small force to aid a small town that was under siege and was met by a small army of rebels and was defeated, retreating back to join us.

Chastened by that defeat, and with news the enemy was recruiting and expanding, Michael waited until we had an overwhelming force, perhaps ten thousand troops, before he took to the field again.

We were not too concerned by the first small defeat. We knew our enemy well, and the Lombards were good soldiers but not so good as us. All the reports said there were only a few thousand of them nearby as they were scattered all over southern Italy, conquering new land and besieging imperial or allied strongholds.

The governor decided to strike with his full army while the rebels were spread out, hoping to catch a few and destroy them one by one. It was not a plan that Harald disagreed with, and we marched out of Bari with high confidence in quickly putting down the rebellion.

We headed north up the eastern coastal plain, towards a coastal town and imperial stronghold called Vieste that was under siege and had sent a request for aid. We progressed without any resistance for four days, but nor did we expect any for the nearest reported rebels were a hundred miles to the north.

We reached a river called the Ofanto that came down from the mountains on our left side and wormed across the rich, broad plain towards the sea. It was easy to understand why the empire wanted to retain this land. It was rich and lush farmland,

and there were towns and villages everywhere with much of the land under freshly sown crops.

There was an ancient stone bridge across the river, broad enough for eight men to walk abreast, and the army crossed it in marching column with us in the rearguard, onto a flat plain framed with low hills to our left and front. Some of the scouts brought us word of unknown armed men watching us from those hills. Being the cautious man that he was, Michael sent fifty mounted scouts forward to investigate, while the army stayed on the flat, open ground near the river and waited in lines in the gentle heat.

Those mounted men came back over the low rise at a gallop, shouting and waving their signal pennants in warning.

We were at the front of the column of march, and the Greek and local troops were behind and to the sides of us.

The strategos Michael looked around nervously and Harald jogged over. 'Your orders, Strategos?'

Michael looked deeply uncertain. 'We don't know what the threat is,' he said tentatively.

'We must assume it is their full army,' Harald replied.

'It might not be.'

We had not expected to encounter the enemy yet, and Michael was clearly unprepared for the surprise. Perhaps his previous defeat had shaken him much more than we could have known.

The argument was cut short as the enemy army, their ambush discovered before they could spring it, appeared over the crest of the low hill in full battle order, a long line of infantry, flanked on either side by large blocks of cavalry.

Harald simmered in frustration as the strategos stared at the enemy. 'They shouldn't be here.'

'They are,' said Harald curtly. 'What are your orders?'

Michael looked back at the bridge we had just crossed, only several hundred paces behind us. 'Perhaps we should retreat over the bridge?'

'Retreat?' said Harald in fury. 'We came here to fight them. Why would we retreat?'

'But we are not prepared for battle.'

'We are always ready for battle,' Harald said firmly, not losing his cool, moving over to hold the reins of the strategos's horse as if to steady the man with the beast. 'There will not be time to retreat, we will be caught crossing. We must fight.'

'Really? Yes.' Michael stammered.

Harald was starting to get flustered. Precious time was being wasted, officers were milling around waiting for orders and the enemy was coming towards us across the plain with intent.

'Strategos, what shall I do with the Hellas theme?' shouted one officer. The Italian officer in charge of the levies gestured angrily, and Michael withdrew into his own space. Harald started to look anguished.

The enemy was closing, half the distance between us and the hill was gone.

'There is no time to plan an attack, no time for orders,' Michael muttered. 'No, we must defend. Defend here. We will hold the bridge,' He finally said, standing a little higher in his stirrups and looking nervously around the gathering. 'Form into line, Greek theme on the right, Italian theme on the left, Guard in the centre.'

'Form up into line of banda!' roared Harald to our Varangians, as the army burst into activity around us.

'We should attack, Strategos,' Harald said to Michael. 'As soon as we are able.'

Michael looked around as officers raced away to take orders to their units. 'I will send you further orders,' he said, not acknowledging Harald's advice. Then he turned his horse and rode away with his small entourage, leaving Harald fuming in his wake.

Harald looked at me and then at our lines, which were already forming into a disciplined wall of bandon, each four men deep and up to fifty across. In the centre with us were Styrbjorn's fourteenth and the eighth. On the left were Ulfr's seventh – the Sea Spears – with the tenth and twelfth banda outside them. The second with Sveinn, the seventeenth and two other banda on our right.

I watched the enemy army as they approached, and instead of lining up opposite us and readying themselves, they did not stop their advance, only speeding up.

'Who are they?' I asked no one in particular, aghast, as several thousand enemy cavalry wheeled away from the approaching enemy army and arrowed in towards our flanks, not wasting any time.

Harald stared at the approaching enemy horsemen with disaster. 'Normans,' he said. And then he was shouting more orders to get the guard into the line of battle.

'How can they be the Normans? There are so many of them!' I said, but Harald was gone, walking off down the line.

Our men, disciplined and battle-ready, were soon fully formed and arrayed, but the local levies on the left were not even finished forming when the Norman cavalry hit their wing.

And it disintegrated.

* * *

The panicked local men, taken completely by surprise by the speed of the enemy attack, and with the least experience or time to react, had not formed up properly and the mailled fist of the Norman cavalry shattered their line like a dry, rotten stick. Real fear blossomed in my heart as a third of our army completely collapsed without a fight.

But on our right, the experienced Greek regulars had formed their lines properly, and the archers started putting a hail of arrows into the milling mass of horsemen on that flank. The Normans all turned to retreat out of arrow range at some unseen signal, and then, without warning, turned on the spot, the entire formation, and changed direction, angling around to attack the exposed right end of the line.

The Greeks were veterans of the Sicilian campaign or men who had fought in Italy for years and won many victories, both in the field and in difficult sieges. They were amongst the best troops in the empire.

They held firm in perfect ranks as the Normans charged at them, banners proudly flying over their heads, and archers starting to pick saddles clean and tumble horses in the onrushing enemy attack.

The Norman cavalry hit the Greeks with a ferocious crash and the screaming of horses and men, and the end of the Greek line buckled and twisted as the power of the Norman charge dug deeply into it.

Somehow, by sheer force of willpower and savage bravery, the Greek ranks held, re-formed and repelled the Norman charge. The Normans broke off and wheeled back again, only to reveal that right behind them the mass of infantry was coming, in numbers equal to the battered Greeks.

From near where the strategos Michael was, the horn blew the signal for our army to withdraw.

'Damn his cowardice! Why won't he fight?' said Harald. He looked around at our long line, then at the mass of Greeks already starting to retreat across the plain.

'Now they will be trying to retreat behind us.'

'Should we cross first?' I asked.

Harald shook his head. 'No, there are too many of us. If we break our ranks we will all be caught together at the crossing and slaughtered. We will have to cover the rest of the army while they retreat. Damn him.'

He snapped a finger at me and pointed to the left. 'Go to the wing. Tell the two left banda to align to cover our flank where the Italians are breaking.'

I ran along the whole line until I reached the left, where Ulfr stood with his seventh bandon, with the twelfth outside him.

He saw me coming and jogged out of the line to meet me. 'What's the order, Eric?' he said without a hint of nerves. Fleeing Italian levies were streaming past now, headed for the bridge while the Norman cavalry was occupied further out in the plain, breaking any remaining resistance and harassing the survivors. Only the sheer number of routing men was keeping the enemy cavalry busy, but it would not last. A huge number of the broken men, cut off from us and being driven by the enemy cavalry, had abandoned their weapons and were trying to swim the river. Hundreds of them were struggling in the current, and few were making it to the other side. I looked away from them in disgust back to Ulfr.

'We are going to hold while the army retreats through us. Pull in the left flank, get tucked into the river and don't let the enemy get around you. When the rest of the army is across, retreat in towards the centre with us.'

Ulfr looked around. 'We are likely to be fighting all the way during that retreat. Nasty work.'

'That's all we can do.'

'I'd rather we attacked, easier.'

'We can't attack now,' I said.

'True enough.'

I clasped arms with him. 'Good luck, Komes. I will see you at the crossing.'

'Or in hell,' said Ulfr with a laugh, and then he turned to his men and started shouting orders.

I ran back to the centre and found the Greeks flowing through the gap between the back of our line and the river, the veteran Greek soldiers trying to keep their formations as they retreated.

From in front of us, towards the tail of the retreating Greeks, there was the sound of heavy fighting.

'It's about to get very messy,' I said to Harald.

'Yes. The men are ready to close the gap on the right when the time comes.'

'And what if our allies are still in the gap?'

Harald looked at me with his lips pressed into a thin line. 'The men are ready to close the gap regardless.'

I swallowed nervously and nodded. When we closed the gap, anyone who approached the line would be considered to be an enemy and cut down. The wall would hold. That was the sacred duty of any Norseman in battle then, as it is today. You hold the shield-wall until you fall, or are given new orders.

The Greeks streaming through the gap became less and less organised, and the sounds of the fighting came closer and closer.

Governor Michael and his entourage came across, and they stepped aside and stopped next to Harald. Michael's eyes were wide and he was breathing hard.

'What is your plan, Harald?' the governor asked. 'I told you we should have retreated.'

Harald ignored the attempt to blame him for the fiasco.

'My plan is to save as many of your men as possible, and then retreat over the river.'

'Good man, good man,' the governor mumbled, looking around. Then he looked at his men across the river, and I could see how badly he wanted to join them.

Harald saw it too, and I suspect he wanted nothing more than to be rid of the Greek general so he would not interfere. 'You should go with your men. They need to be organised on the far bank or they might flee. I will need your cover when I retreat.'

Michael nodded with unseemly enthusiasm. 'Yes, yes. You are right. I shall do that. Hold here, Protospatharios,' he added as if it had been his idea.

Then he trotted away on his horse with his officers, and we went back to staring at the rout that was developing before us. The pennants and helmets of the Normans were wheeling and flowing over the heads of the broken Italians on the left, getting closer and closer as they hunted the rearmost portions like sharks in a school of fish.

We had seen just a few hundred of them do this to the Sicilian Arabs a few months before, and it had been magnificent to watch them pick an army apart. But now we were on the wrong end of several thousand of their spears, and I was having real doubts we would be able to hold them.

Finally, we were tested as several hundred Norman horsemen charged at a spot in our line on the left, forming up into an arrowhead on the move like a flock of sparrows, and hammering into our banda.

A wall of spears and shields rose to meet them. Horses tumbled, men were thrown like children's toys, and the line shook with the shock of it and then closed and re-formed with roars and hacking long axes.

The Normans pulled back, chastened, and went for easier pickings amongst the Greeks and Italians.

'Good work, guardsmen!' roared Sveinn, ignoring the slumped figures behind our line who did not rise again to rejoin their comrades. There was nothing we could do for them.

Harald watched the Greek retreat on the right become a rout, and he judged the moment. Finally, as the retreating Greeks thinned out and the last part of the army still in formation, a hastily assembled rearguard, was still a hundred paces away and retreating towards us under heavy attack by enemy infantry, he roared at the seventeenth bandon to close the line.

There were some shocked faces at that. Five hundred or so brave Greeks were fighting their way towards us in a block, and we were condemning them to death. But Harald could see what the Greeks could not – that two large groups of Norman horsemen were forming up on either side, ready to charge in behind the doomed rearguard and come for the gap between the army and the river.

The seventeenth bandon and two others pushed into the flow of refugees, closing off the gap even as the enemy horse started to move towards us, around the flanks of the desperate survivors.

The urgency in our ranks increased and men pulled and shoved Greek soldiers out of the way, filling in the gap towards the centre, shoving and kicking aside everyone who got in their way. A hundred or so men, many without weapons, were left on the wrong side of the wall, looking back in terror over their shoulders as the horsemen roared in.

One of the panicked Greeks grabbed at a shield and tried to pull it out of the way. The guardsman behind it drew back his spear and put it in the desperate man's chest.

The Greek went down with a look of horror and indignation,

and then the remaining Greeks shouted in fear and protest and more of them tried to get through, pleading and clawing.

'Clear the line!' shouted Harald, and there was a flurry of violence as we cut down anyone within range, even as the Norman attack arrived.

I was right behind the line this time, and it looked like they were riding straight at me. The Normans simply rode over the few Greeks stranded between the two forces and the leading men stood in their stirrups to lean forwards and thrust their long spears at our faces over our shields, turning their horses as they did to skim along the front of the wall rather than try and crash through it again.

Our spears and theirs traded wounds, but theirs were longer and they were moving with the weight of men and horse behind, so when they struck they would rip through scale and maille and flesh and put men down with devastating wounds.

A rider who made such a hit would drop his spear and wheel away, and another would take his place.

Some of them misjudged it, or a brave guardsman would duck forwards and cut at their horse's front leg, spilling mount and rider onto the ground, but far more of our men went down than theirs, and Harald shouted his orders for the line to start retreating, pulling back from the flurry of horsemen and making it harder for them to attack us.

The whole guard shrunk and contracted towards the crossing in a bowl shape, not able to break the line even for a moment because the waiting swarm of Normans was ready to pounce on any opportunity.

Two of the banda on the right divided to go around a clump of rocks, and when they rejoined they were misaligned. A group of the Norman knights lunged for the gap, and, in a howling torrent of horses and armoured men, broke through the ragged line.

There was a palpable shiver of panic that ran through our ranks as some of the Normans broke through and got into the open ground behind us, in amongst the last of the fleeing Greek infantry, and I could hear the komes of the seventeenth screaming at his men to seal the gap even as more enemy tried to force their way through.

Harald shouted at a neighbouring bandon to send spare men to help, but even as he did, the Normans who had broken through turned their horses and charged right back into the mess, cutting the komes and flag of the eighth down even as he shouted orders, then knocking his standard down into the dirt along with its dying holder.

'Go and take over the seventeenth!' shouted Harald, shoving me, and I nodded without argument and ran over towards the fighting where the men of the seventeenth, who were called the Lion Pride for their tenacity and ferocity in some long-past battle, were reeling from the attack and the loss of their commander.

Men from the rear ranks of our formation poured into the shoulders of the gap, trying to seal it even as more Normans, seeing the opportunity, charged in to widen it.

I arrived at the fight and plucked the lion banner of the seventeenth from the ground and tucked it into my shield hand. 'Seventeenth bandon, to me!' I shouted, and men looked up and saw the banner flying and moving into the gap, and they followed it. Because that is what the banner is for.

I vaulted a dying horse and was nearly skewered by another as he passed, ducking under the spear and hearing it rip through the banner over my head, rending the proud lion in half. Encumbered by the banner pole I shoved its spiked end into the dirt next to the downed horse and set my feet as others came to join me, and we tried hacking into the heaving mass of enemy knights in front of us.

The fight was vicious and short. I held my shield high and stabbed at horses, unable to properly reach the men atop them. But each time a horse came at me I was forced to give ground by their bulk and flailing hooves and the long, lancing spears of their riders.

The gap was widening, the pressure was intense, and we were losing.

Someone grabbed me by the shoulder as we retreated and the defiant lion banner fell again, knocked over by a sidestepping horse as its rider cut down with an axe and killed a guardsman stone dead through his helmet.

'The eighth is closing behind us!' a voice shouted, and I looked to my right and found that the two flanking banda on the right had pulled in, going around the mangled mess of the seventeenth and re-forming a new line shoulder to shoulder with the eighth bandon in the centre.

Two things occurred to me, one good and one bad. Good, that they were re-forming the line; bad, that I would be on the wrong side of it.

I looked at the fighting around the fallen lion banner. My feet were leaden, even as the unseen hand tried to pull me back. 'Go, Eric!'

I felt my feet starting to stumble backwards, even as the guardsmen of the Lion Pride tried one more time to counterattack the ever-increasing number of horsemen that were crashing into their battered ranks.

I saw some of them look back at me, and they knew what I knew. Anyone who stood their ground was not going to get another chance to flee.

Those heads turned back to the fight. Someone retrieved their banner and they waved it aloft to an audible roar of defiance. I was pulled back into the main line, my traitorous feet abandoning the lions of the seventeenth as they crumpled in around their banner and showed us all how they had earned their name, even as the victorious Normans hemmed them in and cut the banner down for a final time.

There was no time to mourn or rage as the seventeenth died. We were pulling back towards the crossing now and in the centre, around Harald, a vicious fight had developed as the enemy infantry, finished with the Greek rearguard, assaulted the centre in massed ranks.

The guardsmen of the Warborn, the fourteenth bandon that had been Harald's first comrades in the guard, stood shoulder to shoulder with Sveinn's second bandon and lashed back at the Lombard troops.

The attack was half-hearted. The Lombards were already tired from the fight with the Greeks, and perhaps some of them had been in Sicily and knew our reputation. Our long axes and spears reaped a terrible price from their ranks for the audacity to assault us, but as we retreated we too left a tithe of our blood and our men on the ground.

Few men in a retreating shield-wall rise once they fall. The badly wounded are trampled and left behind.

As our whole force shrank towards the bridge our line shortened and thickened, and even the Normans' attacks on the flanks lost enthusiasm. Behind us, I saw with horror and outrage that the Greek troops had not waited to cover our crossing. What remained of the army was retreating at full speed, heading for the shelter of the mountains behind us. They had even abandoned the baggage train that had been waiting to cross.

'The bastards are leaving!' I shouted as I reached Harald.

'I know.'

'What do we do?'

'We retreat across the river and hold the bridge.'

I nodded. There was no other option.

We started peeling ranks off the back of the line and sending them across to re-form on the other side. The enemy made one last concerted attempt to get between us and the river, prying at a flank with horsemen and infantry, but the twelfth repelled the attack with a vicious counter-charge that first halted the enemy advance and then shattered it, driving it back in a chaotic and bloody melee. I watched glumly when the fighting was over, and it seemed perhaps only half of the twelfth returned to the line.

But they had bought the rest of us time, and one by one the banda crossed the river, until the fourteenth and the second walked across the bridge backwards, shields up, the exhausted Lombards declining to fight us all the way across.

We formed up, guarding the crossing, and licked our wounds. We could not march away, because the Normans would cross behind us and then ride around, surrounding and trapping us.

So we stood there in ranks, facing them across a hundred paces of ancient stone.

Finally, a trio of horsemen walked down the far bank and slowly rode over the bridge.

'William,' muttered Harald, seeing the banner above them.

'And Arduin,' I said in shock, seeing the Lombard mounted next to William. 'Mercenary whores.'

'Harald! Ah, I knew it was you!' William shouted jovially as he rode up the bank on our side. He did not stop twenty paces away in safety and shout his demands; the arrogant bastard just dismounted and came to greet Harald like we were still friends on campaign.

Harald was immobile, his face a mask of anger.

'That was magnificent, really. I thought we had the whole army, but you held us. God, what a fight you gave us,' William said with a broad smile.

'The fight is not over, Norman.'

William looked a little disappointed. 'Harald, your masters have abandoned you.'

'I am holding the bridge so they can retreat.'

William's eyes narrowed and he stared at Harald for a moment. 'No, you did not volunteer to sacrifice yourself for these cowards? Not after what they did to us in Sicily.'

'I follow orders. What do you follow, William? Here you are, killing men who thought of you as a friend.'

'The killing was mutual, Harald, let me tell you. A hundred Norman families have lost glorious sons today.'

'Then go home and mourn with them.'

'Ah, I don't have a home to go to, Harald. I need to get across this river now, don't die for it.'

'Why, why are you here? Is that traitorous whore paying you?' Harald pointed at Arduin, who sat up in his saddle and glowered.

'As a courtesy, yes, and probably using Greek money too!' William smiled. 'But no. We are here for our own reasons. I joined up with some of my countrymen and told them a tale of a lovely island, rich, weak, ripe for the picking and with a terribly pleasant climate.'

Harald stared at him. 'You really intend to take Sicily?'

'Yes.'

'How would you take it from the empire? You don't have the men to overcome our garrisons.'

'No, that is why I needed to lure your garrisons over here,' William said with a smile. Harald tried not to react. 'I'm right, aren't I? That army retreating up the mountain behind you was made by stripping Sicily of its troops.'

Harald's scowl just deepened, and William made an exclamation of triumph and turned to the third man. 'I told you it would work.'

'So what, you have your victory. Turn around and leave, go to Sicily.'

'I can't do that, Harald. You see, we made a deal with Argyrus here.' He pointed at the third man. 'He is the leader of the rebellion. I should have introduced you.'

'I don't care which traitor is in charge. Save your breath.'

William laughed. 'Well, he gets Italy, I get Sicily. So, I need to help him destroy what is left of that army first.'

Harald nodded. 'None of this matters to me. You aren't crossing this river. If you wish to, try it.'

'Harald, be reasonable. You have to march away eventually, and when you do, I will have you.'

'I can hold this bridge until the sea drains and the sky falls.'

'I will just find another way around it.'

'Then go and do so,' said Harald contemptuously. 'I have made my choice and will not be cowed.'

William was silent for a moment, looking almost sad. 'Are you really willing to die for them? The men who treated us all so poorly, who banished you to this far-flung land they don't even care about? Why, Harald?'

'Because I am loyal.'

William rubbed his face and exhaled in frustration and wry amusement. 'Gods, what a man you are! I love you like a brother, really I do. In fact, I love several of my many real brothers a good deal less.' He shook his head and looked at Harald sadly. 'It would be such a shame to have to kill you and your brave men, truly. But I have my own duty, and you are in my way.'

'If your plan is to kill us with anything other than boredom, I suggest you stop talking and get on with it.'

William's face tightened. 'You are really going to make me do this, Harald? After all we have done together?'

'I am not making you do anything, William. It is greed alone that is your mistress.'

'Ah, true, true. And spoken by a man equally besotted with her.' He turned and heaved himself back into the saddle, looking around our ranks sadly one more time, speaking loudly to ensure many of the men would hear his words.

'For the love and respect I have for you, Harald, and the desire not to watch our brave men waste each other's blood at the behest of the Greeks, I will make one final offer: You may leave unmolested, march away with your weapons and your pride, as long as you promise to take no further part in this campaign. Go home, Harald. Go home to Norway, or just to Constantinople. I care not. If you do, I promise not to cross this bridge until this evening, and you will be able to say you stopped me and did your duty. I hope you find space in your great pride and honour to be satisfied to hold me here long enough to let those cowards get to safety and let me finish them on another day.'

He looked at Harald firmly. 'This is my final gift to you, my friend. Give me your answer soon, or we will be coming to take it from you.'

Then he turned to the two Lombards, who did not look at all pleased with the offer. The one called Argyrus argued bitterly for a moment, but William simply held up his hand to stem the argument and rode away across the river.

Harald watched them go for a moment and then looked at me.

'What will you do?' I asked.

I could see his mind was racing, seeking the narrow path to victory that he always did. 'Let me think. We can still win this.'

My eyes ran along our ranks and I saw Rurik standing there, watching, one bloodied hand holding his spear. His gaze bored into mine.

'They will expect many things, Eric. But he has made a mistake by giving us this time. It is a weakness we can seize upon. We will get the men watered and rested. We can still win this.' He grabbed me by the shoulder, eyes wide and afire like the Harald of old. The great leader who led us through the black marshes and the desperate battles with the Pechenegs, who had taken us to the river Jordan and back, who had won impossible victory after impossible victory.

But those were fights for survival. And this was for nothing but pride, for an empire that had abandoned us to die.

'Harald,' I said softly, but he ignored me.

'Yes, we could have some men sneak upriver and swim across, we could make the enemy believe there is a surprise attack on their flank, take their focus from the bridge.'

'Harald!' I said more sternly.

'If we can get among their Lombards, we could scatter them and face the Normans alone.'

'*Harald!*' I snapped, grabbing him by the shoulder. He stopped his musings and looked at me in confusion. I turned him to face the long ranks of bloodied, exhausted men who stood on the bank. The surviving veterans of his Varangians.

'What?'

'Harald, enough.'

'What do you mean?'

'Look at them, really, look at them!'

Harald looked from me to the ranks of listening men, standing there in proud silence, waiting for his decision.

'We might win, Harald, we might. God knows, if anyone can find a way to win here it will be you. But how many of them will be left standing afterwards? Will you truly order them into this fight again?'

Harald recoiled. 'Are you suggesting our men will refuse?'

'God, no. They will die for you and their oaths, to a man.'

Someone hammered their spear against their shield in agreement at that, and the sound rippled down the ranks as others joined in.

'They will do it, Harald… But don't make them.'

Harald looked at me again and his face was pained, his eyes full of hurt like I had stabbed him. 'You want me to accept defeat?' he stammered.

'These men have done more for the empire than it could ever deserve. I'm not asking you to accept defeat, Harald. I'm begging you not to sacrifice them all for a victory that will mean nothing. Even if you win, the corrupt cowards who control the palace will abandon this land just to see us humiliated by its loss.'

Harald looked around again, the energy flowing out of him. He looked at his men, every single one of whom was locking eyes with him, defiant but exhausted. I could see it in their eyes, and so could he. They wanted to leave, but they were too proud to say it.

He cast his eyes across the river to where the Normans and the Lombards stood and his face went into a rictus of pain and shame. 'You do not know what you ask of me, Eric. To return to the capital as a coward? To be shamed by the loss of Sicily and Italy? How will I recover from this? How will I ever return home with the stain of this? Men will say I gave up without a fight and ran.'

'No man here will ever tell such a story, or let it be told in their presence. These are the ones who matter, the ones who were with us for three years of war. Look at us, Harald. We did impossible things, achieved victories no other men could achieve. But we were not meant to win this war, and we protect nothing by dying here in its name. The Greeks abandoned us. Let us not dignify their cowardice with our deaths. Our men dying here will not win your brother's throne.'

That final attack broke him, and Harald could not meet my gaze. He took a last look along our ranks with his shoulders hunched and his hand white on his sword hilt.

'Can you bear it?' he asked, raising his voice. 'Can you follow a man who ran from a battle we still had strength to fight?'

There was silence.

'Shall we go home with our weapons and our wounds, and risk men saying that the unconquerable spirit of the Varangians was finally broken in this place? That the oaths we took were cast aside?'

No one moved for a while, and then Sveinn stepped forward. He looked up and down the ranks, his chin held high. 'My oaths are to protect the emperor, but he is not here. My duty is to defend his empire, but his own officers have abandoned this field of battle. We gave many of our brothers so that the general and his army could escape. And they have. We have done our duty when he failed in his and he does not deserve us. We would storm the depths of hell, Protospatharios, if you saw reason to order it. But if you ask me what to do, I say we go home, tend our wounds, sharpen our axes, defend the emperor and wait for a fight that matters to silence any who doubt our honour or our resolve.'

He looked up and down the ranks, waiting, and then another man stepped forwards and planted his spear-butt in the dirt, and another, and then the whole mass of the guard stepped forwards in a ragged wave and Harald's head sank in sadness, while mine was awash with relief.

I put my hand on his shoulder to comfort him. 'Do you want me to take our answer to William?'

Harald shook his head. 'I will bear that burden myself,' he said, his voice cracking.

He took a spear from the man behind me and walked down from our ranks towards the river. Across the narrow stretch of water, the entire army of the Normans and Lombards was watching.

Harald stopped on the first stones of the bridge and raised the spear above his head, turning his head left and right to take all of them in, and then, holding the weapon out to present it to the enemy, he dropped it. The steel-tipped pole fell to the ancient slabs, where Roman armies had marched for over a thousand years, and where no Roman army would ever march again, and its wood thrummed and its steel head chattered against the stone, and then it lay still and quiet.

The Lombards and the Normans let out a great cheer as they saw the signal of our submission, and the first great defeat of Harald's life was sealed.

21

TINGHAUGEN, NORWAY; SPRING 1098 AD

'Harald surrendered rather than continue to fight?' one of the astonished audience asked Eric.

Eric pursed his lips in annoyance. 'He did not surrender. We marched from the field with our weapons and our banners, as no man who surrenders can do.'

'He surrendered the field,' someone else said.

'Yes,' replied Eric with a strident nod. 'He did, wisely, for that field was worth nothing compared to the lives of his men, and he had the strength to recognise that. Many times Harald sacrificed men for ground, for position, for wealth or for power. It is the way of great rulers. But that ground held no value for us, and even if we had won, we would have had to retreat, and the blood spilt would have been for nothing.'

'Could you have won?'

Eric smiled wryly. 'Some of our men argued, for years afterwards – grumbled you might say – that we could have won if we had continued the fight. I think it is pride because we were in a terrible position with no hope of it improving. But there are always those who believe Harald would have found the impossible victory, as he so often did. For a long time, I was one of them.'

'But not now?'

'No.' Eric shook his head, pulling his cloak around himself more tightly to ward off the increasing cold. 'I am certain now that if we had defied William he would have destroyed us.'

'Would that not have been honourable? Fighting to the end as he did outside Yorvik?'

Eric shrugged. 'Honour is often what men make of it. I say that there was more honour in saving his men from a doomed campaign than in sacrificing them just so that others could say he acted well. We were willing to die for an honourable cause, but what honourable cause was there in Italy? None. We were betrayed by our masters, sent there to die fighting against friends of ours who had been betrayed the same. There is scant honour in accepting that.'

The man who had questioned Eric so stridently looked at the ground in contemplation and nodded slowly. 'I can accept that.'

'I am so glad,' said Eric with a sarcastic grin, and men laughed gently at the over-earnest warrior who had questioned it. The man looked defiant and annoyed but did not speak again.

'So, what did you do?' Ingvarr asked, leaning in towards Eric.

Eric looked at the boy and nodded. 'Yes, let's continue, for I feel I am nearly finished for the day as the last sunlight falls on us here, but there is one last great event to tell.'

* * *

As we sailed through the enclosed sea south of Constantinople and the city finally came into view, glittering on the horizon, the mood was glum indeed. Harald expected to be arrested when we landed as Maniakes had been; the rest of us we were merely returning to the city twice defeated and out of favour.

We had left imperial Italy in turmoil. The remains of the army had returned to Bari with the governor, the rebels were rampant in the countryside and many strongholds simply surrendered without a fight, seeing that no help would come.

From Sicily, word had reached us that most of the towns we had captured had surrendered to the emir of Sicily, except Syracuse and Messina, although we later found out Syracuse had surrendered while we were sailing and the news just had not arrived yet.

So we arrived back in the city after three years of campaigning with nothing to show for it, our names and reputation tarnished by what looked to the outside world like endless defeat, despite the fact we had lost only a single battle and won many great victories.

What can I say? Life is not fair, and John was both cunning and powerful. He had beaten Harald utterly, his ploy to ruin him with an impossible campaign had worked, and all he had had to do was sacrifice the rump of a long-denuded province.

We sailed into the small but beautiful harbour beneath the Boukoleon palace alone in our lead ship, leaving the rest of the guard out in the bay to avoid an appearance of armed invasion, or to give anyone an excuse to claim it. The royal harbour was magnificent, nestled in an angle of the wall under the old summer palace looked over by a lighthouse on one side and the palace on the other, forming a three-sided space with docking for a dozen ships on marble-paved quaysides. The palace itself was a three-storey building with a magnificent marble-arched frontage sitting right above the docks, adorned with flags and flowers and drapes bearing the emperor's and empress's seals.

Two huge, carved stone lions stood on each side of a wide balcony where the emperors of the past had stood to greet important visitors or returning armies, before the newer parts of the palace had been built and taken over in importance and use.

A processional gateway led up past the side of the massive building, leading into the heart of the palace complex.

When we came into the dock, a small party of Varangians was waiting, with Aki at their head. The ramp was put out, and Harald and I walked down it to meet with the second sword of the Varangians. His face was drawn.

'Harald, we did not have news you were arriving until this morning. Why are you not in Italy?'

'Because the governor in Italy abandoned us, so we left.'

'That is not what he reported.'

Harald shrugged. 'The words of liars and cowards do not concern me, nor should they you. In any case, Aki, I do not answer to you, so be careful how you address me.'

'I am asking what I was ordered to ask, and I am also to tell you that you are not allowed to enter the palace.'

'I see. I will be arrested, then?'

Aki shook his head. 'No. But you and the banda with you will remain outside the palace unless you are ordered to return.'

Harald stepped closer. 'The head of the imperial guard is ordered to abandon his duties?'

Aki nodded and I could see the distaste in his face.

'And you command in my absence. So, finally, you are taking over the guard, Aki. I congratulate you on your achievement.'

'It is not my doing or choice,' spat Aki. 'Don't play stupid, Harald. You know why this is being done and you know I have no choice.'

'I'm sure you are unable to do anything about it,' replied Harald callously. 'What banda do you have here?'

'None except the first. All the others are out of the city.'

Harald was stunned. 'One bandon to defend the palace! Aki, I left half a dozen here. What in God's name has happened?'

'They were all sent away for fear of disloyalty. A fear caused by your actions, Harald. The Vigla has taken over our duties.' He shrugged helplessly. 'We are being replaced as the emperor's personal guard, Harald. As all the imperial tagma before us were.'

He stared at Harald accusingly, and Harald only grew more incensed.

'This is not my doing. I did nothing but uphold our oaths!'

'You meddled in politics, Harald. And now we all suffer for it.'

'Horseshit! I intervened to ensure the safety of both the emperor and empress when they were plotting to kill each other!'

'And where did that get us?' Aki asked, gesturing around them. 'Cast out, unable to do our duties, replaced.'

'All except you, Aki. How quickly you adapted to a new master, removing men I appointed without my permission, giving orders to the entire guard.' Harald shook his head in disgust but Aki just looked tired.

'You can blame me all you like, Harald, if it makes you feel better about your own mistakes. But either way, I have orders bearing the imperial seal that you and your men are not to enter the city, and neither of us can disobey them.'

'So where do we go? Back to Italy?'

Aki looked uncomfortable. 'You may use the training grounds outside the golden gate. We are not recruiting any more, so they are empty. Take your ships to the beach west of the walls and unload there.'

'Are we allowed to even enter the city?'

'Not under arms. Although your men are not expressly forbidden to enter for their own purposes I highly advise you avoid even the impression of a potential threat. Things in the palace are extremely tense. This Bulgarian rebellion has the entire city on edge. Things are not as they were when you left, Harald.'

'So we are kept out, but close enough to keep an eye on, eh?' said Harald sarcastically.

The two men stared at each other and then Harald turned his back on his second in command and angrily waved me back aboard the ship.

'Wait!' said a voice, and we both turned to see Styrbjorn coming down the steps to the dockside. He had a slight limp, but he looked well-recovered.

I grinned and Styrbjorn dodged past Aki's men, smiling from ear to ear.

'Room aboard for one more?' he called out.

'Styrbjorn, you don't have orders to go with them. You are not released yet.'

'Fuck off, Aki,' said Styrbjorn cheerfully. 'My men are out there in the bay and I'm going with them.'

Harald laughed and embraced the komes. 'It's good to see you again, and walking too!'

'I'll never be surefooted as a goat again, that's certain,' said Styrbjorn. 'But I can make do as long as we don't have to climb any mountains.'

'Harald, he is not supposed to be going with you!' Aki called.

'Aki, I'm the commander, this is one of my officers, and I care less than a cat's fishy fart for your opinion on it. Do you have an order bearing the imperial seal saying Styrbjorn cannot come with me?'

Aki just glared at us.

'I didn't think so.' Harald waved to the crew to take up the ramp. 'Come, let's go to the training grounds. If Aki wants you back, he can fucking swim after us and get you, the wet whoreson.'

Styrbjorn giggled like a child and came over to me, giving me a violent embrace.

'How are you all? I hear everything went wrong after I left. It's to be expected; I was always the one cleaning up your messes.'

'Ah, so this is your fault then, is it?'

'Yes, it seems so,' said Styrbjorn with a serious nod. 'I lost two toes and the empire lost two provinces, all because some dying arsehole dropped an axe on me.'

'You should have moved your foot, then.'

'It was dark!' protested the grinning man. 'And I was busy killing his friends.'

We carried on laughing and talking and exchanging stories as the ship left the dock and our fleet sailed off the few miles to the sweeping bay west of the city, where we unloaded and went to the guards' sprawling camp there. We found it empty but for a few older officers and invalided men who maintained the camp. The rest had been sent west to help reinforce the army fighting the Bulgarians and to secure various strongholds.

What Aki had said was true. The guard was being stripped of its role as the imperial guardians. It was sobering. That status was what gave us our power and wealth. Harald was miserable and retreated into his new quarters without leaving much in the way of instructions for the men.

Afra came to greet Styrbjorn in the camp as we settled in and the wiry man gave him a folded note.

'What is this?' asked Afra.

'Ah, a palace servant gave it to me. An odd, little balding man.'

Afra grinned. 'Thorir! Hah, he is a servant now, eh?'

'Was it Thorir? Bah, it is so hard to be sure. But he asked that I give it to you.'

'Thank you Styrbjorn. I'm glad you have returned to us.'

'Life in the palace was so boring.'

'Not if you knew the wrong people.' Afra gave Styrbjorn a friendly thump and unfolded the note, grunted and handed it to me. I read through it and my eyes widened.

'I will have to tell Harald this.'

'You think he needs to know now? He will do something stupid.'

'Yes, but I have to tell him anyway. You remember what happened last time we tried to keep this kind of news from him.'

'I do, which is why I gave that note to you and made it your problem. Come, Styrbjorn, come have a drink with me!' said Afra with performative enthusiasm, leaving me with his brother's note and a sinking feeling in my stomach.

* * *

I found Harald walking the camp perimeter. Just a hundred yards away the vast white and red banded walls of the city loomed over the moat. The great triumphal gateway, a monumental construction of sheer white marble walls, sat shining in the sun with its vast, resplendent gold-plated gates. That gate usually only opened to allow victorious emperors or armies to process through, and its gleaming doors were firmly shut.

The evidence that the city was preparing for war was clear. The moat had been repaired, the walls were manned, and all the ground in front of the walls was being cleared of any bushes, trees or cover by large bands of workers.

'What?' Harald said disinterestedly as I jogged over and got into step with him.

'A message from Thorir, in the palace.'

Harald's eyes flicked over to me. 'And?'

'He says trouble is brewing nearby to the west but the palace is trying to keep it quiet. The rumours are that the rebellion might be spreading, or a new one starting much closer to the city.'

'The Bulgarian war is three hundred miles away; they cannot pass into the lands close to the city without being noticed. Perhaps it is just bandits taking advantage of the lack of troops in the area.'

'Perhaps. It is not clear.' I cleared my throat nervously because I knew he would not take the next item of news well. 'It is not all, though. He has spotted Maria in the palace.'

Harald looked at me sharply as if he had been stung. 'Maria is in the city?'

'Yes.'

Harald put his hand to his mouth to think. Maria had been exiled after our return from the Holy Land, as part of Harald's agreement with the emperor and empress. She was a close ally and supporter of Theodora, Empress Zoe's sister, and had organised at least three attempted rebellions on Theodora's behalf, trying to usurp Zoe's power.

Harald had discovered that Maria was, in fact, playing a duplicitous game and that Theodora was only being used by the charming noblewoman in order to get herself into power alongside a puppet emperor of her choosing. Maria was of distant royal blood, intelligent and beautiful, younger than Zoe, and it was not an impossible plan.

Harald was so particularly upset because Maria had tried to recruit Harald himself to be that rebel, and the two had been lovers. Harald had loved her like no other woman before or since, and when he had refused to be her pawn, she had cast him aside and let her faithful dog of a mercenary leader, Bardas, try and murder him. Bardas was the executor of Maria's plots. The sword arm for the weapons she could not herself wield, and had always held a fierce hatred for Harald since Harald humiliated him while they were both in service in the Rus. A hatred Harald returned with burning passion once Maria had allowed Bardas to try and kill him.

Maria's betrayal had hurt Harald more deeply than any battle wound. He had never allowed himself to get close to another woman since.

Even without his personal feelings, the fact that Maria was in the city again meant something was happening. The problem was knowing what. After their last failed rebellion, Maria and Bardas had joined forces with John and the emperor in a plot to replace Zoe with Theodora, while at the same time, Zoe plotted to have her sister killed to avoid that very threat.

It was all a terrible and tangled battle for power, and in the end, Harald had ended both plots, saving Theodora, but preventing John from putting her on the throne in Zoe's place.

Maria, like Harald, was not someone who laid their ambitions aside. I think that is part of what made him love her so deeply. If she was in the city, Zoe was almost certainly in danger.

'Give me the letter,' said Harald, and I handed it over. He started studying it. 'Is there any indication Thorir knows what Maria is doing?'

'No.'

Harald grunted and cast the letter aside, then let out a bark of fury and frustration. 'I wonder if she has some connection to the Bulgarian rebellion? She may have incited it or allied herself with its leaders. Perhaps she hopes to use it to get Theodora on the throne with a tame Bulgarian emperor as her husband. And here I am, out of the city, unable to question her.'

'Thorir will keep investigating. He will find the truth.'

'I am sure he will try, but another possibility is that John is himself trying to replace Zoe with Theodora again, now that he has the power. Perhaps that is why the guard has been cleared out of the city. Either way, Zoe is in danger.'

'It will still not be so simple to get to her. Aki, for all his faults, will protect Zoe.'

Harald stared at the floor. 'I am not so sure. Perhaps John has corrupted him too.'

'Harald, surely you cannot believe Aki will betray his oaths?'

'Why not? Perhaps he has decided a side must be taken and has joined the emperor's. Think about it, Eric. He is the last senior officer of the guard left in the city. He has been carrying out John's orders without question, without my authority, scattering our men to the winds, purging the first bandon of anyone who might resist.'

I struggled to believe it, but Harald's argument was powerful.

'All he has to do now is order the first to stand aside while John arrests Zoe, and who will stop them?'

'The people! He would need a very strong reason to remove Zoe; she is very popular.'

Harald nodded. 'Perhaps that is the only reason why it has not happened yet. But with the war coming so close to the city, the people might be too afraid to resist it.'

I shivered at the thought of it. If Zoe was removed, our future would be grim indeed.

'So what do we do?'

Harald huffed. 'I don't know. If we go back to the palace in force to secure Zoe's position and arrest Maria it will be called a coup. In fact, I expect John hopes we will attempt to do that. I will ask Afra to get a message to the empress, asking her what to do. Perhaps she will have some orders for me. If she feels threatened, we will go to the palace and protect her, consequences be damned.'

That made me flush with fear. Harald was on the verge of taking sides, of not only becoming involved in a civil war but perhaps even starting one.

* * *

Harald eventually got a reply from Zoe. I didn't read it myself and he was reluctant to describe it in great detail, but his frustration turned into despondency. 'We are to stay here and wait for orders,' was all I could get from him.

A week or more passed, and there were more open rumours about the trouble to the west, and of the renewal of fighting in Hellas theme, where the Bulgarians were once more advancing through Macedonia and into Greece.

We received a visitor that we had absolutely not expected: John. He came to our camp with a significant detachment of the Vigla guard to speak to Harald.

Harald was so desperate for information or action that he accepted the visit without any fuss and he stared at the eunuch with great intensity while the slim man smiled in pleasure at our helplessness.

'You look older, Harald. Defeat has aged you.'

'And you still look like a hairless boy, and boast like one too.'

'All the more embarrassing for me to have defeated you, then.'

'Defeated me? You sacrificed an entire province and ruined a successful campaign just to inconvenience me. The empire cannot survive any more of your victories,' Harald replied coldly.

John still smiled, basking in Harald's outrage. 'I do prefer you like this, diminished and angry.'

'Are you so vain you just came here to gloat, or do you have something to say?'

John nodded lightly. 'Enough with the preliminaries, then. Yes, I am sure you have heard that the Bulgarians have revived their campaign in Hellas.'

'We have.'

'Well, you may not know that it appears they may have managed to incite a smaller rebellion much closer to the city, in the foothills of Thrace, little more than a hundred and fifty miles away.'

'Of course, I have heard that,' said Harald drily.

'Really? Hmm. Well, we are not sure if it is bandits, mercenaries, or some of Petar's rebels who have managed to come across the mountains undetected, but the emperor is concerned that this fire might grow, and spread, and cause panic in the city.'

'Why don't the thematic forces deal with it?'

John shrugged. 'They are busy in Greece. In any case, we prefer that you go and deal with it.'

Harald nodded. 'So, now I understand your visit. You dislike me being this close to the city, and want an excuse to get rid of me.'

'We understand each other perfectly,' said John with a satisfied smile. 'Your loyalty is in serious doubt, and although the emperor is not quite ready to have you arrested or stripped of your command, your lurking outside the city walls like a malignant shadow is making some of his supporters nervous.'

'My loyalty is only in doubt to those who do not understand the concept of loyalty to someone other than themselves. So I understand your confusion perfectly.'

'Don't be petulant, Harald. It's unbecoming. If you are so loyal, you will do as commanded.'

'Do you have a—'

'Sealed order?' said John quickly. 'Of course.' He snapped his fingers at an attendant who produced a sealed scroll. 'Just as you like it.'

He handed the scroll over and Harald looked at it with surprise. 'Zoe's seal is on this order. How did you force that?'

'We didn't. The empress agreed on this matter and gave it her blessing.'

'Why should I believe you? I don't understand why the empress would send her guard away, with so many enemies around her.'

'I don't care what you believe, Harald. I am sure you can have your people in the palace check with Zoe.' He looked at Afra, who was standing nearby. 'Your brother, Thorir, I believe?'

Afra's face clouded over and he went rigid in shock.

John smiled in intense satisfaction. 'I must admit, he took me a great deal of time and effort to discover. A very good spy. I wish he were mine.'

'If you have harmed him, eunuch...' grated Afra, still rooted to the ground.

'No, there was no need. Now that I know who he is, he is harmless. I will let you keep him. I will even let him stay in the palace. Consider it a gift.' John turned away from Afra without a care. 'Now, you have your orders, Harald. Carry them out or face the consequences.' He stepped in to whisper to Harald. 'Personally, I am hoping you refuse.'

Then, without allowing Harald a counter, he turned brightly on his heel and left.

There was a stony silence as Harald glared at the departing

eunuch, and Afra stared at the ground with a sick expression on his face.

Harald was the first to recover, and he broke the dual seals on the orders and quickly read them.

'We are ordered to march east to end this new rebellion. We will have men and supply support from some of the thematic forces of Thrace. They will meet us here in three days and we can march.'

He rolled the scroll up and looked at the city gate again, his pulse pounding in his temple. I was astounded by how well he had taken the whole thing. The Harald of old would have flown into a rage.

'So what do we do?' I carefully asked.

Harald gave me a look that showed how stupid he thought that question was. 'We do as the emperor and empress instruct – we march east and crush this brewing rebellion before it can threaten the city.'

'Of course,' I said hurriedly, and with quite some relief.

'But we won't wait for these thematic forces. We will do this ourselves and alone. Gather every single man fit to march. We leave first thing tomorrow. And Afra, get Thorir to check with Zoe. No need to be secretive about it now. I need an answer tonight.'

Afra nodded.

My mouth gaped open. 'Tomorrow? But we have no supplies, carts, mules...' I stammered to a stop as I realised Harald knew all this and didn't care.

'We are in friendly lands and we will find or buy what we need as we go and take only what we can carry. We will take no Greeks or allies to abandon us or sabotage us as they did in Sicily. We still have ships here and we will sail along the coast to the nearest port to this trouble and march inland. We will have to put two hundred men in each ship, but only for a day and it will save us three days' marching. The more quickly we do this, the faster we can be back to protect Zoe. Come!' He turned and strode away, filled with purpose, and Afra just smiled sadly at me and shrugged.

He was right. The only thing to do with Harald in this situation was strap on your sword and follow him.

22

We received a short note back from the empress late that night. Harald read it out for just Afra and me to hear.

'Araltes, I agreed to allow you to be sent on this mission because the threat from this rebellion is real, and although my husband and his brother are too proud to admit it, yours are the only men in the area likely to be able to deal with it. Be thorough and ruthless, my dear prince, and come back to me. Use this opportunity to remind the people of your loyalty and worth, and perhaps you can stand at my side again soon.'

Harald stared at the letter in the firelight, and I saw his face contort with emotion. He finally nodded to himself. 'This may be our chance to start erasing the stain of our defeats.'

I nodded.

Afra looked worried. 'Thorir is concerned. He thinks there is more going on, strange happenings in the palace and the Vigla guard.' Afra looked sad. 'But he is watched day and night now and has lost all his sources. He is blind to exactly what is happening.'

'Then we cannot worry about it. We can only do as we are

ordered.' Harald rose to his feet. 'Go and get some rest. We will get little in the days to come.'

We headed east the next morning. First, we sailed about eighty miles west along the coast to a port called Rhaedestus, where we left our ships and started the march inland. We marched quickly and without a baggage train to hinder or comfort us. I can tell you honestly, it was a delight. It was the old way of war of our Northern ancestors, one that we had forgotten in the highly organised campaigning of the empire and the Rus. We had only ourselves, our weapons, and the silver we carried.

We drank from wells, ate freshly slaughtered goat and mutton bought from shepherds with solid silver that made their eyes go wide like a cat's, and slept under trees on the earth or, if we were lucky, hastily collected bundles of leaves or straw.

We marched twenty miles a day, and the men chatted and laughed and sang, for truly it was good marching through lush country in the early summer sun and we were all just glad not to be in the heat and rocky hills of Sicily.

For three days we marched, moving out of the broad, coastal plains of Thrace and into the highlands and valleys on the border with Macedonia, following rumours and reports of rebellion, and it was there we found our first burned village, the embers of it still smoking, sending up twisting, idle wisps into the air. There was not a living soul to be found, although the dead were scattered all around.

We found four such villages that day, each as completely destroyed as the last.

'This looks like the work of bandits, not rebels,' Harald said with distaste, examining the ruins in the last one.

'No, my friend. Bandits very rarely kill the vine, for then it never again bears fruit,' replied Afra with an assured shake of his head.

'Don't speak in riddles, Afra. What do you mean by it?'

Afra waved his hand around at the scene. 'Bandits steal, sometimes they kill the strong, but they rely on the weak to continue producing the things they need. This reckless destruction and killing, this serves no purpose for a bandit.'

'Killing everyone and destroying everything in defenceless villages isn't the work of rebels who wish to earn the people's support.'

Afra raised his eyebrows and nodded noncommittally. 'True.'

'Then why? What is the purpose here?'

'Perhaps just to spread fear.'

Harald shook his head in disgust, staring at the ragged body of an old woman that was draped over a low wall. 'Or to commit monstrous crimes that can be blamed on someone. Let's move on, we need to catch these men before this spreads any further. We will have the answers we need then.'

The next morning a small town came into view further up the valley. It was unwalled, and smoke was rising from several of its buildings. Not the grey wisps of cooking fires, but the dark, black smoke of burning homes.

But more than that, we saw a small force, perhaps fifty men, with a few horses, outside the town on the west side. They were breaking camp. We saw them before they saw us, and they formed up into a disciplined bloc when they did, but showed no fear.

'They are no bandits,' said Harald, and he pointed at the banner flying over them. 'That is an imperial banner.'

'Rebels can fly false banners,' said Sveinn.

'Perhaps, but we outnumber them and they are not fleeing. Let's go and find out who they are.'

We marched down the narrow road in close formation until we were close to the other unit. We were not flying our imperial banner or our bandon flags. Harald didn't see the purpose in letting it be known who we were in advance.

'Have their commander brought to me,' Harald said to Sveinn. And the stern komes nodded and went forwards with his bandon, bristling with menace. We saw the commander of the opposing unit refuse at first, but then Sveinn simply had a dozen men take him, and his men – outnumbered so heavily – decided against any foolish resistance.

Sveinn escorted the man over to us, and we could hear his protests, then he was not so gently shoved in front of Harald, and both men went still.

'Bardas?' spat Harald in disgust as he recognised the Greek. 'What are you doing here?'

Bardas looked at Harald in confusion and fear. 'Harald. How are you here?'

'Ah, you thought I was in Italy, then?'

'Italy...? Yes.' Bardas's eyes flicked between Harald and the rest of us.

Harald chuckled. 'Well, I was sent here to end the rebellion. Imagine my pleasure to find you instead. Is this rebellion your doing, Bardas?'

Bardas's eyes went wide and he struggled against Sveinn's grip. 'I am no rebel!'

'Then what are you doing here, in this burning town?'

'I was sent here, just like you.'

Harald paused, and a little of the leering happiness came out of his posture. 'With fifty men? Sent by whom?'

'The palace. We serve the same master, Harald. And this isn't all of my men.' He pointed vaguely at the town. 'I was just scouting.'

Harald leaned back a bit, tucking his thumbs into his belt. He looked unsure, and Bardas looked resolute.

'Then where are the rebels?'

'They marched north into the next valley yesterday morning, according to the survivors we found. Maybe three thousand of them.'

Bardas was tense, looking around us, breathing hard. It was hardly surprising. Even if he were innocent of any crime there, he was guilty of plenty in the past. Harald stared at the Greek for a little longer and then turned back to us.

'I believe him,' I said. 'He and fifty men didn't take this town.'

Harald shrugged. 'I would have done it with fifty.'

'He isn't you,' said Afra.

'Such true words are rarely spoken,' said Harald with a smile.

'We know Bardas works for Michael, but our orders did not say any other forces would be here.'

'It is not unlike John to send another force with the same orders; he has done it before. It might even be prudent,' Harald said with a sigh of disappointment. I knew he was hoping for an excuse for violence.

'What I am telling you is the truth, Harald,' said Bardas loudly, interrupting us, recovering a little of his poise now and spreading his arms in annoyance. 'Let me go about my duties.'

'And then what?' said Harald, turning on the short, curly-haired Greek.

Bardas pointed east. 'I will return to my men, and come back with them to chase these rebels down.'

'How long will that take?'

Bardas did some quick calculation in his head. 'Probably two days' riding there and back. You could wait here for me to join forces with you.'

Harald laughed. 'Two days? The rebels will be long gone. No, this is a warrior's job. We will do it alone.'

'Harald, this is my mission,' protested Bardas, but the protest seemed weak. 'Wait here for two days. We can help you.'

'Never, Bardas. Never. You crawl back to the palace and tell them real soldiers have, once again, done what you could not.'

Bardas looked furious, but perhaps also slightly relieved. He straightened up and nodded. 'Fine. I see your pride still rules your head. I will leave you, then.' It was almost a question, and he didn't actually move until Harald gave him a disgusted nod.

'Do not return here. I will not risk you ruining this fight with either incompetence or sabotage.'

Bardas swallowed hard at the insult, but then took the opportunity to leave as Sveinn let him pass.

'Extra men might have been useful,' Afra was foolish enough to say.

Harald just glared at him. 'Come, let's go north and run these rats to ground.'

We turned away from Bardas and his small party, which hastily started marching west, and we went up towards the pass that led into the next valley.

* * *

'Well, he was telling the truth,' said Afra as we crouched on a low ridge and watched the camp in the valley below us that next evening.

'Those may well be rebels, but it isn't three thousand of them,' I said.

'Maybe one thousand,' said Sveinn, staring intently at the ant-like figures below.

'There may be multiple bands, or the townsfolk overcounted. It doesn't matter. Let's deal with these this evening, and make sure to take prisoners who can tell us where the rest are.'

'This evening? You want to attack now? It's almost dark.' Sveinn looked unsure. 'It might be better to attack in the morning, let our men rest and sleep.'

Harald scowled. 'I will not waste another day. Let's take them now and be done with it. They look like they are barely soldiers. Their camp has no wall. We will do it at dusk. Let the men rest briefly until then.'

His tone brooked no argument, and we all nodded and went to our banda with the orders.

* * *

What should I tell you of that fight? Bah, it is not worth the recounting. The enemy were not real soldiers, just bandits and farmboys. Our thousand killers came up out of the darkness and went through their camp like water over a stone floor, and it was over before you could have said a good prayer. I think we only lost a single man.

Sveinn brought over a terrified, bloodied bandit as Harald and I stood in the centre of the enemy camp.

'This is their commander?' asked Harald derisively while he wiped the blood of a rebel off his sword with the dead man's tunic.

'I saw him giving some orders, so I assume he isn't lying,' replied Sveinn, towering over the defeated rebel like the spirit of vengeance.

'I... I beg your mercy, Strategos, please,' blabbered the man.

'You will be begging me to remove my sword from your guts unless you tell me where the rest of the rebels are!'

'The rest?'

The man shrugged helplessly again. Harald whipped out his seax and grabbed him by the scruff of the neck, putting the tip of his seax into the man's stomach, right around his belly button, grinding it into the soft flesh a little.

'The other two thousand men that were with you at the town to the south. Where are they?'

'What two thousand men?'

Harald gazed around at the darkening camp. 'This can't be all of you. Where is the commander?'

'The man who paid us?'

'Yes, the man who paid you! Who, a Bulgarian? Is he here? Take me to him!'

'No, he isn't here. We left him two days ago.'

Harald swore and looked at us. 'So that will be where the other two thousand men went – they split after entering this valley.' He kicked the prisoner. 'So where did he and his army go?'

'He stayed at the town after we were finished with it, he said he was going to raise more men, he told us to march north and keep raiding, that he would be back.' The prisoner looked confused for a moment. 'But he didn't have two thousand of his own men. He only had about fifty. And he is not Bulgarian, he is Greek.'

There was a stunned silence.

'What?' Harald stared at the prisoner as a mask of anger and outrage etched itself into his face. Then he closed his eyes in frustration. 'Bardas!' he howled through gritted teeth.

'He is with the rebels,' I said in shock. My head was swimming.

'That means this rebellion was created by John, using Bardas,' said Afra.

'Why? What is the point? This paltry army could do nothing but burn a few villages. This was no threat. It was obvious we would defeat this,' I said.

Harald looked up at us, real fear in his face.

'That's the point,' Afra said with a sick expression. 'We're here, not in the city. That's all it is.'

'This pathetic rebellion was just a desperate plan to draw us away,' Harald said, his eyes flicking as his mind raced.

'But why was Bardas still here when we arrived?' I asked.

'He couldn't have believed we would get here so quickly from the city. That is why he was so shocked to see us – not because he thought we were still in Italy, but because he thought we were several days' march away and that he had time to escape.'

'Bardas and his men are marching east, and he expects us to be chasing these rebels. He still has all the time he needs,' said Harald.

'Time to do what?' I asked.

Harald looked at me and his face was drawn. 'To get to the palace without us there to defend it.'

Harald stared back down the valley, then looked down at the rebel leader and shoved his seax into the man's chest, giving orders while the bandit wriggled and gurgled around the steel. 'Kill anyone who is left. We march tonight.'

'We will never catch them,' said Sveinn. 'They marched east while we marched west. They will be two days ahead of us already, and they are mounted!'

'We can't catch them, but maybe we can still reach the city first. We will march all day and part of the night. We will take ships at Rhaedestus and sail to the city. We can make it to the ships in three days if we have the minimum of rest. Then cross to the city on the fourth. It will take them three or four more days to ride to the city. We still might get there first by using the ships.'

'Three days? We can't march to Rhaedestus in three days! It took us five days marching to get here,' I protested.

'We can,' snapped Harald, 'because we must. And those who drop out will be left behind. Pray that Bardas takes a day to rest before he goes to the palace, or that he is held up. We can do nothing about it other than march like the wind. Come, we are wasting time. Let's move!'

'We could find a horse and send a warning!'

'To who? Who do we trust? The Vigla guard? They must be part of the plot. John will have sealed the city. He knows about Thorir and no one will be allowed to see Zoe. What can she do even if word reaches her? She is a prisoner. No. We must go there ourselves, there is no other way.'

Harald set off down the slope towards the gate and Sveinn followed him without question. Afra looked defeated. I grabbed his shoulder. 'You think we are already too late?'

He just nodded, his face distraught. 'I am so sorry, Eric. This is my fault.'

'Why?'

'Thorir and I have failed. Perhaps I could have prevented this.'

I squeezed his shoulder and pushed him down the slope in front of me. 'You can't know everything, Afra,' I said, but I don't think I sounded convincing even to myself.

* * *

We marched for half the night, slept poorly, and got up at first light and marched again. We stopped occasionally and briefly to drink and then marched some more. We barely ate. There was no time to cook anything, anyway, and we survived on what we could pick up as we went for the first two days, which was not much.

A few men started to drop behind on the second day. Most of them caught up that night, but we quickly lost most of them again in the morning. It was only a few. Most of us were hardened by the Italian campaigns and although we suffered, we kept the relentless pace Harald set.

Even Styrbjorn, whose maimed foot troubled him more and more the further we went, just gritted his teeth and limped along with us.

On the third day, we managed to buy some bread, cheese and olives in a large village, enough for everyone to have a small meal as we marched again. We reached Rhaedestus on the third day towards dusk, exhausted and hungry, and marched straight down into the harbour.

We all simply dropped down on the docks, bought food and ate it, then slept like dead men around the waterside.

23

Our tiny fleet of ships, overloaded and protesting, carried us away in the first hint of light the next morning. By the blessing of God, the wind was good and behind us, and we swept along the bay in a loose gaggle, praying the traitors would not have any of the imperial navy out to stop us. But there was nothing in our way, and by afternoon we had the city in sight.

The palace lay there, serene and beautiful under the shadow of the Hagia Sophia and its domes. From the sea, all looked peaceful and normal, but we could see nothing of what lay behind its walls.

Harald led us into the royal harbour under the Boukoleon Palace, and I noted with dismay that it was completely unguarded. It was never unguarded. Something was deeply wrong.

'At least Bardas and his men aren't holding it against us,' said Afra unhelpfully.

Harald cajoled the reluctant skipper of our ship to practically ram his vessel into the harbour, and then we poured out of it like ants onto the dock, forming up behind Harald as he cast a quick glance behind to check the rest of the Varangians in their heavily laden ships were coming alongside too.

'Up to the top, secure the gate,' barked Harald, and we ran up the stairs in the shadow of the seafront palace with its twin stone lions standing their perpetual watch over the harbour. The gate was half closed but not sealed. Inside, a dead Vigla guardsman was sprawled on the cobbles.

'He is barely dead; the blood is still fresh,' said Harald, bending down.

As he said that, a half dozen armed men came around the corner of the nearest building inside the palace grounds and stopped dead as they saw us. We stared at them in outrage. They were not Vigla or Varangians.

There was a moment of indecision, and then they turned and fled.

'After them!' shouted Harald, and we pounded across the flagstones and up the ornamental path beside the church of Saint Sergius, following the traitors as they fled up the hill towards the imperial residence.

There was the thunder of armoured men behind us as hundreds of Varangians poured up the harbour stairs and into the palace grounds in our wake. We passed more bodies on the second terrace of the palace grounds, mostly Vigla and a pair of Varangians, mixed in with some of the traitors. Someone had tried to block the path upwards and died in the attempt, although it was unclear which side had been attacking and which defending.

We kept going as the men we were chasing turned a corner around the high wall that surrounded the inner gardens. We could hear the faint sounds of shouting and fighting now, coming from deeper in the palace, towards the main entrance.

We rounded the corner of the walled enclosure and found

the gate to the palace gardens, the gate that Harald and I had sometimes used to visit Zoe. It was shut, but the first bandon guards who normally stood there lay slaughtered beside it. They had died at their post.

Harald looked back. 'Styrbjorn! Take a hundred men and find a way to climb this wall and clear the gardens. They might be trying to get into the palace from there.'

'Yes, Commander!' shouted Styrbjorn, and he started peeling off some of the men behind us to find furniture or ladders or anything they could use to get over the wall. Two men started hacking at the thick wooden door with their axes.

Harald kept on going with me right behind, breathing hard and my heart fluttering, praying we weren't too late but assuming we were.

We reached the main entranceway to the inner palace complex and found the scene of a terrible fight there. Dead and dying Varangians of the first bandon were clumped together around the broken gates, a thick ring of dead and wounded traitor soldiers around them.

A brave stand had been made there by the men of the emperor's shields, but it had been in vain. From the inner courtyard beyond, through the open and blood-spattered gates, was the sound of heavy fighting.

We ran towards the gate and Harald stepped over to a moaning Varangian who was slumped against the pillar beside the archway. I went over and saw who it was.

'Aki!' said Harald, and the man opened his eyes weakly. He looked confused.

'Harald? How?'

'What happened here?' Harald asked.

'Fucking... treason. In the palace. You must... stop them.'

Harald looked up and waved at those who were gathering around. 'Get into the palace! Get to the empress! Move!'

Dozens of our men poured through the archway with Sveinn at their head, and Harald turned back to Aki.

'I tried, I tried,' Aki mumbled.

'Who did this?' Harald sounded pained.

Aki shook his head gently, blood seeping from a wound in his chest in bubbling waves. 'Some of the Vigla... turned on us. We fought them but they opened the Chalke Gate, and some fucking unit of Greek soldiers poured in. Too many to stop, so we fell back to the palace.'

'Who ordered this? Who leads them?'

'I... I don't know. A Greek. Get in there, Harald,' Aki said, weakly pawing at Harald's arm. 'I tried, I tried to stop them.'

'I will.' Harald stood up. 'Someone get this man to the barracks!'

With a last look at Aki, we pushed on past the carnage and into the outer palace courtyard, where a few bodies were scattered haphazardly around. The buildings on our left and right stood open and empty, and the sound of fighting was coming from the gate to the inner courtyard ahead where a thick group of our men were struggling to get through the archway, cutting and hacking at the enemy, who were already inside and now trying to keep us out.

Harald and I shoved our way into the fight and Harald looked over the fight as Sveinn turned to shout at us over the din.

'Varangians are still fighting inside the palace!' he called, and I let out a huge breath of relief.

Our men were laying into the traitors with ferocious aggression, axes flashing and falling on the Greeks, who were armoured in heavy lamellar and looked like any regular tagma infantry. But they were not ready to fight our men, and they were crumbling under the assault of the baying, howling, furious Varangians.

All of us in that fight had crossed over the bodies of our loyal dead to get here, to reach their killers. I had never seen our men fight like that, with such wild abandon that they were barely even defending themselves, just cutting and hacking and clawing at the enemy like the stories of the pagan-mad berserkers of our ancestors.

Even as we looked, the rebel defence of the doorway crumbled under the pressure of our furious assault, big axes cutting heads and limbs from the bodies of the traitors, scattering maille rings and lamellar plates in sprays of blood and bone.

'Get to the empress!' roared Harald, and the men bellowed and surged forwards again.

Suddenly we were pushing forward and the lines intermingled and pulsed. I threw myself into the fight, desperate to break them before they overcame whoever of the first bandon was still alive and fighting inside the palace.

I attacked one bloodied Greek with the edge of my shield, hammering it into his face and wearing his weak return thrust on my armour. I used the shield to knock his weapon aside and then put my spear into his chest so hard it burst through between his plates and stuck fast inside his sternum.

He went down with an open mouth and took my spear with him. I pulled my sword across my body from my scabbard and cut upwards at an enemy who was coming to take advantage of my open side.

I cut hard through his face, from chin to forehead, ripping the helmet from his head with the blade.

I kicked the screaming man aside and pushed through, hacking deeper into their formation, cutting them down as they started to look over their shoulders and find a way to escape. The look of broken men.

God, how I fought that day. I was filled with rage. I was at the peak of my strength and speed and my brothers were howling like wolves behind me and no blade could touch me. I was a demon amongst lambs.

But as I slaughtered them, someone grabbed the back of my armour and pulled me into line. 'Are you trying to get yourself killed?' an angry voice said in my ear, and I looked around to find Afra staring at me. I had left the main formation behind in my blood rage.

'Eric, on me!' shouted Harald from behind, and I shuffled through the ranks like a guilty child.

'I need my officers here,' he snapped, and I just nodded. He was scanning the fight in front of us. Then his eyes lit up and he pointed at the back of the enemy force. 'Bardas!' he said excitedly.

I looked and saw Bardas there, cajoling his men, trying to get them to resist us even as he sent more into the palace to finish the fight there.

'He is trying to buy time to get to Zoe.'

'We need to get to the entrance and cut them off.' Harald looked to the left, where our line was forcing its way towards the palace doors. 'That's where we focus our attack, quickly.'

He looked around. 'Ulfr!'

The big Icelander looked over. 'Commander?'

'Left side, palace doors. Get your men over there and clear the interior before it's too late. Now!'

Ulfr raised his bloodied axe above the crowd to acknowledge, and he roared at the men around him to form up for a push.

They broke out of the wall in a mass, howling like the killers they were and carving a bloody path through the Greeks towards the doors. Bardas shouted at his men to stop them, and the fighting was nasty. I saw half a dozen or so of our guardsmen go down, not having the benefit of being in a line where they could have defended themselves and their comrades properly.

But for every guardsman that fell in the manic attack into the wavering enemy lines, another two poured through the gap, cutting and kicking and killing, and the enemy formation recoiled from the violence like a living thing. They could not match our ferocity or our anger, or the terrible steel storm of our axes and swords.

Finally, Ulfr's men reached the palace door, and Harald grinned in triumph as they started fighting their way into the palace. The rest of us pushed the main enemy body back further into the courtyard, separating them from their doomed fellows inside the buildings.

We watched as Bardas conferred with a few of his men, and then he cast one dirty look at us across the fight before he took twenty or so men and ran through the open doors of the hall of nineteen; the ornate imperial reception hall.

Harald's smile faded. 'Bastard coward!' he shouted. 'He is going to escape!'

'No, he is trapped,' said Afra beside us with a wicked grin.

'He can escape through the door at the back of the hall, into the corridors that lead to the back of the palace.'

'No, he can't. That door is always locked.'

'They will break it down.'

Afra shook his head and laughed. 'They would need all week. It is one of the secrets of the palace that I learned while I was in the first, Harald. That door looks like wood, but it is wood clad over a core of iron and bronze, with locking bars the width of my arm set into the stone. It is built that way so the emperor can escape from that room if there is ever an attack, and then go through the tunnels in the Hippodrome to safety with no possibility of pursuit. Bardas has trapped himself in that hall, believe me.'

As we stood there Ulfr appeared from the entrance to the palace, bloodied and exhausted. He walked over to us and nodded. 'The enemy inside is done, and my men are hunting the last of them, clearing room by room.'

'And the empress?'

'Alive and under the guard of Styrbjorn. He reached her through the gardens. Her quarters were untouched. The emperor lives, too. Men of the first were still defending his rooms when we got there.'

'The traitors were attacking the emperor's quarters?' Harald said in confusion.

'Yes, Protospatharios,' replied Ulfr.

Harald looked perplexed, and I saw him put it from his mind as he turned to look over the ranks of our men, who were still pushing forward against the failing Greeks. 'Men of the Varangian guard! Forwards to the hall! Death to the traitors!'

'Death to the traitors!' the guard roared, and then stamped forward again, axes flashing and swords thrusting, and the traitors' ranks started to break. There was no way out of the courtyard behind them, just the entrance to the hall and the blank wall of the inner palace colonnade. Bardas had closed the hall's doors behind them, leaving his men to buy him time with their deaths.

Ha, the fool. We had all the time in the world.

Traitor soldiers started stumbling back. Some threw down their weapons and begged for mercy.

'No prisoners!' bellowed Harald, his blood up, screaming at the men from under his shining helmet, and the surrendering men were ruthlessly cut down. The enemy formation finally disintegrated and there was a wild cheer from our ranks as our men swarmed over them, killing with abandon and hunting the last of them into the corner of the courtyard.

Harald ignored the last of that fight and examined the doors to the hall.

'Can we break these?'

'Yes,' said Afra. 'They are not strong, just decorative.'

'Bring me axes!' called Harald, and some men started working on the area around the great bronze lion-headed handles that sat proud on the beautifully decorated and gilded doors.

Several years' work of a skilled craftsman was pulped in moments, reduced to kindling, and the intricately carved panels shattered and fell away, leaving the bare structure underneath around the lock, which soon gave way to the heavy blows of the axes.

There was a snap and a groan, and the doors parted, swinging open to reveal the hall. Inside, at the far end, several Greeks were hacking at the door behind the raised area of the emperor's couch, which had been rudely shoved aside, the curtain concealing the door, torn.

I could hear their blades ringing as they bounced off metal, and knew what Afra had said was true.

The men at the far end of the hall looked at us with the terror only a living being that is trapped and knows it is about to die a terrible death can express, and Harald stalked into the hall, calmly cutting aside the one delusional fool who charged at him to try and stop him.

'Bardas!' he roared into the towering, echoing, marble-clad hall as he ripped his sword from the dying Greek's neck.

The Greek soldiers took one look at Harald, advancing down the aisle like the god of vengeance, with dozens of our guardsmen at his back, and they cowered back, tripping over couches and huddling around the door, frantically calling to their comrades to break it down.

Harald pointed his sword at Bardas. 'That one is mine. Kill the rest.' And then he charged.

It was stupid, really. One man charging into twenty. But I never doubted for a moment he would fight his way through them, and neither did they. The fight was completely gone from them. They were scrambling over each other to get to the door, impervious in their panic to the obvious fact that there was nowhere safe to run to.

I think barely a handful of them even raised their weapons to defend themselves as Harald speared into them with me and our men at his back.

He ripped one out of the group and threw the desperate man into our ranks to finish, eyes locked on Bardas, who stood on the emperor's dais, his feet planted on the glorious, red-veined marble and his wide eyes focused on Harald as his death approached.

Harald's sword sang, and his enemies parted before him like sand before rushing water. We killed everyone that he passed until he was standing at the bottom of the shallow steps leading up to the platform.

'Bardas,' he spat.

'Harald! I have told you before, we answer to the same master. Stop this!' His words were confident but his voice was wavering.

'Be quiet, coward, and fight me.'

'Harald, listen to me,' Bardas pleaded.

'Fight me!' yelled Harald, and Bardas, to his vague credit, brought his sword forward to swipe at the commander of the Varangians.

Harald took the blow on his shield and stepped forwards, up the steps, not even using his own blade, just parrying again and again with his shield, before contemptuously dropping his sword to the marble with a clatter.

He forced the Greek back until they were both on the top platform, Bardas's sword still hacking and swiping, but Harald just took the strikes on his shield and armour, batting the increasingly desperate blows aside before punching Bardas in the teeth with his shield rim, scattering fine droplets of blood onto the beautiful marble as Bardas reeled away in pain.

Every one of Bardas's men was now dead or dying, ignored and forgotten as we watched Harald toy with his prey.

'You thought you could abandon me to the Pechenegs, traitor,' Harald snarled as Bardas backed away, his sword hand pressed to his face.

Bardas suddenly thrust, hard and true, straight for Harald's face, but Harald was equal to it and snapped his head to the side, bringing his shield up and hammering it into the outside of the smaller man's elbow, eliciting a pained yelp as the Greek's hand went numb and the sword flew from his grasp.

'You thought you could kill me like a dog in the streets of Kyiv.' Harald panted as he spoke. 'You came to the palace to kill my men, my brothers who have served the empire while you raided and despoiled its people?'

He strode forwards again, forcing Bardas up against the back of the lavish hall, the Greek man's head hitting the stone through the purple drapes that covered the wall.

'You bring steel and violence to despoil the palace, you try to kill the empress of the Romans... And yet you still expect me to listen to your deceiving words, your lying tongue!' Harald roared in outrage.

Bardas tried to shove Harald back with his shield, but Harald dropped his own and grabbed the rim of Bardas's shield with both hands, wrenching it around to his left and breaking Bardas's left arm with a nauseating snap.

The Greek traitor howled with pain and held up his empty sword arm to try and halt his attacker.

'Harald, please, listen!' he wailed. 'We serve the same master!'

But Harald was past listening. He grabbed the outstretched hand with his right and then brought his left up in a vicious strike to the outside of the elbow, bending the traitor's arm in half the wrong way. Bardas screamed like a dying boar.

He slumped against the wall, eyes wide in shock and mouth hanging open, babbling at Harald to stop between sickly, hacking breaths.

Harald grabbed the front of Bardas's armour with one hand and pressed him against the wall to stop him collapsing, and then slowly drew his seax from the sheath at his back.

'I will not hear another word, coward!' Harald spat, and he brought the seax up horizontally and put it, edge first, into Bardas's open mouth so that the edge cut into both corners. He leaned into the blade as the smaller man wriggled in terrified, shaking spasms, each movement only making the blade bite deeper as it slid through both of his cheeks.

Harald held the traitor against the wall like that, hanging off the blade, while he glared into Bardas's horrified, pleading eyes.

'I always knew it would end like this, with me cutting your lying, traitorous tongue from your body.' And then he grabbed a handful of Bardas's hair and pushed the blade, cutting back and then ripping it down, cutting through the traitor's tongue and on down, shearing his lower jaw from his head and ripping out the front of his neck.

Bardas twitched and gurgled, his eyes pinned open as he

drowned in the blood that pulsed from the ruin of his lower face, held up by his hair against the wall as his life splashed onto the rich purple fabric of the torn wall hanging at his feet.

His broken arms pawed more and more weakly, and his eyes never left Harald's, who did not break his gaze until they faded, and the gurgling and pawing stopped.

Then Harald let go of the black, wiry hair and Bardas's body slumped to the ground in a heap.

I don't think I have ever seen Harald look so satisfied in all the time that I had known him. He turned and looked out over us with a fond smile.

There was a stunned silence as he came down the white marble stairs, now flowing with red rather than veined by it.

Even for men of war and violence, we were shocked by the sheer hatred and spite with which he had killed Bardas. I had never seen anything like it.

'You have all upheld your sacred oaths and regained your honour today. Never again will we be cast from the palace, I swear it. Tend to our wounded, bind any traitors who remain alive for questioning later, and guard the inner palace against any further attacks. Ulfr – go to our barracks and secure it. Hopefully, our men there are alive.'

It was a kindness, because if Ulfr's cousin Halldor was in the palace, the barracks was where he would be, and Ulfr would be desperate to go and find out if he lived or if the traitors had cleared the barracks first and killed all of our sick and wounded.

Then my prince came over to me and smiled. 'Let's go and see the emperor.'

* * *

We walked out of the hall of nineteen and into the charnel house of the inner courtyard. Men were already dragging the bodies aside, and taking away wounded guardsmen.

We walked over towards the palace doors, and two bloodied and exhausted-looking men of the first bandon came cautiously out to meet us.

'Protospatharios,' one of them said in greeting. 'What are your orders?'

'Keep the imperial residence secure, as you have so faithfully. I will go to the empress and emperor in turn and talk to them.' Harald looked around. 'Where is your komes?'

'Dead. He was with Aki at the gate. I am his second.'

Harald nodded sympathetically. 'How many of you are still fit to fight?'

'Not many. Twenty? The fighting was terrible. Dozens of us were taken in the first moments and the fight at the Chalke Gate. Most of the rest fell defending the palace. We were moments from defeat when you arrived. I'm sorry, Commander. We were unprepared for the betrayal of the Vigla.'

'Do not be sorry, brother. You did your duty. My men will replace yours where needed. Take however many you need. You have done well and will be rewarded.'

'Thank you, Commander. I must ask, is it over? Is there more of them to come?'

Harald thought about it for a moment and shook his head. 'It is unlikely. They did not have time to gather more. But remain alert, it is not impossible. Where are the rest of the Vigla? How did they let these traitors secure the gates?'

'Most of the Vigla were despatched to quell a riot outside the walls. I don't know what happened after that. Some of the remaining Vigla turned on us and then these bastards stormed through the Chalke Gate, out of nowhere. We barely got the doors of the inner palace closed in time.'

'Despatched by who?' Harald said, his brows narrowing.

'I don't know.'

'I see. Thank you, Komes.'

The man looked confused. 'I am not the komes, Commander.'

'You are now. The first is yours. Get to your duties.'

The man straightened up and nodded.

Harald turned to me and nodded his head to follow, but as we did, there was a commotion at the outer gate and we looked around to see a man in a cloak leading a woman in, and a guardsman moving to block him.

Harald peered at them and Afra spoke up. 'That's Thorir!'

'Let them through!' shouted Harald, waving at the guards who had blocked the pair.

'Who does he have with him?' I asked.

Thorir half dragged his unwilling prisoner along and presented her to Harald. He was dressed as a servant, and although the woman he was dragging wore simple clothes you could see by their quality and her bearing that she was not.

'I caught her trying to sneak out of the palace through the Hippodrome tunnels. I thought you would want to speak to her.'

Harald smiled and put a finger under the defiant woman's chin, lifting it slightly.

'Hello, Maria.'

24

Maria's eyes blazed as she glared up at Harald.

'I thought you might be involved in this treason,' Harald said.

Maria just wriggled against the unkind hands that held her, and Harald motioned to Thorir to release her.

'I was not. Let me go. What reason do you have to treat me like this?'

'Your dog Bardas is dead. I killed him,' said Harald with relish.

Maria swallowed hard.

'It's what we do with traitors.'

'Will you kill me too then, Harald?' she asked, meeting his eye with a great deal more courage and confidence than Bardas had. God, she was beautiful, even then. Perhaps more so then.

'I wouldn't have to consider it if you had just obeyed me and stayed away from the city. But you can't stop, can you? You can't help yourself.'

'Really, Harald? You criticise me for coming back to the city when I was ordered not to, for getting involved in politics and seeking power? What a hypocrite you are.' She glowered at him and Harald laughed.

'That is a fair point, and well made. Anyway, no, I will not be killing you. There are questions to be asked, your conspirators' identities to be discovered. And then a trial, I am sure.' He looked at her sadly. 'I think you will wish I had killed you.'

Maria looked like she might be sick, but she managed to stay on her feet.

'Take me to the emperor, then. For his judgement.'

Harald looked at her wryly and then shook his head. 'No. You would like that, wouldn't you? I think he would not be a fair judge in this... situation.'

Harald was being careful what he said in front of so many of his men, not daring outright to suggest that to hand Maria over to the emperor was effectively to hand her over to her co-conspirator – John.

'It is my right to plead my case to him. I am a noblewoman of the empire.'

Harald nodded slowly. 'That might be true. But I think one imperial family member is as good as another. Let's take you to the empress instead. I feel she might be more... interested, in hearing the truth from you.'

Harald smiled and firmly took hold of Maria's arm.

'Come then, Eric. Let's see Empress Zoe first, and then it will be time to face the emperor and his brother.'

He pushed Maria along in front of him and turned to talk to Afra. 'Go and make sure no one enters or leaves the emperor's quarters until I get there. No one. Do you understand?'

Afra nodded and headed off into the palace.

We went through the blood-spattered doorway into the palace. Maria covered her mouth in horror when she saw the dozen or so bodies that had been dragged to one side, their blood smeared and pooled on the flagstones.

'It's not what you expect, is it, when you plan such things? You don't imagine the blood and the shit and the cries of dying men that emanate from your plotting,' said Harald in a dark tone.

Maria just turned her head away from the ghastly sight and sobbed once.

'Now you have to see the consequences, the bodies stacked like firewood. Not the last consequences for you, I suspect,' he added.

I remembered, three years before, when Harald had quietly confessed to me that he still loved Maria and that he exiled her because he couldn't trust himself around her, even after her betrayal.

Clearly, three years apart had hardened his heart. He was leading her to her likely death, and he was calm and even a little pleased. Well, a lot had happened to him in the intervening years, but I couldn't help feeling it was wrong to have such glee.

We reached the doors to the empress's quarters and Styrbjorn was there. He looked at Maria in curiosity but jerked a thumb through the closed door. 'Empress Zoe is safe inside with some of my men. We are guarding every entrance.'

'Good man. Stay here. Zoe will want to have a talk with my friend here, alone.'

Styrbjorn nodded nonchalantly and rapped on the door, which opened from the inside to reveal another pair of guardsmen, incongruous in their filthy, road-worn equipment inside the empress's beautiful anteroom.

Harald pushed Maria past them and Styrbjorn ordered them to wait outside, leaving the three of us alone. The usually spotless floor had been trampled on by dozens of dirty soldiers' boots, but otherwise, the place was undisturbed. There had been no fighting in there; no traitors had reached Zoe's inner quarters.

We went through and found the empress in the fountain room, staring out of a window. She looked up and her expression was alarmed when she saw us. She looked utterly terrified.

'Basilissa. The attack is over, and I bring you one of the culprits.'

'The culprits?' she said with odd confusion, looking between Harald and Maria.

'Yes. I believe John organised this attempted assassination, and conspired with Maria and her mercenary, Bardas, to carry it out. But I am sure, under the right questioning, she will confirm the truth of it.'

Zoe looked at Maria intently, her alarm fading. 'I see. And tell me, Harald, how you came to be here to stop this attack? I thought you were in the west fighting the rebels?'

'We defeated them quickly, and then marched very hard,' said Harald with a pleased smile.

Zoe looked at him carefully and then at Maria. She gestured to the woman. 'Maria, come here.'

Harald kept hold of her. He looked at Zoe in confusion. Nothing about her reaction was what I expected, and clearly Harald saw it too. 'What? Basilissa, she might be dangerous yet.'

'She isn't going to kill me here, in my quarters, with you standing next to her. Let her go.' Zoe spoke softly but with absolute authority. Harald reluctantly let Maria go and she walked over to Zoe with her head bowed and stood beside her.

'You may go now, my child. Through that door behind me. Hypatia will show you to a room where you can stay and be safe.'

'Basilissa? What are you doing?' said Harald in outrage.

Maria turned and smiled sweetly at Harald. 'Thank you, my dear, for not taking me to the emperor.'

Zoe gave her a reproachful look and she bowed her head and disappeared through the door, leaving Harald gaping like a landed fish.

Zoe stood there and stared at him, and her face was angry and sad.

The pieces finally tumbled together for me. I remembered Bardas's dying words: 'We serve the same master.'

'It was you,' croaked Harald, as if he had been run through with a spear. 'All of this... this was you. The traitors weren't trying to kill you; they were going for the emperor.'

'And you ruined it,' spat Zoe with real venom, her face transforming in an instant into a furious mask.

Harald took a step forward, his hand moving to his sword in his anger, and I grabbed at his arm as Zoe's face lit up in alarm.

'Harald, don't,' I hissed.

He stopped, but he did not back up. 'How could you do this? My men were sworn to you, they fought and died out there for you, and it was you who killed them? They died to protect you, and yours was the voice that ordered their deaths?'

'I tried to make sure you were away!' said Zoe angrily. 'John, in his stupidity and petty fear, cleared the city of your men and gave me one final opportunity to save myself. So I made my plans. It took months. Months! When you arrived back to the city unannounced just before the plan was to commence I tried to make sure you were far away, but you returned! Why couldn't you just stay away, Harald? I created a rebellion for you to go and subdue. If you had just stayed there you would have returned to find me the sole ruler of the city. We could have rebuilt the empire together, you and I, ended the corruption and the decay and the squabbles of petty men. But you returned. Why did you return?'

'I came back to protect you!' replied Harald in a pained,

guttural moan. 'And what of the first bandon? They never left the city, they were always going to die. Those are my men out there, my brothers, their bodies are stacked outside your *fucking door*!' Harald jabbed a finger at the empress and two of her attendants appeared from another room, short Greek swords in hand, and Zoe held up her hands to restrain them.

'I'm sorry, Harald, but men die for us. That is the way of the world. How many men have died for your desire to rule Norway?' Her eyes blazed with the accusation.

Harald swallowed and froze. It was true; he couldn't deny it.

'That is different! They died fighting our enemies, not by my own orders!'

'They died the same!'

Harald shook his head, furious with the comparison. 'But why, why did you have to do this? Why resort to this?'

'I was trying to save the empire from John! He has abandoned the imperium of my fathers to rebels and traitors, and I can do nothing! I am a prisoner in these walls, Harald. At his order. He is emperor in all but name. It was only a matter of time before he had me killed or replaced, and then the useless spawn of his brothers would rule what was left of this empire until they finally destroyed it! My birthright, my father's empire!'

She shouted the last part and nearly choked, such was the strength of her emotion, and Harald visibly backed down.

'How could I let him do that? What wouldn't you do, Harald, to make sure your brother's kingdom wasn't lost to cowards and traitors?'

'I would do anything,' said my prince without hesitation.

'And you judge me for doing the same? For doing what needed to be done?'

Harald stepped back like he had been stabbed, and his face fell. 'I...'

'You would conquer half the world to have the throne of your country back, and such is your right. But so would I!'

Harald tried to compose himself. 'It is true, Basilissa. And I am sorry. I was just... shocked. I was so certain John was behind this. To find out it was you... If I had known...'

'Why would it be John? John wouldn't need an assault on the palace to kill me. He could do it himself with Michael watching and no one would lift a finger!'

'My men would, they would have put themselves between his blade and you and died to protect you.'

Zoe's anger also softened and she nodded. 'I know, Harald. But there were too few of them left to protect me for when John finally made his move. And it grieved me to betray them. It grieves me even more that it was all for nothing.'

'For nothing?' Harald asked, looking at her.

'It's over for me now, isn't it, Harald? Your gallant attempt to save me has condemned me.'

Harald looked aside and thought about it, staring into the fountain for a while.

'Who knows?'

'Who knows what?'

Harald stared at her. 'Who knows this was your plot?'

Zoe blinked and considered it. 'Bardas, Maria, a couple of my closest followers, and everyone in this room.'

'That's it?'

'That's it. Maria and my followers I could keep quiet. But Bardas will confess, if questioned.'

Harald huffed a short laugh. 'Bardas won't be questioned. Not in this world.'

Zoe's face brightened as she saw a glimmer of hope. 'Then perhaps we can keep this secret. What do you propose?' She looked utterly desperate, forlorn, helpless. I couldn't help but feel a single pang of sympathy, which I quickly and furiously quashed.

'You cannot trust Maria.'

'I don't need to.'

'Why? She was allied to your sister Theodora and abandoned her. Then she was allied with John, and apparently, you managed to persuade her to change sides yet again. How could you trust her after that?' Harald said in bewilderment. 'She will betray anyone or anything if she thinks it benefits her.'

'Yes, but that is how I can trust her. I trust her to follow her self-interests, and I offered her what she wanted.'

'And what was that?'

'To be my heir.'

Harald's eyes bulged. 'Your heir?'

'Yes. She wants to be the empress and I will not have children. So I will adopt her, formally, and she will finally have what she wants. I was going to let her marry Michael's successor after this was over but...' She gave Harald a tired and pointed look. 'She will have to wait a little longer for that chance.'

Harald thought about it for a moment. 'If you adopt her, let alone let her marry the next emperor, then she stands to benefit from your death.'

Zoe smiled. 'True, so it seems like I will need a devoted protector who doesn't trust her to keep me safe. Anyway, Maria's loyalty won't matter unless I can survive today. My life is in your hands, yet again. How will you save me from Michael learning the truth, Harald?'

Harald tapped his finger on his lip and tilted his head to one side. 'We could blame it on your sister Theodora.'

I think I might have choked. I was still fuming, beyond angry that Zoe had caused the deaths of so many of our men. Yet here was Harald, already over it, making plans with the traitor to cover up her tracks.

Both of them heard the noise and turned to me, and Harald had the decency to look embarrassed.

'I'm sorry, Eric. What other choice do we have?'

'Taking the person who tried to murder the emperor and slaughtered our comrades to justice!' I said indignantly, ignoring the quiet inner voice that sympathised with her.

'Be careful, guardsman – that is your empress you are talking about,' said Zoe with a withering glare.

I looked from her to Harald. 'Our oaths are to the emperor and empress both; you cannot ignore this attack.'

'No, but nor can I deliver the empress to be executed.'

'Then our duty is to the throne itself, to the continuation of the empire!'

'And how will that continue with John controlling the palace? Giving away the empire province by province?' asked Zoe, and I ignored her because it was a good point and I was furious and imagining killing her with my bare hands to cover my uncertainty.

'Remember what we are doing here, Eric,' said Harald.

'I honestly cannot, Harald. I am not sure that you do, either.'

His eyes narrowed and he nodded slowly. 'We have to take a side here now. There is no longer any choice. If we hand over Zoe, John will remain in charge of the empire unopposed, we will be exiled and we will return to Kyiv to live out our lives in obscurity, without the money or the power to return home unless as Yaroslav's pet.'

I grimaced; it was not a good prospect.

'But If we allow Zoe to remain on the throne, and ally with her to control John and Michael...' He paused and looked pointedly at the empress.

'You will be richly rewarded,' she said, smiling for the first time.

Harald looked at me. 'I do remember why we are here, Eric. Truly. And I remember what you said in Italy by that wretched river about taking our men home, not wasting their lives. What could waste their lives more than failing in our task when so many have already died?'

I glared at him, hurt and angry, because I knew he was right. The men Zoe had killed were dead, and nothing could change that any more than the men whose bodies we had left beneath Sicilian soil could be brought back to life, laughing and joking and telling drunken stories of their glory.

The men who had died were gone, and Harald needed Zoe alive and in power in order to achieve his aims.

I shook my head angrily, the denial of it burning at me. 'This is not right, Harald.'

'Yet it is what we will do,' Harald said. 'I am sorry. It will be hard for you, but you will follow me in this.'

'Others will work out the truth. Afra, Thorir at the least. This secret is too big to keep.'

'I will speak to the brothers. They will get in line. This is what they do.'

'They are more honourable than you think.'

'And they are more pragmatic than you think.'

I crumbled and accepted that the decision was already made.

Zoe looked back at Harald with new intensity. 'Go to my husband, convince him that Theodora was behind this. And find a way to get rid of John, or at least remove him from power. Or this will all happen again.'

'I will. But you need to understand, Empress, that I will have requests later, and they will be granted.' Harald gave the empress a hard look and she tilted her head softly in acceptance.

Harald looked back at me with a hard expression. 'Come, Eric. I need you looking like a man who just helped me save the empire.'

I clamped my mouth shut and looked away from him, distraught.

I have told you, being Harald's man was not an easy path, it tested every part of my honour, my courage and my soul. They call me Eric the Follower and damn you all, I earned that name.

25

We walked back through the palace towards the emperor's quarters, and I tried to hold my tongue as we passed the scene of several small but bloody battles. Varangians had made desperate barricades in corridors and doorways. Piling furniture and tearing down parts of walls to block access and create a point they could defend.

Some had been successful.

Others had not, and even then our comrades were carefully clearing their bodies away.

We went through into the emperor's quarters, and the new komes of the first was there, along with twenty or so guardsmen from many different banda, who stood shoulder to shoulder around the doors to the emperor's chambers like the loyal brothers they were.

The Greek traitors had not made it this far, and the hallway was pristine, out of place in that battlefield of the palace.

'I need to see the emperor,' said Harald to the new komes, who nodded and motioned to his men to move aside.

We went through the doorway and antechambers into the

emperor's vast, octagonal bedchamber. Michael was sitting on his bed, drinking something steaming from a cup an attendant was holding for him.

He looked up as we approached, and I was shocked. For a man of little over thirty years, he looked frail and withered. His face was pale and he looked nervous.

'Harald! What is happening? Is it over?'

'Over? It's probably *his* doing,' said John, who was hovering near the bed.

Harald addressed John first. 'If this was my doing you would be dead, not merely ungrateful.'

Then he looked at the emperor. 'Basileus. The attack is over, and the assailants are dead or captive and the city is secure.'

Michael slumped in relief, and a smile spread across his sickly face. 'Thank God. What happened? Who did this?'

'We believe it was Theodora's faction, attempting to seize the palace and take power.'

Michael looked aghast. 'Theodora?' He looked at John. 'I thought you said we had an agreement with her, that this wouldn't happen again?'

John stared at Harald thoughtfully and then shook his head. 'I do, so I don't believe this is the case. No, not Theodora. What evidence do you have, Harald?'

'The confession of the leader.'

'Bring him here, I would like to hear it myself,' said John with a dismissive wave.

'I don't take orders from you, John, but if you wish to check yourself, he is in the hall of nineteen. My men will escort you there to see him if you wish.'

John looked at Harald suspiciously and then back at Michael. 'I will return quickly.'

Then he swept from the room, giving Harald a dubious glare.

Emperor's Axe

The moment John was out, Harald quickly walked over to the emperor's bed and got down on one knee beside it. 'Michael, the true problem here is not Theodora, for her people surely did this without consulting her. The problem is the man who sent your guard away from the palace and left you vulnerable for his own selfish ends.'

'John?'

'Yes. Why did you allow him to dismiss us?'

'He said you couldn't be trusted, were foreigners who cared for nothing but gold.'

'And have we not proven that wrong? My men died for you today, by the hundred. We took sacred oaths to defend you and we have. We were banned from the city and then sent to a distant province, yet when we heard you were in danger, we marched a hundred miles in three days, barely pausing to sleep, eating almost nothing, to sail here and rescue you. What further proof of our loyalty do you require?'

Michael put his head in his hands and sobbed. 'I'm sorry, Harald. Oh God, John was so sure you would side with Zoe and betray me, and I believed him.'

'Never. I do not take sides. I could kill you, right now, claim the rebels did it, and make Zoe empress, could I not?'

Michael looked up from his hands nervously, and then around the room. He suddenly realised the danger. 'But you wouldn't?' he squeaked nervously.

Harald shook his head and drew his seax, pressing it into the terrified man's hand. 'If you believe I could betray you like that, kill me now. Take my life and trust my men to continue to serve you, for they earned that right today.'

Michael stared at the huge knife as if it might attack him, his eyes wide and his breathing hard. Then he pushed it back towards Harald with trembling fingers. 'I believe you, Harald. I am sorry that I ever doubted you.'

Harald nodded sagely and put the knife back in its sheath.

'I don't know if John is unfaithful, or merely a fool, but he sent us from your side and made you vulnerable.'

Michael nodded miserably.

'He sent us to Sicily and Italy, and in his jealousy and spite he sacrificed those provinces in order that we might be lost with them. Do you know this, Michael? Or did he hide it from you?'

Michael looked up at Harald and I thought the shame might break him. 'I know it,' he whispered. 'John said it was necessary, that we could cleanse the empire of traitors like you and Maniakes, and that we would take back the provinces later. But then the Bulgarians rebelled, and... Everything is out of control and I cannot stop it.'

Harald nodded and I saw the blood vessel in his temple throbbing with anger at Michael's weakness, but he controlled his expression and his voice. He took the emperor's hand in his. 'The thing that you must first control – and defeat – is the man who whispers in your ear that everyone else is a traitor.'

'Harald, he is my brother. He is the reason I am emperor.'

'No, Michael – he is the reason you are *not* the emperor,' said Harald firmly. 'He uses you as a farmer might use a donkey. He has all the power, and you bear all the burden.'

Michael looked horrified.

'He has taken over every aspect of imperial power, and though I am sure he cares for you, he cares for himself far more.'

'But, he protects me from Zoe.'

'I will protect you from Zoe. I already have, and always will,' said Harald with such conviction that even I believed him.

Michael's eyes lit up, and he even smiled a little. God, he was such a weak man.

'Truly?'

'Truly. I have sworn to it, and my word is iron.'

Michael nodded. 'What do you want me to do?'

'I simply want you to be the emperor, Michael. I want you to find it in yourself to rule, not be ruled. I want to help you take back the empire from these rebels and traitors, under your leadership. I know you can finally be the man you must always have wanted to be. Is there greatness in you, Michael?'

Michael straightened pathetically as he sat. 'Yes!' he whispered, almost daring to believe it.

'Then be that man!' said Harald with a rumbling force, dragging the frail emperor to his feet. 'Take control of your empire, be the ruler the empire needs in a dark time!'

'Yes!' said Michael, barely managing to keep the squeak of excitement out of his tone.

'I will protect you, but I will not control you as others would. I will be your shield and your sword, your strength and your vengeance, but not your mind! I will follow your orders, not whisper them like poison in your ears.' Harald drew the seax again, the heavy, bright blade. 'This oath I swear!' And he dramatically sliced the blade across the meat of his own palm, drawing dark blood that ran from his hand in a rivulet, Michael's eyes watching in rapt fascination.

Now, perhaps you all know already, but blood-letting is not involved in the secret ceremony of oath-taking we Varangians hold when we join the guard. But Michael didn't know that, and he was rapt and completely swept away by it. He stared at Harald in inspired glee, even as the door behind us slammed open, and his brother came scurrying into the room again.

'He is dead!' John shouted angrily.

'Who is dead?' Michael said, looking at his brother in confusion.

'The traitor leader. Harald sent me to interview a dead man, one apparently he himself killed!'

'You didn't ask me if he was alive,' Harald said calmly, without taking his eyes off the emperor. 'I would have told you if you had. I just told you where to find him.'

John came over to Michael's side and put his hand on the emperor's hand, staring at Harald in triumphant spite. 'You have heard enough from this man. Send him from us. I am sure he was behind this whole affair, probably just to try and earn your favour. A pathetic attempt.'

He tried to lead Michael back to the bed, but he was surprised when Michael resisted.

'Come, brother, there has been enough stress on you today. You must rest.'

'You always say I must rest,' said Michael in a detached voice.

'Yes, you are sick.'

'Maybe I am sick because I always rest, and do not attend to my duties.'

'Nonsense, Michael. The doctors say you need rest, and I am happy to attend to your duties while you recover.'

'I will never recover, John. And you know it.'

'There is always hope. Come, to bed.'

'No,' Michael said and pulled his hand away.

John reached for the emperor's arm again but before he made contact a heavy hand grabbed his wrist, calloused fingers pressing into his soft flesh.

'The emperor gave an instruction, eunuch,' Harald rumbled. 'Do not touch him.'

John looked up at Harald in outrage. 'Get your hand off me!' But Harald didn't react so John turned to his brother to protest. 'Order this brute to release me!'

Michael looked at them both for a moment, torn, but then he

shook his head. 'No. He is right. You were not listening to me. You never listen to me.'

John suddenly realised how dramatically the situation had changed, and his face rippled with shock and fear. 'But, brother, I just do what is best for you.'

Michael shook his head angrily. 'No, you do what is best for *you*.'

'Brother?'

'Be quiet, John, and listen to me.'

'Michael, you can't.'

Harald clamped his other hand over John's mouth, and the eunuch's shocked eyes looked up at Harald's monolithic form. 'The emperor said to be silent,' Harald whispered with deathly intensity.

Michael looked fraught as his brother wriggled and squeaked in Harald's hands.

'Release him, Harald, please?' Michael asked.

Harald let go of John instantly, and the shocked man backed up a few steps.

'As you command, Basileus,' Harald said, bowing his head and stepping back to stand by Michael's side.

Michael looked thrilled and a little surprised at the deference and instant compliance Harald had shown. It was really a masterful performance.

John saw it too, and his face clouded over with fury and fear. 'What has he told you, Michael? What lies has he spoken?'

'He has told me nothing but the truth I already knew, John.'

'Lies!'

'No. All he has done is supported me, and made me remember who I am, who I can be.'

'He has tricked you!'

'Be quiet!' Michael shouted, his pale face reddening. 'Or I will have him silence you again!'

John stammered to a halt, and he shot a look of pure poison at Harald.

Michael calmed himself and adjusted his fabulous tunic before he spoke again.

'John, by my order you are stripped of all your titles, power and positions. As recognition of your service, and our familial ties, you will not be tried for your treason in enabling this attack on the palace.'

'Enabling?' croaked John, and Harald took half a pace forward but Michael restrained him with a gesture and Harald stilled, allowing the emperor to wield him with utter obedience, something I could see was thrilling Michael, to have such power and violence at his fingertips to command.

'Yes. You sent my loyal guard away from the palace and left me vulnerable.' Michael said.

John sagged but did not reply.

'I will be the emperor, for as long as God gives me on this earth. I will fulfil my duties, not trust them to another. I will lift up this empire to its past glory and I will...' Michael suddenly slowed, and his eyes bulged and his raised hand shook, then his body twitched.

'Oh, no,' whispered John, as the emperor fell to the floor and started convulsing.

'Michael!' cried John, and several of the emperor's attendants rushed to Michael's side as Harald and I looked on.

'What is happening?' said Harald in alarm.

'Get out of the way, oaf!' John said, kneeling by his brother and putting his hands under Michael's head as the emperor's eyes rolled and his hands clutched at thin air. Bubbles started pouring from his mouth and his breathing became ragged.

'Have you poisoned him?' snapped Harald in fury.

'No! If he died you would kill me; I need him alive more than you do. Now back away!'

Harald took a step back, completely thrown by this sudden turn of events.

John cradled his brother's head softly, showing genuine care. 'This is a sickness. It happens to him from time to time and we know what to do,' said John, and Harald finally backed away from the thrashing Michael with a look of shock and distaste.

'Get the doctors!' shrieked John, and another attendant rushed from the room.

We stood there in silence as the emperor's people supported him, and as the doctors blew the smoke of incense into his face and rubbed a lotion on his forehead as the emperor's convulsions died away and disappeared.

Finally, they put him back in his bed, and Michael recovered his sensibilities, but he was pale and his voice was weak when he finally spoke.

'I'm sorry you saw that, Harald,' he whispered.

Harald was still shocked, but he tried not to appear so. 'Do not worry, Basileus.'

'You must keep it a secret. The people cannot know I have Caesar's curse.'

'Caesar's curse?' Harald looked around.

John looked up as if Harald were simple. 'Julius Caesar, the first ruler of the empire, had this sickness. He kept it a secret lest the people think him weak.'

Harald's eyes narrowed. 'And people now know this Caesar had this sickness?'

'Yes.'

'And he was a great man?'

'Yes.'

Harald shrugged. 'Then it is a mark of greatness, no? Given by God?'

'Caesar was a pagan,' said John with contempt.

Harald shrugged. 'You do not have to believe in God for his work to be real.'

'Well said, Harald. But still, I would prefer you keep my secret,' said Michael.

'I will. What are your other orders, Basileus?'

Michael sighed and then looked at John. 'I need you to take my brother away, somewhere safe and comfortable.' He gave John a sympathetic look. 'Do not harm him,' he added, sternly, and Harald nodded.

John's face fell. 'Brother, how could you do this to me?'

'You overstepped, John. You tried to make a token of me, bent my empire to your personal desires, and it nearly killed me and my realm. I need to rule without you for a while and repair the damage. Then, when it is settled, we will be brothers again and you will return to my service.'

John seemed slightly relieved at this, and Harald kept his disappointment hidden.

'Go with the guard commander now. I will send men to ensure you are well looked after.'

Harald gently took hold of the eunuch's arm, and John surrendered to his grip.

'He will be well accommodated, Basileus. As befitting the brother of the emperor.'

'Thank you, Harald, for everything. Now please go, I must rest after my sickness strikes. Come to me in two days, and we will discuss the revival of the empire's fortunes.'

'As you command, Basileus.'

Harald led John from the room with me following, and we made our way through the shattered, blood-soaked halls of the palace. The men had made a lot of progress clearing the bodies away, but only so far as to stack the traitors in the courtyard like bushels of wheat, while the dead Varangians were laid out in sad rows on their cloaks, weapons on their chests.

'Behold, the men that you would claim were disloyal, who died for your brother,' rumbled Harald as John looked at the rows of fallen heroes. 'How ashamed you must feel to have said that, for you would be dead if it were true.'

'I never questioned the men's loyalty, only their leader.'

'Maybe, but I came a long way to save the emperor, John, I lost a great number of my men to do it, and if you accuse me of being unfaithful to my oaths again, I will break one for the first time and take your life in compensation for the insult.'

John had the good sense not to reply, because he knew Harald was capable of it.

We walked out of the palace and John sighed. 'You are much smarter than I thought, Harald. I congratulate you on your victory.'

'And you are not as smart as you thought, John.'

John smiled wryly. 'It is not over, you know?'

'Oh, I know, but, unlike you, I already know how the next round will end.'

'Do you?'

'Yes,' said Harald with quiet confidence, and then he waved at Afra, who was walking down the path towards us. The old bandit came over and looked at John with interest.

'You need him to be found floating in the Golden Horn tomorrow?' Afra said with a smile.

John shrank back in fear at the ease with which Afra joked about his murder.

Harald smiled. 'Sadly not. The emperor orders that he be isolated somewhere, somewhere comfortable and safe.'

Afra shrugged with disappointment and stared at John. 'Shame. You put some friends of mine in the sea with sliced throats. I long to return the favour. But short of that, I look forward to being your gaoler.'

John just shrank back a little and looked at Harald pleadingly. 'My brother ordered that I should be well looked after!'

Harald smiled down, his wolfish, victorious smile as he handed John over to the old bandit. 'Oh, John, I assure you that you will be very well looked after.'

26

A week later, Harald and I stood on the harbourside as Halldor stepped into the longship behind the rest of his crew.

I was sad to see him leave, but the Icelander's wound was terrible. His eyesight was afflicted and he would never lead men into battle again. Instead, he was taking the long voyage home, loaded down with gold and silver, including a beautifully decorated sword and scabbard that had been a personal gift from Harald.

Halldor turned to look at us from the ship, and his broken face cracked into a half-twisted smile. 'I will still be the most sought-after husband in Iceland!' he said, hefting his fabulous sword.

'I believe you, Halldor,' said Harald with a laugh.

Then Halldor ordered the crew to cast off, and the longship moved out into the water, bound for Kyiv with another deep load of our silver and gold, where they would leave Halldor to continue his journey home and return to us.

Michael had rewarded the entire guard handsomely for saving him, and we were one big step closer to the wealth we needed to regain Norway. Not only that, but Harald was a hero of the empire again. Although the emperor ordered the attempted assassination to be downplayed, too many people were aware of it to hide it completely, so the city knew that some rogue traitorous soldiers had tried to kill the emperor and empress and that the brave men of the guard under Harald had defeated them.

We had buried nearly two hundred guardsmen who had died in the fighting together under a great tomb outside the city beside the guard's training ground, with Aki at their head, so that everyone who approached the main gate of the city would see the monument to the protectors of the palace.

Harald and I stood there in companiable silence as the ship rowed away.

'You know, I had a thought,' I said.

'Hmm?'

'Bardas. He really was on our side, after all, he was Zoe's man. Not a true traitor.'

Harald grunted. 'Maybe, but do you claim he did not deserve his fate?'

'Oh, no. We found him slaughtering our men. He deserved every bit of it.'

Harald nodded. 'I only wish I had killed him sooner, or that I could do it again.'

'But Zoe was the culprit, not Bardas, and you have forgiven her.'

'I won't forget it,' said Harald. 'I may forgive her, I may understand her reasons, but I saw our men lying there in rows, I helped turn the soil to put them in the ground. Don't worry, Eric. I will not forget.'

I nodded. 'Good. Because I heard about your visits to her

quarters in the last few days. The ones you didn't take me along for.'

Harald stiffened and I laughed. 'So it is true?' I turned to grin at him. 'You really are, aren't you?'

Harald glared at me. 'How do you know?'

I shrugged. 'I have knowledgeable friends; nothing much happens in the palace without them knowing.'

'Ah, Afra. Afra found out and told you.'

I shook my head in mock indignation. 'Afra? No, Afra would never dare to come to me, his best friend, and tell me our prince was secretly ploughing a furrow into the empress of the Romans.'

Harald punched me in the shoulder, hard enough to hurt. 'Don't talk about her in such base terms,' he growled, and I could see he was truly angry.

'I remember you telling her you would have requests that she would grant, but I didn't think one of them would be allowing you into her bed.'

'It is not like that. I did not request it.' He paused. 'It was she who led us down that path, not me.'

'And did you go willingly, or are you just expanding your duties to her?'

Harald glowered. 'Willingly. Now stop provoking me.'

'Sorry, but I had to know if you cared,' I replied, rubbing my throbbing shoulder. 'You really have strong feelings for her, don't you?'

Harald looked indignant, but he nodded slowly. 'She is a wondrous woman. Unlike any I have ever met. But also this allows me to be close to her, to help control her.'

'Very close to her, I understand.' I laughed at him softly and he smouldered. 'Are you sure she isn't using you? She has seduced you for a reason. She isn't in this for love, Harald.'

'I know,' he said. 'We both know it. We are both using each other, we both need each other's support. She tells me things as a lover that she would never tell me as an empress.'

'So you get what you want from her?'

Harald nodded.

'And what about what she wants? She wants you to stay, you know that, right? She wants you to stay and help her rule after Michael is dead. She has no interest in giving you what you need to leave and letting you go back to Norway. She is allowing you into her bed because she wants to trap you there between her legs. This isn't love for her, Harald; this is politics conducted without clothes.'

Harald stared out to sea, after the receding ship with our treasure in it. 'I know it. I won't forget what we are here for, Eric. I swear it. My home is in Norway, not in the bed of an empress, however glorious she might be.'

I wasn't entirely convinced, but I had done my duty to our men by reminding him and could push it no further.

'And what of Maria?'

'What of her?'

'Do you still love her?'

Harald thought about it for a moment. 'I don't know. Perhaps, but not as before. The empress has ordered me to be at peace with her newly adopted daughter, so I am. But Thorir is watching her and her people carefully, and I am ready for her next betrayal, even if Zoe is not.'

I nodded. 'That is good.'

'So, what do we do next? Your plans must extend beyond lazing away your days in the empress's bedchamber.'

'Actually, a few weeks of that seems like a very pleasant thought, after all we have been through.' Harald smiled, and I almost believed him.

'Pfft, you will be bored within the month.'

'Yes, it is true – I feel it already. But I have spoken to Michael, and he is intent on a campaign against the Bulgarians. He wants to lead it himself, with me as his strategos.'

'Really? Strategos?'

Harald smiled broadly. 'Yes. No more being seconded to a Greek general, no more politics. He is ready to unleash me on his enemies with the full power of the empire in my hand.' He glowed in that moment, standing there, almost rippling with the pleasure the thought of that power gave him. His first command of an army, the full weight of the empire of the Romans to command.

'When?' I said, with breathless excitement at the thought.

'Soon, just a few weeks while the troops are gathered.'

'A summer campaign, then?'

'Well, summer and autumn. The emperor wants the rebellion over by winter, to not allow it to drag into another year.'

'Why?'

Harald's smile faded a little. 'Because he is not sure he will see another year, and needs a victory, a legacy to leave.'

'You sympathise with him?'

Harald laughed and nodded. 'I do, a little. I do not claim that I will mourn him, but when we arrived he was a drunk and a womaniser, absorbed with parties and debauchery. This illness and the attempt on his life have sobered him. What he speaks of now is his legacy and his empire, the glory and security of his people.' He shrugged. 'I can respect that. Even at this moment, he is trying to become a better man.'

'That will make it difficult when Zoe plots against him again.'

'And I will be there to prevent her doing so. I never said any of this would be easy, Eric. But if it were, there would be far less glory in it. Anyway, speaking of Zoe, she has invited me to see her this afternoon. Now that you know about my new relationship with her, you can come and keep watch outside her quarters to make sure we are not discovered.'

I laughed, and then my laughter faded as I realised he wasn't joking.

'You want me to stand guard at the door while you lay with the empress?'

Harald grinned slyly at me. 'Yes.'

I scowled at him and shook my head in disbelief. We started walking away from the docks.

'Is there no one else? I had my own plans,' I added hopefully, for Harald was not the only one who had found a woman in the city, although mine was a beautiful and energetic serving girl from our favourite tavern, not an empress. We were very different men, you see, despite our closeness.

'Then cancel them. This is a vital diplomatic mission, Eric, and I need my most trusted friend to ensure it is kept a secret,' Harald said with sickening joy and a smug smile.

'What a life you lead, Harald. What a life you lead.'

'*We* lead, Eric. We lead. Isn't it glorious? Now, we mustn't be late. Zoe gets terribly irritated if I am late, and she will take her anger out on me in terribly creative ways. Do you know the strange behaviours of the Roman nobility in the bedroom? I bet that you do not. It is nothing like our own people, let me assure you.'

'Harald, please,' I protested, feeling a little nauseous.

But he was enjoying torturing me far too much to stop. 'It is a long walk through the city, and I will explain it to you. Honestly, some of the things she does. She has a servant in the room at all times to hand her iced drinks. Can you imagine that? She just watches us, waiting for a signal. It is quite strange. Not that that is the only thing she has the servant do.'

'Harald, for the love of God!' I tried to put my mind in a different place as he joyfully recounted to me his adventures in Zoe's quarters, and it was, as he promised, a long and disturbingly enlightening walk back to the palace.

On my mother's name, I hated that man sometimes. It was easier to follow him into the thick of the most ferocious battle than it was to suffer that long walk through the city. We arrived at the empress's private quarters and Harald gave me a look and a wink before heading inside which made me want to punch his teeth out.

But I didn't, of course. Not because I was sworn to him. The time when my words alone bound me to his side was long gone by then. I stood watch on that door and exchanged knowing looks with Zoe's own guard while Harald risked his life to bed an empress because I loved him like a brother, and would have laid down my life without a thought to save his.

He was sometimes a fool, hot-headed and callous. But he was the greatest of men, with the ambition and vision that only the high kings of the world can even aspire to. He lived his entire life with the relentless pursuit of legacy and glory, with all the despair and sacrifice and magnificence that goes with it.

He demanded everything from those who served him, their unbreakable devotion and often their very lives, but in return, we marched in the footsteps of a giant and knew glory and infamy that no other man can ever aspire to. We bled for his desires and watched friends and comrades die for his rise. But in return, for as long as we draw breath, we earned the right to say, 'I walked with Hardrada' – and all men know what that means.

EPILOGUE

Eric smiled sadly around the field and pulled his blanket around himself more tightly. The last rays of the sun were on the mountains behind the town, and their warmth was long gone from the meeting field.

'I think it is time, my friends, to admit that I am defeated, that the cold has breached the walls of my flesh and fought its way right into the citadel of my bones. Retreat is the only option, retreat into the hall the way my balls have already retreated into my stomach.'

There was a ripple of laughter from the assembled men, sitting on the great rows of benches or crowded around the margins, for so many had gathered that there was not enough room in the gathering place for them all to sit.

'Will you continue the tale inside?' asked Ingvarr hopefully.

Eric smiled and shook his head. 'No, not tonight. I have rudely interrupted this great meeting every evening so far and I know you all secretly wish to talk and drink and swap tales of home with those you have not seen for months or years. So, you should do so, and this old man will cease his rumblings about the past.'

Ingvarr looked disappointed, but Jarl Hakon stood from his seat near the front and nodded gravely.

'I am glad you admitted you were cold, and saved me the shame of admitting it first. I am longing for the comforts of the hall and a good mug of ale.'

Eric smiled and gestured comically to the audience to get up and leave, and there was a ripple in the seated ranks as men stood and stretched, talking to their fellows and heading to the hall, many of them thanking Eric as they went.

'It was a fine story, Eric, as always. Surely, we must be coming towards the conclusion?' said Jarl Halfdan, walking to the front as Hakon helped Eric to his feet.

Eric smiled graciously at the lord of Tinghaugen. 'I do find the story takes longer to recount than I remember. The excitement gets into me and I feel I must recount every detail, but maybe tomorrow will be the last, although I will only continue if men want me to do so. Do you wish me to stop, Jarl Halfdan? I hope I am not offending you with my tales?'

Jarl Halfdan smiled and looked around them at the mass of men headed into the hall to drink and talk. 'I think if I tried to stop you there would be a murder, and then a new lord of Tinghaugen.'

Eric laughed and waved the notion away humbly. 'No, no. It is just a story to pass the time while we wait for the Thing.'

'Don't be so modest, Eric. You tell tales of power and powerful men; don't pretend innocence at the influence you are exerting.'

Eric looked at Halfdan and saw that although he was smiling, there was a hardness behind the pleasantry. Hakon and Ingvarr, still standing to Eric's side, felt the tension rise too and looked on awkwardly.

'I seek no influence, Jarl Halfdan,' said Eric disarmingly.

'You have it whether you seek it or not, Eric. But I wonder what you will do with the power you have accrued over the men of this gathering. Will you support your king?'

Eric looked taken aback. 'My life has been nothing but service to my king.'

Halfdan nodded and stepped forward and put his hand gently on Eric's wizened shoulder. 'True, and no man doubts it. But do you serve the king that is living or the long-dead king you have resurrected these last nights with your fine tales? Beware the dead one does not interfere with the plans of the living.'

Eric looked at Halfdan with something approaching regret. 'I am sorry you think that is even possible, Lord Halfdan. King Magnus is Harald's grandson and living legacy. My loyalty is as strong now as it ever was.'

Halfdan smiled and embraced Eric, speaking quietly in his ear so that only the old man could hear.

'You go to great lengths in your stories to portray yourself as far less clever than I know you to be, Eric Sveitungr. And I note you still did not answer the question as to which king you serve.'

Then he patted Eric on the shoulder and glanced at Hakon and his son before walking away towards his hall.

'What happened?' Ingvarr said, even as his father Hakon tried to hush him.

Eric laughed and waved it away. 'Oh, nothing. Politics. Men with power see threats everywhere, even where they do not exist. It is in their nature. In fact, I would say that it is important to do so, for if you do not see the false threats, you certainly will miss some real ones.'

Ingvarr nodded slowly, but his furrowed brows showed he did not really understand.

'Come, let's go inside, Ingvarr,' said Hakon.

'Eric, will you come with us?' asked the boy earnestly.

Eric thought about it for a moment. 'Well, I had intended to go early to my bed tonight, but I am thirsty. One mug of mead, perhaps?'

'Just one, then,' said Ingvarr with a pleased smile, turning to walk towards the hall.

Eric winked at Hakon.

'Just one?' asked Hakon as Eric watched Ingvarr leave. 'I'm not so old as you but I have heard that said many times before, I can't remember it ever being the truth!'

Eric smiled knowingly. 'Just one cup, just one night of storytelling. It's remarkable how our intentions often matter little.'

'Or that we never meant them in the first place. Will it really just be the one this time, Eric?'

Eric's smile deepened. 'You should come with me and find out.'

And then the cheerful old man started his slow meander towards the hall, passing through the last of the crowd, as several who had waited for the opportunity shook him by the arm to thank him.

'What do you think, boy?' Hakon asked his son.

'I think we should go and drink,' replied Ingvarr earnestly.

'Ah, well, that is not what I meant, my boy.' He gave his son a friendly clap on the back, pushing him towards the hall. 'But also, in my experience, it is never a bad idea.'

They started walking, among the last headed towards the hall.

'What did you mean, then?' Ingvarr asked as they walked.

Hakon sighed. 'Oh, it was a question of politics. Let's leave it to another day though, eh?'

'I want to know now.'

Hakon laughed. 'Patience my son, Eric hasn't finished, and I'm sure we will find out tomorrow.'

AFTERWORD AND HISTORICAL NOTE

The latter part of Harald Hardrada's time in the Roman Empire, as depicted in this book, is one of the best and most richly sourced times in his life. Some of his campaigns in this series, such as his earlier adventures against the Pechenengs and his travels to Syria and the Jordan, are reliant on single sources, often very vague in details.

However, his campaigns in Sicily and Italy are very well-sourced by multiple, independent writers. He is mentioned in the sagas, of course, in particular, the so-called 'Morkinskinna' saga which is one of the first and most detailed chronicles of the Norwegian kings of the period. There is also substantial material in the Heimskringla of Snorri Sturluson (much very similar to the Morkinskinna). However, these sagas are openly biased and often fantastical, and on their own are not 'accurate' sources.

In writing this book I was lucky that Harald's participation was confirmed by both Norman and Greek writers. His participation in Georgios Maniakes' spirited but ultimately unsuccessful attempt to return Sicily to Byzantine rule can thus safely be considered part of the historical record, not the semi-mythology that a lot of the sagas sometimes seem to be when they are the only surviving source.

From the Morkinskinna and Heimskringla, there are three remarkable stories of Harald Hardrada using cunning and trickery to capture three Sicilian fortresses. In one, he notices birds that return to a town to roost every evening, and sets some on fire, watching as they return to roost and set the town ablaze. On its face, this is slightly ridiculous, so I tried to adapt that story to make it more plausible (although it still stretches credibility somewhat).

I gave the same treatment to a story of him and his men holding a mock funeral and gaining entry to a 'large town' by that deception. That story I (and others before me) attribute to Syracuse, because although it is known they captured the city, it is not known exactly how or when. This is where I brought William 'Iron-arm' in, who was also with Maniakes in Sicily but is not mentioned in the Icelandic sagas. He is reported by Norman sources to have gained his name in single combat with the emir of Syracuse. And so those two stories were wedded.

The third story, and most realistic at face value, is how Harald captured a strong town above a river by tunnelling through the riverbank and up inside the fortress, spewing forth 'like demons who had emerged from the ground'. For that one, I merely filled out the picture the sagas already paint.

One thing that is difficult when writing using the sagas as a primary source is that they ascribe all success and glory to Harald, and paint all other named figures as useless, cowardly, perfidious and lesser. This obvious bias means sticking to the sagas entirely would be silly, so for example with George Maniakes, who is scorned utterly by Snorri and the Morkinskinna, I

Afterword and historical note

tried to give him a more balanced telling. It's apparent from imperial records that he was both an experienced and successful general, but also clear that he was a terrible politician and frequently feuded with his subordinates and eventually turned rebel. Sticking to the caricature of Maniakes in the sagas and ascribing all successes to Harald would have been a historical disservice to a much more interesting and flawed character.

The locations and general scheme of many battles depicted in this book (Rometta, Troina and Montemaggiore) in Harald's campaigns in Sicily and Italy are also very well-known, unlike at earlier times in his adventures. The battles described in this book are almost all (apart from the fictional assault on the palace at the end) real historical events that Harald was cited to be present for.

You can still visit the ancient quarry at Syracuse where Harald keeps his (fictional) prisoner in this book and where he and William seal their partnership in blood. You can also visit the ancient Greek fort that stands on the low ridge above the ancient heart of the city, stand under that ruined tower where Harald himself perhaps once stood, and walk in the tiered benches of the theatre where I depicted Maniakes as having his headquarters.

During the writing of this book, I was able to visit the ancient city of Constantinople (now Istanbul), walk some of the old walls, visit the Hagia Sophia and sit in the entrance of the Golden Gate. Unlike Eric, I can't say that I walked with Hardrada, but I very much enjoyed retracing a few of his footsteps. Istanbul is well worth a visit for anyone interested in the Byzantine Empire's history.

None of the men who led the war in Sicily and Italy in the events told in this book had happy endings to their ambitions.

Maniakes was executed for leading a futile and ill-judged rebellion in 1043, desperately trying to realise his goal of becoming emperor. The Emir of Sicily was deposed soon afterwards by his own people, and years of civil war followed. After Argyrus defeated them, the Byzantines did what they so often did and simply bought him, luring him to their side with promises of power and money, turning on his own people. He spent the next twenty years fighting a losing war for the Romans, being Capetan of Italy for over fifteen years until shortly before the final defeat.

Michael Dokeianos's brief and failed governorship of Italy did not survive his defeat at the River Ofanto. Demoted and recalled to Constantinople, he was captured fighting against Harald's old enemy, the Pecheneg, a decade later. Paraded before the enemy leader, he defied them and, managing to seize a sword, is said to have cut an arm from the enemy chief before he was overpowered and killed.

William Iron-arm's dream of a Norman state in Sicily and southern Italy came true, although he did not live to see it, ignominiously and prematurely dying from an unknown illness in 1046. From what little we know of him I see so many similarities with Harald: A life of adventure and seeking of reputation and glory, the desire to rule, and great military skill. The army he commanded inflicted two serious defeats on armies Harald and his Varangians were part of (condensed to one in this book for brevity), as his Norman knights and their supporting infantry fought outnumbered and yet triumphed on each occasion. To achieve that against the Greek veterans of Sicily, and Harald's fearsome Varangians, he must have been a superlative general indeed.

It must also have been quite the shock to Harald, who had never been defeated like that before, and particularly for it to happen at the hands of a man he may well have considered a friend.

But that brings me back to something Jarl Rognvald said to Harald in the first book – that great rulers have no friends, only allies and enemies, and those two classes are easily interchangeable.

Spare a thought for Arduin the Lombard, perhaps the most sympathetic side character in this story. His efforts to lead and protect his people were betrayed again and again, and after the whipping and shaming by Maniakes portrayed in this book, his alliance of revenge with the Normans only led them to betray him in turn. After the success of the rebellion of 1041, he disappears from the record books as the Normans took control of his lands, and Arduin was doomed to obscurity and an unknown fate.

But Harald's story survives the events of Sicily and Italy, where so many other great men fell from grace forever. Even as his time in the empire is coming to a close Harald has the most climactic and history-changing events of his service with the Varangian guard yet to come.

The weakened emperor Michael is ailing but seeking redemption. Zoe is bruised and battered, her power having been on the verge of being extinguished but now perhaps secured with Harald at her side. The once all-powerful eunuch John has spectacularly fallen from grace and finds himself imprisoned with nothing to do but plot his return to power. The power of the rebel Bulgarian emperor Petar Delyan grows, with the entire rebellion united under his rule, and it may yet expand to become a threat to the capital itself.

And astride it all stands Harald, whose oaths and honour have been stretched to their very limits. The crown of Norway is calling to him, but as the final struggle for power in the palace of

Constantinople draws near he will have to survive its chaos, find a way to resist Zoe's temptations, and escape with the men, wealth and reputation he needs to reclaim his brother's stolen throne.

Eric Sveitungr's tale of Harald Hardrada's service in the Roman Empire is building towards its fateful conclusion.

ABOUT THE AUTHOR

JC Duncan is a well-reviewed historical fiction author and amateur bladesmith, with a passion for Vikings.

Sign up to JC Duncan's mailing list here for news, competitions and updates on future books.

Visit JC's website: www.jcduncan.co.uk

Follow JC on social media:

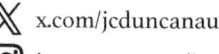 x.com/jcduncanauthor
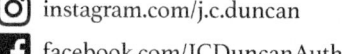 instagram.com/j.c.duncan
facebook.com/JCDuncanAuthor

ALSO BY JC DUNCAN

The Last Viking Series

Warrior Prince

Raven Lord

Emperor's Axe

WARRIOR CHRONICLES

WELCOME TO THE CLAN ✕

THE HOME OF
BESTSELLING HISTORICAL
ADVENTURE FICTION!

WARNING:
MAY CONTAIN VIKINGS!

SIGN UP TO OUR
NEWSLETTER

BIT.LY/WARRIORCHRONICLES

Boldwood

Boldwood Books is an award-winning fiction publishing company seeking out the best stories from around the world.

Find out more at www.boldwoodbooks.com

Join our reader community for brilliant books, competitions and offers!

Follow us
@BoldwoodBooks
@TheBoldBookClub

Sign up to our weekly deals newsletter

https://bit.ly/BoldwoodBNewsletter

Printed in Great Britain
by Amazon